GARDENS of the SUN

GARDENS *of* *the* SUN

PAUL McAULEY

an imprint of **Prometheus Books**
Amherst, NY

Sci Fic
McAuley

Published 2010 by Pyr®, an imprint of Prometheus Books

Inquiries should be addressed to
Pyr
59 John Glenn Drive
Amherst, New York 14228–2119
VOICE: 716–691–0133
FAX: 716–691–0137
WWW.PYRSF.COM

14 13 12 11 10   5 4 3 2 1

Library of Congress Cataloging-in-Publication Data

McAuley, Paul J.
    Gardens of the sun / by Paul McAuley.
        p. cm.
    Sequel to: The quiet war, 2009.
    First published: London : Gollancz, an imprint of Orion Publishing Group, 2009.
    ISBN 978–1–61614–196–7 (pbk. : alk. paper)
    1. Imaginary wars and battles—Fiction. 2. Space colonies—Fiction. I. Title.

PR6063.C29G37 2010
823'.914—dc22
                                                                        2009047957

Printed in the United States on acid-free paper

For Stephen Baxter,
and for Georgina, *encore, toujours*

PART ONE
WAR DAMAGE

I

A hundred murdered ships swung around Saturn in endless ellipses. Slender freighters and sturdy tugs. Shuttles that had once woven continuous and ever-changing paths between the inhabited moons. Spidery surface-to-orbit gigs. The golden crescent of a clipper, built by a cooperative just two years ago to ply between Saturn and Jupiter, falling like a forlorn fairy-tale moon past the glorious arch of the ring system. Casualties of a war recently ended.

Most were superficially intact but hopelessly compromised, AIs driven insane by demons disseminated by Brazilian spies, fusion motors and control and life-support systems toasted by microwave bursts or EMP mines. In the frantic hours after their ships had been killed, surviving crews and passengers had attempted to make repairs or signal for help with lasers pried from dead comms packages, or had composed with varying degrees of resignation, despair, and anger last messages to their families and friends. In the freezing dark of her sleeping niche, aboard a freighter sliding past the butterscotch bands at Saturn's equator, the poet Lexis Parrander had written in blood on the blank screen of her slate *We are the dead*.

They were the dead. No one responded to the distress signals they aimed at the inhabited moons or the ships of the enemy. Some zipped themselves into sleeping niches and took overdoses, or opened veins at their wrists, or fastened plastic bags over their heads. Others, hoping to survive until rescue came, pulled on pressure suits and willed themselves into the deep, slow sleep of hibernation. In one ship people fought and killed each other because there were not enough pressure suits to go around. In another, they huddled around an impedance heater lashed up from cable and fuel cells, a futile last stand against the advance of the implacable cold.

Many of the ships, fleeing toward Uranus when they'd been killed, had planned to pick up speed by gravity-assist maneuvers around Saturn. Now they traced lonely paths that took them close around the gas giant and flung them out past the ring system and the orbits of the inner moons before reaching apogee and falling back. A few travelled even further outward, past the orbits of Titan, Hyperion, or even Iapetus.

And here was the black arrowhead of a Brazilian singleship approaching the farthest point of an orbit that was steeply inclined above the equatorial plane and had taken it more than twenty million kilometres from Saturn, into the lonely realm where scattered swarms of tiny moons traced long and eccentric paths. Inside its sleek hull, a trickle charge from a lithium-ion battery kept its coffin-sized lifesystem at 4° Celsius, and its mortally wounded pilot slept beyond the reach of any dream.

A spark of fusion flame flared in the starry black aft of the singleship. A ship was approaching: a robot tug that was mostly fuel tank and motor, drawing near and matching the eccentric axial spin of the crippled singleship with firecracker bursts from clusters of attitude jets until the two ships spun together like comically disproportionate but precisely synchronised ice-skaters. The tug sidled closer and made hard contact, docking with latches along the midline of the singleship's flat belly. After running through a series of diagnostic checks, the tug killed its burden's spin and turned it through a hundred and eighty degrees and fired up its big fusion motor. The blue-white spear of the exhaust stretched kilometres beyond the coupled ships, altering their delta vee and their high, wide orbit, pushing them toward Dione and rendezvous with the flagship of the Greater Brazilian fleet.

2

Sri Hong-Owen was on Janus, climbing the outer slope of a big crater stamped into the moon's anti-saturnian hemisphere, when General Arvam Peixoto reached out to her. "Get back to the *Glory of Gaia* as soon as possible," he said. "I have a little job that requires your peculiar expertise."

"I have plenty of work here. *Important* work," Sri said, but she was speaking into dead air. The general had cut his end of the connection. She knew that if she tried to call back she wouldn't be able to get past his snarky aides, and she also knew that she couldn't risk the consequences of disobeying him: out here, in the aftermath of the Quiet War, Arvam Peixoto's word was law. So she switched to the common channel and told the three members of her crew that she'd been recalled.

"Drop whatever you're doing and pack up. We're leaving in an hour."

"We're already on it, boss," Vander Reece said. "We got word too."

"Of course you did," Sri said, and switched off her comms.

Despite the encumbrance of her pressure suit she was poised like a dancer in the vestigial gravity of the little moon, tethered to the static line she'd been following up the bright slope. Below her, a stretch of flat terrain planted with vacuum organisms that somewhat resembled giant silvery sunflowers tilted toward the close horizon. Above, a scalloped ridge stood stark against the black sky where Janus's co-orbital partner, Epimetheus, hung like a crooked fingernail paring. The two moons chased each other around the same track beyond the outer edge of the A Ring, one always slightly lower and faster than the other. Roughly every four years, the faster moon caught up with its slower partner. As it approached to within ten thousand kilometres, gravitational interaction kicked the faster moon into a higher, slower orbit and dropped the slower moon into a lower, faster orbit and the race started over, no end to it. A celestial version of a futile metabolic cycle. A crude metaphor for Sri's life after the Quiet War.

This was her second solo outing on Janus's surface, a long trek to patch-work gardens of several dozen variant species of vacuum organism that covered the inner slopes and floor of the crater. They'd already been mapped by drones, but Sri had been looking forward to rambling through them, taking samples, searching for anything that might give her further insights into the mind of their creator, the great gene wizard Avernus. Well, too bad. Arvam Peixoto had twitched her leash, and like a good little pet she must come running to see what her master wanted. So Sri bit down on her resentment and regret, collapsed her long-handled pick and hooked it to the utility belt of her pressure suit, and swarmed back down the slope, following the line through the stands of sunflower vacuum organisms.

Their black stems towered all around her, topped by silvery dishes that focused the dim light of the sun—one-hundredth the brightness of sunlight incident on Earth—onto central nodes whose heat-exchange systems drew up liquid methane and warmed it and pumped it back down into a labyrinthine network of mycelial threads that ramified through the regolith, absorbing carbonaceous compounds and rare earths and metals that were deposited in scales elaborated around the bases of the stems, ready to be picked and refined. The sunflowers crowded close together, dishes set edge to edge in a tiled canopy that obscured most of the sky, stems rooted in a scurf of fallen scales and clumps of blocky ejecta. Despite the exiguous gravity, traversing the Stygian undercroft of this dwarf forest was hard work. Sri was sweating hard inside her pressure suit and feeling a quivering exhaustion in her shoulders and calves when at last she broke free and swarmed up the shallow slope of another crater rim, following a well-trodden path toward the tug that squatted on a landing platform a short distance from a pressure dome.

Inside the dome's transparent blister, lights brighter than the shrunken sun illuminated a green, jungly garden—another of Avernus's sly little miracles. A preliminary survey had shown that the bushes, creepers, grasses, and sprawling trees of the jungle shared the same genome: all were different phenotypic expressions of a single artificial species, creating an intimately interlinked self-regulating biome. Sri's old mentor, Oscar Finnegan Ramos, would have thought this phenotype jungle a vain and silly exercise, a waste of a great talent. And he would have been wrong, as he'd been wrong about so much else. Sri was learning all kinds of novel techniques and tricks from her investigations of Avernus's gardens, finding inspiration for her own work, beginning to get the measure of the contours and amazing range of the gene wizard's mind.

Principles and elements of ecosystem construction developed and elaborated by Avernus had enabled Outer colonists of the moons of Jupiter and Saturn to establish robust and stable biomes in their cities and garden habitats and oases on the moons of Jupiter and Saturn; the vacuum organisms she'd designed, congeries of cellular nanomachines able to grow and reproduce on the moons' cold and airless surfaces, provided dependable supplies of CHON food, metals, fullerene composites, and every kind of complex organic compound. Avernus had expected little or no reward for her work and had withdrawn from ordinary life, an aloof genius protected by a small circle of acolytes, absent-mindedly conjuring miracle after miracle. But despite her long self-imposed exile, she had realised that humanity was approaching a crucial crossroads. A hundred years ago, when Earth had attempted to extend its hegemony over them, the pioneering generation of Outers had fled from the Moon to Mars and Jupiter's second-largest moon, Callisto. Shortly afterward, the nascent colonies on Mars had been H-bombed by the Chinese Democratic Republic, but the Outers on Callisto had survived and prospered, spreading to other moons of Jupiter and to the Saturn System, building cities and settlements, experimenting with novel forms of scientific utopianism. Previous attempts to heal the rift between Earth and the Outers had failed, but these failures had not mattered much. Earth had been preoccupied with repairing the damage caused by catastrophic climate change; the Outers had become inward-looking, absorbed in the creation of works of art or in scientific research with little or no practical value. But this equilibrium had been threatened by the expansionist ambitions of the rising generation of Outers, and Avernus had allowed herself to become one of the figureheads of the movement for peace and reconciliation, ploughing vast amounts of personal kudos into collaborative projects meant to strengthen bonds between the two branches of humanity.

The peace effort had been sabotaged. There had been a short, swift war. The Outers had been comprehensively defeated. Expeditionary forces from Earth's three major power blocs had taken control of every city and settlement on the moons of Jupiter and Saturn. A few Outers had managed to escape into the outer dark; Avernus had disappeared into the vastness of Titan's icescapes.

Sri had been unable to persuade Arvam Peixoto to mount a full-scale search for the gene wizard. The men and women under his command had more important things to do—securing the cities and major settlements on Mimas, Enceladus, Tethys, and Dione, policing and caring for their populations, repairing damaged infrastructure, and installing new administrations. Sri had been given only the vague promise of some kind of help in the indefinite future, and use of a pod of autonomous drones. They were ferociously smart hunters that could synthesise fuel from the hydrocarbons in Titan's atmosphere but were pitifully inadequate for the task of locating a single person squatting in some spiderhole on a smog-shrouded moon with a surface area of more than eighty-three million square kilometres. Sri had set them loose with little hope or expectation, and turned to searching out and exploring the gardens that Avernus had scattered across inhabited and uninhabited moons, elegant fusions of whimsy and theory that would take years of hard work to catalogue, analyse, and understand.

But the secrets of the gardens of Janus would have to wait. Sri helped her crew pack equipment and samples and load them into the lockers of the little tug, and one by one they cycled through the airlock into the cramped cabin where they'd been living for the past week. Sri strapped herself into the crash couch next to Vander Reece and he lit the motor and Janus fell away behind them, quickly lost in the glory of the rings. Six hours later, the tug entered orbit around Dione and rendezvoused with General Arvam Peixoto's flagship, the *Glory of Gaia*. The tug matched delta vee with the big ship and crept close and fired a harpoon tether and reeled itself onto a docking spar, and the spar contracted like a chameleon's tongue and delivered it to a cargo bay.

Sri gave her crew precise instructions about handling and storage of their collection of specimens and went off to find her son. After ten days in the vestigial gravity of Janus, the 0.05 g imparted by the ship's spin felt like lead in her bones. The hot stale air stank of ozone and old sweat, like the locker room of a municipal swimming pool; the corridors and companionways were crowded with soldiers and civilians. A shipload of advisers and civil servants had arrived from Earth while Sri had been working on Janus; in Berry's cubicle two men she didn't recognise were sleeping in cocoons hung on the walls. She backed out, called the quartermaster, and learned that Berry was no longer on board: he'd been reassigned to a habitat formerly owned by the Jones-Truex-Bakaleinikoff clan, down on the surface of Dione.

Sri didn't need to ask who'd arranged this, or why she hadn't been informed. Arvam Peixoto had refused to allow Berry to leave the *Glory of Gaia*, keeping him hostage to ensure Sri's absolute and unconditional loyalty; now, without bothering to consult her, the general had dispatched Berry to some tented habitat on a moon not yet fully pacified. With a cold star of indignation and anxiety burning in her chest, Sri swarmed down the ship's spine and badged her way past a marine guarding the hatch to what had been the officers' wardroom before Arvam Peixoto's staff had appropriated it.

Walls and ceiling padded with red leather; couches and side tables bolted to the floor; the general and half a dozen officers and civil servants over in one corner, studying spreadsheets scrolling through a big memo space. No one acknowledged Sri's entrance, and she knew better than to interrupt. Arvam Peixoto was a bully who loved to pick and pry at other people's weaknesses; if she confronted him head on, he'd use her anger against her. And besides, there was no point in picking a fight she couldn't win. No, she had to be calm and cool and strong. For the sake of Berry. For the sake of her work. So she snagged a bulb of coffee and sank into a sling chair and diverted herself by reviewing and collating the last of the data that her crew had gathered on Janus. The close attention required to parse the information soothed her; she had more or less regained her equilibrium when at last one of the aides floated across the room and told her the general had a few minutes to spare.

"Here you are at last. I was beginning to think you'd forgotten about me," Arvam Peixoto said.

He was a handsome, vigorous man in his sixties, dressed in his usual many-pocketed flight suit. He'd shorn his hair since they'd last met, cut off his ponytail and clipped what was left to a crisp snow white flattop. A pistol was holstered at his hip: the one he had used to murder a man right in front of Sri, once upon a time.

"Perhaps you've forgotten that I was working on Janus," Sri said.

14

"I don't believe I've been there yet. Have I been there yet?" Arvam said.

"No, sir," one of the aides said.

"Is it worth a visit?" Arvam said to Sri.

"I have plenty of work to do there. May I ask," Sri said, trying to keep her tone light and friendly, "why you sent Berry to Dione?"

"Oh, the ship's no place for the boy," Arvam said. "It's too crowded, and there's nothing for him to do except get into trouble. Where I sent him, it's being made over into my headquarters. It's been thoroughly checked out, and it's quite safe. A big garden with lawns and fields, trees and lakes. Just the kind of place for a healthy, active boy, yes?"

"I'd like to see it. Your people might have missed something."

"I'll tell you all about it after dinner tonight. The Pacific Community liaison secretary is paying a visit and for some reason he is eager to meet you. You can tell him about your gardens, and perhaps he'll let slip some useful information about the situation on Iapetus."

"This is why you interrupted my research? To make small talk with a PacCom official?"

"That's one reason. I also have a new project for you," Arvam said. "A very important project. Come with me."

Sri and a comet-tail of aides followed the general to the medical bay and a curtained alcove at the far end where a young man lay in a slanted bed. A white sheet was tucked tight as a drumhead across his legs and waist; the black band of a heart-lung machine was clamped across his chest. His head was shaven and bandaged and his eyelids were taped shut, there were tubes in his nose, and a dripline attached to his arm looped up to a sac of liquid hung from the bulkhead beside him. The sac quiveringly pulsed at intervals, like a sluggish and fretful jellyfish.

Arvam told Sri that the young man was Lieutenant Cash Baker, single-ship pilot and war hero. "He was wounded in combat. Brain damage. I want you to fix it."

"I'm flattered, of course. But what can I do that your excellent and highly experienced medical staff can't?"

"You rewired his nervous system during the J-2 test programme. Also, it's your fault he died."

After a heartbeat's hesitation, Sri understood what the general meant. "He was flying the singleship that attacked Avernus's tug."

"Yes, he was. But he may be useful to me, so you will have to find it in yourself to forgive him."

Lieutenant Cash Baker had piloted one of the singleships sent to intercept and destroy a chunk of ice flung at the Pacific Community's temporary base on Phoebe, at the beginning of the war. His ship had been damaged by the ice's automatic defence system, but it had managed to partially repair itself and as he'd fallen back toward Saturn he'd targeted an Outer tug that had escaped from Dione. The tug had been carrying Avernus, and Sri Hong-Owen had been in hot pursuit. When Cash Baker had ignored a direct order to call off his attack, it had been necessary to activate a suicide program buried in his singleship's control system. In the aftermath, the singleship had plummeted through the plane of the ring system, a speck of basalt travelling faster than any bullet had pierced its hull and shattered into dozens of fragments, and one of those fragments had shot through the lifesystem and drilled Cash Baker's visor and skull and brain. The lifesystem had put him in hibernation and saved his life, his singleship had been located and retrieved, and now General Arvam Peixoto wanted Sri to help the medical team tasked with repairing his brain damage.

"We need heroes who can drum up support back home by telling stirring stories of extraordinary acts of bravery. This man is an excellent candidate."

"He is a fool who very nearly murdered Avernus."

"I'll deal with his story, Professor Doctor. Your job is to fix him up. I don't care if he can't move from the neck down, but he has to be able to speak in full sentences without drooling. Think you can do that?"

The chief surgeon told Sri that the fragment of basalt had struck the pilot just above his left eye, burning a path through his frontal cortex and corpus callosum and clipping the lower edge of the visual cortex before exiting his skull. The fragment had been just a couple of hundred microns across, but it had been travelling very fast: shock waves had destroyed or killed everything in a track averaging seven millimetres in diameter. Damage to the frontal cortex and visual cortex was trivial and could be easily repaired by insertion of glial and totipotent fetal cells. There would be some memory loss, but no serious side effects. But the damage to the corpus callosum was more problematical. Passage of the fragment had severed large numbers of reciprocal connections between the two halves of the brain. If this wasn't repaired, the surgeon said, the right side of the pilot's brain would be cut off from the dominant left side, a separate mind with its own perception, cognition, volition, learning, and memory but lacking the ability to speak, able to express

16

itself only through nonverbal reactions. He would not be able to integrate the right- and left-hand sides of his visual field, and might suffer "alien hand syndrome" and other dissociative effects.

After studying high-resolution tomographic renderings of the damage, Sri proposed a radical solution. She had helped to design the artificial autonomic nervous system that enabled singleship pilots to plug directly into the control system of their ships and to briefly boost their neural processing speeds during combat, and she believed that she could use this to reroute connections between the two sides of the pilot's brain and reunite his mind.

She had plenty of other work to do, of course. She wanted to visit the garden habitat that the general had taken over for his headquarters and make sure that her son was safe and happy. She wanted to return to Janus and complete her survey of the phenotype jungle and the sunflowers and the other vacuum organisms, work up the data and thoroughly examine it and compare it with the data sets gathered from her inspections of other gardens. Then she would head out to the next garden, and the one after that. . . .

No, there was never enough time to do everything she wanted to do. But although she'd been bullied into doing it by Arvam Peixoto and it wasn't anywhere near the top of her list of priorities, she enjoyed discussing the redesign of Cash Baker's augmented nervous system with the ship's surgeon. He had extensive experience of brain and nerve reconstruction, there was a definite intellectual bond between them, two minds into one, and she felt a spark of resentment when one of the general's aides appeared and reminded her of the formal dinner.

The aide escorted Sri to a senior officer's cabin, waited outside while she showered and put on uniform coveralls and slippers, then led her to the wardroom, where senior officers and civil servants and the guests from the Pacific Community were already seated at the long table. As Sri settled into her seat between the ship's captain and the PacCom liaison secretary, Arvam Peixoto gave her a stern look across a centrepiece arrangement of lilies and roses that must have been shuttled up from some garden on Dione—perhaps from the habitat where Berry was now living.

Sri found most social occasions tedious. Trivial chatter and pointless and suffocating etiquette overlaying crude status displays. Alpha personalities like the general strutted and preened; everyone else flattered him, reinforcing their positions in their stupid little hierarchy, watching each other for possible faults and failings. Ape behaviour. Sri couldn't play these games. She lacked in every measure the vivid, forceful, and confrontational personality of the typical alpha male, and wasn't the kind of wily social networker, able to build up cadres of loyal followers and keep them in line by Skinner-box reward-and-punishment games, typical of alpha females. Although her reputation gave her some social cachet, these occasions always reminded her that she was a wild card tolerated only as long as she continued to be useful. And to be useful she needed to work, not waste her time on chitchat and posing.

Then there was the political dimension. Less than a decade ago, the Pacific Community and Greater Brazil had almost gone to war over control of the Hawaiian islands. Both power blocs had stepped back from armed confrontation and had slowly restored diplomatic links, but a great deal of mutual antipathy and suspicion still remained. And although it had cooperated with Greater Brazil and the European Union during the brief war against the Outers, the Pacific Community had come late to the campaign and had made only a minimal contribution, and its intentions were still obscure. Arvam Peixoto wanted Sri to wheedle some morsels of useful intel from the PacCom liaison secretary, and although she liked that kind of game even less than ordinary social discourse, she had to play along for the sake of her son, and for herself.

Fortunately, the liaison secretary, Tommy Tabagee, turned out to be sufficiently intelligent and witty to keep her mildly amused throughout the long and formal dinner. A slight, limber man with coal black skin and a Medusa's crown of dreadlocks, he was very proud of his Aboriginal ancestry and fanatically dedicated to reconstruction and remediation of his native continent, telling Sri about what he called his modest contributions to the levelling of cities and erasure of every sign of the sins of the age of industry, a great work that would take centuries to complete.

"It won't ever be the same, of course," he said. "For one thing, the climate is still completely buggered. There are places where it hasn't rained for a hundred years. But we must let the land find its own direction. That's the important thing. And we have had some small successes. Before I was assigned here, I had the honour of working with a crew in Darwin that was restoring a portion of the Great Barrier Reef. Using real corals to replace the artificial ones. Oh, it will never be as glorious as it once was, but if it works half as well as they claim, it has some small potential."

Sri questioned Tommy Tabagee about the artificial corals, startled him with a few insights and ideas. Around them the other guests ate and drank and chattered, and marines in white jackets brought plates of food and took away empty plates and refilled glasses. Tommy Tabagee drank only water and ate quickly and neatly, like a machine refuelling, telling Sri that people like her were desperately needed back on Earth and it was a pity she had to waste her time out here.

"I wouldn't call investigating Outer technology a waste of time," Sri said. "I learn something new and useful every day."

But Tommy Tabagee didn't take the bait, telling her instead that he'd also learned a thing or two in his brief time in the Saturn System.

"Best of all, as far as I'm concerned, was discovering that these moons have their own songlines," he said, and explained that songlines had been the key to the survival and civilisation of his ancestors. "In the long ago, my people lived in a country that was mostly scrub or desert, with scant and unpredictable rainfall. So they had to lead a nomadic existence, moving from waterhole to waterhole. These not only supplied food and water, you understand. They were also places where neighbouring tribes met to conduct ceremonies and exchange goods. Using a barter system very like the Bourse which regulated the economies of the Outer cities and settlements before the war, as a matter of fact. So they were important in all kinds of ways, and they were linked by paths called songlines, because the principal trade was in songs. Each tribe had its own song cycle and traded verses with other tribes. Trade in goods was secondary to the trade in songs. And the songs, you see, they defined the land through which they passed."

"They were maps," Sri said.

She was thinking of the web of static lines that her crew had laid across the moonscape around the phenotype jungle's pressure dome, the gardens she hadn't had time to visit.

"Exactly so," Tommy Tabagee said. "A man could cross hundreds of kilometres of desert he'd never before visited, using the information in songs he'd learned from other tribes. *He* wouldn't have seen it that way, of course. He'd have said that he dreamed the land into existence as he sang. Which was why he had to get the song exactly right. Of course, the land here is even more unforgiving. No waterholes, and no food. Not even air! But the Outers have scattered oases and shelters across their moons, and in my opinion it is possible to think of the routes between them as songlines. I'm pleased to say that the Outers on Iapetus are very receptive to this notion. They are very intimate with their territory and they navigate by landmarks, just as my ancestors did."

"Is that why you're here? To learn the songs of Iapetus and all the other moons?"

19

Tommy Tabagee's playful smile revealed a notch between his front teeth. "I hope you're not making fun of my cultural inheritance, Professor Doctor."

"I didn't mean to," Sri said. The stuff about songlines and dreaming the world into existence was mumbo jumbo that mythologised a basic survival strategy, but she believed that it revealed something useful about the Pacific Community's plans for the territory it had seized.

"I hear you're interested in the gene wizard Avernus," Tommy Tabagee said, smartly changing the subject. "Do you know we have one of her gardens on Iapetus?"

It was a small tented oasis on the anti-saturnian hemisphere of Iapetus, he said, near the mountainous ridge that girdled the moon's equator. The ground inside had been planted with stuff that looked like bamboo: tall black stalks that stiffly swayed and rattled in random gusts generated by the air-conditioning. Every thirty days the stalks sprouted banners of every conceivable colour and pattern, died all at once, and released the banners, which swarmed and blew in a great cloud in the gusty air. Compatible banners exchanged genetic material by folding themselves together and forming a patchwork chimera that pulled apart into two halves that fell to the decaying mulch left by the stalks. And then new stalks arose, and the cycle began again. An endless round of growth and reproduction that generated fleeting patterns of random and unrepeatable beauty.

"Maybe you can tell me what it means," Tommy Tabagee said. "Because I'm buggered if I can."

"I don't think it means anything in particular. Apart from its own intrinsic meaning, that is."

"So it's a work of art, is it?"

"Avernus likes games," Sri said. "And her games are both playful and serious. They're an expression of the whimsical side of her talent, and they also explore the possible expressions of the limited number of natural and artificial genes currently available. Evolution has been doing just that for more than four billion years on Earth, a little less in the ocean of Europa. It has produced many intricate and marvellous wonders, but they are a mere drop in the sea of the information space that defines every possible expression of life. Avernus's gardens are expeditions beyond the edges of current maps of artificial genetics. She is creating new territory, just as your ancestors believed that their songs created the territory over which they walked."

Tommy Tabagee thought about that for a moment, then said, "You like her, don't you?"

"I admire her."

Sri felt a little flinch of caution, wondering if the spry little man knew just how badly she had been humiliated the only time she and Avernus had met.

Instead, he asked her about the gardens she'd discovered and explored, and they talked pleasantly until white-jacketed marines moved forward to serve coffee and Arvam Peixoto rose to make a short speech about the necessity for cooperation between Earth's three great powers. When the general was finished, Tommy Tabagee told Sri that now he'd have to sing for his supper, and stood up and gave a graceful response. And then the dinner was over, but before Tommy Tabagee left he told Sri that he'd met her green saint once.

"Oscar Finnegan Ramos, that is. He was a fine fellow. I was sorry to hear about his death."

Sri's flinch was stronger this time. Sharp as a needle stabbing her heart. According to the official story, Oscar had died of sudden-onset multiple organ failure, one of the signature syndromes suffered by those kept alive by longevity treatments. Until recently, Sri had believed that only she and Arvam knew the truth, but a few days before she'd left for Janus she'd found a handwritten note on the fold-down table in her cabin.

I admire your bold move. If you ever need help, contact me.

Sri had recognised the round, childish scrawl at once: it was Euclides Peixoto's, a cousin and rival of Arvam's who had been given oversight of one of her projects before the war. She'd swabbed the note for DNA, had failed to find any, and had destroyed it. She hadn't told Arvam about it, even though it meant that one of Euclides's agents must be on board the flagship; she'd been badly burnt by the internal politics of the Peixoto family once before and she didn't ever again want to become involved in their intrigues. But now she was struck by the unpleasant thought that Euclides might have been spreading rumours about Oscar's death to weaken Arvam's position, and wondered if Tommy Tabagee knew or suspected that she had killed Oscar so that she could escape the tangle of intrigue that had threatened to trap her and throw in her lot with Arvam Peixoto and the war effort.

She told the PacCom liaison secretary that Oscar's death was an untimely loss, to herself and to the Peixoto family and the scientific world; if he noticed that her face had stiffened into a mask he gave no sign of it, saying that Oscar had been a fine man who had contributed so much to the great cause.

"If you have half his scruples and a quarter of his talent, you're all right by me, I reckon."

After Tommy Tabagee and the rest of the Pacific Community delegation had returned to their ship, Arvam Peixoto intercepted Sri and asked her what she and the liaison secretary had been talking about.

"The two of you were as thick as thieves."

"Isn't that what you wanted? He told me that they found one of Avernus's gardens on Iapetus. More or less invited me to visit."

"I don't think so," Arvam said.

"I might learn something useful about the PacCom's plans."

"They'll feed you a mess of grey info and naked propaganda while subtly pumping you for useful information. And besides, you're a valuable asset," Arvam said. "I'd look like a damned fool if I let you go there and you decided to defect."

Sri couldn't tell if he was joking or not. "I'm sorry that you think I'm too naive to be trusted."

"You're the most intelligent person I know. But you don't know much about people. One of my aides is writing a summary report about your tête-a-tête with Mr. Tommy Tabagee. Check it over, add any comments you feel necessary, sign it, and have it on my desk tomorrow morning," Arvam said. "Oh, and you can tell me how you plan to fix up our hero pilot. It's about time you started earning your keep."

3

Some fifty days after he'd defected, the spy at last returned to Paris, Dione.

It had not been an easy journey. He'd fallen from orbit in a stolen drop-shell, skimming through a hole in the Brazilian surveillance-satellite network, landing inside a small impact crater in the high northern latitudes of Dione's sub-saturnian hemisphere, walking away across a frozen, gently undulating plain. He was short of air and power and had to reach a shelter or an oasis as quickly as possible. He knew that his former masters would be searching for him and that he faced disgrace and execution if he was captured, yet in those first hours of freedom his heart floated on a flood of joy. All around, beyond the shell of his pressure suit, with its intimate chorus of clicks and whirrs, the tide of his breathing and the thud of his pulse, the moonscape stretched silent and still, lovely in its emptiness. The dusty ground glimmering golden-brown in the long light of the low sun. Saturn's swollen globe looming half full above the curved horizon, bisected by the black scratch of the ringplane, which printed crisp shadows across smoggy bands of butterscotch and peach and caught fire with diamond light as it shot beyond the gas giant's limb toward the tiny half-disc of one of the inner moons. He felt as if he was the emperor of all he surveyed. The only witness to this pure, uncanny beauty. And for the first time in his brief and strange life, master of his fate.

He'd been shaped before birth, molded and trained and indoctrinated during his strange childhood, dispatched to Dione before the beginning of the war on a mission to infiltrate Paris, sabotage its infrastructure, and soften it for invasion by Brazilian forces. He'd carried out his mission to the best of his considerable abilities, but his sojourn amongst the Outers had changed him. He had fallen in love, he'd begun to understand what it meant to be truly human, and then he'd betrayed the woman he loved for the sake of his mission. But now he was free of every obligation and duty toward God and Gaia and Greater Brazil. Free to be anything he wanted to be. Free to find Zi Lei, and save her from the aftermath of war.

And so he bounded along in exuberant kangaroo hops, chasing his long shadow across the plain. Several times he misjudged his landing and tumbled and fell amongst spurts of dust, wrenching his wounded shoulder. It didn't matter. He bounced to his feet and bounded on, eager and happy, reaching a shelter some sixty kilometres from his landing spot late in the long afternoon.

Hundreds of these tiny unmanned stations were scattered across the surfaces of the inhabited moons, insulated fullerene shells buried in ice and surrounded by fields of tall silvery flowers that transformed sunlight into electrical power, providing basic accommodation where hikers and other travellers could stop for the night. The spy ate a hasty meal, fed a little sugar solution to the halflife bandage that covered the raw bullet wound in his shoulder, then swapped his Brazilian military-issue pressure suit for the shelter's spare—it fit his lanky frame better, and its lifepack had a longer range—and filled a slingbag with supplies and hiked on toward a crater rim that stood at the horizon. He walked up the long apron of the slumped ridge and near the top found a good hiding place in a deep cleft between two house-sized blocks that had been shattered and overturned by the ancient impact, and unrolled an insulated cocoon and climbed inside it and fell into a deep and dreamless sleep. He slept for sixty hours, through Dione's long night and most of the next day, and woke and headed out to the next shelter, where he showered and ate, recharged his suit's batteries and topped up its air supply, and walked on.

He travelled like this for more than forty days.

The land dropped in a series of broad, benched terraces into Latium Chasma, a long linear trough carved by a catastrophic flood of ammonia-rich meltwater early in Dione's history, before the little moon had frozen to its core. He hiked along the broad plain of the chasma's floor, moving from shelter to shelter, sleeping in shallow crevasses or in the deep shadows of embayments in the gouged and pleated cliffs of the trough's eastern wall. He was certain that he was still being hunted, but although Dione was only a little over a thousand kilometres in diameter it had a surface area of four million square kilometres—half the size of Australia—and the Brazilian forces were small in number and would be mostly deployed around Paris. Even so, he would now and then spot in the black sky swiftly moving points of light crossing from west to east, and feel as exposed as a bug crawling across a microscope slide.

Every day the spy risked tuning into the military band for a few minutes, listening to chatter, trying to work out how the occupation of Dione was unfolding. The Brazilian flagship was still in orbit around the moon, and Brazilian marines were free to move everywhere on its surface, challenged only by a few deadender holdouts—and these were being eliminated one by one. Paris, the self-proclaimed centre of resistance, had been badly damaged. Its tent was ruptured and most of it lay open to freezing vacuum. More than half of its population had been killed; the rest had either fled or had been taken prisoner. And now the Brazilians were rounding up Outers from oases and habitats scattered across Dione and transporting them to temporary prison camps outside the stricken city.

If he was going to find Zi Lei, the spy thought, he would have to go to Paris. It was his first best hope of finding her, and if she wasn't there he would look everywhere else.

One day he climbed the rim of a big crater that cut across the trough and at the top saw, far across the great circle of the crater's floor, a steep-sided pyramid of construction diamond panes and fullerene struts lit up within and crowded with tall trees. Another day he walked past the outer margin of fields of vacuum organisms like pages of dark and twisted characters printed on the pale land.

His wound healed and he wrapped up the halflife bandage and folded it away.

At last, the cliff of the eastern wall slumped downward and the floor of the trough rose, cracked in blocks and little ravines. He'd reached the southern end of the chasma. He'd walked almost a quarter of the way around the little moon.

Someone had cut a trail through the chaotic landscape. The spy followed it across the tops of broken blocks and over ravines bridged by elegant spans of fullerene composite. He walked around the broad, uneven ridge at the edge of a small crater and climbed a natural ramp of consolidated debris onto the rolling, cratered plain beyond.

When he reached the next refuge, he found that it had been cleaned out and left open to vacuum. Tire tracks and bootprints marked the dust all around, and the vacuum-organism flowers had been chopped down. Certain that the Brazilian occupying force was responsible for this despoliation, feeling lonely and hunted, he walked on. He had no choice.

Four hours later, he was approaching an oasis whose angled tent was pitched on the low rim of a crater some five kilometres across. There were no lights inside and the three sets of doors of the main airlock stood open and the gardened interior was dark and frozen. The spy believed that the place had been raided and cleared out by the Brazilian occupiers some time ago, and although he was by now low on air and power, he spent a good hour scouting its perimeter before he dared walk in.

He found spare batteries and air in the airlock of one of the outlying farm tubes. Better still, he found a rolligon hidden under camouflage cloth in a shallow pit dug at the edge of a broad field of tangled black spikes. He spent the time interrogating the vehicle's AI, but it couldn't tell him anything useful, so he dozed until shadows had everywhere crept out to cover the moonscape, and then he started up the rolligon and drove up the shallow ramp at one end of the pit.

Navigating by the soft light of Saturnshine, scarcely brighter than starlight, the spy drove due south, with the ramparts of Eumelus Crater doubling the horizon to the west. Using the rolligon was a big risk, but not as big as hoping to rely on resupply from refuges and caches that the occupying force was now targeting. At last he picked up a road that stretched away in a dead straight line toward the equator, the usual graded construction of ice gravel laced with fullerene mesh, thirty metres wide, absolutely level, and with transponder guides set along one edge so that he could surrender control to the rolligon's AI. He performed a set of stretches and isometric exercises to loosen the rigid bar across his shoulders, went into the galley and steeped a sachet of lemon tea in a beaker, and returned to the driving chair and saw a line gleaming at the horizon.

It was the railway that girdled Dione's equator, a single track elevated above the plain on pylons like a tightrope bridging the western and eastern horizons. Built, like the road, by the patient and unceasing labour of gangs of construction robots. The spy took back control of the rolligon and stopped a little distance from the elevated track, looking all around, wary again. The railway was important. It could be a target. Something could be watching it. . . .

To the east, far off, a faint light gleamed. A star perched at the vanishing point of the railway's ruled line. The spy used the zoom function of the rolligon's monitor. The star dimmed as it expanded; details emerged. It was a bullet-shaped railcar, its rear capped with a cargo space, its nose a diamond canopy over a pressurised cabin. It had been heading west, away from Paris. Now it sat flat on the superconducting magnetic track and the door of its cabin gaped open.

The spy sipped lemon tea as he thought things through. The power had cut off and the railcar had grounded and its passengers had climbed out. That much was clear. But where were they now? And who were they? Brazilian or Outer? At last, with less than an hour before dawn, the spy took the wheel of the rolligon and bumped off the road and drove across the dusty ground parallel to the elevated railway, toward the stationary railcar. The nape of his neck and his palms were prickling, but he couldn't not look. He was hoping that someone else's bad luck would give him what he needed.

He spotted a muddle of bootprints around the base of the support pylon closest to the grounded railcar and stopped the rolligon and pulled on his pressure suit and climbed out and cast around. The bootprints resolved into a path that followed the railway east, in the direction from which the railcar had come. Five sets of tracks either side of something that had left a broad trail in the icy dust.

The spy called up a map and realised that the railcar's passengers must be heading for the nearest station, some fifty kilometres away at the rim of Mnestheus Crater. He looked toward the horizon but nothing moved there. Everywhere was as silent and still as it had ever been.

He climbed the rungs stapled to one side of the pylon and walked down the track to the railcar and stood at the open door for a little while. One of the floor panels was missing and there was blood on another part of the floor and on two of the big cushions that had served as seats. The blood frozen and black in the cold vacuum.

Someone had been wounded, then. And his companions had taken the floor panel and used it to drag him along with them. The spy wondered how much air they'd had, wondered if their wounded comrade had survived the trip.

There was only one way to find out.

A few minutes after he'd started up the rolligon and set off parallel to the railway, the sun sprang above the horizon directly ahead, as bright and sharp now as it would be at noon because there was no atmosphere to attenuate or diffuse its harsh white light. The railway strode straight on, its pylons stepping amongst a string of small impact craters and growing taller as it crossed a broad and shallow depression. The spy lost sight of the track left by the railcar passengers when it bent to the north, around the outer edge of the craters. He backtracked, spotted a bright yellow cannister someone had discarded, picked up the trail, and went on.

After a few kilometres, the trail of bootprints and scrape marks bent north again and crossed the low rim of a medium-sized impact crater. The spy stopped the rolligon and looked all around, the elevated railway skylined behind him, the moonscape all around utterly still and empty. He locked his helmet over his head and climbed down and followed the bootprints up the crater rim to the top, where a flat sheet of fullerene composite, the missing section of railcar floor, stood upright at one end of a mound built of loose ice-rock rubble. He unpacked the rubble at the foot of the sheet and uncovered a helmet, its faceplate blind with frost.

The pressure suit had been powered down and the body inside was frozen solid. The spy had a little trouble unlatching the helmet and felt relief wash through him when he saw that the corpse was male, its face white and hard as marble. He uncovered the body down to its waist and jacked his patch cord into the pressure suit's service port and studied the personal files stored in its memory. The dead man was Felice Gottschalk, born in a garden habitat called Dvoskin's Knoll and currently a resident of Paris, an apprentice architect and sonic artist, twenty-three years old, no children. Perfect.

He did not give another thought to the dead man, or to the people who had dragged him with them until he had died and then had buried him here in the hope that they could one day come back to retrieve his body, or tell others where to find it. He did not wonder whether they had reached the safety of the station or had run out of air or power and died somewhere out on the empty plain. His curiosity was strictly practical. With the exception of Zi Lei, he was interested in people only inasmuch as they were useful or dangerous to him.

So without ceremony or second thoughts he carried the corpse to the rolligon, stashed it in an external locker, and drove south and east. The railway sank beneath the horizon behind him. When he saw the long gleam of an ice cliff at the horizon he turned toward it.

The cliff, created by tectonic fractures when Dione had cooled and its icy crust had contracted, was more than a hundred metres high. Part of it had collapsed, forming a small, shallow basin. The spy drove up a lobate apron of consolidated mass-wasted rubble and parked in the shadows under the grooved face of the basin and interred Felice Gottschalk's corpse deep in the dusty rubble, where no one would ever find it.

He microwaved and ate a portion of rice, black beans, and shiitake mushrooms, then set to work, merging his biometric and DNA profile with the biographical data in Felice Gottschalk's files and porting everything to the ID chip in his pressure suit. This fake identity would pass any casual check made by the occupying forces, and if he could reach one of the caches he'd set up while he'd been living in Paris he would be able to alter his appearance and change his fingerprints with injections of halflife collagen. The spy dozed in the driver's seat, luxuriating in idle but pleasurable fantasies about Zi Lei until nightfall, and then he drove on toward Paris.

He was certain that he would find Zi Lei there. If she'd managed to escape from the immediate vicinity of the city during the war she would by now have been caught in the occupying force's sweeps and transported to one of the prison camps. And even if she had managed to evade capture so far, if she was hiding out in some remote oasis or shelter, he would find her. Even if it took the rest of his life, he would find her.

—●—

Now, at last, the spy had reached the dead city.

He'd driven as close to Romulus Crater as he dared and hiked in over the rim some thirty kilometres west of Paris, to one of the caches he'd set up before the war. He'd subjected himself to a few minor cosmetic alterations and altered his ID accordingly, picked up a memory needle containing back-up copies of his demons, and after night had fallen he'd snuck across the ancient landslips and fans of mass-wasted material to a vantage point just two kilometres from the city's perimeter.

The long tent slanted down the inner slope of the crater's rim and ran out across the flat terrain beyond. Buildings stood up inside it, starkly lit. The farm tubes were dark and the land all around was dark too—apart from the spaceport, which seemed to float in the glare of hundreds of floodlights. Three Brazilian shuttles stood on landing pads. Beyond them, a crew of giant construction robots were working on a skeleton of new tent.

The spy dozed until the sun's tiny disc appeared at the horizon and the moonscape was immediately tangled with shadows. He looked all around, alert and eager, and spotted a tiny gleam to the northeast. It was the dome which housed the research station where Zi Lei and other members of the peace movement had been held prisoner. The healed wound in his shoulder itched. His body, remembering.

Zi Lei had come to him for help after martial law had been declared and the city's wardens had begun to arrest prominent members of the Permanent Peace Debate. He'd drugged her, forced her to swallow a transmitter, and betrayed her to the city's wardens because he'd needed to find out where the peaceniks where being held—he'd been instructed to locate the gene wizard Avernus and the traitor Macy Minnot, both prominent supporters of the peace movement. Although he'd been wounded while escaping from the city at the beginning of the war, he'd managed to reach the makeshift prison, sabotage its security system, and deal with the guards . . . but then things had gone badly wrong. Someone had knocked him down with a tranquiliser dart, and he'd been left behind when Zi Lei and the other prisoners had escaped. He had a hazy memory that she'd bent over him as he'd faded into unconsciousness, that she'd whispered that she knew that he was a good man. He hoped it was true. He hoped that she would forgive him when he found her.

He watched as military vehicles drove up to the farm tubes that ran alongside the city. Figures in blue pressure suits—Brazilian soldiers—clambered out and moved toward the airlocks at the ends of the tubes. After a little while, people in Outer-style pressure suits emerged and were chivvied into lines by the soldiers, some marching off to the vacuum-organism fields pieced across the plain beyond the city, others marching through the freight yards toward the big airlocks at the eastern end of the city.

When all was quiet again the spy wormed his way closer and found a hiding place in a small crevasse close to the road between the city and the vacuum-organism fields. He dozed for several hours and came fully alert as lines of prisoners, shepherded by guards on fat-wheeled trikes, shambled past. As the last line went by, he rose up and tagged onto its end, following it along the road to the farm tubes. There were no headcounts or ID checks. He followed the Outers into one of the airlocks, the door guillotined shut, and that was it. He was back where he belonged.

4

Cash Baker was woken by degrees. Surfacing to a confusion of light and clamour, sinking back, surfacing again. He knew that he had been badly injured and that he was still gravely ill, but he didn't remember what had happened. The surgeon in charge of his recovery and rehabilitation, Doctor Jésus McCaffery, told him that his singleship had been attacked by Outer drones. One of the drones had exploded close to his ship and a fragment of debris had punched through the ship's hull and pierced Cash's head. His ship had saved his life by putting him in hibernation; after he'd been rescued, Dr. Jésus and his crew had kept him in an induced coma, repaired the damage by regrowing parts of his brain and modifying the artificial nervous system that had enabled him to fly combat singleships, and then brought him back to consciousness in a series of carefully managed steps.

Dr. Jésus or one or another of his aides had to explain this several times. Cash would fall sleep and wake up and try and fail to remember what had happened to him. Sleep was dreamless. Waking was like being in a bad dream he was unable to escape. He didn't know why he was strapped to a bed in a medical ward, and whole slabs of his life were missing, too. According to Dr. Jésus, he was suffering from retrograde amnesia. The memories were still in his head, somewhere, but he had misplaced the codes that accessed them. As he recovered, some of his memories would gradually return, Dr. Jésus said, but the doctor couldn't or wouldn't say how much would be forever lost.

Cash slept a lot, and spent most of his waking time striving to master the basic chores of body maintenance. The medical aides applauded him when he successfully voided his bowels or guided a spoon to his mouth without spilling more than half its cargo. They lavished praise on his ability to remember short strings of unrelated nouns, or to count backward from one hundred in units of three or seven. He met every challenge with the same determination and vigour he'd applied to basic pilot training, the test-pilot school, and the J-2 test programme, and his recovery was astonishingly fast. Within days of being returned to full consciousness, he was out of his bed and testing his ability to walk in a straight line. He had a swirling limp and a tendency to drift to the right, but he gritted his teeth and got the job done in less than two hours, and then he slept around the clock.

An intelligence officer paid him a visit, told him that he was a hero, and showed him two files, crisply edited and saturated with brash patriotic fervour. The first documented the descent of a pair of singleships, one of them apparently his, into the atmosphere of Saturn. Operation Deep Sounding. A demonstration of the capabilities of the Brazilian J-2 singleships that had ended in a thrilling hairsbreadth escape from a fiendish plan by the Outers to destroy them. The second followed the trajectory of a chunk of ice that a gang of Outers had flung across the Saturn System toward a base that the Pacific Community had established on Phoebe, the largest of the gas giant's flock of eccentric outer moons. Cash and two other singleship pilots had been dispatched in hot pursuit. When they'd caught up with the rogue chunk of ice there'd been a brief but furious battle with its automated defences. Cash's singleship had been damaged and he had been grievously wounded. According to the file, his noble sacrifice had allowed his companions to plant a nuclear bomb that had blown the ice to harmless fragments. And he had been rescued and, thanks to the intervention of skilled surgeons using the very latest technology, his life had been saved and now he was recovering from his injuries, a true hero of the Quiet War. The file ended with video of General Arvam Peixoto, commander-in-chief of the Brazilian/European joint expeditionary force and acting head of the Three Powers Authority, leaning solicitously over Cash lying in the bed where he was lying right now, asking him how he was feeling. Cash, watching, winced when he saw his lopsided smile, the obvious effort with which he lifted his arm, thumb quiveringly erect.

Cash didn't remember the general's visit and he didn't remember the action against the chunk of ice or the descent into Saturn's atmosphere. And he didn't recognise some of the people who came to visit him, although they clearly knew him. He remembered his best buddy, Luiz Schwarcz, sure, and Caetano Cavalcanti and a couple of other guys from the J-2 test programme, but he had no recollection whatsoever of several others, including the severely beautiful blonde woman, Colonel Vera Flamilion Jackson, who claimed to have flown with him on the two missions celebrated in the files.

When he asked Luiz Schwarcz about their bunky Colly Blanco, Luiz's mouth turned down and he said that Colly was dead. He'd flown a rescue mission and he'd been shot down. The first casualty of the Quiet War.

Cash was a casualty of war, too. He was improving physically every day, but his head still wasn't quite right. He suffered from violent headaches and was prone to sudden rage, crying jags, and depressions that leached everything around him of colour and value. Meanwhile, he exercised, did his level best to ace out every one of the memory and reasoning tests that Dr. Jésus's crew set him, and slept.

Luiz Schwarcz stopped by Cash's little cubicle whenever he could. He smuggled in forbidden luxuries: a pouch of cachaça, squares of chocolate, a fresh peach. He also brought, at Cash's request, a mirror. Cash had already seen himself in his sickbed at the end of the second file. He believed that he was prepared for what the mirror would reveal. But he wasn't. The file must have been doctored. Cosmetically tweaked. He'd looked pretty bad in the file, but he looked even worse in the mirror. He looked like his father. He looked like his goddamned father in his last days, dying from a wildfire carcinoma that had turned his lungs to black slime.

"You look like a man with a hole drilled right through his head," Luiz said. He was sitting on the edge of Cash's bed because there was nowhere else to sit, a wiry man with coffee-brown skin and a hairline moustache, trim and poised in pressed blue coveralls. "You're the only person I know stubborn enough to survive that."

"I'm not sure I did. I mean, I'm not who I used to be."

"You're a certified grade-A gold-plated hero," Luiz said.

"I'm a fuck-up who screwed the pooch."

"It was a hairy mission. And you went in close and took out the booby traps. The rail guns and the drones. If you hadn't done that, we couldn't have planted the nuke that blew the chunk of ice to dust and splinters. And if you want to talk about screwing the pooch, that would be down to Vera and me. Because we weren't able to rescue you when your ship jagged off."

"No hard feelings on my part. You had to complete the mission," Cash said.

"We completed it. And then we should have come after you—"

"You did what you had to do," Cash said, riding a hot spurt of anger. "You had to leave me. Big deal. Get past it. Because I'm fucking sick of hearing you apologise."

"You're tired," Luiz said. "I'll come back later."

"Yeah, fuck off, why don't you," Cash said. He knew that he was being unreasonable but was unable to stop himself. Hearing himself say, "It's what you're good at. Fucker."

It was like he was possessed. Like the women in church back home, collapsing when the preacher pressed the heel of his hand against their foreheads, writhing on the floor, speaking in tongues.

When Luiz came back the next day, Cash apologised, but his friend waved it off.

"Não é nada."

"It ain't nothing," Cash said. "I have to get past it. I have to get back."

"You will," Luiz said, although his soft sad gaze contradicted him.

They talked about the war. According to Luiz, it had started long before a gang of Outers who called themselves Ghosts had aimed that chunk of ice at Phoebe. And the military phase, the attacks on Outer cities and settlements and ships, had really been the last stage of a cunning and intricately planned campaign. Before the Brazilian/European joint expedition had arrived in the Saturn System, diplomatic and trade missions had persuaded some of the Outer cities to stay neutral. To give in; surrender without a shot. As for the rest, spies had infiltrated the cities and sabotaged their critical infrastructures. Crops packed tightly in greenhouse farms had begun to die, depriving the cities not only of supplies of food but also of oxygen; water had been contaminated with psychotropic drugs, and air with influenza viruses; the information nets had been polluted with demons that denied service or saturated the nets with propaganda messages; power supplies had become untrustworthy. By the time the military phase of the war had begun, the populations of the cities had been demoralised, sick, and exhausted from dealing with faltering or failing life-support systems. Most had surrendered at once. Only Paris, Dione, had put up any kind of resistance, and it had fallen inside a day.

Luiz told Cash that he and the rest of the singleship wing had spent their time chasing down Outer ships that had been attempting to flee the Saturn System. Most of those had been unarmed; the rest had been no match for the singleships. Still, more than half the refugees had managed to escape. Right now they were hiding out at Uranus. And no one knew how many of them were out there, or what they were planning to do.

"Why haven't you gone away?" Cash said.

"Away?"

"I mean after them."

"We're too busy here," Luiz said. "We're good at blowing things up. It's what we trained to do. But we're not so good at putting things back together again. And fixing the damage to the cities is child's play compared to dealing with the Outers."

Luiz told Cash that he'd been put in charge of a taxi service, shuttling marines and civilians and equipment between various moons. The Saturn System was now governed by the Three Powers Authority. The Pacific Community had established a small base on Phoebe and controlled the scattered settlements on Iapetus; the Europeans had been given charge of Rhea; Greater Brazil owned the rest. All the tiny and mostly uninhabited moons, as well as Mimas, Enceladus, Tethys, Dione, and Titan.

"Plus we're arguing with the PacCom over who controls Hyperion," Luiz said. "No one lives there, but it's become a sticking point."

"Bullshit politics."

"Remember we nearly went to war with them over Hawaii?"

"I'm not that fucked up."

"They didn't come here to help us out. We didn't need their help. They came here for a piece of the action," Luiz said. "The question is, what are they going to do with what they have? And what else do they want?"

"If there's going to be another wart, another *war*, I need to make better fist," Cash said, and pretended that he didn't see the quick tremor that passed across Luiz's face.

One day, General Arvam Peixoto visited Cash in his hospital bed and presented him with a medal and his captain's bars—that was when Cash found out that he had been promoted, and that he was going back to Earth. The general told him that people back home needed to know about how the war had been won. He wanted Cash to act as an emissary or ambassador for the expedition. To explain the heroic work being done here, and to tell his own story.

"I don't remember too much of it right now," Cash said.

"Don't worry about that. I have people who can help you. It'll be a fine little assignment. You're a hero, Captain, and you'll be treated as one. You'll tour the major cities, meet VIPs at parties and receptions, drink fine wines and eat steak each and every night. And women, Captain, I don't have to tell you that women love a hero, eh? All you have to do is make a few speeches, answer a few questions. And my people will write the speeches and coach you, and because they will be asking the questions, you will know the answers. A fine assignment, yes? And one that you fully deserve. What do you say?"

34

5

Every day, the Brazilians brought more people to the dead city. Their search parties spread out across the face of Dione, entering and securing every garden habitat, oasis, and shelter, rounding up the inhabitants and transporting them to Paris for processing: a brief interrogation, confirmation of identity, injection with a subdermal tag. An industrial process, inflexible but efficient. The city's net and every copy of its database had been destroyed or corrupted during the war, but the Brazilians had assembled a list of malcontents by trawling news boards, public forums and private discussion groups, personal mailboxes, and registers in the nets of cities that had survived the war unscathed. Anyone who had ever been a member of any civic agency, had served on Paris's council or any of its committees, or had spoken out against reconciliation with Earth, whether in private or in public, was dispatched to the maximum-security jail, formerly the city's correctional facility and now much expanded. Of the rest, pregnant women and women or men nursing babies were sent to a maternity camp; everyone else was told that they could either work for the Three Powers Authority or spend the rest of their lives in a prison camp.

Almost half the prisoners supported the doctrine of nonviolent resistance and refused to work. At first, the Brazilians attempted to break their spirit. Refuseniks were subjected to public strip-searches, random beatings, solitary confinement, or even, in the early days, execution. The guard would order the prisoners to line up and then seize two or three of them and drag them to an airlock and cycle them through into vacuum, but this practice was abandoned when prisoners began to follow the guards and their victims, demanding to be cycled through too. If anyone in one of the barracks was refused rations, the rest went on a hunger strike in sympathy. If the guards selected someone for a random beating, other prisoners would volunteer to take their place. And so on. At last, the Brazilians gave up on attempting to convert the refuseniks and left them to their own devices, supplying their barracks with minimal rations and life support, locking them down in quarantine.

The spy chose to work. People who practised nonviolent resistance might be honourable, principled, and brave, but they were also crazy. They would weaken and die in their isolated barracks, and their principles would die with them. In any case, it was nothing to do with him. He was neither an Outer nor a Brazilian. Neither prisoner nor occupier. He was a free man. He had given himself up to the Brazilians freely because it gave him the best chance of finding Zi Lei. He knew that it was a stupidly dangerous quest, but it gave his new life a shape and a destination. He had been trained all his life to be someone else: to wear the skin of an assumed identity and infiltrate the enemy population and carry out a secret mission. That was what he had done before the war, when, working in the skin of Ken Shintaro, he had sabotaged Paris's infrastructure. And that was what he was doing now. Despite the deprivation and fear and hard work, he was quietly content.

In the first weeks, the spy and his fellow prisoners, all single, childless men, worked twelve hours a day every day in the ruins of the city. Supervision was minimal. They were left to their own devices when they weren't working, and organised themselves into crews assigned a variety of housekeeping tasks: taking turns at cooking, laundry, and general maintenance, nursing those who'd been wounded in the battle for Paris and its aftermath, collecting and recycling urine and feces, tending the fruit bushes packed into the farm tube that served as their quarters, and passing out harvested fruit to supplement their CHON food rations.

The spy was immediately welcomed into this little community. The Outers weren't naive or credulous, but they were naturally hospitable and hadn't yet learned to suspect and distrust strangers. And besides, it was obvious that, with his etiolated build, opposable big toes, and simple secondary hearts pulsing in his femoral and subclavian arteries, he was one of them, and his story about his search for his friend Zi Lei chimed with their strong sense of romance. He told them that she had been arrested and incarcerated before the war, that he had tried and failed to find her during the confusion of the attack on the city when battle drones and troops had fallen from the sky and quickly overwhelmed the defences that ringed the city's perimeter, and that he had been searching for her ever since.

No one in the farm tube had known Zi Lei before the war, or knew if she had survived it. And the Brazilians kept men and women apart, so there was no easy way of discovering if she was a prisoner, in one of the work crews or, more likely, amongst the refuseniks. The spy bided his time. He had been taught how to be patient. But he couldn't stop wondering where she was and if she was all right. He supposed that his tender helpless yearning meant that he was in love.

The spy's work crew had been tasked with collecting the bodies of citizens killed when the Brazilians had taken Paris. The Brazilians had broken in at either end of the city's tent and advanced toward the centre amidst fierce hand-to-hand street fighting. The city's defenders had blown up and set fire to the public buildings in a last desperate stand, and then the tent had been ruptured and the city had lost its air. Half the population had died. Some ten thousand people.

The crew worked in the lower part of the city, amongst manufactories, workshops, and blocks of old-fashioned apartment buildings. It was where the spy had lived as Ken Shintaro before the war, and he found it strange to return to it now. Power had been restored, but the city was still in vacuum and everything was frozen at −200° Celsius. Trees stripped of foliage and branches by the hurricane of explosive decompression when the city's tent had been ruptured stood naked and frozen hard as iron along the wide avenues. The halflife grass that turfed the avenues and the plants in the parks and courtyard gardens was frozen too, slowly bleaching in the stark light of the chandeliers.

Most buildings had been damaged during the battle; few had retained their integrity. There were bodies in apartments, in central courtyards, in basements. Fallen where they had been caught in the open, huddled around doors, in bed niches, inside airlocks. Those who had been wearing pressure suits when they had died were the easiest to deal with. The rest were statues frozen to the floor or to furniture or to each other, heads and hands swollen and blackened by pressure bruising, faces masked by blood expressed from ears and eyes and mouths and nostrils, eyes starting, swollen tongues protruding. Men and women and children. Babies.

The crew secured samples of frozen flesh for DNA analysis and logged and bagged any possessions, then pried the bodies free by using crowbars and wedges and loaded them onto sleds that were driven out of the city through airlocks whose triple sets of doors stood permanently open. Construction robots dug long trenches in the icy regolith beyond the eastern edge of the vacuum-organism fields, and the bodies were dumped into them without ceremony and covered with ice gravel—as if the Brazilians wanted the evidence of their atrocities to be erased as quickly as possible.

After all the bodies in public areas had been removed, the clearance work became a macabre treasure hunt. Searching through apartment blocks room by room. Looking in basements and service tunnels. In storage lockers and cupboards where people had sought refuge or had tried to hoard a last few sips of air. Everyone worked in a haze of exhaustion. They averted their gazes from the faces of the dead as they levered and pried and cut. They cursed the stiff and awkward corpses, sat down and wept, and were chivvied back to work by the Brazilian guards.

There were dreadful stories of people finding loved ones, partners, parents, children, and in any case the work was an unceasing horror. Many people in the salvage crews committed suicide. A few dramatically, by unlatching their helmets or throwing themselves under the treads of one of the construction robots that were demolishing badly damaged buildings; most by finding some hidden spot and disabling their air scrubbers. It wasn't so bad, people said. You became woozy as the carbon dioxide built up, and passed into merciful sleep.

The suicides went into the trenches, too.

One day, the spy was lined up with the rest of the crew near one of the big airlocks, everyone shivering with fatigue inside the shells of their pressure suits, waiting for their armed escort to march them back to the farm tube, when a sled glided by and something caught his eye. A woman lying on top of a pile of bodies, her unmarked face pale and hard as the face of a marble statue, a stiff banner of black hair, little tucks in the outer corners of her eyes, a small uptilted nose. It was her. It was Zi Lei. He broke ranks and chased after the sled and caught up with it, and with a shock of relief saw that the dead woman wasn't Zi Lei after all. Then two guards crashed into him and knocked him to the ground. They hauled him away to the punishment block and stripped him and beat him halfheartedly and threw him in a cell and left him there all night without food or water. And in the morning they gave him his pressure suit and put him back to work.

No one on the crew said anything to him about his moment of craziness.

The spy had been in the city for more than sixty days and still had no news of Zi Lei. By now a kind of telegraphic system had been established amongst the prisoners. Crews sometimes mingled while working on large projects and could exchange news by using a form of sign language to talk to each other right under the noses of their guards. Everyone asked after everyone else, establishing a roll call of the living and the dead and the missing. Zi Lei was one of the missing. No one knew anything about her. It was as if she had dropped off the face of the world.

Perhaps she had.

One day, the spy's crew spent an entire shift searching for bodies and turned up only one. The following three shifts they found no bodies at all. And then, without warning, they were redeployed to work in the vacuum-organism fields.

38

Many of the city's farm tubes and its microalgal and dole-yeast cultures had been destroyed during the war, and most of the crops that had been planted out in new or refurbished farm tubes were not yet ready for harvest, so tracts of vacuum organisms south and east of the city were being ripped up to provide CHON for the foodmakers that supplied the prisoners with basic rations. One day this work took the spy's crew close to the little dome of the research station where Zi Lei and others in the peace movement had been held prisoner. He'd hiked there to save her, and that had been the last time he'd seen her. And here he was again, helping to scrape up stiff lichenous growths from dusty ice, with the dome sitting on a low ridge in the middle distance, gleaming against the black sky. Remembering what had happened there when he'd been someone else.

By now, the damage to the city's tent had been repaired, and it was being repressurised by atmosphere plants that split water into hydrogen and oxygen, stored the hydrogen for fuel, and mixed the oxygen with reserves of nitrogen and carbon dioxide. At first, the carbon dioxide fell as snow, but it sublimed as the city slowly warmed, and then the temperature crept past the melting point of water-ice. The whole city began to thaw. What had once been a frozen morgue was now a ripening charnel house. Trees shed bark and branches as their icy cores melted. Every plant wilted and deliquesced into slime. Bacteria and fungi whose spores had survived the freezing vacuum multiplied tremendously and a great stink of rot and mold filled the tent. Drones equipped with methane probes located bodies that had so far escaped detection. The spy's crew returned to their grim task for a few weeks, and afterward were put to work repairing the surfaces of streets shattered by explosions during the bitter fighting and clearing away the rubble of collapsed buildings.

It was a hundred and fifty days since Paris had fallen. Air pressure inside the city's tent was now at four hundred millibars, thin but breathable. Power had been restored to most areas. The river was running again, fed by a waterfall at the top of the city and tumbling over the rocky watercourse that ran between slopes of dead trees and dead parkland in the slanted half of the city, flowing through the centre of the flat built-up area of the lower half and disappearing underground into pipes that recirculated it back to the top. The pace of reconstruction work picked up as more and more prisoners were brought in from outlying areas across Dione. Work crews cleared rubble and chopped down dead trees. Repaired the railway terminus at the top of the city, and the big airlock complex at the bottom. Patched up apartment buildings.

The spy's crew was rehoused in one of the old square-built apartment blocks at the edge of the industrial zone, very similar to the block in which he had lived when he had first come to the city. Where he had first met Zi Lei. Other crews moved into neighbouring blocks. Only men at first, but then women and children. Families and friends fell into each others' arms. Slowly, that quarter of the city came back to life. Entrepreneurs set up makeshift cafés on corners, serving tea and snacks, or cultivated small patches of herbs and vegetables. There were stalls where goods could be exchanged. An informal index of kudos was established. Along the banks of the river, people erected memorials to their dead, making little sculpture gardens from rubble and glass, setting plaques in the embankment wall, raising painted flags and pennants on wire-whip staffs that blew and doffed on cross-currents of air-conditioning. They painted murals across bullet-riddled walls. There was a fashion for embroidering tiny but elaborate abstract patterns on the sleeve-cuffs of standard-issue coveralls. There were poetry recitals, song-fests, and discussion groups on science and philosophy.

But the bulk of the city was still shabby and battle-scarred. The halflife turf that paved streets and avenues was dead and crumbling to dust; parks and gardens had not been replanted; many buildings were still badly damaged and uninhabitable. Curfews and other restrictions were strictly enforced, power was cut in apartment blocks from ten at night until six in the morning, and Brazilian drones constantly patrolled the middle air between the high vault of the tent and the flat rooftops of the old part of the city. Deadly glittering things that moved with a lazy hum, strobe lights blinking. At night, the red threads of their tracking lasers stitched empty streets and avenues. Sometimes Brazilian patrols would stage night raids on apartment blocks, waking everyone and searching rooms, confiscating possessions and tossing them down to the courtyard, trampling precious garden plots, making random arrests. Most people would return two or three days later, dazed with lack of sleep and the aftereffects of veridical drugs. Some never returned at all.

The Brazilians had moved into the city too, zoning off everything west of the burnt-out ruins of the Bourse and the City Senate, turning the central part of the city and the sloping park beyond into a kind of fortress or forbidden zone inside a perimeter of heavy blast walls and tangles of smart wire. A tented and relatively undamaged apartment building that had retained its integrity when the main tent had been breached was converted into suites of offices and became the seat of the new government of the Saturn System. A regular traffic of tugs and gigs ferried Brazilian and European officers and civil servants to and from orbit, and they were conveyed at speed through the city to what was now called the Green Zone.

When Outers began to be recruited for menial tasks in the Green Zone, the spy began to ingratiate himself with his guards. Unlike most of the Outers he spoke fluent Portuguese, and in addition to his usual work he ran errands for the guards and pretended not to mind whenever he became the butt of their stupid practical jokes. At last, he was granted a brief interview with a security officer, and was put to work in the Office of Collateral Damage Assessment, checking translations of files recovered from the spex and slates of dead Outers.

As soon as he could, he inserted one of his little zoo of demons into the Brazilians' net, a data miner that quickly returned with the results of its searches amongst the great registers of the living and the dead. Zi Lei's name was not listed with the dead; nor was it on the lists of refuseniks and members of the general labour pool. And although the spy's demon presented him with pictures of some twenty-three young women culled from files and security footage, none had more than a passing resemblance to Zi Lei, so it was unlikely that she was living under an assumed identity. It took a little longer, and deployment of two more demons, to break into the hardened and deeply encrypted communications system and send copies of his data miner to the administrations of the other moons under Brazilian control. Zi Lei was not registered on Mimas, Enceladus, Tethys, or Titan.

The spy refused to consider the possibility that she was aboard one of the dead ships still in orbit around Saturn. No, she was alive. She must be. Perhaps she had escaped on one of the ships that had managed to head out to Uranus. Or perhaps she had fled to Rhea, or to Iapetus. Rhea was controlled by the European Union, and Iapetus by the Pacific Community: there was no direct connection with their nets. Or perhaps she was still on Dione, part of the active resistance movement whose members had infiltrated the city or lived in refuges not yet discovered by the occupying force. The spy inserted a demon in the Brazilian net and tasked it with scanning every frame of the city's security camera footage for Zi Lei, and began to reach out to sympathisers of the resistance.

Every day brought rumours of some act of sabotage, or harassment of the occupying force. Squads searching remote refuges were ambushed; explosive devices were buried beside roadways; once, several civilian advisers in the Green Zone were killed by a remote-controlled bomb. The explosion was close to the building where the spy was working. The hard thunderclap knocked him out of his seat; when he picked himself up, he saw a column of black smoke unpacking in the air toward the roof of the city's tent. Within an hour, soldiers swept through the offices and like every Outer working in the zone the spy was arrested, beaten, and briefly interrogated. His assumed identity held, and two days later he and the others were allowed back to work, although it now took more than an hour to navigate the increased security at checkpoints, and all workers inside the Green Zone were subjected to random stops and searches.

At first, the spy's cautious inquiries about the resistance met only with dead ends and denial. A few men and women seemed sympathetic and told him that they would try their best to find out about Zi Lei, but no one ever got back to him. One day, on his way home from work, he was cornered by two men. Both wore fabric sleeves over their heads, with slits for their eyes and mouths. One held a knife at his throat while the other, much older, told him that he was making too much noise about things that were not his concern. He could have disabled or killed both of them inside thirty seconds, but he pretended to be shocked and frightened. He told the older man that he was desperate to find the woman he loved, that he had a position in the Green Zone and could be of help. He had access to useful information, and he would do any kind of favour. All they had to do was ask.

The man shook his head. "That's why we can't trust you—because you work for them. Stay out of our business. Find your woman without involving us."

The spy let the two men walk away, marking their gait. That was how he recognised the younger man a few days later. He followed him to where he lived and learned his name. He was still keeping track of the young man, hoping he would lead him to other members of the resistance, when the Brazilians arrested three women and claimed that they had planted the bomb in the Green Zone. There was a show trial, the accused were found guilty, and the next day every member of the general labour pool was assembled on the dead lawn of the city's largest park to witness the execution.

The spy stood near the back of the crowd, watching the young man he'd been following, planning to follow him afterward. The three condemned prisoners, barefoot and dressed in new blue coveralls, were led out onto a stage by Brazilian guards who moved with the delicate clumsiness of those unused to Dione's low gravity. An officer read out a brief statement, warning that any further acts of treason or sabotage that threatened the reconstruction of the city and the restoration of order would be met with extreme force. The spy wasn't listening. He didn't even react when the three women were shot in the back of the head, one after the other. He had seen, on the far side of the great crowd, someone he knew. Keiko Sasaki, the woman who had been a friend and caretaker of Zi Lei before the war.

It was impossible. He'd mined the Brazilian records for information about everyone Zi Lei had known: Keiko Sasaki's name was in the lists of the dead. And yet there she was.

As the shock of recognition faded, the spy realised that there could be only one reason why she was registered as dead and was living in the city under another name: she was a member of the resistance. Despite the risk, he decided there and then that he must talk to her as soon as possible.

It took him less than twenty-four hours to establish that Keiko Sasaki worked in the city's hospital and lived in the same apartment block as the girlfriend of the man he'd been following. The spy doubted that it was a coincidence, and decided that it would be too dangerous to confront her there. Instead, three days after he'd seen her at the execution, he walked up to her in the hospital and slapped a narcotic patch on her neck and caught her when she collapsed and dragged her into a storeroom.

When she came around she struggled briefly against the plastic ties he'd used to bind her wrists and ankles to shelving, crucifixion style. She made noises behind the halflife bandage clamped over her mouth.

He showed her the knife he'd fashioned from a shard of fullerene, told her who he was, and told her that he'd kill her if she screamed when he removed the gag.

"I won't tell the Brazilians that you are all part of the resistance. I don't care. I only care about Zi Lei. Nod if you are willing to talk."

Keiko Sasaki bobbed her head up and down. She was a slender woman who seemed to have aged ten years since the spy had last seen her. Her face was gaunt and her eyes were bruised and sunken, but her gaze was angry and bright, and she didn't wince when the spy ripped off the halflife bandage.

"I heard you'd died, Ken."

"And I heard that *you* had died. Yet here we are. Where is she?"

"What have you done to your face?"

"Where is she?"

Keiko Sasaki flinched when he dented the skin under her left eye with the point of his makeshift blade and said quickly, "I don't know where she is, but she has family on Iapetus. I heard that after she escaped from prison she tried to get on one of the ships leaving Dione. Whether the ship reached Iapetus, or whether it was one of the unlucky ones, I don't know. I do know that if she managed to reach Iapetus, if she's still alive, she will be safe from you."

"She didn't tell me that she'd come here from Iapetus."

"You didn't know very much about her at all, did you? You didn't even know that she was suffering from schizophrenia until I told you," Keiko Sasaki said. "You weren't interested in her as a person. You were interested in her as an object of your obsession. You believed that you were her friend, that you were in love. But in truth you were two lonely and confused people who were thrown together in the middle of a crisis when emotions were heightened."

"You are trying to hurt me. It won't work."

"I'm trying to tell you the truth."

"I want to help her."

"Wherever she is, alive or dead, she's beyond your help. But listen. You can help us. You can join us. You obviously have the skill to create a false identity, and you obviously needed to do it because you're on the Brazilians' shit list. That means you can be useful to us. We need people like you, Ken. Resourceful people. Survivors."

"Ken died in the war. I'm Felice Gottschalk now. And when I walk out of this room I will be someone else, and you and your friends will never find me."

"If you help us, then in time it might be possible to find Zi Lei. You help us; we help you."

"Don't worry, I'm not going to kill you. I killed a man once, and I never want to do it again," the spy said, and quick as thought slapped a second patch on Keiko Sasaki's forehead and caught her as she slumped sideways.

He walked out of the storeroom as a Brazilian marine, Ari Hunter. Trooper Hunter was a skin, a few entries in the files of the Brazilian military, but he wore the spy's face and fingerprints and retinal and metabolic patterns, and he possessed the spy's DNA. He also looked like an Outer, but that didn't matter. He only had to deal with the AIs and robots that controlled the security gates and the garages. They believed that Ari Hunter required a rolligon because he was on a mission to investigate an anomalous signal near the northern end of Latium Chasma.

This time the spy could drive across the surface of the little moon without worrying about being targeted by the Brazilians. His mission was logged and approved—although he would not be making the return part of the journey, of course. He planned to retrieve and refuel the dropshell and quit Dione. It wasn't an ideal craft, but he couldn't risk stealing anything else. It had just enough thrust to reach escape velocity, and then he could spiral out to Iapetus in a long, lazy orbit that would take more than a hundred days. That was all right. He had plenty of air and water and food, and would spend most of the time drowsing in hibernation. And when he woke, he would set out again to find the woman he loved. It was a holy mission. Nothing could stop him.

6

Loc Ifrahim deserved a world of his own. Instead, they gave him a junkyard full of dead ships.

When the war had kicked off, most of the Outer ships in the Saturn System had been killed by encounters with singleships or drones or mines. Now, robot tugs were locating and intercepting these hulks, modifying the long and erratic paths they traced around Saturn, and nudging them toward Dione, where they were parked in equatorial orbit to await the attentions of the salvage gangs.

A dozen agencies commissioned and loosely controlled by the Three Powers Authority were attempting to reconstruct damaged infrastructure in the Saturn System, find gainful employment for tens of thousands of displaced Outers, set up Quisling administrations and police forces, harness the skills of Outer gene wizards, engineers, scientists, and mathematicians, and reboot the economy using a centralised command-and-control model. All this required a robust transport network, and because it was too expensive to build ships from scratch, repair and refurbishment of those damaged in the war was an essential part of postwar reconstruction planning. Loc Ifrahim was responsible for civilian oversight of the salvage operation, reporting directly to the TPA Economic Commission, a key role in work that was crucial to the success of the occupation. Nevertheless, he felt short-changed and slighted.

Before the war, as a member of the Brazilian diplomatic service, Loc had worked in most of the cities on the major moons of both Jupiter and Saturn. He'd been part of the commission that had drawn up tactics used in the war; he'd helped to lay the groundwork for the deal that had kept Camelot, Mimas, neutral. And in addition to his official duties, he had been carrying out clandestine work for General Arvam Peixoto. He'd not only fed the general useful information, but had also gotten his hands dirty on several occasions. And he was a genuine war hero, too. He'd been kidnapped by Outers and held hostage in a prison outside Paris, Dione, but had managed to escape at the outbreak of war, reach the Brazilian flagship, and disclose important information about the whereabouts of the gene wizard Avernus. It was not his fault that Avernus and her daughter and members of her crew had managed to escape, and yet he was certain that he was being punished for it.

When the war ended, Loc could have chosen to return to Earth, either accepting a modest promotion within the diplomatic service or resigning and becoming a consultant for one of the companies bidding for construction or security work in the Outer System. Instead, he'd made a riskier but potentially highly lucrative move: taking up Arvam Peixoto's offer of a job as special adviser. It paid well enough, but Loc soon realised that the general had no real plans for him and simply wanted to keep him close. Because he knew too much. Because he was an asset that might be useful at some point in the future. Loc spent some time on advisory and intelligence-assessment committees, but his main duty—oversight of the salvage operation—amounted to no more than pushing files to and fro, participating in exhaustive debates about insignificant matters, and spending far too much time in orbit around Dione in a cramped little facility staffed by Outers and controlled by the Brazilian Air Defence Force. He should have been governing a major city, or running one of the relief or reconstruction agencies. Instead, he spent most of his time harassing Outers and Air Defence officers about repair and refurbishment schedules, and taking the flak for slippage in schedules, slow delivery times, and slipshod workmanship.

In short, his work was tedious and onerous but gave him little power or influence, effectively excluded him from the main action, and didn't offer any opportunities to make any real money. The ships had been packed with people fleeing the war, but their personal possessions had little value. The original Outer economy had been based on utility rather than scarcity, and the Outers prized above everything else nontransferable knowledge and experience, and what they called kudos—personal ratings in a bartering system based on favours, good works, and small kindnesses. The only things of value on board the dead ships were works of art, but these were mostly sold off cheaply, as souvenirs. Loc, who knew enough about Outer art to know that he knew very little, had snagged a few nice pieces but couldn't sell them for what they were worth: people from Earth were largely ignorant of Outer traditions and aesthetics, so there was as yet no established market for their art.

46

Meanwhile, young blades from the great families, with little or no experience or knowledge of the Jupiter and Saturn systems, were being parachuted into positions that were rightfully Loc's. The only way for ordinary people to get ahead of the game was by marriage or adoption, but Loc, who had been born in the slums of Caracas and had worked his way up the ladder of the diplomatic service by skill and cunning and ruthless ambition, had spent far too much time in the Outer System instead of on the cocktail circuit in Brasília. He knew that he wouldn't be able to woo and win a woman with even a minor degree of consanguinity unless he gave up his ambition to make his fortune from the spoils of war and returned to Earth. And he wasn't prepared to do that, not after enduring years of hard work, hazards, and humiliation. So he had to suck up the insult of his present position and hope that in time he would be properly rewarded for the favours he'd done for Arvam Peixoto, or that he'd discover some rich opportunity and mine it for all that it was worth.

"We'll all come good in the end," his friend and colleague Yota McDonald said, after Loc had vented at great length and with fine passion about his latest humiliation at the hands of the Economic Commission.

"I don't want early retirement on a government pension. I want the preferment and promotion I've earned," Loc said.

The two men were sitting on a café terrace that overlooked the silken slide of the semicircular waterfall that plunged into a seething basin of wet rocks and ferns and the jewelled cushions of giant mosses. The basin fed a river that ran away downhill between stands of newly planted saplings toward the Green Zone at Paris's midpoint. The terrace, with its quaint wooden tables and white umbrellas, stands of tree ferns and black bamboo, and strings of fairy lanterns, was the preserve of senior civil servants, diplomats, and military officers. Its food—shrimp and fish grown in the city, lobster tails and steak shipped at tremendous expense from Earth—was excellent. In one corner of its terrace a guitarist and flautist played delicate choro numbers that floated on a cool breeze invigorated by the iron tang of falling water. It was one of the most pleasant places in the city, redolent of the privilege Loc craved, but he slouched sulkily in his sling chair, a slender, dark-skinned man dressed in a tailored canary yellow suit and a pink shirt open to his navel, oiled black hair done up in a cap of short braids tipped with ceramic beads. A dandy whose handsome face was spoiled by an air of jaded cynicism that he no longer bothered to hide.

His companion, Yota McDonald, was a sleek, plump young man who before the war, in Brasília, had worked alongside Loc in the commission that had analysed information about the cities and the main political players in the Jupiter and Saturn systems and had developed the asymmetric "quiet war" strategies that had proven so effective in taking down the Outers. Like Loc, Yota had a taste for gossip about the failings of his superiors, but he lacked Loc's ambition. He was content with his position in the middle grade of the diplomatic service and looked forward to returning to Greater Brazil in a couple of years' time, when he would use the bonuses he was assiduously banking to get married, and the contacts he had made to win a well-paid job as an adviser in the private sector.

"You are smart and shrewd, but you feel that you must have everything at once," he told Loc. "Try patience, for a change."

"I want to get what I deserve before I die," Loc said.

"Of course. But destroying yourself in the attempt to win it makes no sense."

"Perhaps I have already destroyed myself. I have given up my health and my marriage prospects in service to God and Gaia and Greater Brazil. So winning fame and fortune is all I have left. My only reason for living. Yet I am frustrated at every turn by men who have grown rich at my expense. Fools who know nothing, who can do nothing, who have suffered nothing. Fools whose only virtue is to have been born into the right family. Lucky sperm. All they have to do is reach out and pluck the golden apples that dangle in front of their faces. And most of the time they get someone else to do it for them."

"We are lucky enough, considering who we are. Look how far we've come!"

"Yes. But not yet far enough."

Yota skillfully changed the subject, telling Loc about the latest row between General Arvam Peixoto and Ambassador Fontaine over treatment of Outer prisoners.

"Our ambassador is still struggling to impose any kind of 'normalisation' on the general and his merry men," Yota said. "Did you hear that he wants to mount a punitive expedition to Uranus?"

"Military command and the Senate have vetoed it; he is threatening to do it anyway," Loc said. "And you know what? He's right. We know that every kind of Outer malcontent is skulking out there. And every day we leave them alone they grow stronger and bolder. We have to deal with them now, before they decide to deal with us."

"Don't let anyone in the security service hear that kind of talk," Yota said. "It's defeatist."

"It's the truth."

Yota shrugged. "Even so, it could get you sent back to Earth."

"Nothing could get me sent back to Earth. It's punishment enough that I remain here," Loc said.

"Now your grievances are showing again," Yota said amiably.

"There has to be more to it than this, Yota. You deserve more. I deserve more. And most of the people who are making good, they don't deserve it at all."

Loc was thinking of Colonel James Lo Barrett, the officer in command of the salvage yard—a lazy, self-satisfied bully of a man with no regard for schedules or the minor details that kept the project running right, bombproof because he was one thirty-second consanguineous with the Nabuco family. The latest slippage in the salvage work had been entirely due to Colonel Barrett's *laissez-faire* attitude, but it was Loc who'd had to explain it to the subcommittee of the Economic Commission.

Yota took a sip of brandy from his oversized glass and said, "Here's something that might please you. It seems that Professor Doctor Sri Hong-Owen is increasingly out of favour with General Arvam Peixoto. She's spending too much time out in the field, working on those exotic gardens, when she should be providing the general with technological miracles he can profit from."

Loc had already heard about this, but it was good to have it confirmed from another source. As far as he was concerned, it was not only important to succeed—it was also important that your enemies should fail. And he believed Professor Doctor Sri Hong-Owen shared a large part of the responsibility for his present plight, for she'd whispered poison about him in the general's ear after the gene wizard had escaped, when in truth it had been entirely her fault. She was obsessed with the hunt for Avernus, and it was a delicious irony that this obsession, coupled with her self-regarding arrogance, might yet be her downfall.

He said as much to Yota, hinting about the small part he'd played in cutting her down to size, smiling and shaking his head when Yota asked him to elaborate. He liked secrets; liked to make people think that he had an inside angle on everything.

"I have allies in unexpected places," he said. "One day soon, perhaps, I'll be able to tell you more. But not yet. It isn't that I don't trust you, Yota. But I don't want to put you in danger."

"Of course not," Yota said, clearly believing that this was another of Loc's revenge fantasies.

It was and it wasn't. After the humiliation of his appointment, Loc had reached out to a cousin and rival of Arvam Peixoto. He'd met the man before the war, when they'd both been involved in one of the projects of the failed and little-mourned peace and reconciliation initiative meant to enhance trade, cultural exchange, and mutual understanding between Greater Brazil and the Outers. The project had failed; Loc, working clandestinely for Arvam Peixoto, had played a small part in its failure. But when it became clear that he would never be properly rewarded despite all he'd done, he had begun to make tentative approaches to Arvam's rival, feeding him little bits of information, such as the truth about the hero-pilot who was promoting the war back in Greater Brazil, and doing a few minor favours. Nothing much so far, although one errand had been amusing—slipping a handwritten note to Sri Hong-Owen that suggested it would be in her best interests for her to look for a new sponsor. Luckily, the bitch hadn't taken the hint. Loc hoped that she'd stick with Arvam Peixoto until the day of reckoning came; he very much wanted to have a hand in her downfall, even though he couldn't see any way of profiting from it.

Meanwhile, he was stuck on the dreary round of his dead-end job, rotating between Paris and the orbital salvage yard. Dione's elegant shipyard, a gossamer web dotted with workshops and cradles, had been destroyed during the war. Its replacement was a grim utilitarian lash-up of modified cargo cylinders, with noisy air-conditioning, an ineradicable odour of stale cooking and chemical toilets, and little privacy. Loc had to bunk in his tiny office, with his aide snoring on the other side of a betacloth curtain; the rations were military MREs; the recycled water reeked of chlorine, and showers were rationed to two minutes once every three days. Colonel James Lo Barrett, the soldiers of the security detail, and the Outer salvage crews didn't seem to mind the appalling living conditions, but Loc loathed the place and would have spent as little time as possible up there if he hadn't had to cover for Colonel Barrett's deficiencies.

The salvage yard hung in the middle of a Sargasso Sea of derelict ships. More than sixty of them now, and one or two still arriving every week, even though it was a year and counting since the war had ended. Their shapes sharply silhouetted against Saturn's foggy bulk, flashing like fugitive stars as they tumbled slowly through black vacuum. Those damaged beyond repair were stripped of reusable components, their fusion and attitude motors were dismounted, and their lifesystems, hulls, and frames were rendered into chunks of scrap metal, fullerene composite, and construction diamond. But most were powerless and frozen but otherwise intact, killed when their cybernetic nervous systems had been zapped by microwave bursts or EMP mines during the investment of the Saturn System. Salvage and refurbishment of these brain-dead ships was fairly straightforward, apart from having to deal with the remains of the dead.

General Arvam Peixoto had refused to mount any kind of expedition to rescue the crews and passengers of the crippled ships. There were too many ships in too many orbits, and the risk that rescue crews might be attacked by survivors was too great. So every ship was a tomb, because those trapped on board without power and life support had either committed suicide, suffocated, or succumbed to the relentless cold. Before salvage could begin, the dead were located and documented and removed, along with all their possessions, the black boxes containing the ship's logs and flight data were handed over to an intelligence officer for analysis, and any cargo was inventoried and offloaded. Then the hulk was guided into a cradle where crews of men and robots replaced AIs and control systems, overhauled and quickened the lifesystem, checked attitude motors, and gave the fusion motor a static test before the ship was inspected by flight technicians, certified, and handed over to the transport wing of the Three Powers Authority.

The salvage work went slowly because there was a shortage of skilled Outer volunteers, and the Air Defence Force claimed that the only flight technicians it could spare were the surly pair who certified the salvage work. The job Loc detested would last for at least two years. Maybe more. But then a chance to redeem himself came out of the empty black sky.

—●—

Loc was in Paris, recuperating from another bruising session with the Economic Commission's subcommittee, when his aide called and told him that one of the salvage crews had found a live body.

It was late in the evening. Loc was dining with Yota McDonald. They'd finished a bottle of expensive imported wine and were working on their second brandies, so Loc was a little thick-headed, saying stupidly, "A live what?"

"A passenger. One of the salvage crews found a live passenger."

The crew had been working on a shuttle that had passed too close to an EMP mine. Its AI and control systems were stone-cold dead, but the rest of it, apart from some kind of fast-growing vacuum organism that coated much of the exterior shell of the fusion motor, was undamaged. The crew had cleared corpses from its lifesystem and unloaded cargo from its hold and had been stripping back the vacuum organism's thick black crust when they'd found a bare patch on the skin of one of the insulated tanks that had supplied reaction mass to the attitude motors. In the centre of the patch was a circular cutout, fixed in place by a thick seam of glue on the inside of the tank. When the crew removed it, they discovered that the tank had been drained. In a plastic bubble nestling between two of the anti-slosh vanes and filled with foamed aerogel at a pressure of 100 millibars a little girl slept inside a pressure suit.

Her body temperature matched the suit's internal temperature, 16° Celsius; her pulse and respiration signs were slow but steady. A quick ultrasonic scan showed that her blood was circulating through a cascade filter connected to the femoral artery of her left leg. There was also a small machine attached to the base of her skull, and a line in the vein of her left arm that went through a port in her pressure suit's lifepack and was coupled to a lash-up of tubing, pumps, and bags of clear and cloudy liquids—a continuous culture of dole yeast growing in a cannibalised foodmaker powered by a trickle charge from a fuel cell. And the fuel cell was connected by superconducting thread to the vacuum organism, which absorbed sunlight and generated a small amount of electrical energy.

The aide told Loc that the girl had been waking from deep hibernation when the crew had found her.

"The revival process seems to have been triggered by a sensor that reacted to the change in the shuttle's delta vee when it was taken out of its orbit. Someone on the shuttle must have put her to sleep, hoping that she would be rescued."

"I better come up there right away," Loc said. "Tell Barrett to leave her as she is. Don't wake her. Outer children are smart and resourceful. As dangerous as their parents."

Excitement and self-interest were burning away his alcoholic fug. He was wondering why the little girl had been hidden away in the drop tank. If someone had put her into hibernation, hoping that she would be rescued, why not leave her in plain sight?

"She's no longer here," the aide said. "Colonel Barrett decided that he didn't have the facilities to deal with her, and sent her down to the hospital in Paris. I'm sorry, Mr. Ifrahim, but he didn't bother to tell me. I didn't find out until after the crew filed their report."

"When was this?"

"She went down in a gig three hours ago. As I said, I didn't find out about this until the crew—"

"Debrief them. Talk to them one by one and get every detail of what they found. And document the continuous culture and her pressure suit. Document everything." Loc was about to ring off when he had a thought and said, "Do you have a photo of her?"

"Barrett didn't—"

"The crews' pressure suits are rigged with surveillance cameras. Check the files, find a good shot of her face, send it straight to me. Get on it now," Loc said, and took off his spex and signalled to one of the waiters and ordered a double espresso.

Yota asked if there was anything he could do.

"You can order transport. I need to get to the other end of the city right away," Loc said, and called the hospital.

The city's main hospital, badly damaged by fire during the war, had not yet been repaired, so its medical services had been relocated to a converted warehouse at the eastern end of the city's tent, close to the freight yards. The place was in uproar when Loc and Yota arrived. After Loc's call, the hospital's supervisor had checked the pod where the little girl was being treated: she had disappeared, a nurse lay unconscious in the pod, and something had shut down the hospital's surveillance system. Soldiers and drones had set up a perimeter and were going from pod to pod, room to room. Loc found the captain in charge and told her that the little girl was very dangerous but under no circumstances should lethal force be used.

By now, Loc's aide had transmitted a video clip from the shoulder camera of a member of the salvage crew. There'd been a clear shot of the girl's face through the faceplate of the helmet of her pressure suit, and Loc had recognised her at once. Avernus's daughter, Yuli.

The captain was a sturdy, competent young woman who listened calmly to Loc's brief explanation about who the girl was and where she had come from. "She could be anywhere in the city now," he said. "Patch me in to your superior. I want to call an immediate curfew, lock down every possible exit, and flood the place with drones."

"She knocked out the hospital's system, but the cameras on the streets were still working," the captain said. "I had an AI process their footage. It found no trace of her."

"Then she used the service tunnels. There's a maze of them under the city."

The captain shook her head. "We have good surveillance down there, too. Ever since we found a posse of rebels hiding in one of the pump rooms. Fixed cameras, bots, and autonomous drones. So far, none of them have picked her up. She's still in the hospital, sir. Be patient."

"Evacuate the patients and staff. Seal it up, flush knock-out gas through the air-conditioning, then send drones in to look for her."

"We'll find her, sir."

"She's no ordinary little girl, Captain. She's a monster."

They stared at each other. Then the captain said, "I'll need to get authority from my CO."

"I'm in charge," Loc said. "If anything goes wrong, I'll carry it."

He would be in a bottomless amount of trouble if he fucked up, but he didn't care. He needed this prize so very badly.

The captain, Bethany Neves, was young but wouldn't be intimidated, and insisted on contacting her commanding officer before she began the evacuation. Her soldiers sealed off the building and escorted staff and patients out through the main entrance one by one, past a gauntlet of drones and armed marines. It took more than an hour. The lieutenant colonel who had command of city security arrived and tried to take charge, but by then Loc had managed to talk briefly with Arvam Peixoto and the general had given him control of the operation, telling him, "Find her and bring her to me. Alive or not at all."

At last, the evacuation was complete. The doors were sealed and a narcotic gas was introduced into the air-conditioning system. Loc had a bad moment, picturing the girl calmly putting on a breathing mask and attaching it to an oxygen cylinder. He told Captain Neves, and she said that the gas worked very quickly.

"One whiff and you're out cold. She won't have time to realise what's happening, let alone do anything about it."

"She could have guessed what we planned to do."

"We'll find her and bring her out alive," Captain Neves said.

It took thirty minutes for the gas to infiltrate every part of the converted warehouse. Drones moved through rooms and corridors, and located a heat spot in a service duct close to the entrance.

Loc insisted on going inside with Captain Neves, a squad of marines, and a medical technician. He didn't want to do it but knew he must or else lose his authority. Parched by booze, caffeine, and adrenaline, he had a bad case of the shakes as he crept after the others. They were all wearing full-face masks and white nylon oversuits. Three marines aimed pulse rifles at the duct while a fourth cut into it with a power saw, peeling back a big flap of plastic, exposing the girl huddled unconscious amongst water bottles and ration packs. No doubt she'd planned to wait out the search and then slip away. The technician slapped a tranquilliser patch on her forehead and fastened a mask over her face, and one of the marines lifted her out.

A slender figure dangling limp and helpless in the man's arms. Loc's prize. His ticket to a better place. His way back in.

1

Sri Hong-Owen didn't hear about it until a news bite hit the nets: a brief announcement that Avernus's daughter Yuli had been taken into custody following a collaborative action between the civilian administration of Dione and the military, soundtracked over video of a tall young girl dressed in an orange jumpsuit and sitting at a table in a bare room with two burly marines behind her. Propaganda no doubt meant to dishearten the resistance. No details about how or where she had been captured, or whether she had given up anything useful about her mother. Sri tried to reach out to Arvam Peixoto, but couldn't get past an aide who, even though the line was strongly encrypted, refused to give her any information "for obvious security reasons."

Sri was on Titan, exploring one of Avernus's gardens. It had been located just six weeks previously by one of the autonomous drones: a small tent capping a shaft drilled into a volcanic dome west of Hotei Arcus, giving access to domains of ammonia-rich water seething with a complex ecosystem of halflife prokaryotes. She ignored Vander Reece's advice, told him he was in charge of the crew until she returned, and flew north in one of the dirigibles to Tank Town.

The journey covered some seven thousand kilometres and took a little over two days. Flying under the hazy orange sky across a vast desert of transverse dunes neatly combed in parallel rows hundreds of kilometres long, built from crunchy grains of frozen gasoline and shaped by prevailing winds that blew steadily from west to east, with long shallow slopes scalloped and sculpted on the upwind sides and steep slip faces on the downwind sides. The sun, a pale spotlight blurrily magnified by the dense atmosphere and ringed by shells of diffused light, tracked across the dense orange smog that sheeted the sky, slowly descending toward the western horizon through Titan's long, long afternoon. At last, a low range of hills appeared out of the haze: outliers of the northern uplands, a rumpled province of ammonia-water ice carved by the lightning forks of dry river channels and dappled with thousands of lakes, some little more than shallow ponds, others small seas the size of North America's Great Lakes. It was midwinter. Methane accumulated during the summer rains was evaporating from the lakes, leaving behind ethane doped with benzene and complex hydrocarbons. The larger lakes had shrunk inside their contoured beds and some of the smaller ones had dried up completely. The braided river channels were dry too. This dark, rugged landscape spreading away under the omnipresent orange haze, the tops of ridges and low domed hills palely gleaming where ammonia-water ice had been stripped of overlying organic material by aeolian erosion and runoff from the methane and ethane rains.

Tank Town squatted on the shore of one of the largest of the lakes, the Lunine Sea. The Brazilian base was a few kilometres to the north, a segmented structure built from discarded cargo shells and raised on fat struts and wrapped in silvery quilted insulation, its fission pile lofting a pale plume of steam bent by the constant wind. The traffic master refused to lay on a special shuttle, so Sri was stuck there, buzzing with frustration like a bee in a bottle, until the scheduled supply run arrived. She tried and failed to get information on the capture of Avernus's daughter, collated her field notes, and paid a visit to Tank Town's mayor, Gunter Lasky.

The old man was of the pioneering generation which had fled from the Moon to the Outer System, and the first person to have established a permanent home on Titan. One hundred and thirty-eight years old, he'd outlived three wives, and his children, grandchildren, and great-grandchildren comprised a significant proportion of Tank Town's population. He was boastful and vain, an old pirate king acting out the myths of his cunning, idealism and intestinal fortitude, but he was still a potent force in Titan's micropolitics. He and two of his sons had brokered a neutrality deal with the TPA and claimed to know as much as anyone in the Jupiter and Saturn systems about Avernus. But he told Sri now that he knew little of any importance about Yuli, saying that the girl had never visited Titan.

"She isn't as young as she seems, I can tell you that. Did you ever meet her?"

"Once," Sri said. "From a distance."

It had been two years before the war, at the opening ceremony of the biome at Rainbow Bridge, Callisto. Sri had designed the biome's ecosystems and had been looking forward to showing them to Avernus, who'd helped to underwrite the cost of its construction. But the ceremony had been disrupted by the appearance of the corpse of a murdered man, carried by drones across the surface of the biome's central lake, and in the subsequent confusion Avernus and her daughter had vanished. Sri had chased them to Europa, but had been recalled before she could make contact. The memory still rankled, a significant portion of her vast store of frustration. Sometimes it seemed that she had been chasing Avernus half her life.

Gunter Lasky said, "How old did Yuli seem then? Eight? Nine? She will seem no older now, I bet, even though Avernus popped her out of an ectogenetic tank more than twenty years ago. Raised her in one of her gardens, as if they were castaways on some desert island. Avernus was given to long disappearances then. Before she became involved in the peace movement, before she returned to the public eye and installed herself in Paris, she was a recluse. A hermit. Hardly ever seen. Mostly communicating through her so-called entourage, although they didn't see much more of her than anyone else. It isn't that she can't bear to be around people, or that she doesn't like them. What it is, she doesn't need them. But I suppose she must have been lonely, so she made herself a daughter. . . ."

The old man fell silent. Lost in some distant memory, staring out at the chthonic landscape beyond the big diamond window, where habitat drums three or four storeys high and capped with steep conical roofs were raised on stilts amongst vivid green farm tubes. Beyond the little settlement, fields of black crusts, spikes, and giant fins stretched away under orange haze toward the dry shore of the Lunine Sea. Gunter Lasky and Sri were sprawled side by side on a mound of low cushions amongst big-leaved tropical plants and vines growing in gravel beds set in the floor, Sri nursing a glass of mint tea, Gunter sipping wine made from grapes he'd grown himself, the only grape vines on Titan. He was a skinny, pale-skinned old satyr with an abundance of white hair and a white beard plaited with coloured strings, wearing only shorts cut down from a suit-liner, a swirling mandala tattooed in black ink on his chest, earrings looped around the rims of his ears, and a chain strung between rings in his upper lip and his eyebrow.

"By making a daughter, I suppose you mean that Yuli is a clone," Sri said, prompting him.

"Hmmm. Most say so, but I don't believe it. The young people who worship Avernus can't believe that anyone as old as she is could ever have had sex, but we were lovers, once upon a time. Did I ever tell you about that?"

"You told me that you've known her a long time," Sri said. She was excited and intrigued by this unexpected revelation, but wary too. This could be another of the old man's tall tales, a skillful blend of fact and misinformation to divert her from an important truth.

"Our little fling was more than eighty years ago," Gunter Lasky said. "Long before I settled down and married my first wife. But it is clearer to me than yesterday. Yes, for a season or two, when this world was as yet mostly unexplored and Tank Town was no more than a landing platform and a single dome, we were lovers as well as collaborators. I taught her about lovemaking and she taught me about designing vacuum organisms. So it's not impossible that Avernus got herself pregnant by the usual means, although I imagine that she would have used the poor man as a sperm donor, nothing more. She's chilly that way.

"Oh, she was passionate in the act," the old man said, with an exaggerated and astonishing lewd wink. "But afterward she'd go away inside her head, no use asking what she was thinking. She was brilliant, of course. And vivid and a lot of fun, when she wanted to be. But more often she was moody and remote, impossible to live with. Although we *did* live together for a little, and worked together, too, building a new home on a new world. A world we explored hand in hand, so to speak, and made our own. But she had interests elsewhere. No one world can hold her for long, let alone one man. Not even me. You understand, I know. You and her, you're somewhat alike."

"Did she ever talk with you about her daughter?"

"I only saw Avernus a handful of times after Yuli was born. And—you may be astonished to hear this—I always respected her privacy. I didn't pry. I heard stories, of course. That Yuli was a clone, yes, many times. That she'd been cut to be some kind of immortal superhuman. All kinds of nonsense, none of it remotely true. What I can tell you is that Avernus has grown strange in her old age. She had a mystery about her, of course. Tossing off hints and half-formed ideas that would take us ordinary mortals years to understand fully. Making us think hard about everything she said. I didn't always appreciate it at the time, but I realise now that it was good discipline. After all, thinking is what makes us human, eh? So by making us think hard she was making us more human. While she became, well, not less than human, but different. Which is why the young, with their strange ideas about driving human evolution in every possible direction, worship her.

"So I imagine that Yuli must have had a strange childhood. Growing up with only her mother. And it's hard for me to think of Avernus as a mother. . . . You know, of course, the irony of her chosen name. Avernus was a volcano in Italy, a place where poisonous fumes meant that birds crossing over it fell dead from the air. Avernus: without birds. Without life. And she who fashions life for places with poisonous air or no air at all took the name of that place, you see? Because she transforms killing airs to life. A clever woman, a genius. Yes! No denying that. But odd. Living at a slant to the rest of us. In her own world, with her own codes and principles."

Sri suspected that Gunter knew more about Yuli than he claimed, but she wasn't able to get past his little act. He told Sri several stories about Yuli that she'd heard from other sources, asked questions of his own. How had Yuli been caught? Where was she being held, and in what conditions?

"I'm certain that she is being treated humanely. Whatever Outers might think, Brazilians are not barbarians."

"Don't hold out any hope that she will tell you where her mother is hiding," Gunter said. "She probably does not know. And even if she does know, she will not tell you. No matter what is done to her."

"I will find Avernus sooner or later," Sri said. "With or without her daughter's help."

Gunter laughed. "You are so serious, and so certain of yourself. Just like Avernus!"

"I certainly know that things may go badly for your people and the rest of the Outers if my search is prolonged. For all the reasons we have discussed several times before."

Sri knew that the old man was withholding all kinds of vital information. He and Avernus had once been lovers, they'd explored Titan together, and Avernus had continued to visit the moon, on and off, for almost a century. She'd borrowed blimps and construction robots from the Tank Towners, and Gunter would have kept track of her comings and goings—he'd probably ridden along with her many times, too. Yes, he knew much more about Avernus and her daughter than he'd ever admit, but he was also stubborn and wily, and threatening him wouldn't achieve anything. As far as he was concerned, the Brazilians were not conquerors but guests. Visitors who should be forgiven their presumptive arrogance and treated politely and hospitably. He would tell Sri only what he wanted to tell her: no more, no less.

Saying now, "Like Avernus, you don't really understand people. So please allow me to give you a little advice. You are anxious and eager to learn what Yuli knows, not only because it will teach you much about Avernus, but also because your general is growing impatient with you. Because you spend too much time studying Avernus's gardens instead of doing what he wants. You think that you can help him by talking with Yuli. But she will not talk. Not to his people, not to you. I have never met her but this I know. Because she is her mother's daughter. So be patient. Let the general fail without you. Do not let your eagerness and anxiety and ambition drive you to become part of his failure."

"I won't fail," Sri said.

"Well then, I can't wish you luck," Gunter Lasky said. "But I can say that I hope to see you again."

His smile, fond and gentle and sad, touched for a moment the part of Sri that had loved—that still loved—her murdered mentor. But she had no time for sentiment. She had work to do.

———————●———————

At last the shuttle arrived. Sri rode it up through the sky's orange haze and fell toward Saturn. Dione's icy crescent hung small and sharp beyond the outer curve of the rings. After a single orbit around the little moon the shuttle stooped down to the spaceport outside Paris, and Sri rode the railway east around the equator and transferred to a rolligon and drove along a new four-lane highway to the tented crater formerly owned by the Jones-Truex-Bakaleinikoff clan, which General Arvam Peixoto had confiscated and made over into his headquarters.

Sri thought it was typical of Arvam's theatrical arrogance to set up his official residence on the moon whose chief city had been at the centre of the resistance to Earth's incursion into the Saturn System, and in a place inconvenient to reach and vulnerable to attack. It was an unambiguous signal of his determination to stay, demonstrating to the Outers that the TPA could commandeer anything it chose; and it was also a deft piece of symbolism. The matriarch of the Jones-Truex-Bakaleinikoff, Abbie Jones, had enjoyed a stellar level of kudos because of her exploits in the far reaches of the Solar System, and it was here that the infamous traitor Macy Minnot had made her home after defecting.

The area around the habitat was in the throes of a massive transition. A military spaceport was being constructed ten kilometres to the northeast; the four-lane highway that linked it with the habitat cut past the fortified bunkers and fields of satellite dishes and tower aerials of the command centre that controlled and monitored all traffic in the Saturn System, past icy ridges that Outers had sculpted into a fantasy of animals and heroes and castles, now much knocked about by target practice and military training exercises. And then the dome of the habitat's tent reared into view, neatly fitted into the slumped rim of a circular impact crater. Chandelier lights strung high inside its web of giant diamond panes and fullerene composite supports burned brightly against the naked black sky, brighter than the sun; the green thread of the rim forest was hallucinogenically vivid in the moonscape's ashy desert. It was beautiful, but appallingly vulnerable: a single missile or smart rock could rupture the dome's integrity and every living thing inside it not destroyed by the blast would be killed by exposure to freezing vacuum.

Arvam and his staff occupied the mansion at the centre of the habitat's gardens, groves of trees, and ponds and meadows. A rambling structure that looked as if it had grown piecemeal, towers and wings and domes in a dozen clashing styles carelessly tacked together and linked by haphazard walkways and ziplines and dogtrots. The general's office was a big, round, white room cluttered with gymnasium equipment, including a rack of fixed weights and a treadmill wheel, several memo spaces, a scarred table cluttered with all kinds of handguns and rifles, and a long low cage in which a dwarfed tiger paced back and forth on tiptoe, tail lashing, yellow eyes bright as lanterns, baring its teeth at any secretaries and aides who came too near. In the middle of this organised chaos, Arvam Peixoto lay prone on a bench, stripped to the waist, a masseur working oil into his shoulders. Because of Dione's vestigial gravity, Arvam was strapped to the bench, and the masseur's feet were stuffed into loops tacked to the floor.

The general was in a good mood, calling loudly to Sri when she entered, asking her if she needed any kind of refreshment after her journey. "We just turned up a cache of excellent white wine in an oasis a couple of hundred kilometres south of here. Try a glass."

"Where is she? Can I see her?"

Arvam smiled at up Sri, his chin resting on his folded forearms, his gaze cold and sharp. "Always business, always straight to the point. I don't hear from you for months and months. It is impossible to make contact with you. And now here you are all of a sudden, making demands."

"I've come to help you."

"If you know something we don't, you should write up a memo. I can assure you that it will receive serious attention from the people I've put in charge of the case."

"I know more about her mother than anyone else. I know that she may be much older than she seems. I know that she isn't human. And I know your people will fail."

The general closed his eyes as the masseur worked on the knots in his shoulders. At last he said, "This isn't about your quixotic quest to find Avernus, Professor Doctor. This is an important matter of security."

"Which you made public knowledge."

"To prove to the tweaks that no one can hide from us."

"It won't do you any good unless she talks. And she isn't talking, is she?"

"My people know exactly what they are doing. They can make the very stones sing." Arvam grunted as the masseur twisted an elbow into the flesh between his shoulder blades. "But there is something you can do for me, now you're here. Talk to the crew analysing her hiding place, and also the crew working on her genome. Translate what they've found into plain speech and report back to me."

"And then?"

"And then we'll see if we need your help. But there's something else you need to do before you get to work," Arvam said, raising his head and aiming his steady, slightly cross-eyed gaze at Sri. "Go visit your son."

———◆———

It was an awkward encounter. Sri hadn't seen Berry for six months. She'd been too busy, unriddling the secrets of the phenotype jungle on Janus and the various gardens discovered on Titan. He had to be encouraged by his governess, a slim young soldier, to go to his mother, and he was stiff with shyness and resentment when Sri gathered him into her arms, answering her questions in monosyllables and shrugs. He'd put on three centimetres and was broader in the shoulders and chest. A boy-man with a shock of black hair and a pale face. Looking at Sri and glancing away. Sly and shy.

Sri dismissed the governess and took Berry for a walk in the belt of forest that girdled the rim of the garden habitat. Tether lines were strung everywhere, but Berry was fully accustomed to Dione's low gravity—one sixth of Titan's, one thirtieth of Earth's—and bounded ahead of Sri like a gazelle. He showed her a herd of shaggy-coated miniature cattle grazing amongst long grass in a grove of sweet chestnut trees, pointed out an albino pheasant, a string of quail chicks jittering along after their mother, a rushy pond where terrapins sprawled on a half-submerged log and giant dragonflies skated over the water's unquiet skin.

Sri thought that the carefully planned and planted forest reeked of nostalgia for Earth and a consequent poverty of imagination, but for her son's sake she affected an enthusiasm for this petty little paradise, the dwarfed animals cut for cuteness and domesticity, the formal gardens and fake wildernesses. Berry was as capricious and exhausting as ever. He chased after the dog-sized cattle and scattered them far and wide, threw stones at the pheasant, would have stamped on the quail chicks if Sri hadn't restrained him, and she had to wade in after him when he splashed into the pond and tried to snatch up one of the terrapins.

Sri stepped on her impulse to correct her son then and there. She'd have a severe talk with the governess later. Berry needed discipline and a strong framework of routine, and it was clear that the young woman had been slack and indulgent. Meanwhile, Sri allowed Berry to lead her up a long path through stands of turkey oak and white pine to a grassy saddleback ridge that had a fine view across the entire garden habitat. He showed her a wooden ramp that jutted above a steep plunge to the treetops of the rim forest, and said that he had flown from there. It was easy, he said. You were strapped under a kind of kite, and you ran out, and the air took you up and out.

"You did that? You really flew?"

Berry nodded solemnly and told Sri that other people wore suits with wings from their wrists to their ankles and flew like birds. He said that he wanted to try that ever so much, but the general had said he would have to wait.

"But I don't want to wait! I want to be a bird!" he shouted, and bounded away across the top of the ridge, arms out, wheeling this way and that and making noises like a combat plane on a strafing run.

Sri calmed him down and they walked back and ate supper and splashed in a warm pool together before Sri allowed the governess to put him to bed. Afterward, she gave the young woman a severe lecture about allowing her son to risk his life and told her that from now on any kind of flying was forbidden.

The young soldier lifted her chin in defiance. "You'll have to take it up with the general, ma'am. He supervises Berry's education."

But the general had left Dione for Xamba, Rhea, where he was meeting with the city's mayor and the commander of the European forces to discuss problems caused by passive and nonviolent resistance to the occupying forces. So Sri set aside her anger and got to work on the tasks she'd been assigned.

She read a summary about the discovery of Yuli's hiding place in one of the dead Outer ships, the rig that had allowed her to survive more than a year of deep hibernation inside an empty fuel tank, how Loc Ifrahim, of all people, had thwarted her attempt to escape from the hospital after she'd been revived. The tank in which the girl had hidden herself had been detached from the shuttle and brought down to Dione's surface. Now it lay under a canopy in a secure area in the military spaceport west of the habitat, a sphere six metres in diameter, half covered with the black scurf of a lichenous vacuum organism and propped on scaffolding like a gigantic Christmas ornament. Sri was shown the hatch cut into the tank's skin and the nest that Yuli had made inside, neatly stashed between two of the anti-slosh vanes that honeycombed the interior. The vacuum organism that coated part of the tank's exterior was a deep, glossy black, smooth as spilled paint in some places, raised in thin, stiff sheets and vase shapes like mutant funeral-flowers in others. The technician who had sequenced its pseudoDNA told Sri that it was a fast-growing variant of a common strain that absorbed sunlight and generated an electrical charge.

"Something like point six watts over its entire surface. Not very much, but enough to supplement the battery the girl was using to run her equipment. And of course it was still growing. In another year it would have covered most of the shuttle," the technician said.

"Using carbon and other material from the shuttle's hull."

"Yes, ma'am. But its feeding hyphae don't penetrate very far, so it would not have damaged the integrity of the ship."

"She planned to stay asleep for a long time," Sri said.

"We believe that she could have survived for at least ten years," the technician said.

"The change in the shuttle's delta vee when it was retrieved started the process of revival."

"Yes, ma'am. A simple tilt trigger. Fortunately, she was found before she woke up."

"She hid herself carefully. She didn't stay inside the ship. So she must have realised that the ship might have been retrieved by her enemies rather than by her friends," Sri said.

She was trying to imagine the foresight and calm with which the girl and the other passengers on the shuttle had made arrangements for her long-term survival. It was impressive. So was the self-sacrifice of the other passengers, all of them members of Avernus's entourage, all found dead and frozen aboard the shuttle. She examined the pumps and filters and yeast culture that had kept Yuli alive, then had a long and interesting discussion with the crew who were analysing her genome and proteome.

It seemed that Yuli was Avernus's biological daughter, not a clone. Also, she possessed a number of intriguing and novel cuts in the genes that controlled development of her brain and nervous system. Her hippocampus was larger than average; the synaptic connections in her reticular formation, her visual cortex, and her neocortex, especially in Wernicke's area, which controlled language processing and speech, were extremely rich; there were subtle alterations to the myelin that sheathed the axons of her motor and sensory nerves. In short, her nerve action potential speeds were ramped up, and her reflexes and her various levels of information processing and decision making were faster than those of ordinary humans. There were other cuts, too. Some were common to most Outers—physiological adaptations to low gravity, alterations to her retinas so that she could see more acutely in low levels of light, and so on—but there were also modifications to the structure of her muscle fibres, mitochondrial ATP production and storage, and the oxygen-carrying capacity of her hemoglobin. And there were extensive tweaks to her metabolism, too. She could synthesise essential amino acids, for instance. Sri discussed everything with the crew, suggested two different methods for determining the girl's true age, and wrote up a summary for Arvam Peixoto.

She didn't tell him about the test she'd performed. A simple cross-match of the girl's DNA against the sample she'd brought from Titan, proving that Yuli was the child of Avernus and Gunter Lasky. If the old pirate hadn't been lying about his relationship with Avernus, Sri thought, if he didn't know that he was the father of the gene wizard's daughter, she might be able to find a use for that bit of information. And if the girl didn't know who her father was, it might be possible to use it as a bargaining point, or to gain her trust.

Sri was granted a meeting with Arvam Peixoto the day after he returned to the garden habitat. They began by talking about Berry. Arvam shrugged off Sri's complaints about the boy being allowed to fly, saying that it was perfectly safe, that he should be allowed to take a few small risks.

"I have three sons of my own," he said. "They had active and healthy childhoods. Much of it spent outdoors. Hiking and hunting, horse riding, sailboats . . . and yes, hang-gliders too. They might have suffered a few bumps and scrapes, but it was important for them to be able to test their limits. Finding out about what you can do, it's part of growing up."

"Berry isn't robust," Sri said. "And he can be a little clumsy at times. Accident-prone."

"Healthy exercise will toughen him up and improve his sense of self-esteem. And this is just the place for it. Safe, and self-contained. Also, when he's given a little freedom to be himself there's a marked improvement in his temper and manners," Arvam said. "And he needs all the help he can get in that department."

"He needs intellectual stimulation," Sri said. "And he isn't getting enough here."

They both knew that this wasn't about the risk to Berry: it was about control. They were like divorced parents battling over custody rights.

"I find it curious that you didn't ever cut him to fix up his little . . . deficiencies," Arvam said.

"It's illegal. Antievolutionary."

"That didn't stop you tweaking the genome of your other son."

Sri felt a cold fist in her stomach. Until now, she'd always believed that no one else knew about the work she had done on Alder. She'd edited his genome very carefully, making sure that his beauty, charm, and charisma did not exceed the human norm, destroying all the evidence.

"Don't worry," Arvam said. "Your secret's safe with me. And besides, if it ever came to it you'd be answerable to worse crimes than a little cosmetic gene-play. So tell me the truth: why didn't you bestow similar gifts on Berry?"

"I left him in his natural state out of respect for his father."

"Ah yes. Poor Stamount. You still wear his ring, I see."

Sri wore it on the third finger of her left hand. A lattice of bone grown from a culture of Stamount Horne's osteoblasts after he had been killed fighting bandits in the Andes. Sri hadn't exactly loved the man, but she had respected and admired him. They had been a good match, and would have done much together if he had lived. He had sometimes been as cruel and capricious as Arvam Peixoto, but his cruelty always had a purpose; unlike Arvam's crude bludgeoning, it had been as honed as a scalpel, and wielded with masterly skill.

"Stamount was a fine man, and I am sure that his son will grow up into a fine man too," Arvam said. "Now, if you have no more complaints to lay at my feet, I'll allow you a glimpse of our prisoner, as I promised."

"She hasn't talked, then."

"Oh, she talks. But so far not about anything important. You can discuss everything with the team who are questioning her. As a matter of fact, their chief is waiting for you right now, in the interrogation suite."

The room where Yuli was being questioned was as bright and sterile as an operating theatre. White walls, white floor, a ceiling that burned with bright and even white light. No shadows anywhere. Everything lit with stark particularity. The girl was encased in a machine like a coffin or an iron lung of the long ago, with only her head showing. An MRI cap clamped over her shaven scalp. Her skin pale and perfect as porcelain. Her eyes large and green. The lids were taped open and a delicate apparatus dripped artificial tears so that her corneas wouldn't dry out, and her head was secured so that she had to stare at the memo space hanging above her, which was presently showing a slow parade of faces while a lilting voice asked her to identify them. She said nothing. Her jaw was clenched and a muscle jumped in her cheek. It was the only indication that she was suffering a tremendous white-hot bowel-ripping agony. The machine was playing on her nervous system like a concert pianist, subtle ever-changing variations and arpeggios that ensured that she could not grow accustomed to the pain.

Standing in the adjacent room, watching her through a polarised patch of wall, Captain Doctor Aster Gavilán, the interrogation team's chief, told Sri that the girl had endured pain induction for more than twenty hours now, yet still showed no sign of cooperation.

"We began with drugs, of course, but they didn't work. Her metabolism is different; her nervous system is *very* different. So now we are using pain, but she has withstood more pain than anyone ever tested in this device. She feels it. I know that she feels it. Elevated levels of histamine in her blood, activity in her nervous and endocrine systems, brain scans . . . she is not blocking the pain at any level. But she hasn't broken. Amazing."

"That isn't what I'd call it," Sri said.

Captain Doctor Gavilán was a dark-complexioned middle-aged woman, plump-breasted as a pigeon. She studied Sri for a moment, her head cocked to one side, then said, "If you are disappointed in our progress, I can assure you we have other resources. Mutilation, for instance. People who should know better talk about the separation of the mind and the body. In my experience, subjects who can withstand substantial amounts of pain break as soon as you begin to brand and cut them."

Sri was sickened by the avid glint in the woman's gaze. "I'm disappointed in your progress, Captain Doctor. And disgusted by your methods."

"This girl is living proof of the Outers' plans to speed up human evolution and push it in unacceptable directions. She has been turned into a monster. A crime against God and Gaia. We came here to put an end to such abominations. It is a holy task, and we must not flinch or hesitate while carrying it out. Think of her as an asset," Captain Doctor Gavilán said, her tone sweet as poisoned honey. "The key to finding Avernus."

Sri studied the little girl locked in the gleaming apparatus, and watched the muscle in the corner of her jaw jump, jump again. "Torture rarely yields useful information," she said.

"The general believes that she will cooperate."

"The general is mistaken," Sri said.

She phoned Arvam Peixoto, explained what she wanted to do, and told him that she could only do it on her terms, without any kind of interference from other parties.

"That sounds like a demand," Arvam said. "Be careful."

"You need my help. Captain Doctor Gavilán is a fool and a fanatic. And her methods are unsound. She has failed to make any kind of progress because she does not understand the nature of her subject."

"Can you guarantee that your methods will yield results?"

"I can guarantee that I will try my best. If it doesn't work, I won't ever ask you for anything else. I'll walk away, and you can let Captain Doctor Gavilán and her little crew of pain kings do their worst."

Arvam Peixoto gave Sri seven days. Yuli was moved out of the interrogation centre, installed in a suite of rooms, and subjected to a light routine of vanilla interrogation sessions by a pair of psychologists. Meanwhile, Sri gave the crew who'd been analysing her genome a new project: identify and synthesise a pheromone that, unlike standard hypnotics and truth drugs, would gain traction in the girl's tweaked metabolism and make her pliable and open to suggestion.

Fortunately, Sri already had a model she could adapt—the mix of subtle chemicals that her elder son secreted from his sweat glands. She and the crew worked up a virtual replica of Yuli's olfactory receptors and tested a myriad modifications of Alder's pheromonal perfume against it, substituting a nitrogen atom for a sulphur atom, adding an acetyl tail or deleting a *cis*-double bond, and so on, and so forth. The most likely candidates were tested on Yuli herself by introducing minute amounts of each one in turn to the air in her suite while she was being interviewed by the psychologists and monitoring changes in her responses to the psychologists' questions and gross physical reactions such as her pupil dilation, and skin temperature and conductance.

Sri drove the crew hard. They worked around the clock for four days, fueled by protein blends, caffeine, and tailored pharmaceuticals, and at last they had a single candidate that, although inducing only small downward revision in the results of standard tests for aversion and antagonism, and correspondingly small increases in cooperation and friendliness, was the best Sri could do in the impossibly tight time frame. She slept for six hours and then, after an intense coaching session with the psychologists, entered Yuli's suite for the first time.

The rooms were small and softly lit, decorated in soothing blues and greens. Flowers growing in pots, lush halflife turf softening the floors, piped birdsong. The little girl sprawled on her tummy on a big bean bag, dressed in clean white coveralls and reading an ancient novel, *Moby-Dick*, clicking through the page on a slate at a fast and steady rate. She didn't look up when Sri came in, and shrugged when Sri asked if she could sit down.

Sri perched on the lip of a sling chair and folded her hands in her lap. "I want to apologise for what happened to you. It was a mistake. They didn't understand you."

"But you do."

"Of course not. But I'd like to try."

"You want to be my friend because you want to get inside my head. And you want to get inside my head because you want to know my mother's secrets. I know who you are, Professor Doctor. You collaborated on the Rainbow Bridge biome with my mother. You were on that barge, the day the biome's lake was supposed to be quickened. You were so anxious and eager to meet her that you were actually trembling. Vibrating. You're vibrating a little now, aren't you? Not just because you are frightened of me, although you are, but also because you think I might bring you closer to what you want most in all the worlds."

Yuli's tone was light and amused. Her green gaze, almost exactly the shade of chlorophyll *a*, was still fixed on the slate. Her hair was beginning to grow back, a faint black stubble on her scalp. A plastic collar was locked tight around her neck; it would deliver a crude paralysing blast if she attempted to attack Sri or did anything that the soldiers monitoring her every move deemed inappropriate.

Sri said, " You see other people very clearly, Yuli. Use that perception to examine your own situation. See how I could help you. And your mother, too."

"A dead man came walking across the water that day. And that funny little ceremony promptly dissolved into chaos. The veneer of so-called civilised behaviour is very thin and brittle, isn't it? Here we are now, being polite to each other. What is it that could shatter that, I wonder?"

"I'm not like the others, Yuli. I'm not part of the military thing they have here. I'm a scientist, like your mother."

The girl yawned, showing tiny spaced teeth in clean pink gums. "My mother isn't a scientist. She's a gene wizard. If you don't know the difference, there's no help for you."

"Science is one of the tools that she uses. Also imagination, and a way of seeing the world at a slant that's quite unique. But science is as fundamental to her work as anything else. I admire your mother's work, Yuli. I want to understand it. I want to understand her."

"I'm not like my mother," Yuli said. "I'm not even a scientist, much less a gene wizard. So I can't help you. I'm sorry, but there it is. You think I'm lying. You think I am the key to your heart's desire. Well, I'm not. And nothing you can say will change that. You might as well save your breath and give me back to the military."

"You and your mother have at least one thing in common," Sri said. "I think you see the world at a slant too."

With shocking abruptness, Yuli rolled onto her back and kicked her legs in the air and knotted her long prehensile toes together. After a moment, she looked over at Sri and said, "She's hiding, isn't she?"

"Yes."

"Where?"

"I caught up with her on Titan. But she escaped."

"This was during the war."

"Yes."

"After we escaped from that dreary prison and those silly people."

"After she left Dione, yes."

"Who was she with?"

"She was alone when I met her, but I believe that two people helped her reach Titan. Macy Minnot and Newton Jones."

Yuli's toes knotted and unknotted. "And where were these two heroes when you confronted my mother?"

"When I arrived, they appeared to be heading away from Titan."

Sri hesitated. She'd never told anyone, not even Arvam Peixoto, the whole truth. But she felt that she had to be candid now; she was certain that Yuli would know if she attempted to dissemble, and in any case candour was the cornerstone of trust. So she gave a brief account of how her attempt to confront and capture Avernus in one of her gardens had ended in utter humiliation. How her secretary had disobeyed her, and she'd had to kill him. How she had been snared by one of Avernus's creations.

She said, "After your mother got the better of me, I saw an aeroshell land nearby. I think it was carrying Macy Minnot and Newton Jones—they came back to rescue your mother. But she didn't need rescuing. A small aeroplane took off, and soon afterward the aeroshell left."

"My mother was flying the plane."

"I think so. I want to find her because I want to help her. Because I think we could create wonderful things together."

"Do you have any children?" Yuli said.

"Yes. Two sons."

"Did you tweak them?"

"I gave my eldest son a few . . . advantages," Sri said.

"Is he here?"

"He's in charge of a research facility in Antarctica."

"Pity. Him and me, we have something in common."

"My other son, Berry, lives here. It might be possible for you to meet him."

"My mother created me," Yuli said. "She isn't what you could call a people person. Really, she doesn't understand people at all. She doesn't even understand herself most of the time. But when Greater Brazil began to make overtures to the Outer System a decade ago, she believed that for the first time in a hundred years there was a possibility of a real and lasting reconciliation with Earth. And she decided that she wanted to become involved. That she could do some good—like the biome at Rainbow Bridge. And because she didn't want to be distracted by all the political maneuvering, she got up a crew of advisers and she made me—made me what I am—to help her explain what people wanted of her and how she could deal with them. But here's the funny thing. *She didn't listen to me.* I would give her advice and she would listen carefully and then completely ignore it. She carried on exactly as she had always carried on. When the so-called joint expedition arrived in the Saturn System and began to behave in a grossly provocative manner, I told her to give up any idea of making peace with Earth. And I told her to keep away from the people who, contrary to all the evidence, believed that war could be averted. But she didn't listen. No, she made herself into their figurehead and sacrificed her freedom on the altar of their principles. Sacrificed my freedom, too. And when war broke out and we managed to get free, I told her to stay with Macy Minnot, who may not be the brightest of people but is a proven survivor. But again: no. She decided that she knew better, and went off on her own. To sulk, I bet. To lick her wounds and try to figure out where she went wrong."

"Very often my advice goes unheeded," Sri said. "I know how frustrating it can be."

She was trying to make a connection with the girl by sympathising with her and seeking to underscore similarities, as the two psychologists had advised. But Yuli laughed and said scornfully, "Do you really, truly think we're in any way alike? Oh, maybe you're like my mother, just a little bit. But you and I have nothing in common. I'll tell you why, if you like."

"Please," Sri said, as calmly as she could.

"I hope for your sake that you didn't change your son too much, Professor Doctor. I hope you didn't make him into a true more-than-human monster. The kind of creature that people like your general quite rightly fear. Because if you did make him into a monster, he will destroy you. That's what monsters do. They aren't grateful for the so-called gifts they've been given. They may love them because they elevate them above the common herd, or they may loathe them for exactly the same reason, but they'll never, ever be grateful. Why? Because those gifts set them apart from everyone else, including their creators. Yes, the old story, Frankenstein and his monster, the stuff of a billion tawdry serials and sagas. But the reason it has persisted for so long is because it contains a fundamental truth: monsters are always lonely, because they can't connect with ordinary people in any ordinary way. People fear and persecute monsters because they are different, and monsters despise and torment people because, despite their weakness and inferiority, they possess the one thing that monsters can never possess: the fellowship of the herd. And so monsters grow contemptuous, and contempt turns to hate, and hate to rage, and then the running and the screaming and the killing and the destruction begins. And I should know," Yuli said, flexing her back and bouncing to her feet, "because I'm very definitely a monster!"

Sri flinched, she couldn't help it, and then Yuli was on her back, arched and straining, making raw animal noises. After a moment, Sri realised that one of the monitors had activated the collar.

Despite the abrupt end to the session, the psychologists believed that it had gone well. "The pheromone had only a small effect, but I think it was significant,"

one said. "Yuli was open and friendly toward you. She engaged in conversation, showed curiosity, and was candid about herself. It's an excellent start."

"She was attempting to assert her own identity," the other said. "She harbours considerable resentment toward her mother, that's been clear from the outset. And she appears to blame her mother for her present situation. We must find a way of sympathising with that, and using it to build a bridge or two."

"I'm not interested in making friends with her," Sri said. "And she isn't interested in making friends with me. I thought that was clear enough."

"But she *was* friendly," the first psychologist said.

"Discover what she wants," the second psychologist said. "Then she may open up and give you what you want."

"She wants her freedom," Sri said. "I can't give her that. And besides, she's already refused it when it was offered to her in exchange for information about her mother. Tell me: does she really hate Avernus? If she does, wouldn't she have betrayed her mother by now?"

"She's conflicted," the first psychologist said. "She blames her mother for her situation, but she's also loyal to her."

"And she knows that by blaming her mother she isn't taking responsibility for herself," the second psychologist said. "Help her to do that, and you will begin to win her trust."

It sounded too pat to Sri. Like one of the Just-so stories made up by evolutionary biologists, simplistic attempts to rationalise quirks of human behaviour by suggesting they were hardwired relics of ancient survival strategies. Nevertheless, she allowed the psychologists to coach her through a couple of scenarios and went back to the suite early the next day. She'd been coolly confident before; now she felt a sharp edge of caution.

Yuli was waiting for her, sitting cross-legged on the big cushion, calm and indifferent. Sri had brought a slate with her and showed the girl videos of the garden on Titan where she'd been working: ragged sheets fluttering in currents in a lead of ammonia-rich water under the volcanic dome, the zoo of different microscopic forms expressed by a single suite of genes.

Yuli yawned, and said that she didn't know anything about her mother's gardens. "She made them before I was born. And afterward, she was too busy to make any more."

"I'm sure you visited some of them."

"If you want to know why my mother made them, ask a plant why it makes flowers. Ask a bee why it makes honey. She made them because that's what she does." Yuli paused, then added, "You're collecting them, aren't you?"

"I'm trying to understand them because I believe it will help me understand how your mother works. How she thinks. And I believe that it will make me better at what I do. Let me show you something else," Sri said, and pulled up the list of changes made to Yuli's genome and highlighted those which had altered her brain structure.

The girl shrugged. "You can't understand someone by cataloguing their genes."

"I'm not trying to understand you, Yuli. I wouldn't presume. But I *am* trying to understand your mother's work. She changed you because that's what she does. She remade you out of the same impulse that lay behind the creation of her gardens," Sri said. "It's all one piece."

"I don't know where she is," Yuli said.

"I believe you."

"If she's hiding, it will be in one of the gardens she didn't tell anyone about. Even me."

Sri showed Yuli more videos, and gave quick and precise summaries of what she had discovered in the gardens that she had so far explored. Yuli watched and listened quietly, and said, "Those are the only ones you know about?"

"Apart from one on Iapetus I have yet to visit."

"There are many more gardens than that," Yuli said, with a perfect imitation of carelessness. "One of them is right here on Dione. I'll take you to it, if you like."

Arvam Peixoto refused to allow Yuli to leave her suite, let alone travel to some remote spot on the surface of Dione. Besides, he said, her offer to lead Sri to one of her mother's hidden gardens was no more than an attempt to create an opportunity to escape: Sri would find nothing but dust and ice out there, or some kind of trap. Sri said that Yuli was more subtle than that, pointed out that she wore a collar that could paralyse her at any time, and suggested several other ways of making sure that she could be controlled. But Arvam's mind was made up.

When Sri told Yuli about the general's decision, the little girl shrugged and said that she would think exactly the same thing if their positions were reversed. "As of course I wish they were."

In their previous meetings it had been as if Yuli had drawn a circle around herself, a wintry fortress she'd defended with barbs of sarcasm and shafts of bitter wit. Now it was as if she had opened the gates of the fortress and stepped outside. As if, overnight, winter had turned into spring. She seemed to be genuinely relaxed, making and maintaining eye contact with Sri, smiling at her small joke.

"I'm sorry I can't do more," Sri said, and meant it.

"Don't be. I'll tell you where it is anyway. As a gift." Yuli recited a set of map coordinates, and added, "Of course, it's a test."

"What are you testing?"

"You, Professor Doctor. I want to see how quickly you can understand my mother's little *jeu d'esprit*."

"And if I succeed? As I will, of course."

"Then we can talk some more," Yuli said.

The coordinates led Sri to one of the bright cliffs created by tectonic fracturing east of Palatine Chasmata. A passage cut between two folds of ice descended to a sealed and insulated bottle chamber some five hundred metres long. Sri burned with frustration while a squad of marines wasted half a day mapping the chamber and the area around it with drones and deep radar, treating it like an unexploded bomb or plague pit until it was at last declared safe and she was allowed to enter and get to work.

She quickly realised that it was another phenotype garden like the jungle on Janus or the microbial biome in the volcanic vents on Titan. It seemed to be a favourite theme of Avernus's. Here, the basic form was a kind of moss that expressed gross and subtle variations of thallus structure, from thick cushions to tangles of filaments or erect shoots like scaled clubs a metre tall in every shade of green or orange, all connected to each other by hyphal threads, like a drawing made by a single unbroken pencil line. This moss garden filled the floor of the chamber from edge to edge, interrupted by chunks of black silicates mined, according to spectrographic and isotopic analysis, from the dark and broken ring that circled Rhea. The light was dim and red, the air cool and damp. Water burbled up from springs near the entrance and fed slow, fat, low-gravity streams that cut wandering lines through the moss and fed deep pools at the far end. In places ferns or grasses or bamboos sprang directly from the moss substrate. Everything shared the same genotype, including the butterflies that hatched from capsules at the tips of the club mosses and fluttered about and died and sprouted new moss filaments, like the grass-scarf-grass cycle that the PacCom liaison secretary, Tommy Tabagee, had once described to Sri.

Within a day Sri had worked up a bare-bones description of the garden. Analysis of every potential form coded in its genome, and the homeobox sequences and transcription cascades that controlled their expression— whether a filament would become moss cushion or fern or grass—would have to wait, but she expected that they would turn out to be variations on the basic pattern. When she returned to the habitat she gave a precis of her findings to Arvam Peixoto. She told him that it was as spare and elegant as the ancient moss gardens of Japan. He said that it was an elaborate joke, and worthless. He was in a bad mood. Several of his soldiers had been killed or injured when a sabotaged building had collapsed in Paris; its skeleton had been weakened by some kind of halflife catalyst that had degraded the fullerene components to sooty powder.

Sri assured him that the phenotype gardens had immense economic potential. "It's a trivial skill to graft genes into an organism so that it expresses a new property. But once I understand how the apparently random expression of phenotype is regulated, I will be able to create varieties of totipotent plants that will be highly adaptable and produce all kinds of different foodstuffs according to need. Apples, maize, tomatoes, all growing on the same vine. Or plants that produce apples one season and tomatoes the next."

She talked for a while, but Arvam didn't seem convinced. "At least you passed the little monster's test. What now?"

"We will talk some more, and more openly, I hope."

"She gave you a little treat and you're wagging your tail like a puppy. Who is in charge of whom?"

"I'm happy to let her believe that she is testing me. It allows her to believe that she has some power over me. It brings us closer together."

"The psychologists think she's trying to play you."

"Of course she is. She doesn't want to be tortured. She wants better treatment. Simple quid pro quo."

"If she wants better treatment, she had better start giving up hard information," Arvam said.

"She's already given me this garden. In time she'll give me much more."

"You have another seven days," Arvam said. "And I don't need any more gardens."

The psychologists cautioned Sri about getting too close to Yuli too quickly, and suggested that the little girl would be more willing to talk freely, more likely to divulge useful information, if Sri didn't visit every day. Sri ignored them. For one thing, their plan was a crude variation of the reinforcement principle of behaviour, like giving a mouse food pellets at random intervals when it completed a series of tasks because that made it work harder than if it was rewarded every time. But people were not mice, and Yuli was not like most people; she would see through this transparent ploy straight away. For another, Sri knew that Arvam's deadline was inflexible, so she needed to spend as much time with Yuli as possible, even if it meant neglecting Berry and the rest of her work.

She discussed the marvellous and intricate details of Avernus's gardens with the girl, and told stories about her childhood: how she'd grown up shy and awkward and lonely in a provincial town where no one else was interested in science; how she had worked so very hard to escape, but because of her lowly birth had been able to win only a post in an agricultural research facility in São Luis; how her work had attracted the attention of the green saint Oscar Finnegan Ramos, who'd given her one of his famous scholarships. She told Yuli about her first true insight, the epiphany that had cracked open a stubborn problem crucial to the development of a novel artificial photosynthesis system. She talked about her two sons, the research facility she had built on the Antarctic Peninsula, the biome she had created there and the biomes she had created elsewhere, including the ill-fated project at Rainbow Bridge, Callisto.

Sri poured out her life to Yuli. Opened her heart. Told her things that she hadn't told anyone else. Trying to make contact. To find common ground. She didn't tell her about the murder of her mentor, but she tried to explain the ambition and frustration that had driven her to risk everything by coming out to the Saturn System, leaving one son behind on Earth, bringing the other with her and giving him up as a hostage.

"I'm lonely," Sri said. "Most really clever people are, at one time or another. And although I'm not as clever as your mother, I'm cleverer than most people. But sometimes I wish that I wasn't. It would have made my life much easier because I would be able to accept an ordinary life and small, ordinary ambitions."

Yuli thought about this and said at last, "I see through the masks people wear in public, and I think faster than they do, and most of the time I can pretty much guess what they're thinking. It makes it hard for me to like them, and that makes me lonely. It makes me feel that I'm the only real person in a toy universe too small to contain me. Is that how you feel?"

"Sometimes."

"I feel it all the time. With everybody."

"Including your mother?"

For a moment Sri thought that Yuli was going to open up, but then the little girl shrugged and said, "No one understands my mother. Not even my mother."

So it went. Sri would spent hours attempting to establish common ground with Yuli, and just when she thought she had established a tenuous empathic bond the girl would retreat into her winter fortress. After three days of this, Sri went to the colonel in charge of security in the habitat and told him what she needed. The man was cautiously doubtful, but he couldn't consult Arvam Peixoto because the general was visiting Baghdad, Enceladus, and Sri put her case with considerable force and assumed all responsibility.

The next day, she met with Yuli at the edge of the forest that ringed the perimeter of the hold. A pair of drones hovered overhead like hawks. The girl's wrists were shackled in front of her and she stood in front of a phalanx of armed guards in black body armour, looking demure and composed and very small.

"I thought you might enjoy a walk," Sri said.

"Why not?" Yuli said carelessly.

The guards and the drones followed them as they ambled through the green shade of the trees. Yuli told Sri that she had been here several times before; her mother had been friendly with Abbie Jones, the matriarch of the Jones-Truex-Bakaleinikoff clan.

"I don't suppose she lives here now," Yuli said.

"I believe that she was moved to Paris."

Abbie Jones was a political prisoner, one of several hundred interned without trial.

"I'm glad she isn't dead," Yuli said. "I liked her. She was almost as famous as my mother, but she wore her fame very lightly."

They talked about the exploration of the fringes of the Solar System that had won Abbie Jones so much acclaim amongst the Outers. They talked about Avernus's visits to the habitat and the little gifts she'd given the clan: the dwarf cattle that roamed the forest; several novel species of flowering plant that grew in the formal gardens beside the habitat's mansion; a redesign of the waste-management system. They sat in the shade of a big cork oak and shared a jug of iced pomegranate juice and a plate of pão de queijos and other savouries prepared by Arvam Peixoto's personal chef.

"This is very nice," Yuli said at one point, "but it would be nicer if I wasn't shackled like an animal and watched by armed men and machines.

Isn't this collar enough? It will knock me down if I try to do anything stupid. And anyway, I promise that I won't."

"The military are scared of you," Sri said.

"And what about you? Are you scared of me?"

"Let's say that I am cautious, because I don't yet know all that you can do."

"No, you don't," Yuli said, looking pleased.

Sri made arrangements to meet her in the same spot the next day, but when she arrived she found not only Yuli and the guards, but also Arvam Peixoto and Berry.

Arvam showed his teeth to Sri and said, "I thought we'd take a walk together. The children can get to know each other."

"You know that she isn't a child," Sri said. She was angry and afraid. Angry that Arvam had presumed like this, exposing her son to danger without any precautions or preparation; afraid that he was doing this to punish her for forcing the security chief to allow Yuli out of her suite.

"Whatever she is, we can control her," Arvam said, and showed Sri the remote he held. "A little demonstration would be appropriate, I think. Just in case."

"Don't," Sri said.

Arvam turned and aimed the remote at Yuli, and the girl fell to the ground in a knot of agony.

"I should make my staff wear those things," Arvam said. "It would keep them on their toes."

"You fit every definition of a fool," Sri told him and went over to Yuli and helped her up. It was the first time she'd touched the girl. Yuli's skin was dry and fever hot, burning through her paper coveralls. Her wrists were fastened by plastic shackles and a short cord.

"This wasn't my idea," Sri said.

"I don't mind pain. It make me stronger. It shows me how much he fears me," Yuli said. She was almost exactly Sri's height. There were flecks of gold in her calm green gaze. "Besides, it's worth it to have a chance to talk to your son. Perhaps I can learn about you from him, just as you've learned about my mother from me."

"That seems fair," Sri said. She was striving to sound calm, but she felt as if she had swallowed a cloud of butterflies.

Arvam told Berry, "You want to show our new friend the terrapins, don't you?"

Berry studied Sri and Yuli solemnly, then shrugged.

"Of course you do," Arvam said.

Berry picked up a stick and thrashed at the tall grasses on either side of the trail as he ankled along. Yuli glided beside him, serene and calm, asking simple, seemingly harmless questions about the habitat while Arvam, Sri, and the guards followed close behind. Berry shrugged or gave monosyllabic answers, and when they entered the oval green eye of the glade that circled the pond he suddenly broke away, running in long floating leaps, splashing into the reedy shallows and commencing to throw clots of mud at the terrapins perched on the half-submerged log. When Yuli moved toward him, Arvam caught Sri's arm and told her to let the children talk.

"Perhaps you son will get her to say something useful, eh?"

"If you want to punish me, punish me. Don't ever again involve my son," Sri said.

"What are you frightened of, Professor Doctor? I thought that you and the girl had become good friends."

"We have an understanding. But I never ever forget that she's a monster," Sri said, and shook off Arvam's grip and stepped away from him before she said something she would regret.

Berry and Yuli were squatting by the edge of the water, talking quietly with their heads close together. As Sri asked one of the guards to patch her into the drones so that she could listen to the children's conversation, Berry suddenly reared up and shoved at Yuli. She grabbed at him and they both fell over, splashing and struggling. Someone bounded past Sri. It was Arvam, wading into the water, picking up Berry by an arm and a leg, pulling him off Yuli and tossing him ungently to one side. Then he stooped to help Yuli to her feet and reeled back, hands clapped over his face, blood running between his fingers, and Yuli shot up out of the water, a long balletic leap that carried her clear across the pond. Two guards ran toward Arvam; the rest chased after Yuli, going right and left around the pond. Berry picked himself up, wailing, and Sri went toward him, shouting to the guards.

"Don't shoot! Use the collar! Don't shoot!"

Yuli ran on, fast and agile as a deer, jinking this way and that, disappearing under the trees. The pair of drones flashed past the guards, chasing after her. A whipcrack echoed out; another. A cloud of doves rose fluttering and tumbling into the bright air above the treetops.

Yuli had snapped off the end of Berry's stick and jabbed it in Arvam's right eye, skewering the ball and fracturing the bone at the back of the socket. If it had penetrated another centimetre it would have lobotomised him. He was rushed to surgery, but the eye couldn't be saved.

Sri talked to Berry for a long time, but he clammed up, stubborn and petulant and scared, refusing to tell her what Yuli had said to make him so angry. Sri expected Arvam to blame her for the disaster, even though it had been his idea to introduce Berry to Yuli, but the general, wearing a black patch over his raw right eye socket, told her that she should put the incident behind her.

"Work on Avernus's gardens. Find something that will lead me to her. Find something that will persuade me that your work is worthwhile."

"What about Berry?"

"He will stay here, of course." Sri started to say that what happened wasn't in any way Berry's fault, but Arvam interrupted her, saying, "You really don't understand people, do you? I'm not going to hurt him. I love him as if he was one of my own sons. Now, go and say goodbye to him, and get back to work."

So that was her punishment. She had lost Alder when she had fled Earth. Now she had lost Berry, too.

As Sri was leaving the mansion, Loc Ifrahim angled toward her through the busy throng of military personnel in the vaulted atrium. "I should have known you had something to do with this monstrous clusterfuck," he said.

Sri met his bright, bitter gaze and said, "My congratulations for having caught her, Mr. Ifrahim. You're a bona fide hero at last. At least they can't take that away from you."

"If you think that, you clearly don't know the general. I'm on my way to find out how he's going to punish me for a mess I had nothing to do with. I have to eat shit over this, and you're free to go back to Titan and your all-important quest. What's it like, being able to float above ordinary human mess? I'm genuinely interested."

"You should go home, Mr. Ifrahim. You're clearly unhappy here, and in my opinion you've already done more than enough damage to the Outer System and its people. Go back to Earth, and get on with your life."

For a moment, a glint of naked contempt showed behind the mask of Loc Ifrahim's handsome face. Then he smiled and said, "Good luck with your work, madam. I hope that you find what you are looking for. Truly I do. But if you cross my path again, if you *ever* interfere with what's properly mine, I will take you down."

"I promise you that I'll do my very best to stay away from you." Sri was too tired and too upset to be angry at his presumption. Besides, he was a fool, so what was the point of trying to teach him any kind of lesson? She turned to the woman who stood at his elbow, a homely young thing with a bristling black crew cut and captain's bars on the breast of her blue coveralls, and advised her to stay away from Mr. Ifrahim. "His bad luck has a way of transferring itself to everyone around him," she said, and moved on.

Loc Ifrahim called after her—he had to have the last word—but she didn't look back.

———●———

Two days later, aboard a shuttle bound for Titan, Sri was still wondering about Yuli's steely resolve. The young girl had almost reached one of the emergency airlocks when the drones had cut her down. Her shock collar had been working perfectly, but when one of the guards had triggered it she'd somehow blocked the pain. Which meant that she could have blocked it while she was being questioned, but Captain Doctor Gavilán's brain scans and bloodwork showed that she had not. She had endured exquisite agony for day after day so that her captors would believe that they could control her with pain. And she had allowed herself to be shocked at least twice before taking her revenge on the man who had ordered her torture, and making her escape bid. She had been a monster all right, but oh, what a monster!

Sri hadn't told Yuli that she had discovered who her father was. There had been no opportunity to speak privately and Sri hadn't wanted Arvam to know what she knew. But there was one person who deserved to know, and after the shuttle touched down on the pad outside the Brazilian base in Titan's high northern latitudes, she drove straight to Tank Town.

Gunter Lasky heard out the story of Yuli's escape attempt and her death without once interrupting. When Sri had finished, the old man said, "Did she suffer at all?"

"She died quickly."

There was no need to tell him about the torture that Yuli had endured. It would be a needless cruelty, and it would also be potent ammunition for the resistance.

"Why did you tell me? It doesn't make any difference now."

"You deserve to know. I didn't come here to trawl for information."

"It doesn't make any difference," the old man said again, with a little more force. "It doesn't make me like you any more, or like Avernus any less. You've come blundering into our lives, trampling over everything we've built, a century of history you don't understand. That you can't ever understand. That's why you'll lose this war, you know. Because you don't understand us."

Another silence. They were both staring through the big diamond window at the charcoal fields of vacuum organisms that sloped away into the sullen orange haze, but for the first time Sri realised that they weren't seeing the same landscape. That she still had so much to learn about Titan, and all the other moons where Avernus had made her gardens.

She said, "I want to understand. That's why I'm here."

"Last time we met, I said that you were a little like Avernus. I think I was wrong."

"I want to be better than her."

"You're certainly more human. That's meant to be a compliment, by the way," Gunter Lasky said. "But I doubt that you'll take it as one."

Sri left the old man with his grief for the daughter he had never known, and flew halfway around Titan to the volcanic dome and the garden that her crew was still exploring. She had plenty of work to do there. No end to it. . . . But she was learning so much. The old man had said that she'd never understand the Outers, much less Avernus. He was wrong. He underestimated her. She would prove that she was Avernus's equal by creating her own masterpiece.

As she worked with her crew, unpicking the secrets of the underground kingdom of polymorphic prokaryotes, Sri thought long and hard about Avernus and Yuli, and began to sketch out the preliminary details of her great work.

PART TWO
THE SCHOOL OF NIGHT

I

U ranus's axis of rotation is tipped at right angles to the plane of the ecliptic: while the other planets in the Solar System spin around the sun like tops, Uranus rolls around it like a ball. When the refugees from the Quiet War arrived, Uranus's south pole was aimed at the sun, and the retinue of moons rotating about its equator inscribed paths like the circles of an archery target, with the blue-green ice giant and its slender graphite rings at the bull's-eye. One by one, a ragtag procession of ships dropped around it and swung out around one or another of the five largest moons in spiralling periapsis raise maneuvers to achieve a common equatorial orbit. An erratic and shell-shocked flock of the dispossessed cleaving close in the lonely dark, chattering each to each, trying to decide what to do next, where they should make their home, how long they should stay.

It was a bitter irony that the Quiet War had driven them to the place where they had long dreamed of establishing new settlements and exploring new ways of living: the three major political blocs on Earth had gone to war against the peoples of the Jupiter and Saturn systems precisely because the Outers, evolving away from so-called base human stock, diverging in unpredictable directions, had been threatening to expand into every part of the Solar System and create a patchwork diversity of posthumans changing human destiny in unimaginable ways, relegating Earth to a powerless and unsophisticated mudpuddle. The Quiet War had been a war against evolution, an attempt to bring every faction of the Outer community under the leash, to put an end to uncontrolled exploration and development, to establish Earth's hegemony over the entire Solar System.

The refugees had managed to escape all that, but they knew that they had won only a temporary reprieve. A year. Maybe two. They were not only an affront to Earth's desire for control and order, but they also possessed stolen technical data about the new fast-fusion motor that, developed by Greater Brazil, had enabled Earth to win the Quiet War. Uranus was twice as far from the sun as Saturn, but it was not far enough to guarantee their safety.

Meanwhile, their ships were low on fuel and their inventory of supplies and equipment was haphazard and short on many items essential for long-term survival. They needed to take stock of their situation, replenish their consumables, and work out what needed to be done to protect themselves from attack.

Uranus's largest moon, Titania, had been briefly occupied some twenty-five years ago. Isolation and internal tensions had broken up the commune and its members had moved back to the Saturn System, but the AI of the tented habitat that they had abandoned in place had kept the THOR fission generator and basic environmental systems ticking over. It would have taken only a little work to make the place comfortable, but it was an obvious target. It was on the map and in the history books, and it was sitting in plain view on a broad flat plain close to the centre of Titania's sub-uranian hemisphere. So the refugees stripped it of everything useful; unloaded the small and widely scattered fleet of robot cargo shells which, having been dispatched at irregular intervals to Titania when it had become clear that war with Earth was inevitable, stood like random megaliths on the plain around the habitat's angular tent; and hauled their loot to Miranda.

Most of Uranus's thirty-plus moons were small chunks of ice or carbonaceous material. One group orbited just outside the outer edge of the ring system; another occupied distant and irregular orbits, wanderers captured by Uranus's gravitational field. And between these two shoals of tiny moons were five massive enough to have achieved hydrostatic equilibrium, contracting into spheres under the force of their own gravitational fields. Four were much alike, balls of dirty ice wrapped around silicate cores, spattered with impact craters, dusted by dark materials flung outward by the chains of collisions that had created the ring system, fractured by varying degrees of ancient geological activity. But the smallest of the larger moons, Miranda, was not only the strangest of Uranus's family of satellites, it was one of the strangest moons in the Solar System: a patchwork of cratered, banded, and ridged terrains broken by mountainous ridges and monstrous fault canyons up to twenty kilometres deep, as if hammered together from pieces of half a dozen different bodies by some inept god who'd afterward slashed and hacked at his botched creation in a fit of rage. An early theory about its formation suggested that it had been shattered several times by massive impacts and the larger fragments had randomly clumped together, exposing sections of the core in some places and sections of the original surface in others, but later research showed that its haphazard topography was the result of intense geological activity driven by tidal heating at a time in the deep past when it had possessed a far more eccentric orbit.

Stretched and kneaded every time it swung close around Uranus,

Miranda had bubbled and blistered and cracked like a snowball wrapped around a hot coal. Eruptions of icy magma had flooded older terrain and created smooth plains. Coronae, huge domes edged with concentric patterns of ridges and grooves, had grown at the top of upwellings of warm ice that penetrated and deformed overlying strata. And after it had settled into its present orbit, it had cooled and frozen through and through. Its surface had contracted and tectonic activity had scored it with deep grabens formed by extensional faulting, while compressional strain had raised systems of ridges and valleys and thrown up escarpments several kilometres high.

This violent geological history had created a varied and chaotic moonscape that, patched with varied terrain, cut by the rifts and grooves of transition zones and gigantic scarps and grabens, provided a wealth of hiding places. The refugees elected to settle in the deep groove of a narrow chasm in the high northern latitudes, and put to work the two crews of construction robots they'd brought with them.

Uranus's moons were somewhat colder than the moons of Jupiter and Saturn, but their surfaces were similar in composition and the refugees were able to draw on a vast wealth of experience in low-temperature construction techniques and biome design developed during the colonisation of the Jupiter and Saturn systems. They located and mined carbonaceous deposits and set up reactors that transformed the tarry material into construction diamond, fullerene composites, and every kind of plastic. Their crew of construction robots—powerful, versatile machines capable of carrying to completion in only a few weeks engineering projects that human labour would have taken a decade to finish—excavated a chain of cut-and-cover tunnels close to one of the chasm's steep walls, beneath a bulging overhang that would hide them from casual optical, radar, and microwave surveys. The THOR fission generator from the old habitat on Titania supplied ample power; the tunnels were efficiently insulated; residual heat that leaked through their layered walls was captured by superconducting mesh and piped away to a point several kilometres beyond the edge of the chasm, creating a pocket lake buried deep beneath the surface that not only provided a supply of potable water but could also be electrolysed to provide oxygen.

Like the rest of Uranus's moons, Miranda was presently orbiting at right angles to the rest of the Solar System, with its south pole pointing toward the sun and the inner planets and its north pole pointing toward the outer dark at the edge of the Solar System. So the site of the refugees' new home was not only hidden from everywhere else in the inner Solar System by the bulk of the moon but was also sunk deep in the permanent darkness of a winter that would not lift until Uranus had rolled halfway around its orbit and its axis of rotation and the axes of rotation of its moons tipped over toward the sun. But that was some forty years in the future, and the future was all but unknowable. The refugees, now calling themselves the Free Outers, settled into their new home and began to rebuild their lives and make tentative plans about what to do next.

To begin with, the Free Outers lived mostly on dole yeast and CHON food harvested from Titania's vacuum-organism fields. Transformed in various imaginative ways by foodmakers, this was more than sufficient to supply their physiological needs, but like all Outers they believed that growing their own provender was a psychological and spiritual necessity. An assertion of the primacy of life over mere matter. An immediate connection with the web of life from which they had come. So the tunnels were fitted out as hydroponic farms from end to end, and people slept in tents and wickiups amongst dense plantings of wheat and maize, rice and potatoes and yams, tomatoes, lettuce and spinach, two dozen species of beans, fruit bushes, tiers of tea and coffee mosses, and an abundance of herbs. There were the usual setbacks and fluctuations in supply to begin with, but after six months of hard work the ecosystem of the underground settlement was reasonably stable.

The Free Outers kept only a few ships on active duty; the rest were stored in pits dug into the floors of neighbouring grooves and valleys and covered with rigid fullerene skins and layers of ice gravel. Desperately short of fuel, they cobbled together a shoal of robot airframes equipped with ramscoops that ploughed the middle reaches of Uranus's atmosphere like basking sharks, sieving tons of hydrogen every hour for deuterium and tritium isotopes and pumping them into storage tanks that, when full, separated from the airframes and ignited chemical motors that gave them just enough escape velocity to spiral outward in minimum energy orbits to Miranda, where tugs intercepted them.

Small automated observatories were established at the south poles of Ariel, Umbriel, and Titania; these moons orbited further out than Miranda, and except for very brief periods at least one of them was always visible in the sky of its northern hemisphere. The observatories forwarded live video of the inner Solar System and raw unfiltered radio transmissions from the occupied moons of the Jupiter and Saturn systems to a monitoring station in a bunker a couple of hundred kilometres north of the tunnel system, where an AI analysed and catalogued everything, and at least one human supervisor kept

90

watch at all times, sifting nuggets of useful information from the general chatter. A small number of clandestine newsloggers transmitted at irregular intervals compressed bursts around ten megaHertz that unpacked into video and text messages, providing information about the activities of the occupying forces and the arrival and departure of ships, updating casualty lists and rolls of those arrested and working in labour camps, and passing on messages from relatives and friends. It was an important link with the cities, settlements, and people that the Free Outers had left behind, but most of the news from home was relentlessly grim. Aided by Quisling governments, the Three Powers Authority was tightening its grip everywhere. The mayor of Paris, the centre of resistance to Earth's incursion, had died defending his city. Many of his supporters had been killed; most of the rest were in prison. Sporadic acts of sabotage were punished by swift show trials and executions. Habeas corpus and other civil rights had been suspended, every city and major settlement was ruled by martial law, and most small settlements had been forcibly evacuated. Gene wizards and other specialists were being forced to collaborate in the systematic plundering of the great archives of scientific and technical knowledge. A century of enlightenment, utopianism, and experiments in every kind of democracy had fallen dark.

The Free Outers could do nothing to help those who had been left behind because they were outnumbered and outgunned by Earth's Three Powers Alliance: they couldn't even reply to messages by relatives and friends, because the risk that the TPA would trace any kind of transmission was too great. And the small radio telescope they'd set up at Miranda's north pole failed to pick up any replies to signals aimed in turn at Neptune and the dwarf planets at the outer edge of the Solar System—Pluto, Enka, Sedna, and so on, places where other refugees might have settled. As far as they knew, they alone had survived to tell their tale. Burdened with the responsibility of preserving the knowledge and traditions of their home, of keeping a little candle of democracy flickering in the outer dark, they hunkered down, kept watch for enemy ships or probes, and engaged in intense discussions about their future.

Many wanted to stay where they were. To keep quiet. To stay out of sight. The TPA had not yet come after them and perhaps it never would, for it was clear that winning the peace was proving to be very much harder than winning the war. But a vociferous minority objected to the idea of spending the rest of their lives squatting in burrows, in perpetual fear that at any moment their enemy might shark in from the starry sky. Besides, most of the

Free Outers were in their twenties and thirties, and many wanted to start families. Several babies had already been born on Miranda; others were on the way. Expansion of their present refuge, or setting up new refuges elsewhere, would soon become a necessity, and it would increase the risk of discovery. No, they could not hope to stay hidden forever; instead, they should move on as quickly as possible and spread into the farthest reaches of the Solar System. To Neptune, whose largest moon, Triton, had an ocean of liquid water wrapped around its mantle. Or to Pluto and its trio of moons—one of which, Charon, also had liquid water beneath its surface. Or even further out, to one of the many other dwarf planets of the true Outer System and the Kuiper Belt. Places impossible for the TPA to attack because the supply lines would be too long and too fragile to support any sustained campaign.

Chief amongst this group was Newton Jones. He commanded a tug and possessed considerable kudos because he and his partner, Macy Minnot, had not only helped Avernus escape, but had also stolen the technical data about the Brazilians' fast-fusion motor. And he was also the son of Abbie Jones, a famous pilot who'd been amongst the first to explore the Neptune System, had been the first person to land on Enka, and had undertaken a solo expedition to the edge of the cometary zone, travelling farther from the sun than any other human. After her great adventure in the outer dark, Abbie Jones had been one of the founding members of the commune that had briefly colonised Titania—Newt had been born there—and after the commune had failed she'd helped to build the garden habitat of the Jones-Truex-Bakaleinikoff clan. She'd been the senior member of the clan, a powerful matriarch, before the Quiet War, and now she was a famous political prisoner.

Newt's detractors said that he'd spent his life trying to escape from the gravity well of his mother's fame—that he was driven to prove that he could equal or better her achievements. He'd been something of a daredevil trader before the war, constantly getting into scrapes and dubious capers, and although he'd proved his worth during the Quiet War and had been a cheerful and energetic leader of the crew that had designed and built the ramscoops that sifted from Uranus's atmosphere the deuterium and tritium needed to fuel the Free Outers' ships, many people suspected that his support for exploration of Neptune and the inner edge of the Kuiper Belt was motivated not by considerations about their safety and best possible future but by his notorious addiction to self-promotion and adventure.

Many of the Free Outers didn't trust his partner, Macy Minnot, either. After all, she was from Earth, and had defected in dubious circumstances:

murder, sabotage, and the abrupt end of a cooperative project involving Greater Brazil and the city of Rainbow Bridge, Callisto. There had been rumours before the war that she was some kind of double agent, that her prominent support for the peace movement had helped to undermine any possibility that the Jupiter and Saturn systems might mount a credible defence against invasion by Earth's three great powers. The taint of these rumours still clung to her, even though she'd been instrumental in saving Avernus and stealing the fusion-motor schematics, and had shared every hardship and had worked as hard as anyone to make the tunnel habitats safe and pleasant places to live.

Macy knew that the people who objected to mounting an exploratory expedition also harboured deep and unshakeable suspicions about her, and she tried her best not to care. She herself was in two minds about the plans that Newt championed. She supported him, and she would go with him if he carried the day, no question, but it meant venturing even further away from Earth and the hearthlight of the sun, and she had already travelled further than most Outers. From Earth to Jupiter, where she had been forced to defect. Then from Jupiter to Saturn when it became clear that if she tried to return to Earth she would be arrested for treason. And then from Saturn to Uranus. But she was certain that the TPA would come after the Free Outers sooner rather than later, and that the Free Outers wouldn't be able to mount a cred-ible defence against a highly trained force with every kind of experience of warfare and overwhelmingly superior resources. That had been amply proven during the Quiet War, when a small expeditionary force from Earth had out-thought and out-fought the Outers on their own territory. The Free Outers who believed it might be possible to engage in a guerrilla war or spin some kind of startlingly powerful weapon system out of the vast repository of the Library of the Commons and take the fight to the enemy were peddling com-forting fairy tales that had about as much substance as a comet's tail. At best, they might be able to mount some kind of Spartan last stand, but it would be a pointless sacrifice. No, from now on they'd have to live by the old maxim of every refugee: silence, exile, and cunning.

Macy was an exile twice over. First from Earth, and now from her adopted home on Dione. And although she had been living in the Outer System for two years before the Quiet War and had now spent more than a year in exile on Miranda, she was still not reconciled to spending the rest of her life under some kind of tent or dome, or inside a tunnel. And she was homesick, too. Sometimes she would pull up a telescopic view of the inner system transmitted from one or other of the observatories hidden at the south poles of Ariel, Umbriel, and Titania. Mercury was lost in the glare of the sun, but the other three rocky planets were clearly visible. Bright Venus, rust red Mars, and the blue disc of Earth, hung in sable black with its pale bride. At maximum magnification, Macy could make out Earth's land masses and oceans—even some of the larger weather systems, such as tropical storms swirling across the Pacific Ocean. She would think of rain lashing down on a rolling seascape that stretched from horizon to horizon, of thunder and wild wind, fingers of strong sunlight breaking through storm clouds. . . . The images rising up strong and clear in her mind, a sweet sharp pang compounded of nostalgia and regret piercing her heart.

If Macy started to think about all the things that she missed she'd never stop. Snow creaking under her boots and a cutting wind pinching her face as she marched with other labourers in the R&R Corps to another day's work dismantling the ruins of Chicago. The sun setting over Lake Superior, sinking beneath a ladder of thin clouds tinged pink in the darkening blue sky, everything reflected with perfect fidelity in the calm mirror of the water. Brassy city sunsets over the rooftops of Pittsburgh. The vast slow sunsets over the Nebraskan plain, and the starry empires mapped across Nebraska's night sky. Sunlight hot against her face, red on her closed eyelids. Rain. Storm waves exploding into foam on a rocky shore. The chirr of grasshoppers in dry summer grass. Cathedral forests. An explosion of pale roses in a dark clearing. Crowds of strangers swirling down brawling streets.

She missed meat. The Outers were vegetarians out of habit born from necessity, and the approximations spun by the foodmakers were nothing like the real thing. Macy dreamed of keeping a few chickens amongst the truck gardens of the habitat. The Free Outers possessed the equipment and know-how to quicken plants and animals from genome maps, and there were thousands of maps of all kinds of species in the Library of the Commons. She probably wouldn't be allowed to kill and cook a chicken—it would confirm every bad notion the Outers had about her—but at least she'd have a supply of eggs. . . .

Currently, some four hundred days after the Free Outers had first settled on Miranda, Earth and Uranus were about as close to each other as they ever got—yet they were still separated by almost 4.4 billion kilometres, a gulf almost impossible to imagine. Macy had enough trouble visualising the distance between the missile silo and trailer park in Nebraska, where she'd grown up in the tender care of the Church of the Divine Regression, and Pittsburgh, where she'd lived after she'd escaped. A lousy two thousand kilometres. And the distance between Earth and Uranus was more than two million times greater. It had taken her three weeks, hitching rides and walking, to reach Pittsburgh; travelling at the same rate, it would take her 115,000 years to cross the gulf between Uranus and Earth. Even if she stole one of the ships, assuming she could learn how to fly one and it had enough fuel, it would take something like twenty-four weeks to make the trip. Yes, Earth was a very long way away. But most of the little worlds beyond the orbit of Uranus hung at even greater distances from each other in a vast cold dark through which the small lives of the Free Outers might fall forever, dwindling to dust and less than dust. It seemed inconceivable that they could build any kind of life for themselves so far from the sun, yet that was what Newt and his little crew of maniacs were planning.

While the rest of the Free Outers had been turning the cut-and-cover tunnels into a comfortable home, Newt's motor crew had been designing and building their first working prototype of the Brazilian fusion motor. Many of the Free Outers had worked in the transport trade before the Quiet War. They'd owned their own ships or had piloted ships on behalf of collectives. They were experts in ship construction and maintenance. But the motor crew were true technical wizards, young and eager and frighteningly intense, and used a battery of psychotropic drugs to sharpen their formidable intelligence, hone their powers of concentration, and work around the clock. They scoured the files of stolen technical data and borrowed most of the Free Outers' memo space to construct a virtual model accurate down to the atomic level. They cannibalised two ships for components and rare metals and used printers to fabricate components and grow the ceramic reaction chamber molecule by molecule. The Brazilian motor required antiprotons to catalyse fast-fusion reactions. At first, the crew discussed mining antiprotons created by reactions between high-energy cosmic rays and Uranus's outer atmosphere, but these were too few and too widely scattered. So instead they had the construction robots excavate a tube a kilometre long, and built inside it a linear particle accelerator that used a quantum diffraction version of a Cochcroft-Walton generator to fire raw quarks at hydrogen atoms suspended in a laser trap. This required the output of fusion generators dismounted from three ships, and some three hundred days' hard work, but at the end of it they had enough fuel to conduct the first test-firing.

The motor crew dug a pit in the icy plain a couple of hundred kilometres north of the Free Outer settlement, filled it with a web of fullerene scaffolding, inserted the prototype motor with its tail pointing upward, and connected it to fuel lines and a mass of monitoring equipment. Then they retreated over the horizon to the control-and-command bunker—they were fairly sure that if there was a containment breach it wouldn't do much more than melt a hole in the adamantine ice, but they were taking no risks—and got ready for the critical moment.

The hot, cramped bunker stank of tension and four a.m. funk. Construction of the prototype had consumed much time and valuable and irreplaceable resources. Everyone knew that if the test failed the rest of the Free Outers would almost certainly vote against resumption of their work. The young men and women sat shoulder to shoulder on the floor, masked by spex, skating fingertips over slates or shaping the air with their hands like so many blind people investigating an elephant. Newt Jones and Macy Minnot were squashed together in one corner. Someone had rigged up a big red button that was linked to the AI that controlled the test rig. Now, with just a minute to go, Newt offered the plastic box that housed the button to Macy and asked her if she would like the honour.

"It's your thing. You should do it," Macy said.

"It's your thing too. And I'm so scared I'll jinx it my hand's cramped," Newt said.

"You don't want the responsibility if it goes wrong," Macy said, but took the box as one of the tech wizards began a countdown that everyone joined in, a jubilant chant reeling backward from ten.

At *zero*, Macy pushed down the button with both thumbs, and in the multiple views tiled in the memo space in the middle of the crowded little room a narrow searchlight shot up into the black sky, so brilliant its blaze of white light scoured all detail from the rugged plain. Everyone cheered and hugged each other and clapped each other on the back. Newt kissed Macy and she kissed him and the room began to shake and rattle as vibrations in the icy regolith raced past. Two seconds later, the AI began to throttle back the motor and the searchlight dimmed and went out. The vibrations died away. The bunker was quiet for a moment, and then everyone began to talk to everyone else, arguing over the telemetry, throwing out and refining thrust parameters and fuel consumption, exhaust velocity and burn efficiency. . . .

There were more tests: days and days of tests. The crew ramped up antiproton production and began to build a second motor. The prototype was unbolted from the static-firing rig and fitted inside Newt and Macy's tug, and Newt took the little ship out on a test-flight that looped around Uranus's outermost moon, Ferdinand. A round trip of more than forty million kilometres, there and back again in less than a day.

After this triumph, Newt and the rest of the motor crew put their plans for a real trip beyond the Uranus system to the general assembly where all matters large and small were decided by debate and free vote. Newt made a passionate speech, using all his considerable charm and fluency; the senior tech wizard, Ziff Larzer, explained that most of the crew would stay behind, manufacturing motors and fitting them into ships, while the expedition was away. But they had to field numerous objections, principally from a group led by Mary Jeanrenaud, who was not only the oldest member of the Free Outers but had been one of the leaders of the peace and reconciliation movement before the war. She commanded a considerable amount of respect, and talked eloquently about the need to conserve resources, to build outward, yes, but only from strong foundations.

"We do not yet have those foundations in place. We are getting there, it's true, but to achieve that goal all of us must work together. I can understand that some have grown impatient and find it difficult to keep a steady course. But we must not falter, difficult though it may seem. For otherwise we are in danger of dissipating our energies and our goals, of rushing off in too many different directions, after too many dreams. And that will leave us divided, and weak and vulnerable."

Mary Jeanrenaud won considerable applause for this, and when it had died down Idriss Barr stood up and ankled to the bottom of the grass bowl. He wasn't exactly the leader of the Free Outers' democratic collective, but he was one of the people who listened to every side of every argument, arbitrated on minor disputes, and generally united the group. Tall and lithe and vigorous, he possessed an easy authority that he wore lightly and carelessly for the most part, but wouldn't hesitate to use when he wanted to make a point or force a discussion in the direction he wanted it to go. He spoke now about their future. They would make a choice today and they must unite behind that choice and joyfully and gladly seize the opportunities it would give them.

"We've done so much here in just a year. It's amazing. And we will continue to amaze ourselves," he said. "We have shown that we can make our home anywhere we choose. We should not be afraid of fresh challenges, because we know that we have the resolve and skill to overcome them. Here at Uranus, and at Neptune, at Pluto, or anywhere else in the Solar System."

Macy was astonished. Previously, Idriss Barr had supported the motor crew's work on the strict condition that they had just one goal: to fit out every ship with the fast new fusion motor so that, when the time came, they could outrun any attempt at pursuit. Now he was calling for exploration and expansion.

"He changed his mind and you knew it," she said to Newt, who was sitting next to her at the top of the grassy bowl. "That's why you've been so calm. You had a secret weapon all along."

"Idriss is a good man who wants the best for everyone. He likes to lead from the rear, and he can be persuaded to change his mind if you show him what other people think," Newt said. "We canvassed people we reckoned were sympathetic to us, showed him the results. Mary and her friends have a lot of kudos, but kudos doesn't mean too much out here. And most of us want to explore and spread out. We always have. It's why we're here."

"My partner the politician."

"It isn't politics. It's common sense. Not much different from figuring out how to pitch the price of a hold full of tea moss, it turns out."

One by one people stood up and descended to the centre of the circle and picked up a small white plastic ball and dropped it in one of two glass cylinders, one tinted red for *no*, one tinted green for *yes*. The proposal to mount an exploratory expedition to Pluto and Neptune quickly gained a clear majority. By the time Macy's turn came and she dropped her ball in the green-tinted cylinder, it was almost full.

Idriss Barr asked if he really needed to declare the count, winning laughter from the people circled around. So it was decided, and because Newt's crew had already made detailed flight plans covering every aspect of the expedition, departure was scheduled for just twenty days later. Food and drink were brought out, several people started up a percussion group, and the meeting turned into a party that lasted late into the night.

They were on their way.

2

The spy spent more than four hundred days looking for Zi Lei on Iapetus. It should have been easy to find her. There were only ten thousand indigenous inhabitants, plus a few hundred people who'd fled from other moons or had been stranded there by the war. And he knew where she'd been born: the farm at Grandoyne Crater that her family still owned, the very first place he visited. Her family welcomed him warmly, for he was a friend who'd known her when she'd been living in Paris, Dione, someone who could tell them what she had been doing before the war and how she had escaped from prison when it had started. But they claimed that they did not know where she was now and said that they'd lost contact with her when she'd left Iapetus more than five years ago.

"She stopped taking her medication," Zi Lei's mother said.

"She believed that she was on a mission," Zi Lei's father said.

They were both olive-skinned and black-haired like their daughter, with the same tuck in the corners of their dark brown eyes. Zi Lei had left without warning, they said. It had taken them some time to discover that she'd hitched a ride on a tug that had returned to Xamba, Rhea, after trading with farms and oases in the region. Her mother had gone to Xamba to talk to her, but Zi had already moved on, to Paris, Dione, and had ignored all attempts to contact her ever since.

The spy told Zi's parents that she had friends in Paris who had encouraged her to take the medicine that kept her calm and suppressed her fantasies, although she had not always listened to their advice.

"Were you happy together?" Zi's mother asked.

"I tried my best to take care of her."

"But were you happy?"

"As much as we could be," the spy said. "She taught me many things."

Talking about his feelings for Zi Lei made him feel uncannily naked. Scared and exposed but also weirdly happy. As if the world and his purpose were completely aligned and in harmony: every atom, every quantum of energy singingly aware that he was in love with Zi Lei and he was on a mission to find her. He'd been on a mission when he had slipped into Paris before the war, of course, but this time he wasn't driven by loyalty and duty but by love. A love he believed to be pure and selfless. All his life he had been trained to complete his mission or die trying. He would not stop searching for Zi until he found her or discovered what had happened to her.

"She isn't always easy to love," Zi's mother said, with a wistful smile uncannily like her daughter's.

"No."

"But you came here anyway," Zi's father said. "My daughter might not be grateful that you did, but we are."

Zi's family promised that they would do all they could to help, but the spy did not entirely trust them and he wasted ten days at their habitat, discreetly searching the gardens and fields under the pleated tent, and the vast fields of vacuum organisms that patched the coal black plain of the crater's floor, until he was certain that Zi was not hiding or being hidden there. All right, then. He would look for her everywhere else.

At a little over fifteen hundred kilometres in diameter, Iapetus was the third-largest moon in the Saturn System, but it was sparsely inhabited and had no large centres of population, only widely scattered farms, small garden habitats, and smaller oases. Although most farms and habitats were located in a belt roughly defined by the thirtieth parallels north and south of the equator, with rather more people living in the bright half, Roncevaux Terra, than in the dark half, Cassini Regio, the spy had a lot of territory to cover. Fortunately, the Pacific Community expeditionary force that now controlled the moon allowed its inhabitants free passage everywhere except Othon Crater, north of the equator in the sub-saturnian hemisphere, where they were building a large base, so the spy was able to search for Zi Lei unhindered and unchallenged.

He travelled in the skin of Ken Shintaro—the old identity he'd used while living his double life in Paris before the war, the name by which Zi Lei had known him. If she heard that Ken Shintaro was looking for her, she would surely come looking for him.

In the beginning he travelled alone, hitching rides from place to place and undertaking various spells of unskilled labour to pay for his board. But then he was given a lift by a gypsy prospector, Karyl Mezhidov, and after he heard Ken Shintaro's story about searching for the woman he had loved and lost, Karyl offered to drive him to most of the places he hadn't yet visited. And so the spy spent more than two hundred days with Karyl, travelling on either side of Iapetus's equatorial range.

Iapetus's most famous physical characteristic was its two-tone coloration: one half covered with water-ice, the other with a layer of black or reddish brown material, mostly carbon-rich dehydrogenated tholins. A dusting of this dark organic material could be found on other moons, including Dione, Hyperion, and Epimetheus, as well as in the F Ring of the ring system, but on Iapetus it formed layers many metres thick. The best current theory was that it had been lofted into orbit around Saturn in the aftermath of the violent destruction of the object whose major remnant, after being considerably modified by subsequent impacts, had become the irregularly shaped honeycomb moon Hyperion. Much of it, in the form of fine, electrostatically charged dust, had been swept up by Iapetus, the next moon in from Hyperion, and had flowed into the floors of craters and had been converted into a tarry crust through chemical reactions driven by the ultraviolet component of sunlight, cosmic radiation, and charged particles from Saturn's magnetosphere. Iapetus's farmers cultivated more than a hundred types of vacuum organism that grew on this substrate and turned it into every kind of organic compound, from CHON food to the complex strands of artificial DNA used in AI chips.

Even if Iapetus had not been divided into dark and light halves, it would still have been notable for its great equatorial ridge, whose isolated peaks and long crests rose in places to more than twenty kilometres above the surrounding plains and extended for more than 1,300 kilometres through the centre of Iapetus's dark hemisphere, running almost exactly along the line of the equator. This gigantic mountain range was a remnant of the moon's early oblate shape. When Iapetus had formed by accretion from the disc of rubble around proto-Saturn, it had been spinning so rapidly that its lithosphere, still plastic because it was warmed by radioactive decay of nucleotides, principally aluminium-26, had been distorted, fattening around the equator. But aluminium-26 has a short halflife and Iapetus was too far from Saturn to be significantly stretched and kneaded by tides, so the moon had stabilised and cooled very quickly after formation, and the bulge at its equator had been preserved like the raised seam at the joint of the two halves of a walnut shell.

The massive weight of the ridge had stressed and compressed the surface to either side. Thrust and high-angle reverse faults had created scarps and ridges, and during thermal expansion of the icy lithosphere early in Iapetus's history, ammonia-water melt from deep in the interior had risen through faults and flooded parts of the surface, forming smooth plains that had been heavily cratered during the period of heavy bombardment, when large bodies like Iapetus ploughed through leftover debris—there were a good number of large impact basins in Iapetus's leading hemisphere, including one more than five hundred kilometres across. Then a violent collision had shattered Hyperion's parent body and spilled dark material across the sky, which had been swept up by Iapetus's leading hemisphere and like a fall of haematic snow had covered and softened the features on half its globe. This deep blanket hid from satellite surveys intrusions and volcanic deposits rich in minerals along the length of the great equatorial ridge: a century of exploration had not yet exhausted them, and gypsy prospectors like Karyl Mezhidov could still make a good living.

Karyl was only a couple of years older than the spy's supposed age of twenty-four, a lanky, gentle man whose long blond hair was brushed back from his sharp face and caught up in a braid woven through with thin coloured wires. The braid hung to the small of his back when he was driving, and he coiled and pinned it up before climbing into his pressure suit. He had a partner who lived on her family's farm, no children as yet. He and his partner planned to start a family soon, Karyl told the spy, and then he'd settle down and build a little dome and grow every kind of fruit bush inside it. But for a little while yet he had to accumulate the credit and kudos he needed to start up his own farm, exploring the badlands on either side of the great equatorial ridge, searching out remnants of stony or iron meteorites, and deposits of phosphates, sulphates, and nitrates left by ancient cryovolcanic eruptions. Although it was a lonely life and often frustrating, with long dry spells when he sank hole after hole in likely terrain yet uncovered nothing useful, Karyl loved the freedom and the unpredictability. Like every prospector he was a born gambler, and the prospect of finding a rich mother lode of valuable minerals or metals, reinforced by the occasional small strike, drove him ever onward across the rugged unpeopled moonscapes.

He habitually played music as he drove. Serial compositions from the twentieth century; antiphonal church music of the sixteenth century; the a cappella religious chants, polyphonic heroic songs, and wild dance music of North Caucasia, the homeland of his ancestors. And he was usually floating on one or other of his home-brewed psychotropics, too. He had a small automated laboratory in the cabin of his rolligon and was continually tinkering with endorphins, attempting to achieve an ideal oceanic state in which world and self melted together. On his best days, he told the spy, he diffused outward into the moonscape and became one with it, and in that state of blissful understanding potential rifts, lodes, and reefs shone out with their own particularity as if illuminated from within.

The spy politely refused offers to sample Karyl's extensive psychotropic library. As it was, the music and the inhuman scale of the moonscapes through which they travelled stirred up strange emotions that threatened his fragile sense of self; he was afraid that if he ingested a tab or slapped on a patch of one of Karyl's drugs he'd lose control and melt and flow away and disappear completely.

They circumnavigated Iapetus twice, first travelling east, to the north of the great equatorial ridge, and then returning west, to the south of it. Across dark plains, through great rifts and ravines, beneath towering cliffs and bluffs, across heavily cratered slopes that swept up to pillowy peaks, some bitten or truncated by impact craters near or at their summits, giving them the appearance of volcanic calderas. The terrain here was more than four billion years old, battered by the great bombardment of the Solar System's violent infancy and by a steady rain of meteorites ever since. The rolligon might spend a day crawling across the floor of a dished crater, climb the steep scarp on the far side, and top out at a broad rim that gave a view across a saddle valley toward the great dome of a peak that stretched from horizon to horizon and rose ten kilometres against the black sky, its flanks pitted by craters of every size and its top dished by some vast impact. And everything was blanketed by dark material that formed smooth crusts, or pavements of giant crazed polygons, or dusty wallows that had to be given a wide berth because they could swallow the rolligon whole.

Mostly, Karyl and the spy kept to the riven and cratered plains that bordered the great ridge, its smooth switchbacks rising beyond the close horizon, isolated peaks floating against the black sky like tethered moons. Guided by a combination of geological expertise and drug-enhanced instincts, Karyl truffled along domes, scarps, and anticlinal folds raised by compressional tectonism, mapped down-dropped blocks flooded by ancient cryovolcanic melts, hunted across ejecta aprons outside craters, or probed their centres. He used radar and sonic imaging to map the terrain to a depth of half a kilometre, or deployed small robots that skittered off on three or four pairs of jointed legs, squatting here and there to drill into the frozen tars of the regolith and take samples of the underlying ice. If it was only lightly contaminated with mineral intrusions, Karyl seeded the ground with vacuum-organism packets that budded and grew and sent down pseudohyphae to absorb and concentrate metals. Rare veins and rifts were stripped out there and then, and loaded onto one of the trailers hitched in a small train behind the rolligon; fragments of meteorites were retrieved by blasting open the ground or sending down serpentine robots that gnawed at the stony or metallic bolides with diamond teeth and pushed the fragments through peristaltic tubes to the surface. Karyl stopped at vacuum-organism fields he'd planted on previous trips, too, and he and the spy suited up and stripped out by hand scales rich in minerals absorbed from the regolith, hard but satisfying work in the absolute stillness of the dark moonscape.

But they spent more time travelling than mining, camping out in the rolligon for the most part, sometimes stopping at farms or oases for a day or two, where the spy would tell his story and ask everyone if they knew anything about Zi Lei, and Karyl would sit with his hosts and drink tea and nibble at sweet and savoury pastries, olives, and slices of watermelon, and dicker over prices for the phosphates and nitrates and breccias and metals he'd collected, gossip about small scandals and marriages and births and deaths, and speculate about the plans of the Pacific Community. Even when he didn't sell anything but digested waste from the rolligon's toilet, the farmers or villagers would give him a surfeit of fresh fruit and vegetables in exchange for hauling goods to one or another of their neighbours, or for a promise for goods or minerals he'd bring the next time he swung by.

The Pacific Community expeditionary force ruled with a lighter hand than either the Brazilians or the Europeans. In all their travels, Karyl and the spy only once met representatives of the occupying force, four polite soldiers in dark green uniforms who were making an inventory of equipment and crops on a farm. PacCom soldiers were confiscating a third of the fresh food grown by farms and oases, so everyone had to supplement their rations with CHON food or dole yeast. Every construction robot had been requisitioned, too—the PacCom base was the size of a small city now, and growing ever larger, a grid of segmented tubes buried under berms of icerock rubble much like the first settlements made on the moons of Jupiter and Saturn a century ago—and there was a regular traffic of ships plying between the Saturn System and Earth, bringing in troops and materiel, and a big factory appeared to be fabricating tugs after the pattern of those built by Outers.

Apart from the confiscation of crops and equipment, and the closure of the moon's net and other communication systems, the occupation had little effect on the daily lives of the Iapetans. And yet everything had changed, and nothing would ever again be the same. The long-cherished belief that the Outers had created a utopian bubble that had floated free of the incessant barbarities of human history, and where every kind of art and scientific research could be endlessly explored and a variety of cooperative political and economic systems flourished in a rich and peaceful patchwork, had proven to be a delusion. Like a biome that had evolved in isolation on some remote island, it had been overwhelmed by the intrusion of vigorous and aggressive forces from the larger world. If the Outers ever regained their freedom, it would not be as before. From now on they would have to be ever vigilant against attack and ready to defend themselves, with everything that entailed.

Everywhere Karyl and the spy went, there was talk of resistance and revolution, rumours of fresh atrocities on other moons, fantasies of escape into the outer dark at the edge of the Solar System. But nowhere was there any sign or news of Zi Lei—except once, when the spy talked to someone who had met her during her brief stay in Xamba, Rhea. It seemed that her parents had been telling the truth about that, so perhaps they'd also been telling the truth when they had said that they had heard nothing of their daughter before or after the war.

The spy's quest was unfulfilled, yet he was not unhappy. He was convinced that he would find Zi Lei sooner or later, and meanwhile he was becoming comfortable in the skin of Ken Shintaro. Learning to be human, forgetting for days at a time the chill and fretful caution that had set him apart while he'd been at work in Paris, the constant low-level paranoia that anyone might be following or watching him, that he was caught in some great game where he didn't know the identities of other players, or any of the rules. Then, he'd been constantly alert, checking his every action for deviancy from the norm, observing and judging not only the people around him but his own self. Now, he was at ease with Karyl—although it would have taken a lot of hard work to dislike the good-natured gypsy prospector—and the other Outers and most importantly with his own self.

The spy had been born and trained to fight for God, Gaia, and Greater Brazil on the Moon. He had never been to Earth, but he had always dreamed of Earth's soft green landscapes and trackless oceans, all stretched out under a sheltering sky of exquisite blue. An ideal approximating paradise. Now, during the long double circumnavigation of Iapetus, he learned to appreciate and to love the intrinsic beauty of its stark and empty moonscapes. How to read in its every form the processes that had shaped it; how its violent history had been softened by the blanket of in-fallen material and billions of years of slow sublimation and microscopic meteorite impacts that chipped and rounded every feature. A great work of time, working on scales ungraspable to the human mind.

Despite its bitter and unrelenting inhospitality, the Outers had learned how to live off the land. Ancient ice as hard as granite was mined and melted for water; water was electrolytically split to supply oxygen. Generations of gypsies like Karyl had seeded parts of the dark plains of Cassini Regio with vacuum organisms that used sunlight as energy and the dark material as substrate to grow and produce every kind of fullerene and organic polymer, and stores of simple organic molecules that could be spun into basic foodstuffs by the rolligon's foodmaker. Other varieties soaked up the weak sunlight and transformed it into electrical energy and stored it in analogues of electric-eel muscle that, when tapped, could supply trickle charges to the rolligon's batteries.

Miracles of nanotechnology, hives, or self-organised swarms of various kinds of self-replicating microscopic machines modifying themselves and their behaviour according to simple rules, the vacuum organisms grew and multiplied in sunlight one-hundredth the strength of sunlight incident on Earth's surface and temperatures as low as −200° Celsius, forming structures like flowers or leafless trees, or scabs or filamentous tangles like giant lichens. Starkly simple forms that harmoniously echoed the spare and brutal beauty of the moonscapes in which they flourished. Driving past the ridge of a thrust fault overgrown with tangles of black wire, or mounting the crest of a slope toward the end of one of Iapetus's long afternoons and seeing a vast prospect of rounded peaks spread out ahead, the light of the low sun throwing long shadows across the dark ground and picking silvery highlights from ridges and the far rims of craters, and Saturn's pastel crescent tilted high in the black sky, caught in the luminous and laminated bow of its rings—the plane of Iapetus's orbit, unlike those of the inner moons, was inclined to Saturn's equatorial plane—the spy would be filled with a sense of wonder and his heart would lift and turn on a flood of happiness, and Karyl would look over at him and smile his gentle, dopey smile and say, "Yeah, ain't it the shit?"

And so they drove, and so they drove. They stopped for thirty days at the farm owned by the parents of Karyl's partner, Tamta. Karyl and Tamta, an elegantly thin and dreamy woman, drifted off to a little oasis some twenty kilometres from the main tent of the farm to renew their vows to each other, as Karyl put it. The spy volunteered for general labour in the farm tunnels, planting and pruning and harvesting, and learned how to make bread. Tamta's parents were second-generation settlers nearing their centenaries; they had three sons and four daughters and a small tribe of grandchildren and great-grandchildren. Tamta was a late addition to the family, born after her parents' youngest child had died in an accident out in the vacuum-organism fields. She was younger than some of her nephews and nieces, in fact, but didn't seem to find it strange.

At last, Karyl and Tamta emerged from their humid little Eden, and it was time to hit the road again. One day the spy realised that the place where he had left his dropshell was only five or six kilometres away, just beyond the curve of the horizon. When they parked up for the night, he stirred into Karyl's white tea a hypnotic he'd manufactured with the help of a demon inserted into the foodmaker's simple mind. Karyl fell asleep before the tea was half drunk and the spy put him in the recovery position and said goodbye with a deep pang of sorrow—he had spent almost a year in the man's company and had grown to know him as well as he knew every one of his brothers.

He hiked off across the dark and level plain, dragging a sled loaded with air cylinders and several flasks of hydrazine. Karyl would be able to follow his tracks and retrieve the sled, but he'd have to forgive the debt of stolen air and fuel, the spy thought—and realised that he was thinking like an Outer. Feeling guilty because he had taken something without first striking some kind of deal. But it was only a small crime, and it was necessary. The spy was as certain as he could be that Zi Lei was no longer on Iapetus. It was time to move on to the next station of his quest.

It took less than an hour to revive and fuel the dropshell; it took most of the stolen hydrazine to reach escape velocity and enter a minimal-energy orbit that would spiral inward and eventually encounter Rhea. And if Zi Lei wasn't there, the spy would go on. He would search the other moons in the Saturn System and if she was not on any of them he would have to find some way of tracking down the refugees who had fled to the moons of Uranus. He would keep searching for Zi Lei for the rest of his life, if he had to.

3

Pluto was currently approaching perihelion. Its highly elliptical orbit was not only carrying it inside the orbit of Neptune; it was also about as close to Uranus as it would ever get—currently, the ice giant and the dwarf planet were separated by less than two billion kilometres. As far as the Free Outers were concerned, there would never be a better time to pay a visit.

The expedition consisted of two ships equipped with fast-fusion motors, Newt Jones and Macy Minnot's tug *Elephant* and the shuttle *Out of Eden*, carrying twenty-four people, six of them children. The presence of children was another reminder to Macy that space was the Outers' natural habitat: not something to be endured or survived but the place where they lived, so they saw no problem in taking their children off on a voyage into the unknown in ships powered by incompletely tested motors. Of course, the older children had more experience of ships and moonscapes than Macy, and could probably cope with any emergency better than she. And the Pluto System wasn't exactly *terra incognita*, for it had been visited and mapped and sampled by robot probes and human explorers over the past two centuries. Even so, the dwarf planets of the outer dark were strange and incompletely understood, and a long way from anywhere else if something went wrong; Macy admired the Outers' fearless can-do attitude and didn't doubt their competence, but she knew that this wasn't exactly a stroll in the park.

Elephant piggybacked on *Out of Eden* for most of the voyage. The shuttle was big enough to give an illusion of privacy to anyone who needed it, and her crew spun a fullerene sphere based on a design excavated from the Library of the Commons to provide additional living space: a transparent bubble some two hundred metres across stuck to *Out of Eden*'s belly like an egg-case, an airy arena where the members of the expedition could play sports and games and eat communal meals with the bright stars shoaled across the black sky all around, laughing and rough-housing as if it were perfectly natural, as if there wasn't killing cold and vacuum everywhere beyond the bubble's thin skin. Macy never could get entirely used to it, always felt a little plunge, a sudden intensification of her perpetual low-grade airplane fear, whenever a child playing tig or good-to-go bounced off the taut polymer.

Newt noticed this of course, and they had a little spat about it. He said that she was worrying needlessly because she didn't trust the competence and judgement of his friends; she said that this was yet another example of the way he dismissed the problems she was having in adapting to the Outer life.

"You were born to this," Macy said. "It's all you know. But I have to think about everything you don't need to think about. It's like having to remember to breathe all the time. Or having to think about keeping my heart beating, because it'll stop if I don't."

"I know that. All I want to do is find a way of helping you get over it."

"It isn't about 'getting over it.' It isn't even about the fact that I'll probably have to spend the rest of my life hidden in some tunnel, or in some tiny cupboard like this," Macy said, gesturing around her at *Elephant*'s cramped living quarters. "It's about air generators and ion shields and everything else. All the stuff that protects us from cold and vacuum and radiation. It's about always being aware that we could all die if just one little thing goes wrong. If you knew what a tightrope was, I'd say that it was like trying to live your life while walking along a tightrope over a drop a hundred kilometres deep. It's not like I'm always thinking about the drop. Sometimes I can forget the drop is there. For days at a time. I can look around, enjoy the view. But then there'll be a little slip, a little wobble, and there it is, right below me. Waiting to swallow me up."

Newt studied her, solemn as a doctor about to deliver an unpalatable diagnosis. Her strange pale long-limbed lover. His sharp face and fine blue eyes. His disordered shock of black hair. "You're homesick," he said at last.

Macy had to laugh, because he so didn't get it. They'd talked about it before, and he always thought, because he'd been brought up in a culture that believed that everything was explicable and all problems had a solution, that it was some kind of temporary panic, a symptom of something else, something they could work at fixing. She'd talked to other Outers about it, too, tried to explain that even when she found some strange and wonderful beauty in Miranda's moonscapes—like the time she'd hiked a trail and scrambled up a fallen block and at the top seen savagely incised terraces dropping more than ten kilometres to a plain gleaming flat and smooth as a frozen sea, running out to the horizon where Uranus hung in the black sky, fat and blue as Earth—even when she dissolved out into something as wonderfully, eerily beautiful as that, the click of a valve or the change in pitch of the fan that blew air across her face inside her helmet could bring her back with a jolt, remind her that if she wasn't cased in her pressure suit she'd die in less than a minute, a race between asphyxiation and freezing solid. . . . Oh, she knew that her pressure suit and all the other mechanisms and systems that kept her alive were proven, reliable, and pretty much foolproof. But it wasn't about trusting them: it was about being utterly dependent on them. It was a hindbrain thing, one of her friends said. A problem of adaptation, another claimed. They'd offered fixes—neural programming, tailored psychotropics, and so on. Nothing had worked. Well, the psychotropics had given her a nice mellow buzz, like a second beer after a hard shift on a hot day, but she didn't want to be buzzed all the time.

So no one amongst the Outers really understood how Macy felt, not even Newt, and now she gave in, as she usually did, no point prolonging an argument for the sake of arguing, saying yes, maybe she was a little homesick.

"I miss the habitat back on Dione sometimes," Newt said.

"So do I. And everyone there."

"Yeah," Newt said, after a brief pause.

"I'm sorry," Macy said, instantly contrite. Newt didn't mention his mother or the rest of his relatives and friends that often, but she knew that the loss was still raw. A large part of the reason why he'd spent so much time trying to get out from under his mother's reputation was because they were alike in so many ways.

He shrugged it off with one of his funny little smiles. "If we'd stayed behind we'd have been thrown in jail too. It wouldn't have changed anything."

"Even so."

"Instead, we came out here to make a new home. Something we can grow into together."

"That's a nice thought."

"We'll do it," Newt said. "It's going to take time to find a place where we can be truly free, but we will. We're going to live a long time, after all. Every kind of thing will be possible. Even returning to Earth."

"We're going to have to live a very long time before that becomes possible," Macy said.

As far as everyone else was concerned the voyage out was a fine, exhilarating time. For forty-two days, as the two ships fell between worlds, they could enjoy true unbounded freedom, and when they finally made orbit around Pluto most of them thought that it was something of an anticlimax.

Pluto is about half the size of Earth's Moon, and twice as big as its largest moon, Charon; they form a true binary system, revolving around a common centre rather than one around the other, not an uncommon arrangement in the Kuiper Belt. In addition, two small dark bodies, Hydra and Nix, orbit Pluto and Charon beyond the edge of a tenuous dusty system of ring arcs created from material knocked off the little moons by collision with Kuiper Belt objects. A compact toy of a system, as orderly and self-contained as an orrery.

Macy thought that Pluto looked a little like Mars. An ochre globe dappled here and there with pale yellows, expansive caps of white frost at its poles, and a low relief surface pocked by craters and slashed by ancient rifts worn into broad, shallow valleys by thermodynamic erosion. And like Mars, Pluto possessed a faint atmosphere. As the frigid dwarf planet crept toward its closest approach to the sun, the slight increase in insolation caused thin layers of frost—nitrogen leavened with traces of carbon monoxide and methane—to sublime. Methane in the temporary atmosphere absorbed infrared radiation, and this greenhouse effect, and the cooling effect of sublimation at the surface, created an inverted temperature gradient: the temperature of Pluto's atmosphere increased with height, and gas molecules at the top had sufficient energy to escape its shallow gravity well, bleeding away into space like the tail of a comet. And when the Pluto System passed perihelion and swung outward on its highly elliptical orbit and winter approached, Pluto's atmosphere would freeze, and fall as frost across the surface. And this cycle of seasonal changes took almost two hundred and fifty years to complete.

After some debate, Newt and two other volunteers took *Elephant* out of orbit and landed close to the equator. Newt stepped down to the surface, the fifth human being to set foot on Pluto, saying casually, "Well, here we are," and the three of them bounced around for an hour and set several drones tracking away across the frosty plain, then took off and caught up with *Out of Eden* as the shuttle went into orbit around Charon.

The dark surface of the smaller component of the binary system was divided between terrain cut by cobweb grooves and terrain pitted like the skin of a cantaloupe, all of it painted by broad, bright swathes of crystalline water ice and dusted with ammonium hydrate frosts in the shadows of crater rims: deep beneath Charon's surface was a shallow ocean of ammonia-rich water that here and there squeezed up through subsurface cracks and erupted in cryogeysers that deposited swathes of fresh frost across the dark surface, marking it in tiger stripes.

The Free Outers agreed that Charon was a place where human beings could live, roofing over troughs and grooves, tunnelling down to the zone of liquid water. Everyone took turns to descend to the surface. Macy went down with Newt, following him out across a lightly cratered plain, the two of them bouncing along in especially insulated pressure suits to the site of the first probe to have landed on Charon, some eighty years ago. An instrument platform slung between three pairs of fat mesh wheels, it stood at the end of a wandering track where its little fission pack had finally run out of energy. Stranded in a charcoal desert struck with little craters whose floors glimmered with pale frost. The close horizon circling around. The sun a brilliant star that even here, some 5.5 billion kilometres distant, so far away it took light more than five hours to span the distance, gave as much illumination as the full Moon, on Earth. Pluto's half-disc hung in the starry black sky, dim and grey in the faint light, capped white at the poles. The two dwarf planets were tidally locked face to face as they circled their common centre, Pluto waxing from full to gibbous to full again every six days.

Macy told Newt that it was a magnificent view, but she couldn't imagine living here. "It's going to get very cold and dark in winter. And it will be hard to reach anywhere else."

"The new motor will make it easier than it used to be," Newt said. "Besides, it won't be midwinter for more than a hundred years. And if we built habitats here, it will always be summer inside them."

"It's so far away from anywhere else. Just this pair of frozen balls waltzing around each other and a couple of tiny chunks of tarry ice dancing attendance. . . ."

"Is this your homesickness?"

"This is something else. I feel like I'm a ghost in a stranger's house."

"Right now, it is what it is," Newt said. "Sure, it's empty and unmarked. But so were Saturn's moons when the pioneers arrived."

"Pioneers," Macy said. "There's a lonely little word."

"That's what we are, like it or not."

The expedition explored Charon for ten days. They located tracts of carbonaceous material deposited by impacts with Kuiper Belt objects and seeded them with vacuum organisms. They launched a satellite that would in time provide detailed topographical and geological maps. And then they began the long voyage back to Uranus. Everyone was bound close by their shared experience, and Macy felt that she was an integral part of the little band of adventurers now. She would never forget Earth, and she did not think that she could ever come to think of the stark and frigid moonscapes as any kind of home. But she was no longer a stranger, here in the outer dark.

4

The spy woke slowly and painfully, trapped in the stiff embrace of his pressure suit, inside the coffin-sized confines of the dropshell. He felt as if he'd been beaten by experts and afterward staked out in the scorching heat of some desert on Earth. Bruised to the bone, joints stiff and swollen. A black headache pulsing like a poisonous spider inside the tender jelly of his brain. His tongue a shrivelled corpse glued to the floor of its foul tomb. He sipped tasteless recycled water through a tube and wincingly plugged into the dropshell's myopic sensorium. He'd slept for seventy-two days and now Rhea was directly ahead, a bright pockmarked globe hanging beyond the broad hoop of the rings and the bulge of Saturn's equator.

The dropshell hadn't logged any radar pings or attempts to make contact: its skimpy little coffin had managed to spiral inward without being detected by traffic control. The spy pulled up the navigation AI, picked his way through the limited options it presented, and chose the least worst compromise. Attitude jets popped and stuttered, Rhea and Saturn swung in the black sky, and then the main motor ignited with a dull thump, a brief burn that would bring him out of orbit to a spot a little to the south of Rhea's equator, on the sub-saturnian hemisphere.

Rhea is Saturn's second-largest moon, a fat ball of water ice wrapped around a core of silicate rock, its leading hemisphere scribed by a gigantic multiringed basin, its dark trailing hemisphere fractured by long tracts of bright cliffs. When pioneering Outers had arrived at the Saturn System more than a century ago, they'd settled on Rhea and excavated tunnels and small caves in the rock-hard water ice of the inner face of Xamba Crater's rim, a primitive little warren that had become the Saturn System's first city. Now the spy's stealthed dropshell fell in a slow, swooning arc that terminated in blocky terrain a little to the east of the outer edge of Xamba Crater.

It was midday. Rhea was passing through Saturn's shadow. In the darkness of this eclipse the spy hiked to a nearby shelter. He planned to rest up for a day, shower, eat a hot meal or two, recharge the batteries of his pressure suit and top up its stores of oxygen and water. But when he reached the shelter he found that the swathe of sunflowers around it had been smashed down and the inner and outer hatches of its tiny airlock hung open and it was cold and dark inside. The AI was dead, the oxygen stores had been vented, the water tank was frozen solid, and the printer and foodmaker were missing. A notice stencilled in red paint on the wall over the sleeping niche announced in English, French, and Russian that the shelter had been closed by authority of the TPA and anyone needing help should contact the waymaster on radio channel 9. And no doubt be arrested as a spy or saboteur, the spy thought sourly. He checked the dark little cave and the trampled area around its hatch in case a bug or two had been left behind to tattle-tale on trespassers, then hiked on toward the softly contoured slopes of the crater's rim.

It was a long walk even in Rhea's vestigial gravity, and he felt horribly exposed in the stark light of the sun's diamond chip, which hung high overhead in the black sky, just beyond Saturn's crescent. He picked his way between bright scarps at the crest of the rim, and trudged down a long valley on the inner slope to the lightly cratered plain of the floor.

Sombre fields of vacuum organisms spread around and beyond the platforms and tents of the spaceport. Berms of bright ice-rubble that no doubt roofed the Europeans' facility were set at right angles to the railway that connected the spaceport with the city, which was buried in a scarp that cut into the crater's rim. Several hundred rolligons and other vehicles drawn up in neat lines. A starfish of farm tubes, each tube a kilometre long, panes darkly polarised.

The spy spent an hour carefully reconnoitring the area all around the farm before breaking into the service airlock of the northernmost tube. He stripped off his pressure suit and disposed of his halflife suit-liner, which stank of old sweat and was mottled with necrotic patches, washed as best he could with soaked paper towels, dressed the weeping sores and rashes that had broken out across his flanks and thighs, pulled on a set of paper coveralls, and ambled between long rows of bean and tomato plants as if he belonged there.

Rhea's days were a little over one hundred and eight hours long, but the Outers who lived there kept to Earth's twenty-four-hour cycle; although it was the middle of Rhea's long afternoon, it was two in the morning in the city and in its farm tubes. The spy found a memo space and loaded a little crew of demons into it, and while they got to work he crawled into the hutch where the farm's robots were garaged, slowly ate three ripe tomatoes, his first solid food since he'd left Iapetus so long ago, and went to sleep. The machines wouldn't bother him, and it was highly unlikely that anyone would check the hutch.

He slept around the clock. When he woke, he found that his demons had established a back door into the net controlled by the European occupation force. Like their Brazilian allies on Dione, the Europeans had cleared everyone from habitats and oases scattered across the face of Rhea and moved them into its only city. A basic search string brought up Zi Lei's records in a couple of seconds. She was registered as a refugee who'd been transported from an oasis called Patterson's Curse some two years ago, shortly after the end of the Quiet War. She shared an apartment with other refugees, worked in a communal kitchen, and had never been cited for violating security regulations. The spy read the brief entry several times. He felt cool and alert but not especially excited. He was already planning what he had to do.

The tag he'd been given in Paris, when his crew had begun salvage work in the city, was still embedded in the humerus of his left arm. One of the demons copied the tag's biometrics into the Europeans' database and faked up an entry that established the spy's stolen identity, Felice Gottschalk, as a bona fide resident of Xamba.

Getting into the city wasn't a problem. All the farm tubes were linked by cut-and-cover tunnels to a central hub, and a short railway line ran between the hub and Xamba's northernmost chamber. The spy arrived at the city's railway station at six in the morning; the soldiers in charge of security had just changed shifts. The spy explained to the pair at the station's check-point that he'd been called out to fix a problem with the central air-conditioning plant at the farm tubes; they checked the log entry that his demons had faked up, showing that he'd left the city three hours earlier, and waved him through.

The city's five fat chambers were buried side by side in Xamba Crater's eastern rim, linked by pedestrian tunnels and a canal system. A second pair of soldiers examined Felice Gottschalk's ID before allowing him to use the long tunnel—floor turfed with halflife grass, curving walls decorated with mock-heroic murals featuring hordes of figures in ancient lobster-style pressure suits constructing tents and vast spaceships or battling unlikely monsters or flying mankites through Saturn's storms—that led to the neighbouring chamber, where Zi Lei lived.

Apartments, shops, cafés, workshops, and gardens were piled on top of each other in steep, terraced cliffs on either side of the chambers, rising above a park filled edge to edge with tents that housed the overspill population of refugees and cut down the middle by a narrow lake where high-sided boats bobbed on slow, fat waves. The chandelier lights were still dimmed and only a few early risers were out and about. A work crew was opening up a communal kitchen set up at one end of the lake. At the end of a jetty, a group of old men and women were moving from one t'ai chi position to another.

Zi Lei's apartment was on a high terrace close to the big transparent endwall that looked out across Xamba Crater. It was night out there, and the crammed tiers rising on either side of the central garden were dimly reflected in the endwall's patchwork of construction-diamond panes.

The spy sat under a fig tree that sprawled across the wall at the far end of the terrace, where he had a good view of the door to Zi Lei's apartment and could watch everyone who came and went. He sat there for a long time, crosslegged, unmoving, ignoring the glances of passersby. He couldn't send Zi Lei a message of any kind because the occupying force's security AIs monitored every call and text. And he didn't want to knock on the door of the apartment because she shared it with six people. When they reunited—this was how he thought of it now—he wanted to speak with her alone. He wondered if she would recognise him beneath his plastic surgery; wondered if she would run to him with a cry of joy; rehearsed what he would say, what he imagined she would say. . . .

Karyl Mezhidov had once asked him if he loved Zi Lei or if he was in love with her. He hadn't understood the distinction then. He did now.

Two people, a man and a woman, came out of the apartment. The spy's heart thumped in his chest, and then he saw that the woman wasn't Zi Lei.

He told himself that in ten minutes he'd give up waiting and go and knock on her door; told himself ten minutes later that he'd give her ten minutes more. And so time passed until a woman came out of the apartment and ankled across the terrace to the cableway that connected it to lower levels. It wasn't her. It was. He knew it was. Zi Lei, slender as a reed in a yellow tunic and white trousers. She'd grown out her hair and it was braided in a gleaming black rope that hung down the small of her back. She was carrying something in a sling that went between her breasts. A baby. She was cupping its head tenderly, stepping onto one of the cableway's little platforms, descending out of sight.

There'd been nothing in her file about a baby; it must belong to someone who shared the apartment with her.

The spy followed her down to the floor of the chamber. When she went into the communal kitchen, he walked straight past, crossed a bridge that arched over the lake, went up one level, and stood at the edge of a terrace that had a clear view across the water to the kitchen. Zi Lei was sitting at a long table with the man and woman who had come out of the apartment earlier. She had unbuttoned her tunic and taken the baby out of its sling and was cradling it in the crook of her left arm as it sucked greedily at her breast.

"A lovely picture of ordinary human life," a man said behind the spy.

He turned, and the man smiled and said, "Hello, Dave."

Before he'd been given the skin of Ken Shintaro and sent to work in Paris, Dione, the spy had been called Dave. And all his brothers had been called Dave too. He had been Dave #8. The man smiling at him was Dave #27. Dave #27 had been the smartest of them all, and he'd also been Dave #8's best friend. Saying now, "You took long enough to find her. I was beginning to think that you were dead."

"I was in Paris," the spy said. "And then I was on Iapetus."

"We looked for you in Paris, of course. You did a very good job, hiding from us."

"I was a dead man."

"You were Felice Gottschalk. You'd changed your appearance, too," Dave #27 said. "Not a bad job, either. Just enough to fool us."

"I was lucky. The city's records were futzed during the war," the spy said.

"And now your luck has run out," his brother said.

They were both pale and thin, and exactly the same height, but Dave #27 had blond hair and the spy's was black, altered by treatment with a retrovirus that had also darkened the tint of his irises. His face was rounder, too, and his nose broader and flatter.

"If you wanted to kill me, I would already be dead," the spy said. "I suppose you want me to come back. Well, I won't."

"We were beginning to think you'd died," Dave #27 said. "But then we arrested a woman named Keiko Sasaki. She was part of the resistance. During her interrogation she gave up many names, including yours. Or rather, she gave up Felice Gottschalk. She told us that he was really Ken Shintaro, and that he was looking for a woman named Zi Lei. Of course, we searched Paris all over again, from top to bottom. And checked everybody's DNA against their biometric records, a very tedious job. We found the false records you had inserted, but we couldn't find *you*. We looked in the other cities we control, and we looked here. We found Zi Lei, but still we couldn't find you. Because all that time you were on Iapetus, the one place we couldn't search. The Pacific Community is supposed to be our ally, but it wouldn't help us look for a poor lost soul who had foolishly defected from his honourable mission. We tried our best to search for you, anyway, but the PacCom administration is careless and arrogant. Its records are incomplete, and the population of Iapetus is still widely scattered. . . . So we set a trap here, because we were certain that you would eventually find out where your woman was living, and come to her."

The spy didn't say anything. He was using his peripheral vision, trying to spot people who might be watching. He was sick and frightened and excited too. Hyperalert. Everything around him bright with its own particularity.

"Don't worry," Dave #27 said. "I'm alone. I was sent here to monitor the general situation in Xamba. Yesterday, one of my demons spotted your activity in the Europeans' net. I dropped everything else to keep a close watch on your friend. And here we are."

"Do the Europeans know that you are here?"

"If you mean, am I here officially, no. They believe that I am a refugee. I am sorry to tell you that you came here too late," Dave #27 said. "After she arrived here, Zi Lei spent a little time in hospital. She hadn't been taking the drugs that controlled her illness—her schizophrenia. She tried to kill herself. She failed, and fell in love with another patient. They handfasted last year. And as you can see, they have a daughter. Born just five weeks ago."

The spy knew now why there'd been no mention of the baby in Zi Lei's file. It had been erased so that it wouldn't frighten him away. So that he would walk unknowing into his brother's trap.

He said, "I'm glad that she's safe."

Dave #27 smiled and shook his head.

"It doesn't change anything," the spy said. "I have my own life."

"You made it your mission to search for her. And now you've found her, and your mission is over."

"I defected. I can't undefect."

"There's nothing for you here. The woman is fasted to another man and they have a child. And whatever it is you think you feel for her, it's part of the false identity given to you before the war. It isn't part of who you really are."

"I'm still finding out who I really am."

"You can't have the woman. What else is there for you?"

How could the spy explain how he had been changed by working with the crew in Paris, by the companionable days spent with Karyl Mezhidov rolling across the dark plains of Iapetus, by sharing food and work and long conversations about nothing in particular with strangers? How could he explain that he could never go home because he was no longer the person he had once been, before the war?

Anyone else would have missed Dave #27's tremor of intent, but the spy had trained in every kind of combat with his brother for almost three thousand days and he had always been a little faster and a little stronger. He swung up his left arm, blocking the punch that Dave #27 aimed at his throat, and chopped at Dave #27's elbow with the heel of his right hand, striking the point where the nerve ran outside the ball of the joint. Dave #27 dropped the syrette he'd palmed and spun and kicked the spy in the hip.

Then they were fighting seriously, countering each other's blows with dazzling speed, each trying to find a weakness in the other's defences. The spy, driven toward the edge of the terrace, jumped onto the railing and kicked Dave #27 in the chest and flipped backward, landing lightly in one of the boats tied up at the edge of the lake, leaping away like a grasshopper as Dave #27 floated down toward him, running down the length of the string of boats with his brother at his heels. The boats rode high in the water and rocked wildly beneath them as they bounded along. Fat low-gravity waves ran out to the far shore where people stood and watched and cheered them on, no doubt believing that the fight was a piece of street theatre.

The spy kicked off from the stern of the last boat in a long, high parabola aimed toward the terrace. He swung sideways over the rail, took five long, bouncing steps down the terrace, and caught hold of the scaly trunk of a pal-metto tree and swung around and saw his brother standing just a few metres away. Smiling at him, wagging an admonitory finger back and forth. The spy snapped a shard from the rim of the big plastic pot in which the palmetto was planted, held it up like a knife, and told his brother to stay right where he was.

"I'll leave," the spy said. "Right now."

"Yes, you will. With me."

"Alone. I'll leave alone. Leave this city. This moon. You can tell them I was never here."

They were both breathing hard. Down the terrace, two men in the trim blue uniforms of the European Army were moving toward them.

Dave #27 saw the soldiers too and said, "Come with me if you want to live."

The spy stepped backward, ready to turn and run. His brother lunged at him and the spy hit him hard with the hand holding the shard of plastic. It was wrenched out of his grip as Dave #27 reeled back, blood spouting between the fingers clamped on his neck. The spy saw the shock in his brother's eyes and remembered the only man he'd killed. One of the lectors. Father Solomon. He'd been ordered to do it, but he had never forgotten the shame and self-loathing he had felt afterward. How it had set him apart from his brothers. All this tumbling through his mind as Dave #27 tottered and slowly and carefully sat down.

When the one of the European soldiers stepped forward and tasered him, the spy was trying to staunch the spurts of arterial blood from his brother's neck. He came around briefly as he was hauled off, fastened upright to a kind of wheeled stretcher. He tried to turn his head against the strap across his forehead, looking for Zi Lei in the crowd that had gathered. And was glad, so very glad, that he couldn't see her.

5

The motor crew had worked up detailed plans for the exploration of Neptune and several of the dwarf planets at the edge of the Kuiper Belt, but after the expedition to the Pluto System returned to Miranda the Free Outers voted against further trips. Neptune's largest moon, Triton, was a highly promising piece of real estate, to be sure, but it had been comprehensively mapped by human visitors and robot probes, and at present Neptune was on the opposite side of the Solar System. There was no urgent need to go there just yet, and it would be a waste of resources and time better used to improve and expand the settlement on Miranda, and to equip the rest of the Free Outers' little fleet with the fast-fusion motor.

Newt Jones wasn't disheartened by the vote against further expeditions. In fact, he was energised by defeat, convinced that sooner rather than later he would be proven right. He worked long hours on the conversion programme and discussed refinements to the design of the motor with his crew of tech wizards. Macy Minnot returned to her work with the biome crew, tweaking and improving and enriching the habitat's ecosystem. And then, just sixty days after the expedition returned, everything changed.

All the Free Outers spent time on the surface of Miranda. Escaping the close common air of the habitat. Exploring the fantastically varied moonscapes on solo trips or with their friends or families. Making the unfamiliar familiar. Laying down hiking trails across heavily cratered terrain and smoother, younger plains, and along the broken floors of the valleys in the parallel grooves at the edges of coronas. Setting up routes that descended deep within the enormous grabens that cut across every kind of moonscape, where rugged cliffs stepped up ten or twenty kilometres to a black sky thick with stars, and setbacks and terraces could comfortably hold small cities. They navigated by global positioning and left only a few traces: pitons hammered in ice cliffs; splashes of pigment that marked paths through the abrupt ridges and interlocked hills and rubble fields of chaotic terrain; a small number of carefully hidden refuges.

Most of the surface of Miranda was water ice, but early in its history the upwelling plumes or diapirs of soft warm ices that had created the massive upthrust domes of coronas had dragged with them significant amounts of mantle material. The survey crew had located several sources of palagonitised silicates, as well as ores rich in magnesium and aluminium, and drifts of valuable phosphates and nitrates. Newt and Macy made several trips out to the ancient cratered terrain of Bohemia Regio, where deposits of ammonia-rich smectite clays had been discovered, and to the northern edge of Arden Corona, where robots were mining seams of silicate rock. Although crops and herbs were grown hydroponically and the habitat's big commons was floored with halflife turf, the biome crew had plans to develop pocket parks, with copses of trees and flowering bushes. Macy lacked pedon tables and other equipment necessary for the manufacture of proper soil, with its horizons and domains and complex interplay of every kind of microbiotia, but the clay from Bohemia Regio, cloddy and highly alkaline in its native state, made a nicely friable compost after it had been modified in a reactor and mixed with humus from the waste digesters. A fine example of how even this apparently inhospitable moon could yield material that could support life in all its rich variety. The silicate rock, on the other hand, was for purely decorative purposes.

On the day that everything changed, Macy and Newt had travelled a quarter of the way around Miranda to Arden Corona, a routine trip of some four hundred kilometres. They flew in *Elephant*. Newt piloted the tug with careless skill, swooping low over bright, gently contoured plains lightly spattered with small craters, then soaring out across a sudden transition zone where the moonscape slumped and heaved in a broken quilt of hills and valleys, a vast frozen landslip tilted toward the foot of a fault scarp more than a kilometre high, its looming face cut by massive vertical grooves—slickensides—that had been incised by friction as the block face had been pushed upward by massive tectonic forces when the moon had cooled.

Newt flew parallel to the scarp's grooved face for more than twenty kilometres, until it fell back in a huge cirque created by an ancient meteorite impact that had excavated billions of tons of dirty water ice, vaporising some, throwing the rest across the face of Miranda or beyond the feeble grip of the little moon's gravity into orbit around Uranus. Newt applied retrojets to brake *Elephant*'s free-fall trajectory. As it dropped toward the base of the cirque, Macy saw a black animal racing across the bright ground below: the tug's shadow, growing larger as they fell to meet it, attitude motors popping as they feathered in to a perfect landing within the cirque's half-circle.

Macy and Newt closed up their pressure suits, wriggled through the airlock one after the other, unpacked the sled, and rode it across slopes of dusty ice under a black sky where Uranus's bland blue crescent lay on its side. The cliffs curved around them, rippled like frozen curtains, scalloped footings rising out of cones of mass-wasted material. Macy and Newt switchbacked up the face of one of these cones to a bench butted against the cliff face, where an automobile-sized mining robot was patiently gnawing into an intrusive seam of silicates, cutting out block after block and piling them in neat pyramidal stacks. Sunlight on Miranda was just one four-hundredth as strong as sunlight falling on Earth—brighter than moonlight, but not bright enough for Macy to easily make out colours. The dusty hummocks of the bench and the cliffs rearing above were mostly shades of grey enlivened by stark black shadows and salt-sharp glints reflected from freshly exposed facets of water ice, and the brick-sized chunks of silicate material looked like iron slag. But when Macy turned on her helmet lamp, the silicate bricks were transformed into glistening blocks of coarsely textured jade, shot through with folds of delicate yellow and carbon black. Perfect material for pavements and low sinuous walls in the little parks planned for the habitat.

She and Newt loaded a sled and hauled it back to *Elephant* and stacked the bricks in the tug's external cargo lockers. After four trips the lockers were full and their work was done. They hiked out across the floor of the cirque, chasing each other in long floating leaps under the black sky. The sun's bright chip was close to the horizon; their shadows stretched and shrank, stretched and shrank as they bounded along, dancing in the ethereal microgravity, delighted in each other's delight. They warmed meals in the foodmaker and ate them and drank a little homemade wine, and made love and lay in each other's arms in the hammock they'd stretched across the living space. Macy snuggled up against Newt, resting her head on his cool bony chest. She could hear his heart beating and feel the pulse of the microheart in the wrist which lay against her neck as he stroked her hair, the short bristles making a crisp sound under his fingers.

"We don't have to go back," he said.

"Mmm."

"We could build our own garden right here. Throw up a tent, fill it full of jungle."

"And chickens."

"Why not? I'd even let you kill and eat one now and then."

"I don't know how you can bear to live with an unevolved barbarian like me."

"Oh, I've eaten meat before," Newt said. "There's a cult in the free zone of Sparta, Tethys. They grow cloned cow meat, mince it up, eat it raw. A sex thing. They drink blood, too. Little sips of human blood."

"Is this one of your stories?"

Newt had all kinds of tall tales from back when he'd been a freebooting trader. Macy reckoned that about half of them contained a pinch of truth, and one or two might even be more or less genuine.

"Maybe one day I'll be able to take you there," Newt said. "Although I have to say that even though I only took the smallest mouthful, I nearly threw up."

"Raw meat, now that's barbaric. We can clone up our own cow meat, and I'll show you how to cook a hamburger. Or broil a steak."

"Corrupt me with your Earthly ways. We'll build a garden here and grow chickens. And have kids. I mean, forget about the chickens, but don't you think it's time we did something about having kids?"

They'd talked about starting a family before, but this had arrived sideways. Macy raised her head and looked at Newt. His face, with its prominent cheekbones and narrow nose, was all highlights and shadow in the soft faint glow of the dialled-down lights. It was impossible to make out his expression.

"Don't joke about it," Macy said.

"I'm not joking. People are having babies all around us. Four since we arrived, six more on the way. Not to mention all the kids who came out here in the first place. Oh, I know what you're going to say, it's too early, we're going to have to move on when the TPA comes calling. But if we stick to that line of thought it will always be too early, until it's too late."

Newt was serious, for once. A rare mood for him, which meant that Macy had to take his proposal seriously. She told him that it was something that she wanted, all right, but she wasn't sure she was ready for it, and they talked it over, rehearsing all the arguments for and against, and fell asleep twined around each other in the deep hammock.

Macy woke when Newt reared up and reached past her and pulled something toward him: his spex. They were making a soft beeping that stopped when he hooked them over his ears.

"What is it?" Macy said, chills chasing over her bare skin. Like everyone in the field they maintained strict radio silence. If someone had sent them a message, it meant trouble of some kind.

After a moment Newt took off his spex and handed them to her.

She put them on. Black letters marched across a flat grey background in front of her eyes: *Possible contact. Return at once. Possible contact. Return at once. Possible contact. Return at once.*

"They must have bounced it off the observatory on Titania," Newt said. "It's the only one above the horizon right now."

Macy clutched at the side of the hammock as he swung off. "*Possible* contact. It means they aren't sure," she said.

"I guess we'll have to go back and find out. Any way you cut it, it's bad news."

"But not the worst. Not yet."

"No, not yet."

The observatories on Oberon, Titania, and Ariel kept high-resolution telescopes trained on the patches of sky through which ships from Saturn, Jupiter,
or Earth had to pass if they were heading for orbit around Uranus. After two
years, with no sign of any ships or sneaky little drones infiltrating the Uranus
System, the Free Outers had begun to think that they were safe. That the TPA
had decided that it was not worth chasing after them. Jupiter was presently on
the far side of the sun and Saturn was drawing away from Uranus—was now
further away than Earth, in fact. These vast distances were a moat separating
them from the rest of humanity. A quarantine. But blink comparison of frames
captured by the telescope of the Oberon observatory showed a fleck of light
moving across the rigid patterns of the star field, and spectrographic analysis
showed that it was fusion light: the exhaust of a ship that had been dispatched
from Saturn and was now decelerating toward Uranus on a trajectory that put
it at just thirty days out from orbital rendezvous.

As soon as everyone had returned to the habitat an extraordinary meeting
was convened in the bowl of the commons where the Free Outers cooked
communal meals and played and talked. They talked for most of the day, and
long into the night. Although the general tone of the discussion was serious
and sober, it was sharpened by an edge of strained anxiety that sometimes
broke out in uncharacteristic catcalls and squabbles. They had made detailed
plans and preparations for this day, and now that it was here they had been
brought face to face with the possibility that they might not survive.

Sitting beside Newt in their usual place near the lip of the bowl, Macy
watched the proceedings with growing impatience burning low in her belly.
Frustration and claustrophobia. She had never doubted that one day the TPA
would move against the Free Outers, but she'd been lulled into a false sense
of security as she and everyone else had busied themselves with turning their
temporary refuge into a home. They'd sat here making gardens and babies,
growing comfortable and complacent, and now that the crisis had arrived
they were wasting time with pointless arguments.

Macy had never had much time for the interminable debates that the
Outers so loved, especially when it was obvious from the get-go what needed
to be done. No point talking about it: they needed a strong leader who'd stand
up and take charge. But Idriss Barr was more concerned with moderating the
discussion than with taking charge, anxious to defer to every point of view. So
they wasted more than three hours debating whether they should stay or leave,

and when they'd voted by a slim majority to leave they immediately settled into another discussion about whether they should head for Pluto or Neptune.

Newt, Macy, and the rest of the motor crew opted for Neptune. Ziff Larzer set out their plans calmly and methodically. Neptune was further away than Pluto, but other refugees might be hiding out there, and its big moon, Triton, was larger and more hospitable than Pluto or Charon. The motor crew had manufactured sufficient antiprotons to fuel all the ships fitted with new fusion motors, and these would be more than enough to transport everyone. They might have to leave behind the unconverted ships and a considerable amount of equipment, but they would be able to take enough to make a new home, and there was the possibility that they could return to Uranus one day and retrieve the rest. As far as Macy was concerned, it was done and dusted, but there was another interminable delay while people quibbled over this or that detail before they all voted again. This time the majority was clear. The motor crew had won the day. The Free Outers would pack up and move on to Neptune.

Before they could leave they had to strip out everything useful in the habitat, collect the final set of fuel tanks dispatched from the robots in Uranus's atmosphere, and prep and load their ships. Macy and the rest of the biome crew spent most of the time harvesting the hydroponic farms, pruning back the gardens and simplifying the habitat's ecosystem so that it would be easier for the maintenance bots to look after. They packed coffee and tea mosses and dried herbs and collected as much seed as they could—it would be faster and easier to grow new crops from seed than from callus cultures derived from the libraries of gene maps—but the rest of the edible biomass went into the bioreactors because they couldn't afford to waste fuel carrying it.

Macy worked with growing regret. She'd put a lot of work and love into the gardens that curved up on either side of the habitat's narrow floor— clumps of dwarf conifers and bamboos, squares of maize and corn and rice, peanut vines scrambling through stands of banana plants, great heaps of express vine, based on kudzu and cut so that different strains bore tomatoes or cucumbers, dozens of varieties of peas and beans, citrus bushes and grape vines, eggplants and onions, containers overflowing with thyme and mint and parsley. A dense green maze, crammed with lush and vivid life. Now all this was cut back to the bone, everything was stark and bare, domes and tepees were stranded on the floor like barnacles when the tide went out, and she could see that the habitat was no more than a tunnel jointed up from half a dozen cylinders little bigger than the airframes of transport planes, no longer any kind of home.

The Outers worked hard, eighteen hours a day, planning to quit Miranda ten days before the TPA ship arrived. They were still working when a nuclear warhead took out the old commune habitat on Titania.

The missile had been shot off by the TPA ship while it was still decelerating toward Uranus. It flared in on a trajectory that gained delta vee as it hooked around the ice giant, and headed straight out toward Titania and detonated five hundred metres above the tented habitat, vaporising it and melting a perfectly circular shallow bowl a kilometre across in the icy regolith. A clear message that the TPA wasn't prepared to negotiate or take prisoners. That they had come here to clean out a nest of vermin.

And so, before the oncoming ship could launch more missiles, the Free Outers abandoned the habitat and boarded their ships in jittery haste. The last of Miranda that Macy saw before cycling through *Elephant*'s airlock was the scatter of decorative bricks she and Newt had dumped from the tug's external lockers. Lumps of slag derelict on trampled dust.

They left without any formality beyond coordination of launch of their ships. Eighteen equipped with the fast-fusion motor, followed by four slower unconverted shuttles packed with as much equipment and construction material as they could carry and crewed by volunteers. Burning up from the floor of the deep groove where the habitat was hidden and from pits hidden in parallel grooves or close to the rims of craters on the rolling plain beyond, flying straight out from the dark northern hemisphere of the little moon into the diluted glare of the sun.

Idriss Barr sent a brief message from ship to ship, saying that they had become pioneers during their sojourn on Miranda and they would always be pioneers, never refugees. But as Uranus's crescent dwindled behind them into the starry black Macy couldn't help thinking that, rather than setting out on a grand adventure, they were simply running away, like rabbits scattering from the shadow of a hawk. One way or another she seemed to have been running away all her life. From the bleak compound of the Church of the Divine Regression, huddled on the dust deserts of Kansas, to the slums of Pittsburgh, where she'd briefly fallen in love before running away again, and joining the R&R Corps. And that had taken her all the way to Jupiter: to Rainbow Bridge, Callisto, where she'd become embroiled in a sleazy little tangle of intrigue and sabotage and murder. She'd blown the whistle on that and had defected, and had been rewarded with incarceration in an uptight little city from which she escaped with the help of Newt, running with him further out to Saturn, and his family home on Dione. Then war had come, and they'd gone on the run for the second time. And here she was, running away yet again.

The observatories on Oberon, Titania, and Ariel, and a satellite left in orbit around Miranda, transmitted views of the TPA ship as it closed on Uranus, describing an aerobraking maneuver through the tenuous outer reaches of the atmosphere that drew a violet contrail halfway around the ice giant, then jettisoning its scorched heat shield and hooking out past Oberon on a periapsis raise maneuver that, inside six hours, brought it into an equatorial parking orbit beyond the broken arcs at the outer edge of the ring system. A spray of drones shot out toward the five larger moons, swung into orbit around them, and quickly located and took down the observatories. The satellite orbiting Miranda transmitted glimpses of nuclear strikes on decoy tents that had been set up on Oberon and Ariel, and then its signal cut out. The fleeing Free Outers would never know if the TPA ship located the habitat, or the ships hidden around and about, or the little refuges they'd scattered across Miranda's surface. All they could do was plough on toward Neptune.

—●—

Think of the Solar System as a clock, with the sun at its centre and the planets sweeping out in rings of increasing diameter around it, moving counterclockwise. Set Uranus at twelve o'clock, with Saturn off to the left at roughly nine o'clock and Neptune all the way across the dial at half past five, on the far side of the sun. More than seven billion kilometres away, a vast gulf that even the ships equipped with the fast-fusion motor would take twenty-seven weeks to cross, while the unconverted shuttles would take much longer, more than two years.

The little fleet forged steadily onward, dropping empty fuel tanks behind them as they rose out of Uranus's gravity well. At last their motors cut out and they were falling free, vanishingly small and faint motes drifting in the great ocean of night.

Most people slept most of the time. Outers had the knack of being able to drop into a deep sleep similar to hibernation, slowing heartbeat and breathing and metabolism, a spark of consciousness remaining so that they could wake up in just a few minutes. But although Macy had been given retroviral treatments to help her adapt to the stresses of microgravity, the hibernation tweak was more radical than adding a few regulatory genes and so she slept in a coffin like the one she'd slept in when she'd first voyaged out from Earth to Jupiter, cooled down to −4° Celsius, at the borderland between life and death.

Waking was slow, and painful. She was briefly aware of choking up pink fluorosilicones that had infused her lungs, and then she passed out. When she woke again, sick, blinded, and nearly paralysed by the universe's worst hangover, she gradually realised that she was in a cocoon hung in a corner of *Elephant*'s living space. Someone swam toward her—it was Newt, saying something she couldn't grasp. Words that were just noise, lost in the distracting thump of her headache. She slept and woke again, racked by bone-deep aches, her stomach clenched and empty, her bowels distended around fifty kilogrammes of concrete.

She was still strapped in the cocoon. A peristaltic line was feeding clear nutrient fluid into a vein in her left wrist. The living space was empty, lit by dim red light. *Elephant*'s motor was making a comforting rumble and pulling about 0.1 *g* sternward. After unplugging the line in her wrist and unzipping the cocoon, Macy tumbled to the padded floor; it took all her strength to haul her aching carcass up the rungs to where Newt and Ziff Larzer and Herschel Wu lay side by side on the crash couches that took up most of the little control blister.

Newt started to get up, and Macy stumbled forward and dropped to her knees and embraced him, breathing in the familiar warmth and smell of him.

"Hey," he said. "How are you?"

"I think I'm alive. More or less."

"You shouldn't be up."

"What do you want me to do—go back to sleep? I've been asleep too long." Macy bumped fists with Ziff Larzer and Herschel Wu and said, "We're all still here, so I guess the TPA didn't try to cut us off."

The three men exchanged glances.

Cold electricity zipped down Macy's spine. "Something happened," she said.

Ziff Larzer said, "We have good news and bad news, and news we're not sure about."

Herschel Wu twiddled his fingers in the air: the memo space in front of the couches opened up and displayed a navigation plot curving through the orbits of moons scribed around a fat planet, tagged with way points, a bead blinking halfway along it. He said, "We're about a hundred thousand kilometres out from Neptune, coming toward the end of a burn that will insert us into orbit."

"Around Triton or around Neptune? I thought we were heading directly for Triton," Macy said.

A telescope view of Neptune's half-globe hung in a corner of the memo space, darker blue than Uranus, differentiated into distinct bands. Pale elongated wisps of cloud. A small black spot capped with a feathering of white cloud rode above the equator, close to the fuzzy terminator line between day and night. The ice giant was girdled by the bright circles of its two prominent rings, and hanging beyond the rings was a tiny disc: Triton, Neptune's largest moon, their new home.

"There's a slight problem," Newt said.

"Is that the bad news?"

"The bad news is, we lost some people," Ziff Larzer said.

"The unconverted shuttles," Newt said. "The TPA hit them with missiles. Nuclear warheads."

Macy's entire skin felt as if it had turned to ice and for a moment everything seemed to drop away from her. She'd known the people who had volunteered to crew the shuttles. Myk Thorne, Tor Hertz, Darcy Dunnant, Hamilton Browne . . . sixteen people, all gone.

Newt was studying her with soft concern; she told him she was okay and he said that she was far from okay.

Ziff Larzer gave up his couch. Macy was persuaded to clamber onto it and she accepted a pouch of lukewarm mint tea that Herschel Wu brought up from the living space: the sovereign remedy for every kind of illness, he said.

"I'm not ill, just half dead," Macy said, but she sipped the tea and, yes, felt a little better. Strong enough to ask about the third piece of news.

"It's to do with where we're headed," Newt said. "Seems there's a bit of a problem."

"A big problem," Herschel Wu said.

"There are already people on Triton," Ziff Larzer said.

"Isn't that good?" Macy said.

"They're Ghosts," Newt said.

PART THREE

THE CHANGING OF THE GUARD

I

"What you still haven't learned after all this time," Frankie Fuente told Cash Baker, "is how to relax."

"I'm pretty relaxed right now," Cash said. "Maybe you should take a picture to remind yourself what it looks like."

"What you are right now is the exact opposite of relaxed. You're wired so tight I could nail your head to one end of a plank and your feet to the other and play a tune on you. And you know what? You're like that *all the time*."

The two men were leaning side by side at the edge of an infinity pool, chest-deep in warm clear water, elbows resting on polished concrete, looking out across restored rainforest that stretched to the horizon under an enamelled blue sky pierced directly overhead by the white-hot nail of the sun. Behind them was the stone-and-glass saucer of the hilltop house owned by the governor of the Bernal family's territory, set amongst manicured lawns and beds of tropical flowers. In a few hours, Frankie Fuente and Cash Baker would mingle with guests at a cocktail party on one of its broad terraces and give short talks about their role in the Quiet War, the plans for reconstruction, and the opportunities presented by opening up the Outers' store of knowledge and exploiting their artistic, scientific, and engineering expertise.

Cash Baker was a bona fide gold-plated war hero, dividing his time between teaching cadets at the academy in Monterrey and public relations tours: giving speeches at schools and universities and rallies, visiting research institutions, shipyards, factories, and munition plants that supported and supplied the Air Defence Force wings at Jupiter and Saturn, and making nice to members of the great families that dominated the political and economic scene in Greater Brazil. It wasn't a bad life. Teaching cadets was useful work; Cash tried to do his very best by them. And promoting the work out at Jupiter and Saturn, that was important, too, and surprisingly easy. He was able to draw on his deep reserve of lollygagging Texas charm to woo his hosts and their guests, and before setting out on the cocktail-and-chat circuit he'd spent a month being trained in public speaking and the finer points of etiquette and social chitchat, from how to eat an oyster to the correct form of address for the wife of a foreign ambassador.

The benefits were all that anyone could ask for. He stayed at some of the best houses and hotels in Greater Brazil, enjoyed every kind of luxury, and met with all kinds of important and famous people. He'd even toured the European Union, visited Paris, Rome, Berlin, Moscow. . . .

But it wasn't what he wanted, which was to get back to the job he'd won by training, hard work, and application of his God-given talent to the virtual exclusion of everything else: flying J-2 singleship space planes in combat. It was what he had been born to do. It was what he had been *made* to do, when he'd been fitted with the neural network that allowed him to interface directly with his bird. To become one with her. And although he knew that part of his life was over, he still ached for it every day.

Physically, he was almost fully recovered, apart from some weakness in his right side, and a slight, almost undetectable limp. But his head still wasn't quite right. His brain had been pierced. The swathe clear-cut through its delicate, intricate forest had been regrown, but his memory was still full of holes: he couldn't remember a thing about the mission that had nearly killed him, or much of anything else about the mission to the Saturn System. And despite a cocktail of psychotropic drugs, he suffered from wild mood swings. He'd be in the middle of some completely routine task—exercising, preparing a lecture, cleaning his shoes—and his vision would blur and he'd feel wetness running down his cheeks: *tears*, stupid tears. Or he'd be picking at his food during a banquet and would have to stamp out the sudden impulse to pick up the plate and throw it at the person opposite, or stab the bore next to him with his fork just to shut the fucker up. Or, and this was the worst thing, the world would suddenly go flat. As if colour and meaning had been sucked out of everything, leaving only stuff like poor imitations of the real thing, people like awkward robots: meat puppets spouting flat gibberish.

He'd been told to expect sudden alterations in his internal weather system; emotional lability was a condition commonly found in people recovering from violent traumas to the head. But no one had warned him about the awful feelings of flat unreality, worse than any species of depression or despair, and he'd suffered in silence because it was the kind of thing that crazy people must feel, and he didn't want to be crazy because they'd never let him anywhere near a singleship or any kind of flying machine ever again, even if he was a war hero. So he hadn't ever mentioned these spells to the psychologist who checked him every month, or told his best friend, Luiz Schwarcz, about them the one time they'd met when Luiz had come back to Earth for a spell of leave before lighting out for Saturn again, and he'd done his best to keep it hidden from his handlers and the men and women who partnered him on the PR tours—the other war heroes.

Frankie Fuente, his current partner, was a cheerful cynic who said that he took the world at face value so that he wouldn't ever be disappointed or surprised by anything. A big man with dusty black skin and a genial manner, he'd been promoted from first sergeant to lieutenant after the accident that had put him on the PR circuit. He and Cash had been getting along just fine for the past three months. They'd both joined the Air Defence Force to escape the dirt-poor towns in which they'd been born, Cash in East Texas, Frankie in the arid badlands of Paiuí where plantations of Lackner trees soaked up excess carbon dioxide from the atmosphere and vultures flew with just one wing so that they could fan themselves with the other because it was so damn hot.

Frankie's PR story was that he'd lost both his arms when he'd been trying to defuse a booby trap that an Outer saboteur had attached to a gig. Truth was, he'd confided to Cash one drunken night early in their partnership, he'd been high on three patches of rize while working in the maintenance bay of the *Glory of Gaia*, and his arms had been severed above the elbows when he'd accidentally triggered a hydraulic ram. He had artificial arms now. The fake artificial arm that covered the new arm growing from the high-cut stump of his left arm, and the real artificial arm that permanently replaced his right arm. The latter, woven from fullerene fibres and covered in halflife skin, could bend like a snake and had a mind of its own whenever he detached it, pulling itself about with its hand, hiding in dark places, and, according to Frankie, driving his lady friends wild in bed.

His real and fake artificial arms crossed on the wet concrete of the edge of the infinity pool, his chin resting on them as he floated in the water, Frankie told Cash, "Here we are with a view that would make a green saint come, in the house of a man so rich and powerful he has, count 'em, not one, not two, not three, but *four* children. And I bet you aren't enjoying any part of it because you're thinking about your speech. Which you've given fifty times already, to my certain knowledge."

"Matter of fact, I was watching that bird soaring over yonder," Cash said.

It was a big bird, some kind of eagle maybe, silhouetted against the blue sky as it turned and turned in a thermal. Cash had been wondering what it would be like to hang out in the airy gulf so lightly and easily, heart pumping quick and hot in a cradle of hollow bones, broad wings outspread, fingering the air with big primary feathers, eyes sharp enough to pick out a mouse twitch a kilometre away. He was allowed to putter around in the little one-lunged two-seater prop planes used in basic training, and that was it as far as flying went these days, but he'd once soared like that eagle. . . .

Frankie turned his head to look at Cash and said in a kindly tone, "You've been in a mood all day. And now that mood is turning into the mood you get before you have to speak. I wouldn't mind that you can't ever relax, Captain, except it makes it hard for me to relax around you."

"You have my permission to go relax somewhere else, Lieutenant."

"You flyboys are all the same," Frankie said. "You all concentrate on the thing you have to do next. That, and maybe the next thing, but no more than that."

"That's what you have to do, if you want to survive in combat."

"Yeah, but that's how you are all the time. You're obsessing about your speech right now, even though it's no big thing. Because, as far as you're concerned, it's not enough to go out and just do it. No, you got to go out and be the best you could ever be, time and time again."

"Better that than screw the pooch."

Frankie grinned sideways at Cash. Sweat beaded the black skin of his broad forehead and shaven scalp. "That right there is what I believe they call the crux of the problem. Because what you don't ever see, what you don't ever *believe*, no matter how many times I tell you, we can't *ever* screw this particular pooch. You give the best speech you can, Captain, and the punters will bathe in your righteous aura of manly courage and applaud your fine display of grace under pressure. Or you give the worst performance of your career, and the punters will still applaud, and feel sorry for you too, because you are so clearly fucked up by what happened to you in the war. You understand? The pooch, it is absolutely and positively no-two-ways-about-it unscrewable."

Cash knew that Frankie Fuente was right, but it wasn't in him to not try to give his best. So that night, dressed in his pressed blues and polished black knee boots, a rack of unearned medal ribbons on his chest and his peaked cap folded under his right arm, he made small talk with members of the Bernal family, industrialists and their uncannily beautiful wives, and a smattering of high-ranking civil servants, and then he gave his speech, hitting the keynotes with pinpoint precision. He told the story of how he had been wounded while attempting to deflect a chunk of ice aimed at a base on one of Saturn's moons, described how the Quiet War had been so quickly and comprehensively won, explained that the cost of waging war around Jupiter and Saturn would be rewarded by exploitation of the Outers' skills, technology, and knowledge base, and reminded his audience that the space industry was important both for the security of Greater Brazil and for the health of the planet. Orbital sun-shade mirrors had done much to ameliorate the effects of the massive amount of thermal energy pumped into Earth's weather systems during the twentieth and twenty-first centuries. And moving industry off-planet, mining raw materials from asteroids and the moons of Jupiter and Saturn, and fully exploiting the Outers' treasure trove of novel technologies, would make it possible to return Earth's land and oceans and atmosphere to their primal pristine state and remake the planet into a preindustrial paradise, Cash said, his voice soaring at the end like that eagle, just the way he'd been taught.

"Man, I don't know why you get so tense beforehand," Frankie Fuente told him afterward. "You're a natural."

"I reckon I scored 7.5 out of a possible 10. A definite could-do-better."

The next day, the two heroes flew in a tiltrotor to Caracas, where they did their thing at a big reception: a thousand high-ranking citizens partying in a gilt and marble hall with a ceiling so high it seemed to generate its own climate. There was a weird undercurrent to the glittering gathering. Soldiers and aides coming and going, knots of men talking in low voices, and then, halfway through the proceedings, an announcement by the host, Euclides Peixoto: he had been summoned to Brasília, but he hoped that everyone would be able to enjoy themselves in his absence. Cash and Frankie gave their speeches, but the applause was thin and halfhearted, and the reception broke up immediately afterward.

Frankie had organised a couple of women anxious to sample the manly courage and righteous auras of genuine war heroes. Cash woke at dawn with a mouth full of cotton wool and panic tolling like a bell in his head. He sat up, heart racing, sweat starting across his flanks. The lithe young woman half asleep beside him sighed and burrowed deeper into the silk pillows and sheets. A moment later, Frankie Fuente came into the room through the French windows that opened onto the balcony of their suite and told him to get his ass out of bed.

"What's up?"

Frankie was bare-chested and one-armed, his white shorts luminous against his black skin. "History is up, Captain. You best come see."

On the balcony, Cash looked out across the grid of streets, giant apartment blocks, and tower farms. Grey in the chill predawn. Spires of smoke rising here and there. The thin wail of sirens. Police drones shuttling through the deep shadows between the blocks and towers; police helicopters beating above the rooftops.

"What is it, some kind of food riot?" he said, but Frankie had already pushed through the billowing white curtains at the other end of the balcony, into his room. Cash followed. Frankie was kneeling low at the edge of his bed, hunting beneath it for his real artificial arm. The room's memo space glowed in one corner, tiled with news feeds. Cash watched for a moment, then said, "She's dead?"

Frankie stood up, holding his writhing right arm in the hand of his short and skinny left arm. "That's what they're saying."

Cash said stupidly, "I met her last year."

Frankie plugged the writhing snake into his stump and it grew rigid and he flexed it at elbow and wrist and there it was, his right arm. An everyday magic trick courtesy of Outer technology. He said, "I met her too. All us war heroes met her at one time or another. But I guess that exposure to our manly auras wasn't enough to save her."

Every news feed was saying the same thing: Elspeth Peixoto, the president of Greater Brazil, was dead. She had died in her sleep yesterday evening; the news had been suppressed until all the members of her family had been informed. She had been president for more than sixty years. She had been one hundred and ninety-eight years old.

Cash thought of Euclides Peixoto last night, his hasty speech and his quick departure. He said, "Well, I guess that's the end of our little tour."

The two men watched the mosaic of talking heads and archive clips that showed Elspeth Peixoto at every age.

Frankie said, "Remember when her husband died?"

Cash said, "I flew over his funeral service."

"Get out of here."

"Swear to God and Gaia. He was Commander-in-Chief of the Air Defence Force. We did a flyby over the cathedral in Brasília. A wing of J-2 singleships in 'missing man' formation."

"Remember how everything stopped for two weeks either side of the funeral?"

"Not really. I was on the Moon."

"This is going to be ten times worse," Frankie said, and went into the bathroom and came out with towels and little bottles of unguents and lotions clutched to his chest. He stuffed everything into his ditty bag and started hunting through the drawers of the chiffonier, tossing things onto the bed. When Cash asked him what he was doing, Frankie said that he might not get another shot at being a war hero, so he was taking what he could right now.

"They'll cancel the rest of our tour, no doubt. But there'll be another one after things shake down," Cash said.

"You got to see the big picture, Captain. Lose your flyer's tunnel vision. Take a long hard look at what this means. The Peixotos are the chief supporters of the return to space, colonising the Moon, pushing back out into the rest of the Solar System. They tried to make nice with the Outers, and when that didn't work they went to war with them. Sure, there were other families involved, they pulled the Europeans in with them, and the Pacific Community tagged along too because it didn't want to miss out. But none of it would have happened without the Peixotos," Frankie said. He was folding up the top sheet of his bed into a tight square. "And the president, God and Gaia speed her soul to heavenly rest, she was a Peixoto. She was in power for sixty years, and now all the other families will be jostling for the top spot. It's going to be messy, it's going to change everything, and while it's going on there will most definitely be no need for war heroes. We're out of business, Captain. When I told you the pooch was unscrewable, I was wrong. *We* couldn't screw it up, but this surely has. What do you think of that picture?"

"I don't think things will be as black as you've painted them."

"I mean the picture over the bed. I reckon it would look nice on the wall of my momma's house. Come over here and hold it steady," Frankie said, pulling a folding knife from a pocket of his ditty bag, "while I cut it out of the frame."

2

Loc Ifrahim was up in the junkyard station, in orbit around Dione, when news of the death of the president of Greater Brazil splashed across the TPA net. It was a shock, but not unexpected. The woman had been almost two centuries old, and in her dotage. And she'd never recovered from the death of her husband. Still, she'd been a power, and now there was a vacuum, and various alliances in the great families would be maneuvering to fill it as soon as possible after the state funeral. Loc began to calculate what it might mean for the TPA. What it might mean for him.

In the days that followed there were reports of riots in several major cities, renewed fighting with wildsiders along the edges of unreclaimed land, and flare-ups of nationalist activity, especially in the territories that covered the former United States of America, where an independence movement calling itself the Freedom Riders had issued demands for immediate secession from Greater Brazil. But these were minor problems, and the government showed no sign of falling over. There was no revolution, no coup. Armand Nabuco, the vice president who'd long been the power behind the throne, a dark prince who had built up his own branch of security, the Office for Strategic Services, and controlled several government offices that weren't answerable to any of the Senate oversight committees, was installed as president pro tem, pending an election.

Armand Nabuco made it clear that he supported the continuing occupation of the Outer System, but six days after the state funeral of the president, while Greater Brazil and the moons it controlled in the Jupiter and Saturn systems were still locked in a period of official mourning, two ships quit Earth orbit for Saturn, and it was announced that General Arvam Peixoto had been promoted and would return to Greater Brazil, and the military authority that dominated the Brazilian presence in the Saturn System would be replaced by a civilian administration led by Euclides Peixoto.

Immediately after the announcement, the general and his senior officers withdrew from all engagements and executive committees. According to the official line, they were preparing for the handover, but there were strong rumours that they had been surprised by cadres of the Office of Strategic Services, were being kept under house arrest pending their removal, and did not dare to step out of line because their families were being held hostage back on Earth.

The groundwork for the swift and ruthlessly efficient decapitation of Arvam Peixoto's administration must have been put in place long before the death of the president. Many people believed that her death had not been due to natural causes but was the culmination of an ingenious plan to seize control of the government. Loc Ifrahim did not. Armand Nabuco had already possessed all the power he required, and he'd been free to act unseen in the shadows behind the figurehead of a beloved president over whom he had complete control. No, he hadn't been responsible for her death, but he would have made extensive plans and preparations to silence or emasculate potential troublemakers and rivals after she died, and to ensure that he would keep control of the power he'd accrued. And Arvam Peixoto would have been high on his list. The general had gained considerable political advantage after winning the Quiet War, and had more or less declared himself a free agent when, despite explicit instructions to the contrary from the Brazilian senate and military command, he'd dispatched a ship to Uranus to search out and neutralise rebel elements, destroying four of their ships and several habitats, and driving a few no-account survivors deeper into the outer dark.

Things might have gone differently for him if this punitive expedition had failed, but he'd proven himself too good a commander and showed every sign of growing too independent. Doomed by his own success, he'd been brought to heel by Armand Nabuco, and now Loc and everyone else in the Brazilian occupation force were wondering what would happen to them when Euclides Peixoto assumed power. It was generally expected that he would remove all those suspected of remaining loyal to the deposed general, but no one knew how deep or extensive the cuts would be, or what would happen to those deemed unworthy of his trust.

Loc was glad, now, that the general had not rewarded him for the capture of Avernus's daughter; glad that it had ended badly and he'd been forced to return to his obscure and humiliating position; glad that after he'd first been slighted by the general he'd had the foresight to reach out to Euclides Peixoto, pass on some tidbits of gossip, and do the man a few small favours.

All in all, Loc believed that he might win considerable advantage from the president's death. Like everyone else, he signed a declaration of loyalty to both the president pro tem and Euclides Peixoto, and could do nothing else but hope that he had not attracted the attention of the OSS. He sent word to his various Outer contacts that they should keep quiet until things had shaken out, and decided that he would keep a low profile too, stay away from Paris, bide his time. Discretion was all.

But then, a week before the ships from Earth were due to arrive, he received a summons from Arvam Peixoto.

Loc decided that ignoring it would be worse than obeying, and besides, it would give him the chance to observe the general's plight at first hand. He might learn something useful. Nevertheless, he was gripped by a chilly dread when he travelled down to the garden habitat once owned by the Jones-Truex-Bakaleinikoff clan, now a prison in all but name. As if he was stepping into the jaws of a beast that could swallow him whole, and spit out his bones.

He arrived at the mansion at the centre of the habitat precisely on time, but was kept waiting in an antechamber for more than an hour. He watched military and civilian personnel come and go in the big room until at last a captain of the OSS, a severe young woman dressed in trim grey uniform tunic and breeches and knee-length black leather boots polished to a mirror finish, came up and told him that she'd take him to the general. Loc didn't dare ask any questions as she led him out of the mansion and they crossed the patch-work of lawns and gardens and orchards. She clumsily hauled herself along the network of tethers, clearly unused to Dione's microgravity; he ankled along beside her like a native, anticipation hollowing his stomach.

They found the general at the edge of the rim forest that circled the perimeter of the habitat, accompanied by a handful of Air Defence Force offi-cers and Sri Hong-Owen's son, Berry. Loc recognised one of the officers: Cap-tain Neves, the woman who'd helped him capture Avernus's daughter, since promoted to the general's staff. Beyond this little party, a handful of dwarfed cattle were grazing in the long grass under a stand of giant chestnut trees. They were the size of large dogs, with shaggy auburn coats and horns that bent at right angles.

Arvam Peixoto seemed to be in a good mood, telling Loc that he was late and had nearly missed all the fun, calling for his gun. One of the officers pre-sented him with an ancient ball-and-powder rifle with a long barrel and ornate chasings on its side plates. He went down on one knee and showed Berry how to load it—an elaborate ceremony that involved blowing into the barrel to moisten it, pouring black powder through a drop tube and tamping it down with a rod, sliding in a round ball seated on a scrap of cloth, tamping again, and finally cocking the hammer and placing a percussion cap on its nipple—and then asked the boy to choose a target. Berry played up to the moment, pointing to one animal and then another, frowning with concentra-tion, finally settling on a cow on the far side of the little herd. He'd grown since Loc had last seen him, was about ten centimetres taller and at least twenty kilogrammes heavier, but still possessed the same sulky and obdurate demeanour, the same loutish slyness.

The general shaded his eyes, studying the animal. "Did you choose it because it's the best, or because it's the furthest away?" he said.

"I know you can do it," Berry said.

The two of them smiling at each other. The general happy to show off his prowess; the boy excited. Both were dressed in sky blue fatigues.

The general allowed Berry to hold the rifle, and took a long swig from his flask. He wiped his mouth on the back of his hand, capped the flask and fastened it to his belt, and took back the rifle and braced himself against the trunk of one of the trees. Glancing over at Loc, explaining that recoil was a serious problem in low gravity: it could knock you onto your back or send you flying, either way you'd miss your mark by a mile.

"And that wouldn't do, would it? Who knows what or who I might hit," the general said. He fitted the stock of the rifle against his shoulder and sighted along its barrel, taking his time. Berry stood close to him, his lower lip caught between his teeth and his dark eyes shining as he studied with grave concentration the shaggy little cow that was obliviously ripping up mouthfuls of grass, neatly spotlighted by a shaft of chandelier light that pierced the canopy of the big trees. When the shot came, it was absurdly loud. Birds flared from the trees all around and cattle jinked away, bounding with surprising grace into a deeper part of the wood, leaving behind the one that Berry had pointed out, lying heartshot in the long grass.

Berry laughed, a hoarse bark, and clapped in delight. "You killed it!"

"Let's go see," the general said.

He handed the rifle to one of the officers and Loc and everyone else followed him through the long grass, ankling heel-and-toe, while Berry skipped ahead, circling the stricken cow, daring to touch its flank, skipping back when it shuddered and gave a profound sigh.

"It isn't dead!"

"Yes, it is," the general said. "It just doesn't know it yet. A bit like the Outers, eh, Mr. Ifrahim?"

"Indeed, sir."

The cow's wet brown eye, half hidden by an auburn fringe, rolled to look up at Arvam Peixoto when he straddled its neck. The general snapped the button on the sheath at his hip and pulled out a knife with a bone handle and a hooked blade. He kissed the blade, caught hold of one of the animal's crooked horns and jerked up its head, and sawed through the taut skin of its throat. Blood welled along the cut, a rich red flood running out across the trampled grass, darkening the knees of Berry's fatigue pants as he knelt beside the animal, leaning close and staring into its eye as if trying to look down the fixed and unfocused well of its pupil to the seat of its little mind and scry the moment when it let go of life. The general dipped his forefinger in the puddling blood, caught hold of Berry's arm, drew him close, swiped his bloody forefinger down the boy's forehead to the bridge of his nose, and told him that he would have the honour of making the kill the next time. The two of them gilded in the shaft of chandelier light like heroes of a tale from the long ago.

Loc couldn't help wondering if this little moment was for the benefit of the boy or for him. Then Berry barked a short raspy laugh, broke free, and bounded away, chasing after the cattle which had scattered amongst the trees, his gleeful whoops rising toward the great panes of the dome's roof that slanted close above the treetops.

Captain Neves went after him, moving with a steady and purposeful gait, while the general told Loc that he was determined to wipe out the herd before he left.

"Denying Euclides a source of succulent steaks is a small pleasure, but I confess that I relish it. We did good work here, Mr. Ifrahim. We might have done much more but for circumstances, eh?"

"I'm sure you're right, sir."

"What do you think of Berry?"

The general's mismatched gaze, one eye dark brown, the other pale blue, was unsettling. The odour of brandy floated on his breath.

"He's growing up," Loc said.

"He has had a difficult childhood. Professor Doctor Hong-Owen may be a genius, but she's about as maternal as a scorpion. I've tried to do my best, but I can no longer take care of him. Nor can I protect him from Euclides, should Euclides decide to use him as a pawn to keep the Professor Doctor under control."

Loc could not point out that the general had been keeping Berry in the garden habitat for precisely that reason.

"So I have a last favour to ask of you, Mr. Ifrahim," the general said. "I want you to take Berry to his mother. Think you can do that?"

"I am always at the service of the TPA," Loc said, trying his best to ignore the OSS officer's speculative gaze, keeping his expression neutral, showing nothing of the anger he felt at having been sandbagged like this. He had more than enough to do without looking after the gene wizard's weird brat, and doing a favour for the general would almost certainly taint him, too. But he couldn't refuse it. Arvam Peixoto was still a power, and he knew enough to ruin Loc if he cared to.

"Captain Neves will accompany you," the general said. "She is Berry's aide, and has proven herself extremely capable. I trust you have no objections."

"Of course not," Loc said, although he had every objection conceivable. Not to Captain Neves; he liked the woman, and hadn't been in any way jealous when she'd been appointed to the general's staff. But it was clear that the general was paying off old scores in his usual sly fashion. Raising Loc's profile, tying him to Sri Hong-Owen. . . .

"Professor Doctor Hong-Owen is on Mimas, with that crew of hers. Looking into yet another of those strange gardens. I'm sure that she'll be happy to be reunited with her son, and it will be a considerable relief to know that Berry is in safe hands," the general said. "I would ask you to stay to

144

dinner, Mr. Ifrahim, but I think you should set out as soon as you can. Goodbye. Oh, and the best of luck."

———————●———————

"Watch and learn," Loc Ifrahim told Captain Neves, six days later. "This is what happens when the Outers are allowed to keep their so-called democracy."

They were standing in front of one of the big sheets of transparent plastic welded to the external framing of the Caucus House of Camelot, Mimas. It was one of the biggest buildings in the city, an open sphere housing six storeys of platforms and capsule rooms, slung from and interpenetrated by the branches of a huge banyan tree. Before the war, it had been the venue where citizens had met to discuss problems and thrash out policies; now it was the administrative headquarters of the transitional government. The occupying force had wrapped it with a plastic skin, cleared foliage and hanging houses and shops and workshops around it, and laid fullerene mesh on the ground between the multiple trunks of the banyan, ringing it with a plaza a hundred metres wide.

At the eastern edge of this open space, Outers were clustered on rising tiers of branches, banners strung amongst them and clouds of light projected into the air—slogans, long texts detailing the latest affronts to their so-called social democracy, video art packed with strobing, incomprehensible but no doubt highly significant images. Someone was shouting through a bullhorn; others were drumming up a storm. Down on the plaza, a number of protesters had shackled themselves in a circle around one of the banyan's trunks, and a contingent of military police in white coveralls and white helmets with mirrored visors were busy amongst them, cutting their shackles with welding pistols and hauling them away.

As Loc Ifrahim and Captain Neves studied this circus, something bird sized flew through the air above the plaza and suckered itself head-first to the plastic right in front of them. Loc flinched and stepped back before he realised what it was; Captain Neves hardly blinked, studying the thing with a narrow and intently serious expression as it began to chant slogans about peace and love in a raucous screech that rattled and shook the huge pane of plastic. Then a drone stooped down like a hawk on a sparrow, plucked the little machine from the plastic, and dropped away toward its handler on the plaza below, where the police had freed the last of the shackled protesters and were towing them away toward a rolligon while the ragged crowd up in the trees jeered and clapped.

"One of the security people told me they do this shit each and every day," Captain Neves said. She had put on her dress blues for the meeting with the city's military governor and stood straight-backed with her hat tucked under her left arm, her buzz cut freshly trimmed, her coffee-coloured face sternly composed. She looked as if she were posing for a recruiting poster. "I don't get it. Why aren't they all locked up?"

"What would be illegal in Paris is a legitimate peaceful protest here," Loc said. "Sanctioned by the city council and the elusive Colonel Malarte."

"It's disrespectful," Captain Neves said. "And doing nothing about it makes us look weak."

"What would you do, if you were in command?"

"I'd disrespect them right back," Captain Neves said.

"That would certainly get their attention. Of course, it might also create martyrs. And martyrs are very effective recruiting tools for causes like this."

"When someone in a squad breaks regs or screws up, no one rats him out. Which is exactly how it should be if the squad is going to hang together. You deal with it by punishing the whole squad. So if a few tweaks choose to misbehave, you should punish all of them. Make them all martyrs. And because I bet they don't have the stones for that, pretty soon they'll start policing themselves."

"If anyone could punish an entire city, it's you," Loc said.

Captain Bethany Neves was several years younger than Loc. Her parents had both been in the Reclamation and Reconstruction Corps, and she'd led a grim, gypsy life as they worked to rewild section by section the vast ruined desert in the heart of the former United States of America. She didn't share her parents' belief that the world could be healed by ripping up the remains of old towns and suburbs, cleaning up rivers and lakes, and laboriously restoring topsoil and planting catch grass and willows. No, she'd wanted to get away from all that, so she'd joined the Air Defence Force and worked her way up through the ranks. She wasn't bright or especially talented, and she didn't know the first thing about playing service politics, but she was a determined and avid student. Loc was amused and flattered by her intense manner and eager questions, and admired the way she dealt with Berry's stygian sulks and volcanic bouts of bad temper. At their first breakfast together, Berry had squirted a bulb of pomegranate juice at Loc. Captain Neves had snatched the bulb from the boy and slapped him hard in one quick motion, and when he'd lashed out at her she'd pinned him down, pulled off her belt and doubled it, and beaten him mercilessly. Later, she'd told Loc that she'd often been left in charge of smaller kids when she'd been growing up, and had quickly learned that swift justice and strict discipline was the easiest option. The trick was to leave welts rather than bruises, she said. Welts faded in a few days, but bruises took much longer to disappear.

Captain Neves told Loc stories about her childhood; he told her edited stories about his adventures in the Outer System. And while they'd been stuck in Camelot, Mimas, for almost a week, waiting for permission to deliver Berry to his mother, one thing had quickly led to another.

Loc always thought of her as Captain Neves rather than Bethany or Beth; she called him Mr. Ifrahim even in their most intimate moments. Their lovemaking was a series of negotiations and concessions. Captain Neves liked to take charge, and Loc liked to play along with her dominance games, liked to pretend to be helpless as she hurt him in various small and ingenious ways: by surrendering to her, sweetly, tenderly, utterly, he found a temporary release from the pressure of maintaining his cool, carefully ambivalent demeanour. And although their affair must have been obvious to everyone around them, he found that he didn't care. For the first time in his life he didn't care what other people thought of him. He wondered now, studying her sharp profile against the glow of chandelier light, if this was what love was like.

They were waiting to meet with Colonel Faustino Malarte, the military governor of Mimas. They needed his permission to travel outside the city, but the man had dodged them when they'd first arrived in the city and then had disappeared off to Paris, to attend the ceremony that welcomed Euclides Peixoto to the Saturn System. And no doubt to consult with the new administration, and check whether or not he should allow Berry to be returned to his mother.

Now, at last, the colonel's secretary came to fetch Loc and Captain Neves, and led them through tall double doors into a hangar-sized office. Dim lamps were scattered around a floor of crimson halflife turf that reacted to footfalls by generating silvery patterns that raced out like ripples on a pond and reflected from the walls in clashing filigrees; walls painted dark green and hung with works of art. Paintings, exotic masks, wooden and resin sculptures like clutches of breasts or phalluses, or the nests of alien creatures, drooping from the false ceiling . . . all of it loot, no doubt. At the far end of the room was a huge fireplace with what looked like but couldn't possibly be a log fire burning in it, throwing warm yellow light halfway across the room. On one side was a desk the size of a car; on the other, a T-stand displaying the chestplate of a pressure suit.

Colonel Faustino Malarte was studying or pretending to study the chest-plate, turning as Loc and Captain Neves came down the length of the huge room toward him. A dark-skinned man with curly black hair worn collar-length and moist eyes set close together over a nose that had been broken once upon a time and skewed slightly to the left, his sky blue uniform woven from spidersilk and immaculately pressed, his shoulders laden with braid, five ranks of medal ribbons splashed across his chest. He was a scion of the Pessanha family, one-eighth consanguineous, a political appointee who'd escaped the OSS purge because he'd never been especially close to Arvam Peixoto. Loc automatically loathed him, as he loathed everyone who had gained a position of power by virtue of birth rather than by talent and hard work.

"I've heard that you have extensive knowledge of Outer culture, Mr. Ifrahim," the colonel said. "Perhaps you recognise this."

He clicked his fingers and a spotlight sprang on, its narrow beam burning on the painting splashed across the convex surface of the chestplate. A great crowd of crystalline rocks shaped like human heads, every one different, dwindled into a misty lane that curved into infinity.

Loc knew at once what it was, but stepped on his excitement, gave the painting his best bored, blank glance and said, "It looks like one of Munk's *Seven Transformations of the Ring System*. Is it real, or did you have it made for you?"

While Colonel Malarte had kept him waiting, Loc had reached out to his old contacts in Camelot and done a little in-depth research. Amongst other things, he'd learned that the colonel had taken an Outer as a mistress, and the woman was an artist who'd served her apprenticeship in Munk's workshop.

"It's no fake," the colonel said, frowning hard at Loc. "As you'll see if you care to study the detail. It's the last in the series. Number Seven. It's said that every person who was living in Camelot at the time Munk made this is portrayed here. You need a microscope to appreciate it properly."

"I confess a profound regret that I was trained exclusively in practical matters," Loc said. "I can understand the work that went into something like this, but I have little training in the appreciation of art."

"It's absolutely necessary if you want to deal with the tweaks," the colonel said. "They're passionate about authenticity and the intrinsic worth of skilled labour and artistic vision. Before the war Camelot was famous for its pressure suits and Munk was the best of the artisans who specialised in decorating pressure-suit chestplates. If I wasn't so busy today I would be delighted to educate you in the nuances of his work."

"Perhaps another time," Loc said.

He was amused by Colonel Malarte's pompous assumption of superiority, and the corny theatricality of the business with the spotlight. The man was as boastful as advertised, a bubble of vanity and hot air waiting the needle's prick. As for his prized piece of loot, Loc thought that it was as obvious and sentimental as a greeting card. But still, it might be useful, by and by. . . .

The colonel ushered Loc and Captain Neves to couches set on either side of a thick sheet of translucent plastic that floated with no visible means of support above the halflife grass—it was laced with iron and levitated by superconducting magnets, the colonel explained—and his secretary served little porcelain cups of frothy bitter chocolate.

Loc mentioned the display outside the building and said that he found it very interesting.

"The protests can be a little noisy, but they're mostly harmless," the colonel said. "The tweaks blow off pressure, and we keep watch on potential troublemakers. Everyone benefits."

"An admirably enlightened attitude," Loc said. "Does Euclides Peixoto approve? I've heard that he's very keen to show that he is better than the general at controlling the Outers. That he likes the sound of a cracked whip."

"You admit that you do not appreciate the nuances of art. Perhaps you do not appreciate the nuances of command either."

Colonel Malarte's smile was a work of art in itself.

Loc said, "My work in the diplomatic service allowed me to visit almost every city on the moons of Jupiter and Saturn. I believe that it gave me some small appreciation of the nuances of the minds of the Outers."

Captain Neves sat prim and neat on the other side of the couch, drinking everything in.

"This was before the war," Colonel Malarte said.

"In which I had the honour of playing a small part."

Colonel Malarte had arrived at the Saturn System six months after the end of the Quiet War, parachuted into a prime job courtesy of his bloodline.

"I think you will find that things are different now," the colonel said. "Now that the so-called superiority of the tweaks has been shown to be nothing of the kind. Now that they have been brought back into the fold, so to speak."

"Their displays and demonstrations look amusing to us," Loc said. "Harmless entertainment. But as far as the Outers are concerned, they are deadly serious. They are not simply expressing frustration, Colonel. They are making a political point, at your expense."

"I know how to deal with troublemakers, Mr. Ifrahim," the colonel said, with some flint in his gaze now. "And I make sure that the tweaks know, too."

"Don't take offence, Colonel. I was merely making an observation, based on my travels amongst the Outers."

There was a small space of silence. Captain Neves fed her subtle smile a sip of hot chocolate. At last the colonel said, "Much as I would like to discuss the fine points of Outer politics with you, my time is limited. Let's get our business out of the way. You want to go to Herschel Crater."

"My colleague and I are escorting the son of Professor Doctor Sri Hong-Owen. Returning him to his mother. A simple task which has taken rather longer than I thought it would."

"I am responsible not only for this city but for everything else on this moon," the colonel said. "It makes for a great deal of work. Sometimes thing slip. And contact with Professor Doctor Hong-Owen and her crew has been at best intermittent. She seems to think that she isn't obliged to make the usual reports, or show any sign of cooperation. But I'm pleased to be able to tell you that my office has made the necessary arrangements. Transit to Herschel Crater and return. Do you know when you will return, by the way? Your travel plans are somewhat vague."

"I'll come back as soon as I have discharged my duty toward the boy. As to how long that takes, well, as you have pointed out, the Professor Doctor is something of an unknown quantity."

"We'll talk again, when you return. You can tell me all about your adventures."

Loc had no intention of giving Colonel Malarte information that could be put to profitable use higher up the chain of command. "Of course," he said. "But I should warn you that it's highly unlikely that I'll be able to understand any of the Professor Doctor's work. She is irresponsible and arrogant, yes, and causes all kinds of problems to those who are supposed to have authority over her. But she is also a genius."

Once they were outside, making their way along the cordway reserved for the exclusive use of members of the occupying force, Loc told Captain Neves that the colonel was a depressingly familiar mixture of unbridled confidence and sheer stupidity. "A typical specimen of the old-fashioned oligarchy. His ancestors made their reputations and fortunes by piracy and pillage; he expects to do the same. According to my contacts, he's smuggling works of art back to Earth. Every senior officer is sending back a few souvenirs, of course, but the colonel is sending back cargo pods stuffed with loot. He takes by main force anything that attracts his fancy, and if the owners make a fuss he throws them into prison. In short, he treats Mimas as if it was his personal fiefdom, and that's why he wants me to tell him all about the garden that Sri Hong-Owen is investigating. He's wondering why she and her crew have spent so long out there. He's wondering what she has found, and whether he can profit from it. And he probably thinks that returning Berry to his mother is a subterfuge. That I'm really going out there to make a deal with Sri Hong-Owen behind his back. So that little bit of theatre was all about making sure that I knew that he suspected I was up to no good, and that he expected me to cooperate with him."

"If she's been keeping her work secret, perhaps she really has found something valuable," Captain Neves said.

"Valuable to her, perhaps. Because of the intellectual challenge. Because of what it tells her about Avernus. But I very much doubt that her investigations will yield anything of immediate commercial value."

They'd reached a platform where another cordway intersected the one they were following. Loc, badly out of breath, heart thumping, suggested that they stop for a minute. He'd spent too much time in zero gravity and had been skimping on his sessions in the centrifuge gymnasium. At this rate he'd never be able to walk on Earth again. . . .

The platform was slung between the crowns of a trio of tall pines. Treetops spread all around them under the diamond light of the cluster of chandeliers hung from the dome's apex. Camelot's cluster of pressure domes was filled edge to edge with a forest of tweaked banyans interplanted with pines and giant redwoods. Streets had been built along tiers of broad branches, and cordways, ziplines and slides linked homes and workshops that spiralled around tree trunks or hung from sturdy branches like exotic fruit. An arboreal low-gravity city, green, hushed, primeval.

"The gardens left behind by Avernus are experiments," Loc said. "Games. There's no point in plundering them for a few trivial tweaks and cuts. It would be like smashing a Fabergé egg and selling the gems used to decorate it. Not that Sri Hong-Owen isn't above doing that, of course. It is how she justifies her work. How she survives. It makes her useful to whoever is in charge. But it isn't why she's doing what she's doing."

"Still, if you told the colonel what she's found," Captain Neves said, "wouldn't that make you useful to him?"

"What good would that do me? People like Faustino Malarte haven't earned their authority, and they express it by bullying and intimidation because they have no insight into how other people think," Loc said. "And because they have utterly failed to understand the Outers, sooner or later they will make some colossal blunder that will threaten everything we've done out here. I think you should stay in the city while I take Berry to his mother. I think you should find out how Malarte gets his loot back to Earth."

"Are you planning to disgrace him, sir?"

"Of course not. It would be suicidal for me to make any kind of move against him, what with him being in charge of an entire moon, not to mention belonging to the upper echelons of the Pessanha family. No, all I want is information, Captain. That's what people like the colonel don't understand. How important information is."

———◆———

The gig's cabin was a fullerene shell perched on top of its motor platform, a claustrophobic closet with no room for seats or couches. Loc stood next to the pilot, with Berry Hong-Owen crammed in behind them, all three strapped into the webs of their crash harnesses and bulked out in pressure suits, globular helmets screwed on, as the frail craft arced halfway around Mimas in a free-fall trajectory.

The little moon was a ball of dirty water ice just under four hundred kilometres in diameter that had frozen all the way down to its silicate core soon after its formation: its ancient, unmodified surface was pocked and spattered by a chaos of craters of every size, like a boiling sea instantly turned to stone. Peering through the slot of the gig's window, it seemed to Loc that he was plunging headlong past a vast pale cliff printed with a random jumble of inky crescents and clefts and staves: slanting shadows cast by blocks and boulders, shadows cupped inside craters, shadows curving around crater rims. He'd patched a slow-release dose of a local smart drug, pandorph, before putting on his pressure suit. Yota McDonald had turned him on to it. It was cleaner and more effective than any of the military smart drugs they'd used back in the good old days before the war, when they'd brainstormed political and strategic scenarios for a government commission. It sharpened his perceptions and quickened his thoughts and gave him a crystalline godlike perspective, a necessary edge that would help him deal with Sri Hong-Owen, and it had the useful side effect of overlaying his usual anxiety and fright at being fired like a bullet across a hostile moonscape with a calm, semi-detached interest in the spectacular scenery unravelling beyond the gig's window.

Mountainous ridges nested in concentric circles rose above the horizon's sharp curve: the rim of Herschel Crater, a multiringed basin a hundred and thirty kilometres across, a third of Mimas's diameter, created by an impact that had very nearly shattered the little moon. The gig dropped past broken terraces that stepped down to the vast scablands of the crater floor, and flew on for thirty kilometres before the top of the crater's central peak appeared. With a brisk rattle of attitude jets, the gig rolled over and turned end for end. The empty desolation of the crater floor swung away into black sky, the gig's motor flamed on with a solid thump, a brief burn that killed the last of its momentum, and the moonscape crept back into view as the gig drifted sideways above the outer slopes of the central peak's western flank, past boulder-fields and the inky lightning bolts of canyons and rifts toward a broad bench where a beacon blinked red in the monochrome landscape. Attitude jets rattled again as the gig adjusted its final approach, and then its shadow raced up to meet it and with a jarring smack it was down, perched on the edge of a landing platform the size of a football field, close to a turtle-shaped shuttle with the green flag of Greater Brazil splashed over its flank.

Captain Neves had given Berry a shot of tranquilliser before the flight, but she'd miscalculated the dose and he was still more or less comatose: it took the combined efforts of Loc and the pilot to maneuver him out of the gig's little hatch. A member of Sri Hong-Owen's crew was waiting for them. A brisk young man named Antônio Maria Rodrigues, dressed in a pristine white pressure suit, helped to carry Berry to the sled parked on the mesh roadway below the lip of the landing platform, and drove Loc and Berry toward a long slope cut by crevasses that radiated from the foot of a vertical arc of cliffs more than a kilometre high. The road slanted down into one of the crevasses, ending in a tracked and trampled apron in front of a large opaque dome pitched at the foot of a sheer wall of granitic water ice.

Loc and Antônio Maria Rodrigues hauled Berry off the sled and marched him to the oval hatch of an airlock set in the base of the dome, cycling through into a cramped antechamber with lockers, racks of pressure suits, and a dressing frame crowded along the walls, lit by glowsticks stuck at random in its spray-foam ceiling. In the greenish underwater light, Loc and Antônio Maria Rodrigues stripped off their pressure suits and, wearing only suit-liners that did little to protect them against the meat-locker chill, helped Berry out of his. The boy smiled dopily at them and asked if they could go on the ride again.

"First we must talk with your mother," Loc said.

"I don't want to. I want to go back."

"You know that you can't. Come with me, and don't make a fuss."

Loc and Berry followed Antônio Maria Rodrigues through a double set of pressure doors and climbed a short steep ramp to a big, roughly circular space under a vaulted roof that shed a pale glow. Paths wandered amongst layered shelves of black rocks cleverly faked up from shells of spun fullerenes, giant cushions of moss of every hue of red and yellow, clumps of tree ferns, and peaty pools of black water ringed with sedges. The air was clean and cold and damp. Winter. Yes, it smelt like winter. . . . Loc felt a sudden aching swell of homesickness, sharply magnified by the pandorph. But this wasn't home. It wasn't Earth, or anything like it. Just another garden in a dome, a tiny bubble of life set in a vast and lifeless desolation. He looked around and declared that although it was pretty enough, he'd been expecting something rare and marvellous.

"This isn't the garden, sir. The garden is in there," Antônio Maria Rodrigues said, and pointed to the far side of the dome, where a black cliff loomed over an inky lake and a slender white bridge arched across the water to a narrow cave cut into the base of the cliff.

Sri Hong-Owen was waiting in one of the hemispherical tents clustered at the edge of the lake. As always, she seemed ageless: severe and rail-thin, her head shaven, her manner cool and self-contained. She was dressed in a silvery, knee-length insulated coat and wore spex with rectangular lenses in thick black frames.

"You look well," she told her son. "And you've grown, too."

Berry shrugged. The clean air of the moss garden had flushed away the residue of Captain Neve's tranquilliser. He was his usual suspicious, truculent self, a flabby boy like a bear cub not yet licked into shape, scowling at his mother through the curtain of long hair that half hid his face, saying, "The general told me I had to come here. It wasn't my idea."

"The general was thinking of your welfare," Sri Hong-Owen said. "How is he?"

They talked for a few minutes, an anodyne exchange with no warmth in it; then Sri Hong-Owen sent Berry off with Antônio Maria Rodrigues to get something to eat and drink, and asked Loc if he needed anything.

He declined her offer. "I was in Camelot just two hours ago, ma'am. Hard to believe, but there it is."

"And now you're here. It's been a while, hasn't it?"

"Yes, it has," Loc said, coolly meeting her gaze. "But it isn't too late, I hope, to apologise for my unseemly behaviour when we last crossed paths."

"Are you still working in that orbital junkyard?"

"Not for much longer, I hope."

"You expect a new position when Euclides Peixoto replaces the general? Or are you going back to Earth with him?"

"I hope to continue to serve as special adviser to the TPA."

"But right now you're working for Arvam."

"On the eve of his departure from the Saturn System, General Peixoto asked me to return your son to your care. I was honoured and flattered to be given the responsibility, and hope that I have discharged it to the best of my ability."

"And what about Colonel Malarte?"

"I'm certainly not employed by him."

"But you needed his permission to come here, and he doesn't grant such permissions lightly. Arvam no longer has authority over the man, and you can't afford to bribe him, so I suppose that he asked you to report on what I'm doing here. A favour for a favour."

Loc didn't flinch. His thoughts were as bright and quick as fish darting through sunlit water; he knew at once that it was in his best interest to tell the truth.

"You see things as clearly as I do, ma'am. Colonel Malarte has expressed, shall we say indirectly, a proprietorial interest in your work. Whether or not it is legitimate is not for me to say. But I can assure you that he does not have any authority over me."

"Well, for once I'm happy to do *you* a favour, Mr. Ifrahim. I will show you what we have found here, and you can tell Colonel Malarte all about it. And then, perhaps, he will understand that there is nothing here that he can exploit, and he will stop pestering me."

"It won't be easy, ma'am. From what I've seen of him, the colonel will have trouble understanding anything more complicated than a petting zoo."

"I'll explain it in very simple terms," Sri Hong-Owen said. "And if you happen to be working on some little scheme to humiliate the colonel because you resent being bullied by him, do bear in mind that I have considerable experience in dealing with his regime."

"It would be very dangerous to plot the downfall of an officer like Colonel Malarte. Not only because it would be treason, but because he is very well connected. Anyone working against him should keep their plans secret—even from potential allies."

"Of course. For once, we understand each other perfectly."

"For once, ma'am, we want the same thing."

─●─

"I wouldn't say that the general has been kind toward me," Sri Hong-Owen said as she led Loc through the cluster of tents toward the bridge that spanned the lake. "And I can't forgive him for using Berry. For holding him hostage to make sure that I did as I was told. Oh, he gave him a home, and a kind of education, but he also filled his head with distasteful and barbaric notions about honour and courage and war. As if the worst expressions of male behaviour are in any way virtuous or good. He suggested several times that a spell of military service would be good for Berry, when he was old enough. Fortunately, he has no say in the matter now."

"Yet he returned your son to you."

"He did it only to spite Euclides Peixoto. Still, as far as my work is concerned he has always been tolerant and understanding. I suppose I must be grateful for that. What do you think will happen to him, when he gets back to Earth?"

"I can't say, ma'am."

"I understand that Armand Nabuco is looking for someone to carry the blame for the failure of the Quiet War."

"Has it failed? I hadn't heard," Loc said, following her up the narrow span of the bridge, holding on to the rails on either side. One misstep in this vestigial gravity and he would fly away and smack down into the lake.

"I see you still have your sense of humour, Mr. Ifrahim."

"Yes ma'am. It survived the war."

"I wonder if it will survive Euclides Peixoto."

"I'm sure I'm beneath his attention, ma'am. Unlike you."

"Oh, he won't present a problem. He needs me. They all need me."

They ducked through the narrow cave entrance and went down a slanting passage lined with spray-foam insulation, the air growing colder as it descended, until at last it opened onto a kind of gallery or viewing chamber with a long window set in the thick insulation. Triple-glazed with diamond panes, it shone with dim red light. A cluster of cameras and monitoring equipment stood in front of it.

156

"This is what Avernus made here," Sri Hong-Owen said.

The window looked out across a huge spherical chamber carved out of the native ice and lit by a point source hung at the apex of its ceiling like a drop of incandescent blood. Its walls curved down to a floor creased with smooth ridges, and the top of each ridge was streaked with dark eddies and swirls and littered with dense copses of half-melted candles, phalanxes of toothlike spikes, heaps of tangled wires or curled scrolls like spun sugar, meadows of brittle hairs, pods of paper-thin fins breaking out of the ice. All these growths stark black in the ruby light, apart from a large candle-copse close to the observation window that was clearly dying from the inside out, its lumpy spires crumbling into pale ash.

"Vacuum organisms," Loc said. "A garden of vacuum organisms."

He'd been expecting something truly exotic. A clone farm of super-human babies. A wonderland full of weird plants and animals. A city of intelligent rats or racoons. But these growths weren't that much different from the vacuum organisms cultivated on the naked surface around every city and settlement on the moons of Saturn.

"They look like vacuum organisms," Sri Hong-Owen said. "But they are not. They are not constructed from bound nanotech, but are spun from intricate pseudo-proteinaceous polymers. I call them polychines. If commercial vacuum organisms are synthetic analogues of prokaryotes—bacteria, Mr. Ifrahim—these are analogues of the *ancestors* of prokaryotes."

"You want to give me a lecture," Loc said. "It would be easier if you cut to the chase, and told me exactly why these things are worthless. They certainly *look* worthless."

Sri Hong-Owen ignored his sally, and told him that the chamber contained a methane-hydrogen atmosphere at $-20°$ Celsius, far warmer than Mimas's ambient temperature. "As for the polychines, they do not possess a pseudocellular structure; nor are they generated by the systematic execution of a centralised set of encoded instructions. Instead, they are networks of self-catalysing metabolic cycles created by interactions between specific structures in their polymers."

"Like carpets, or suit-liners."

"Very good, Mr. Ifrahim. But although halflife materials are self-repairing and can even grow when fed the correct substrate, they encode only a very simple set of on/off instructions and can express only one morphology. The polychines are far more versatile. They are nonbinary logic engines that use a form of photosynthesis to transform simple chemicals to complex polymers.

They can reproduce, and they can even exchange information, although that information is entirely analogue in form. And they possess a limited set of components which obey a limited set of self-organising rules capable of generating new instructions, and, therefore, new properties and even new forms. Once I completely understand how those rules operate in every possible combination, it will be possible to manipulate the polychines to produce predictable states."

"Does that mean you can order them to manufacture useful stuff?"

"This isn't a factory floor, Mr. Ifrahim. It is a puzzle. A challenge. Unlike ordinary living cells or vacuum organisms, polychines lack any form of internal description. We are accustomed to thinking of information as being encoded in the written word, or in the binary code at the base of all computer languages, or in the four-letter alphabet of DNA. In there—" Sri Hong-Owen made a limpid gesture at the cavern beyond the window "—is a world in which information and form are inextricably entangled. A set of analogue computers that generate unique and unpredictable solutions to a single problem: how to survive and grow. Avernus set them up and left them to their own devices, but I will play her at her own game and prove myself her superior. By providing them with the right information to process, it will be possible to force them to produce predictable solutions, as I shall now demonstrate."

The gene wizard stepped up to the cluster of monitoring equipment, conjured a view in a small memo space, and panned across a bare slope to focus on a silvery box slung between four long thin articulated legs. "Run the sequence," she told the air.

The robot jerked forward, stalking stiffly to a cluster of lumpy black spikes that jutted from a frozen puddle of soot. It extruded a nozzle that jetted a brief mist, and the spikes immediately developed a rash of luminous orange blotches.

"That was a spray of N-acetylglucosamine," Sri Hong-Owen told Loc. "It is a common lectin, a protein that specifically binds to a sequence of sugar residues. When it binds to certain sites on the surface of the polychine, it initiates a short metabolic cascade that results in the luminescent display. So although the polychines do not encode any information, they are capable of *processing* information. Each consists of a specific set of polymers, and each polymer exists in one of two states, either on or off, determined by a number of limited rules. For instance, a particular polymer might switch on in the presence of either of two chemical substrates. Or it might require the presences of both substrates."

"Boolean logic," Loc said, a distant memory swimming out of the transparency inside his head.

"Exactly so," Sri Hong-Owen said. "Perhaps there is hope for you yet, Mr. Ifrahim. The reaction you saw was a simple AND sequence: lectin plus binding polymer equals activation of another polymer which produces the luminescence. The polychines are Boolean networks, capable of generating orderly dynamics—fixed-state cycles. One polychine constructed from just a hundred polymer components, each possessing just two possible states, either on or off, would generate ten to the power of thirty possible arrays. If every component receives an input from every other component, the system will become chaotic, cycling through a vast number of states at random; it would take a very long time before it returned to its original state. But if each component receives just two inputs, the system will spontaneously generate order—it will cycle between just four of its ten to the power of thirty possible states. Thus, constrained by spontaneous self-organising dynamical order, the polychines generate fixed-state cycles that are very similar to our own metabolic processes. And because these cycles are capable of processing information, it is possible to generate predictable results by supplying them with the right information. As a first step, my crew and I tested their reaction to a wide range of chemical messengers, just as you have seen. But they are much more than chemical detectors. When two different polychines grow together, interaction between their pseudometabolic hypercycles produces new forms of polychine. And interactions between second-generation polychines can produce a third generation, and so on. The diversity of the system is constrained only by size and by time. We have been attempting to derive theoretical solutions that will define the entire information space, but infinity keeps creeping in."

"A marvellous toy for someone with your interests. But I doubt that it will please the colonel," Loc said.

He was beginning to understand, with a slick of acid pleasure in his heart, that this strange garden was a puzzle and a trap. Something that would take up huge amounts of Sri Hong-Owen's time and attention to no good purpose. She was undeniably possessed by genius, but she was vain and self-indulgent too, obsessed with playing games for the sake of nothing more than play itself.

And yet there was a strange beauty, a pleasing asymmetrical order, to the copses and meadows of spikes and spires, scrolls and sheets, patched across the vast bowl beyond the window. It reminded him of the neatly nested mechanism of the ancient watch his father had worn on his wrist. An heirloom centuries old. Cogs and springs and tiny balances working away at different cycles that somehow meshed to drive the hands around the face at exactly one second per second. Loc had loved that watch, but although his father had often promised that he would inherit it, it had been hocked to pay a debt one day, and that had been that. A harsh but useful lesson. Make no attachments to anyone or anything. Expect nothing except that which you make or win for yourself.

"Do you believe in fate, Mr. Ifrahim?" Sri Hong-Owen said. "Do you believe that our destinies are shaped by patterns and forces we cannot see? Or do you think that everything we do is shaped by nothing more than chance and contingency?"

"I was raised as a Catholic, madam."

"Mmm. That's a nicely slippery answer. I suppose I should expect nothing less. I learned long ago that biology teaches us that chance and destiny go hand in hand. Our bodies bear the imprints of a myriad contingencies that randomly favoured survival and reproduction of certain genes over others. If you were able to run the great pageant of life in reverse to some point in the distant past and set it going again, it would not play out in the same way. It would tell a different story. Reverse and replay it again, and yet another story would emerge.

"This garden of Avernus's is a lesson in the marriage of contingency and destiny. An experiment that is as unrepeatable as life on Earth. As I have said, the polychines lack the equivalent of DNA—an internal cache containing a minimal set of instructions than can be used to reproduce their initial state. If they are destroyed, their past and future will also be destroyed: irretrievably so. They are creatures of an eternal yet ever-changing now. But I will uncover the rules that shape them. I will free them from contingency, and give them a history and a destiny.

"There's an interesting parallel one could draw between this garden and Outer society. The Outers hoped that, by rewriting their genomes, they could escape the limited range of destinies shaped by past contingencies in human history. The war put an end to that grand experiment because we feared that they would develop into something more than human, something that we could not control or contain, something that would affect *our* destiny whether we liked it or not. By examining this garden and others like it, we can understand the breadth of their capabilities. And by understanding them, we can control them. There's your utility, if you like, although I doubt the colonel will be able to appreciate it." Sri Hong-Owen looked at something behind Loc and added, "Come and join us, Berry. Don't skulk around like that."

The boy mooched out of the shadows by the entrance. When Sri asked him what he thought of the garden he said that he liked the robot.

"I like it too," Sri said. "My assistants are setting up a system that will allow me to control it remotely, so that we can continue to study the polychines wherever we are. You'll stay overnight, Mr. Ifrahim. We have to discuss Berry's future."

As if that was any of his concern, Loc thought. But he didn't have much choice about it. Sri Hong-Owen controlled everything here. He'd needed Colonel Malarte's permission to come here, but he needed her permission to leave.

Everyone ate in a tent floored with halflife fur that hummocked into seats and low tables. Sri Hong-Owen's assistants were friendly, extremely intelligent, and highly motivated young people who clearly were in awe of her. Apart from Antônio Maria Rodrigues, they were all Outers; one, Raphael, was an androgyne neuter, tall and disturbingly handsome, yo's flawless skin as pale and translucent as the wall of the tent.

After the meal, Loc asked Sri Hong-Owen why the Outers were working for her. She said that they had been minor gene wizards who'd worked on the biomes of habitats and oases and so on before the war, and were keen to hone and develop their skills by studying Avernus's gardens.

"Do they have security clearance?"

"They respect and admire Avernus's work, and they've been extremely useful in every way," Sri said. "To give just one example, they helped me to find this place. If you want to find something big in Greater Brazil, Mr. Ifrahim, you follow the money trail. Here, you must examine the records of the bourses of the various cities for large exchanges of kudos. Two of my assistants discovered that Avernus borrowed a crew of mining machines some twenty years ago, and further investigation led me here."

"Some say that you're hiding. That you are scared that Euclides Peixoto will send you back to Earth."

"They couldn't have won the war without me," Sri said, with a flash of brittle defiance. "And they seem unable to understand what they have won until I explain it to them, and show them how they can use it and make money from it. I've been 'down here' for the past hundred days because I have been working. But I will admit that I've been out of touch lately. Perhaps you can tell me something of the great changes that have been happening out there in the wider world. Tell me about Arvam. Tell me how he looked when you last saw him."

It was very nearly a pleasant conversation. Loc realised that they were no longer enemies because they had nothing in common anymore. Sri Hong-Owen had her gardens and her obsession with Avernus; Loc had temporal needs that couldn't be satisfied by knowledge for knowledge's sake: neither had anything that the other wanted or needed.

As they talked it grew darker outside, and rain began to fall. As it did for an hour at the beginning of every night, Sri said. But the rain quickly grew harder, a heavy drumming on the taut material of the tent, and at last Sri used her spex to talk to one of her assistants, a brief and irritable argument about the garden's climate control.

"I must deal with something," she told Loc, and rose and left without another word.

Loc stepped to the entrance of the tent and saw her talking briefly with two of her assistants. When the three of them walked off into the rainy dark he followed, certain that something was up. The big cushions of moss gave off a steely luminescence, glowing like the ghosts of small clouds, enabling him to pick his way along a path that had turned into a small stream. Cold water flowed as sluggishly as mercury over his feet, and enormous drops of low-gravity rain drifted down all around; when one smacked down on Loc's head, it was as if he'd been drenched with a pailful of water, doing Gaia knew what damage to his carefully braided hair, soaking his face, and slicking straight off his suit-liner. He knuckled water from his eyes, spat and snorted, and saw the shadows of Sri Hong-Owen and the two assistants float past a shoulder of luminous moss toward the lake.

Loc groped his way to the bridge and pulled himself along it. Fat, slow raindrops smacked against the water below. Braids dripping, cold air stinging his wet face, he crept through the green light of the sloping passageway toward the red glow of the gallery and the echo of loud voices. Sri Hong-Owen was talking to her son, who hung his head and shrugged and snuffled. One of the assistants, the neuter, was nursing yo's eye; the other was bent over the memo space, where virtual screens tiled in the air showed paths smashed through cloudy thickets of wires and a fleet of paper-thin fins showed from several angles the spindly robot pacing in mindless circles amongst the wreckage of a candle-copse. It seemed that Berry had not only managed to get into the climate controls of the moss garden; he'd also sent the robot on a rampage through the polychine garden.

162

Sri Hong-Owen suddenly turned around, called Loc before he could shrink away, and told him that she had changed her mind. He was no longer needed here, she said. He could leave immediately. "Berry is my responsibility. I will deal with him."

Loc couldn't resist a parting shot. "I hope he has not done too much damage, ma'am."

"It isn't serious. And it might even yield interesting results. Go now," the gene wizard said. Her icy disdain had returned in full measure. "Go. There's nothing for you here."

"It's a classic case of acting out," Loc told Captain Neves later that day, back in Camelot. "The only way the boy is able to express his frustration is to smash something."

"You ask me, sometimes people do bad things because they're bad," Captain Neves said. "And Berry is a bad seed, no doubt about it."

"He certainly drew the short straw in the genetic lottery," Loc said. "I understand that the other son, the one left behind on Earth, takes after his mother."

"Not that that's any kind of advantage. I mean, it hasn't done her much good, has it?"

"I almost feel sorry for her. She believes in the supremacy of logic and order. She believes that science is our only salvation. That only science can make sense of the world, and ourselves. Most of all, she believes in control and determinacy. Those weird things in that garden, their unique, unrepeatable configurations, run counter to all of that. They are a game with no purpose or utility, yet she believes that she can prove herself better than her enemy by attempting to control something that, by its very nature, cannot be controlled. It's funny," Loc said. "She can waste as much time as she likes there, but in the end she'll be no nearer to understanding Avernus."

"So you didn't find anything useful out there. Perhaps you should ask me what I found out about Malarte," Captain Neves said.

"I'd almost forgotten about the good colonel. I'm going to have to find a way of explaining that garden to him. It will be like trying to teach calculus to a donkey. Well, what have you been up to?"

Captain Neves explained that she had plugged in to the military police rumour mill and learnt that Colonel Malarte was employing one of the city's senators, a mountebank named Todd Krough, to help him acquire the works of art he was shipping back to Earth. As for the chestplate decorated with the last in the series of Munk's *Seven Transformations of the Ring System*, the colonel had taken it in exchange for guaranteeing the release from prison of the woman who was presently his mistress.

"And probably a spy for the rebels," Captain Neves said.

"Well, this is all very useful," Loc said. "Something good has come out of this trip after all."

"You have a plan, don't you? You're going to can the colonel's ass."

"Malarte is a greedy and stupid man who's a danger to everyone around him. It would be a public service to expose his crimes, but that isn't possible because of his consanguinity. He's a fool, but he's the Pessanha family's fool. We can't move against him directly. But we *can* move against those around him. Not the senator: he might be useful. But the colonel's mistress, on the other hand . . ."

"It would be very humiliating for the colonel if she was exposed. It would definitely weaken him," Captain Neve said, clearly liking the idea. "Only problem is, there's isn't any hard evidence that she's a spy. It will take time, and we'll be working on the colonel's turf."

"We're not going to expose her. We're going to *threaten* to expose her, and to send her family back to prison. Where they no doubt belong."

"And use her to spy on the colonel."

"Exactly. Also, I would be interested in finding out how much she learnt from Munk when she was his pupil. I'm thinking of giving Euclides Peixoto a little welcoming present."

3

After the publicity tour was cancelled Frankie Fuente went home to the state of Paiuí, where he planned to buy a share in a carnaúba palm plantation and spend the rest of his life watching other people make money for him. Cash Baker went back to the academy, and teaching.

At first, little seemed to have changed. There was a month of mourning after the state funeral of the president—flags at half-mast, black armbands, water instead of wine served at meals in the officers' mess. In a short address at his inauguration, the new president, Armand Nabuco, promised a smooth transition and a continuation of the policies that had made Greater Brazil a power for good in an imperfect world. Flare-ups in wildsider activity in the Andes, the Great Desert, and along the border of the northern territories were quickly suppressed; renewed calls for independence by banned nationalist groups like the Freedom Riders came to nothing; antigovernment posters were torn down, graffiti was scrubbed away, links to clandestine sites on the net were purged. And then, the day after the official period of mourning ended, the Office for Strategic Services removed thousands of civil servants and government officials from their posts, and it was announced that General Arvam Peixoto, leader of the expeditionary force at Saturn and acting head of the Three Powers Authority, would be returning to Earth after he had handed over command to Euclides Peixoto.

Many of the officers in the academy wanted to know what Cash thought this meant: after all, he'd not only served out there, but he'd also met the general, more than once. Was Arvam Peixoto the kind of man who'd give up power easily? Had he overstepped the mark when he'd ordered a strike against the rebels out at Uranus? Was he being forced out because he posed a threat to the new administration? Or did it have something to do with the debt that the new president owed to the radical greens, who wanted to pull back from the Outer System, who believed that the ongoing occupation of the moons of Jupiter and Saturn was a waste of resources that would be better deployed on rewilding the planet? Cash said that it all sounded like politics to him, and he didn't do politics. Sure, it meant that the military forces at Saturn would now be under the direct command of a civilian, but the war was over and, like the president said, this was an important step in the normalisation of the situation in the Outer System. He was sorry that the general had lost his command—he was a stand-up guy and a fine leader, and he deserved better—but those were the breaks, up on the exposed and lonely peaks of high command. Sometimes you ate the bear, and sometimes the bear ate you. As far as the people who'd served under the general were concerned, the people who did the actual work of peacekeeping and reconstruction, life would go on much as before.

Cash was quickly proved wrong. A few days after Arvam Peixoto was deposed, everyone in the armed services was asked to sign a loyalty oath to the new president. There was a lot of angry talk amongst the officers in the academy. Some said that it was nothing more than a trivial formality; others pointed out that they'd sworn an oath of loyalty to their country when they

165

had been commissioned, and if they had to make a further declaration of support it should be to the office of president, not to the man who temporarily held it. Arguments grew so fierce that Major-General Lorenz, the commander of the academy, had to forbid all political discussion in the mess. Some people refused to talk to those they disagreed with; two junior lieutenants called each other out in a duel. They fought with knives in the gymnasium and after they'd sliced each other a few times the fight was declared a draw and the two men shook hands and went off to the hospital together.

Cash continued to tell anyone who asked that he wasn't interested in politics, refused to take sides, and duly signed the loyalty oath, along with everyone else. Several weeks later, he was shaken awake early one morning and discovered an OSS captain standing over him with two troopers behind, the three men making a crowd in Cash's bare little room.

The captain told Cash that he wouldn't be arrested as long as he cooperated. Cash, feeling amazingly calm, said that he'd be happy to cooperate once he knew what this was about.

"I'm required to deliver you for debriefing," the captain said.

"They asked you to pick me up but they didn't tell you why, huh? Has my commanding officer been told about this?"

"Of course. You have ten minutes to pack, Captain."

"No problem," Cash said. "I guess I can shit and shave on the way."

"If it comes to that," the captain said, "we can probably find you a shower, too."

A tiltrotor flew Cash from the academy to the big air base on the other side of Monterey, where he was put on board a fat transport plane. A Tapir-L4, the bird he'd flown on resupply missions east of the Great Lakes some thirteen years ago, right after he'd been given his wings and bars. Cash was locked in one of the travel capsules used by high-ranking officers and VIPs—there was a bed, a refrigerator packed with snacks and juice, and a toilet and a shower: that captain had known what he was talking about—and the transport flew him south to Brasília. He arrived close to midnight, and was driven in a government limousine to a government hotel right in the centre of the city and escorted to a room up on the top floor, with a big bed and floor-to-ceiling windows with a view across the parklands of the Eixo Monumental to the white crown of thorns of the Catedral Metropolitana Nossa Senhora Aparecida, floodlit like a spaceship about to ascend into the big dark. Cash supposed that he wasn't going to be taken out and shot. Not yet, anyhow. But he still didn't have clue one about what they wanted from him, or who they were.

166

The next day he was driven ten blocks to the Ministry of Information, where a pair of taciturn OSS troopers escorted him through the service entrance at the rear and rode up with him in an elevator to an open-plan office crowded with uniformed personnel and civilians working at desks and memo spaces. Not one of them looking at Cash as he was taken past them to a small windowless room tucked into a corner at the far end. He was told to make himself comfortable behind the scarred table, and one of the guards brought him a waxed paper cup of iced tea. The room was unremarkable: pale green walls, black resin floor. No traces of blood spray, no handcuff bolt fixed to the table, no visible surveillance. Nevertheless, Cash felt fragile and apprehensive, sitting there with the guards standing outside the open door. As if everything in his life had funnelled down to this moment, this place. A crux not of his own making. One he might not survive.

He'd been sitting there for more than an hour when an OSS officer and a civilian came in, shutting the door behind them. The OSS officer, a colonel, returned Cash's salute, told him to sit back down, and took one of the chairs on the other side of the table. He was a trim man in his fifties and ugly as a toad, with small dark eyes, pockmarked cheeks, and a squashed nose that had taken a few knocks in its time. He swept off his black-billed hat, revealing a shaven scalp with a knotted scar over one ear, set the hat upside down on the table, and said, "I just need you to answer some questions, Captain. Think you can do that?"

"Yes, sir."

Cash knew better than to ask what this was about. He'd know soon enough.

"Ever worn an MRI cap?" the colonel said.

"No, sir."

"You're going to wear one now. It will tell us when you're telling the truth and when you aren't."

"I'll try to answer your questions as best I can, sir."

"You were wounded," the colonel said, and touched his forehead with the tip of his index finger.

"Yes, sir."

"And you have a faulty memory as a result."

"Sir."

"So perhaps you don't always know when you aren't telling the truth. Because you don't always remember what is true and what is not true. Because of your wound. But the MRI cap, it will help us know if that happens."

"I guess I don't have any choice."

"Of course you do." The colonel's smile hadn't changed, but there was steel in his dark gaze.

"I can volunteer for questioning under the cap, or you'll put me in irons."

"You're a fast learner. That's good."

"Well I guess you better bring it on," Cash said.

The cap was a snug fit over Cash's crew cut. The civilian switched on a slate, put on a pair of spex, asked Cash a series of anodyne questions, and at last told the colonel they were ready. For the rest of that day they talked about Cash's career before the Quiet War. Flying transport planes, flying combat planes out across the Pacific during the war of nerves with the Pacific Community, testing the Jaguar Ghost space plane, the J-2 singleship programme. The next day they talked about the expedition to Saturn, and things got harder.

Cash still didn't remember everything that had happened out there. He drew a complete blank on Operation Deep Sounding and the mission he'd flown to divert the chunk of ice aimed at Phoebe. There were plenty of other holes in his memory, too, and the colonel attacked them from every angle while the civilian technician watched the patterns of activity in Cash's brain on a slate and Cash popped sweat and tried to think around a nauseous throbbing that had established itself behind his left eye. The colonel called a break and Cash was given a pill that took the edge off his headache, but then they started over and he still couldn't think straight, growing angry and frustrated as the colonel bored in, asking over and again about the mission against the rogue chunk of ice.

Cash told him everything he knew. He could remember being briefed about it by General Peixoto, and he knew he'd flown the mission with Luiz Schwarcz and the European Union pilot, Vera Jackson. He remembered Luiz telling him about it, but he didn't remember anything from the mission itself. He didn't remember the flight out; he didn't remember the action against automatic defences installed on the ice; he didn't remember being hit, or what had happened afterward. His headache beat behind his eyes, a knot of frustration growing tighter and tighter. He was angry at himself, angry at what had happened to him, angry at the colonel's insinuations and relentless questions, and at last he boiled over and slammed his fists on the table, shouting that he'd been trying to remember what had happened ever since he'd been rescued and revived and he couldn't because the memories just weren't there any more.

The colonel leaned back and studied Cash, fingers steepled against his chin, then told the civilian tech to show the video to Captain Baker.

168

The man turned his slate around and angled it so that Cash could see the full-screen picture of a chunk of pitted ice slowly revolving around its long axis amidst a thinning fog of debris.

"I remember *seeing* this," Cash said. "It's after we took out its rail guns and its motor. I just don't remember being there."

He knew what was coming. It was like a fist on his stomach. The image of the chunk of ice washed with false colours as it was probed by radar, microwave and multispectrum optical telemetry. Views in infrared showed fresh trenches gouged from stem to stern and a hot crater where the fusion motor had been blasted away. Tiny flashes stuttering across its surface as a swarm of drones was launched at Cash's singleship, vanishing one by one in quick blinks of red light as countermeasures started to take them out, and then a solid white flash when the singleship's systems fell over.

"They showed you this so that you understood what you had done to earn your Medal of Valour. You attacked the projectile, you took out most of its defences, but your ship was damaged. But they did not show you this," the colonel said, and reached over and touched a corner of the slate.

A view of a segment of Saturn's rings, backlit because the sun was below the ring plane, the view zooming in across parallel lanes of dust and ice toward the bright spike of a fusion motor's flame and the lumpy shape of an Outer tug. The tug bracketed by targeting grids and little blocks of numbers that detailed its delta vee, the power output of its fusion motor, radar, and countermeasure profiles, and a host of other information. An inset window showing it creeping toward the Keeler Gap, with the arc of the A Ring beyond.

The colonel said, "Do you remember this?"

"No, sir." Cash's mouth was dry. His tongue a lump of wood. "If you're going to tell me this was taken by my ship's cameras, then you're mistaken. My ship was killed out at Phoebe. So was I. Whatever this is, it doesn't have anything to do with me."

"Let's see if this jogs your memory," the colonel said, and touched the screen again.

The clip jumped forward a few minutes. The tug was making a course adjustment and strings of changing numbers along the bottom of the view showed that the ship following it was changing course too, and so were proxies that had been deployed sometime in the interval, snarking after the tug like eager hounds. A text message popped up: details of Cash's service record, an order to disengage.

Cash leaned forward, slick with sweat from head to foot, hands caught between his knees, fingers laced tight. He was quivering all over, like a machine about to tear itself apart.

Another window popped open: the gamma ray laser was charging up. And then everything went crazy. Everything but the visual feed died. Connections with proxies, the gamma ray laser system, radar, flight control, everything. The visual feed yawed wildly, pitching down toward the ring plane, long arcs of dust and ice fragments smashing up, resolving detail, and then the slate flashed white, game over.

The colonel leaned back, studying him. Beside him, the civilian tech sat masked by his spex, monitoring the spark and flicker of Cash's thoughts.

Cash clawed at the MRI cap, ripped it from his scalp, and crushed it in his hands. He felt hollow and sick. There was blood in his mouth: he'd half chewed through the inside of his cheek.

"I never before saw that," he said. "I don't know where you got it, but it's nothing to do with me."

The colonel said, "Do you know a man by the name of Loc Ifrahim?"

Cash blinked, brought up short.

"A diplomat," the colonel said.

Cash shook his head.

"You have never met him."

"If I did, I can't remember. What happened to the ship that was chasing that tug? It looked as if it was hit by some kind of electronic warfare."

"It refused to pull out of the attack that it was making on the tug, so it was neutralised. Loc Ifrahim. The name means nothing to you?"

"I don't remember meeting him." Cash was wondering if this was someone who'd got him in trouble. Someone he had crossed, or disobeyed. Wondering what it had to do with the aborted attack on the tug.

The colonel said, "You don't remember a lot of things, Captain. Let's go over this again."

———◆———

No one came for Cash the next day. The door of his hotel room was locked from the outside. A guard brought in his meals. Half the functions of the memo space were blocked, but he could watch TV. The government channel (all the channels were government channels: this was the official government channel) had a brief item about General Arvam Peixoto returning to Earth, including about two seconds showing the great man in a wheelchair, his face uptilted as he shook hands with an officer. Cash watched and rewatched it, feeling sick. It was obvious that he was being set up to take the general down. The general had made him a hero, a figurehead for the Quiet War. But according to the colonel, Cash hadn't been killed out at Phoebe; he'd somehow survived and turned rogue, disobeying direct orders. . . .

No one came for him the next day, either. The day after that, he was eating breakfast when the door opened and a grandfatherly officer in Air Defence blues came in and introduced himself as Lieutenant Colonel Marx Vermelho, Cash's counsel.

"I didn't know I needed a lawyer. Have I been arrested?"

Cash was still maintaining his calm. He didn't have any control over what was happening, and so far no one had told him why he was here, so he was going with the flow.

"I'm not your lawyer, son," the lieutenant colonel said. He was a handsome old dude with dark brown skin and white hair clipped short around a horseshoe of bare scalp. "I'm your counsel. Here to help you prepare for your appearance in front of the Senate Subcommittee for Extraterrestrial Affairs. How's that coffee? No, don't you get up. I'll pour myself a cup, and then we can take a look at your statement."

It was a brisk resumé of the story that the OSS colonel had told Cash in the interview room. It described the action at Phoebe, and stated that Cash's singleship had been damaged when it had been struck by debris from an enemy drone, but it had managed to repair itself and Cash had plotted a course back to the inner part of the Saturn System and selected a target. He had directly disobeyed orders to disengage, and his singleship had been shut down. It had ploughed through the plane of the rings, and that had been when it had taken a second hit. A speck of basalt had smashed through its nose and shattered into dozens of white-hot fragments. Most had harmlessly expended their energy in the temperfoam insulation that packed the voids in the singleship's interior, but one had struck Cash's virtual-reality visor and drilled a path through his brain.

Cash said that he'd never been anywhere near the rings. He'd been hit by a fragment of a drone. It had killed his ship. Killed him. Lieutenant Colonel Vermelho shook his head and thumbed the corner of his slate, flipping past the statement to a photograph of what looked like a miniature moon, dark and knubbly and pocked with craters.

"That's what did the damage," the lieutenant colonel said. "A forensic team picked it out of the inner casing of your singleship's lifesystem. It's basalt, son. Pyroxene doped with iron and nickel. Saturn's rings are mostly ice, but there are rocky fragments dispersed all the way through them, and this is a tiny piece of one of those fragments."

Cash felt cold, felt his skin trying to contract all over his body. Everything in the hotel room was bright and dead. The blue sky outside the tall windows was as remote as Heaven.

Lieutenant Colonel Vermelho studied Cash with a kindly look, saying, "I know how you feel. I do. But you have to accept that what you think is the truth is only half the truth."

"This is about General Peixoto. You want to take him down, and you're using me to do it."

"I want you to tell the truth."

"You want me to pretend that I remember things that I don't remember."

"No, son. That isn't how it's going to work at all. I don't want you to lie. I want you to tell the truth. But before you do, I want you to understand and accept that you were set up. That you were lied to. The general and his people needed a hero, and you fitted the mold exactly—aside from a troubling little episode where you disobeyed orders and got yourself killed. So they filed off that part of your story and concentrated on the part that made you seem like a war hero. And as far as we're concerned, that's what you are. You were flying a ship that had been badly crippled, but you were still doing your damnedest to go after a legitimate target, and you had no way of knowing that the order to abort your attack was genuine. You did what you had to do, in the heat of battle.

"But, son, you have to come to terms with the fact that you were used. General Peixoto and his people used you. They covered up the truth for their own purposes. Their forensic team recovered the fleck of basalt that killed you, and they kept the black box from your singleship, too. They knew what really happened, and they covered it up because it was inconvenient. You may not remember going after that Outer tug and being switched off, but I can assure you that that is exactly what happened."

"And if I don't?"

"You aren't in a position to make a deal, son. This is airtight. We can do it with or without your cooperation. And if you don't cooperate, we'll have to believe that you were part of the conspiracy. That you went along with it willingly. But if you do the right thing and stand up in front of the subcommittee and make your statement, then you'll be treated leniently. The conspiracy charges will be dropped. You'll be a free man. So, how about we go over this again," Lieutenant Colonel Vermelho said, flipping his slate back to the statement, "and make sure you understand everything."

They went over it again. And again. Two days later, Cash stood up in front of the Senate Subcommittee for Extraterrestrial Affairs and gave his sworn statement. He managed to answer the questions put to him by one of the senators, all rehearsed, all pointing toward a grand conspiracy involving the mysterious Outer tug. Afterward, he banged straight into the nearest bathroom and threw up. Lieutenant Colonel Vermelho took him back to the hotel, ordered a bottle of brandy from room service, drank a glass with Cash, and told him that he would have to stay in Brasília for the next week or so, ready to answer any supplementary questions that the subcommittee might have.

Cash waited three days. He drank the rest of the brandy the first night, and in the morning ordered up a bottle of whiskey and started in on that. He wanted to stay numb. He didn't want to think about what he'd done, what had been done to him. The morning of the third day, two OSS troopers roused him from his bed, stuck him under a cold shower until he yelled uncle, dressed and shaved him, and escorted him to a transport plane that flew him back to Monterey. General Arvam Peixoto was dead. After he had been formally charged with war crimes that included the unnecessary killing of civilians during the battle for Paris and failure to rescue the crews of disabled Outer ships immediately after the end of the war, he'd been released into the care of a senior member of his family. And the very same day he had shot himself in the head with his service revolver.

Two weeks later, Cash was brought in front of a court-martial that lasted just twenty minutes. He was stripped of his medals and rank and given a dishonourable discharge. He drifted north from city to city along the Gulf Coast to Texas, fell in with a gang who smuggled antibiotics, weapons, and equipment liberated from Reclamation and Reconstruction Corps stores. Cash and another ex-Air Defence pilot took turns flying the gang's plane, a little single-prop job with an alcohol-burning motor, all around the edge of the Great Desert. He was drinking pretty hard, cutting back when he was on the job, cutting loose when he wasn't.

One day he was in a cavelike cantina in a flyblown town north of the ruins of Wichita, sitting at the plank bar and working on a bottle of red whiskey. Outside, the sky was yellow with dust lofted from the badlands of the Great Desert. A hot wind blew billows of dust down an ancient highway, past a broken string of flat-fronted buildings patched together from salvaged lumber and standing amongst empty lots like broken teeth. Plastic sheeting over the cantina's single window billowed and snapped. Dust whirled in at the open doorway and hissed across the stamped-dirt floor. Dust was a hot itch under Cash's shirt, in his hair. He'd grown out his hair, kept it back from his eyes with a bandanna. He was half watching the screen up in the corner, the rolling news coming around again to a report about a raid on some nest of rebel scientists in the Antarctic, when someone sat beside him and said, "Been a while, cousin."

Cash turned, started to say he wasn't anyone's cousin, and saw that the man, tall and rangy in the green shirt and blue jeans of the R&R Corps, was Billy Dupree. His second cousin and his best friend, back when they'd been kids in Bastrop. Smiling at him, saying, "So, you been doing anything 'sides growing out your hair?"

They burst into laughter at the same moment, grabbed each other, and pounded each other's back. Billy asked the barkeep for a glass and poured himself a shot of Cash's whiskey and toasted him with it and knocked it back and poured himself another. Cash asked Billy what he was doing out here in the asshole of Hell, and Billy reckoned he might ask Cash the same thing.

"Oh, I'm waiting on some business. Looks like you got yourself enlisted."

"And I heard they turned you into some kind of superman when you were out there flying those space planes."

"Well, I'm grounded now," Cash said and held up his right hand, palm flat. "See that?"

"Looks steady as a rock to me."

"Yeah, but you should see it when I'm sober."

They drank and played catch-up. Cash had last seen Billy when his mother had died, carried away by a massive heart attack in her sleep, Christ, more than ten years ago. Cash had been flying air-support missions for General Arvam Peixoto's campaign against bandits in and around the ruins of Chicago. He'd been granted compassionate leave, hitched a ride in a Tapir L-4 to Atlanta, flown from Atlanta to Bastrop in a creaky old R&R Corps turboprop, attended the funeral in his dress blues, and returned to Chicago the next day.

He had a pretty good idea why his cousin had come looking for him now, and he also knew that Billy would get around to it in his own good time. Meanwhile, he was happy to ramble on about the good old days, talking about what had happened to the other kids they'd run with and the characters who'd hung out at the gym. He told Billy that he wasn't unhappy with his work. The hours weren't regular and neither was the pay, but he got to travel all over, see all kinds of places. "I was married for about a month, in Chihuahua. Hell, I believe I might still be married. We found out we weren't suited to each other so quick we split without bothering with the formalities. Only time I settled down. Now I'm either on the road or in the air."

Billy told Cash that he'd married a while back, had a son three years old.

"Are you really in the R&R Corps?"

"I really am."

"So where are you stationed? Out here?"

"Not hardly. No, I'm in the transport division, stationed back home in good old Bastrop. Me and Uncle Howard and a few others, we signed up a while back."

"Transport as in flying?"

"Some. Also road trains."

"This has to be some scam of Uncle Howard's," Cash said.

Billy studied Cash. There were deep creases on either side of his pale blue eyes, salt in the outlaw moustache that lapped his mouth. They'd grown up a fair bit since they'd hung out together on the block, wasting hours watching the daily street carnival, trapping racoons for the five centavos each pelt brought, running errands for the guys who hung out at their grand-aunt's boxing gym. They'd sparred after hours any number of times on the taut patched canvas of the ring, Billy, with his long reach and sharp quick jabs and hooks, generally getting the better of Cash. He was smarter than Cash too, but he didn't have the application or the jones for maths that had given Cash escape velocity, sent him to the Moon and beyond, to the Saturn System and the Quiet War.

Billy said now, with a sly sideways smile, "I guess you're wondering how we bumped into each other."

"I guess it wasn't by accident."

"Fact of the matter is, we're always on the lookout for good pilots."

"The R&R Corps or you and Uncle Howard?"

"It's kindly the same thing. Uncle Howard is more or less running the resupply warehouses at Bastrop. He wanted you to know there's an opening if you want one."

"Well, you can tell Uncle Howard I appreciate it, but I don't reckon I'm R&R material. No offence. That's just how it is."

"If you're thinking of your past history, we can take care of that. And it don't matter to any of us," Billy said, "because we're your family. And family stick together no matter what."

"I already have a job."

"Not for much longer. Your friends, they've survived only because they've been bribing people to look the other way. But I hear there's a crackdown coming. A purge of corrupt officials. You stick with your friends, you might get caught up in it. It's your choice, cousin, but any time you want you can give me a call," Billy said, and pulled a folded slip of paper from the breast pocket of his coveralls and set it on the bar.

Cash said, "You're looking for a pilot?"

"You bet."

"What kind of planes are we talking about?"

4

April, the Foyn Coast of Graham Land, the Antarctic Peninsula. Winter beginning, the days dying back. The sun nearing the end of its short, low arc across the eastern horizon of the Weddel Sea, falling behind the Brazilian frigate, formerly the *Admiral João Nachtergaele*, now named for the murdered green saint Oscar Finnegan Ramos. The bristling superstructure of the frigate silhouetted against the bloody flare of the sunset as it sleeked in toward the coast, navigating by radar and GPS, cutting through brash ice and shouldering aside small table bergs.

Night had fallen and the snowy mountains that formed the backbone of the peninsula stood faint and pale against the black and starry sky when the ship heaved to a couple of kilometres from the coast and five big inflatables loaded with shock troopers of the 3rd Special Brigade swept out from its stern well. The troopers wore Kevlar armour over cold-weather gear, hunched with their weapons and equipment against freezing spray as the inflatables slammed across the heavy waves. They entered the mouth of a fjord that hooked inland and saw lights spread along the northern shore. Less than a minute later, smart rounds launched from the frigate's rail guns screamed overhead, snaking up the contours of the fjord, very low, very fast. The black night detonated in the orange flashes and thunder of high explosives as the rounds struck their targets with pinpoint precision and the inflatables accelerated toward the shore, where buildings burned above their burning reflections in black water, tossing flames and smoke high into the sky. The inflatables grounded one after the other on a snow-covered strand and troopers jumped out and ran left and right, some toward the labs and the shattered and burning accommodation blocks of the research facility, others toward a house that sat on top of a ridge overlooking the fjord.

Brief firefights erupted in and amongst the lab buildings, but the positions of the defenders were quickly overwhelmed and in less than an hour the surviving scientists, technicians, and other support personnel were sitting in rows on the snowy shore in the glare of tall floodlights, hands clasped on top of their heads while troopers moved amongst them and confirmed identities with handheld DNA readers.

Senior scientists, administrators, and the chief of the station's security were marched up to the house, where Colonel Frederico Pessanha had established his command post. Its terraces had been blackened by rocket blasts and pocked with bullets and one of its glass walls was shattered. It had begun to snow, dry pellets billowing on knifing gusts of wind, and snow was accumulating in some of the rooms. Colonel Pessanha sat in the living room near a roaring fire fed by broken furniture, drinking brandy and watching his interrogation specialists deal with the prisoners. He was unhappy and half drunk. It had become clear that someone had leaked news of the raid. The families of the scientists and support personnel had been evacuated to a camp at the head of the fjord, no bodies had been found in the buildings targeted by the smart rounds, and the defenders had been well armed and had fought from prepared positions. And there was no sign of the man who was in charge of the research station, and none of the prisoners would tell him where he'd gone.

Long after midnight, Colonel Pessanha had two senior scientists and the chief of security brought before him. He made them strip off their clothes and kneel naked and shivering on the white carpet, by now tracked everywhere by the dirty boots of soldiers, and he asked them who had told them about the raid, when their boss had left, where he was hiding. They told him that they didn't know who had tipped them off, that their boss had left two days ago, that he had not told anyone where he was going. Colonel Pessanha drew his pistol and shot the scientists in the head, one after the other, then stood over the chief of security and screwed the muzzle of his pistol into the man's forehead and asked the same three questions again. The chief of security's torso was covered in reddening weals, and his nose was broken and one eye was swollen shut, but he fixed Colonel Pessanha with his good eye and gave him the same answers as before.

"My men will bring your families here tomorrow," Colonel Pessanha said. "They can go free or they can die here. Your choice."

"Colonel, he didn't tell me where he was going and I didn't ask. Put yourself in his position. Ask yourself what you would have done. It would have been the same."

"How did he leave? By boat or helicopter? On foot?"

"I think he left on foot."

"You think? You did not see him leave?"

"He left in the night. He did not take any of the boats and his helicopter is still on the pad. So, yes, I think he went on foot."

"I have heard that he did not leave alone. Is that true?"

"He took two of my men with him."

"You are their commanding officer. Why didn't they tell you where they were going?"

"I am in charge of security, Colonel. I am not in command. No, they did not tell me where they were going. Because I asked them not to tell me."

"You have lived here a long time."

"Eleven years."

"You know the land."

"Of course."

"You've hiked in it. Explored it."

"As often as I could."

"Where would you go, if you wanted to hide?"

"It really isn't possible to hike along the coast. There are too many inlets and fjords. Anyone leaving here by land would have to go up into the mountains."

"That's where he went, eh? A place you know. A cabin. A bunker."

"I don't know where he went. Kill me now, it won't make any difference."

"Kill you? No. Not yet. One of your children perhaps. The youngest is five, I believe. Shall I have her brought here?"

The chief of security cursed Colonel Pessanha until his voice gave out.

"Are you done?" Colonel Pessanha said. "Well then, think carefully. The man I want is no longer your boss. You no longer owe him loyalty. To your family, yes. To him, no. Where did he go?"

"I don't know. Truly. I don't."

Colonel Pessanha turned to the captain who had conducted the interrogations. "These are the same answers the others gave?"

"Yes, sir."

"Confirmed with the MRI cap?"

"If they know anything else, they've buried it deep."

"Then maybe it's the truth. Why not?"

Colonel Pessanha ordered a guard to unlock the chief of security's handcuffs, gave the man a blanket to wrap around himself, sat him in one of the big chairs in front of the fireplace, and poured a glass of brandy and handed it to him.

"You were a soldier before this," he told the man. "We'll talk, one soldier to another. You asked me what I would have done if I had been your boss. Let me tell you. I would not have run away. I would have stayed with my people. I would have fought alongside them. But your boss—he's a coward who ran and left you in the shit. You and your families. You fought well. I respect that. But your boss does not deserve your loyalty."

"We fought only because you attacked us," the chief of security said. "Because you ignored our messages when we offered to surrender. You were knocking at an open door, Colonel. If you had come here peacefully, we would have surrendered peacefully."

"Put yourself in my position. I am in charge of an operation to shut down a research station operated by a criminal gang who are committing every kind of antievolutionary crime and vile perversion against God and Gaia. Making monsters, chimeras of animals and human children. I receive from them a message of surrender. Can I trust it? Can I believe that I can simply walk into this place and not be ambushed? Of course not."

The chief of security drained his brandy glass with a defiant gesture. "We are both soldiers but it seems that we are different kinds of men," he said, and they were his last words.

The glass bounced on the white carpet in the echo of the gunshot that killed him. Colonel Pessanha stepped past the body in the chair to the smashed glass wall and looked out at the black night, absent-mindedly fingering the spray of blood on his black and white camo tunic. A steady wind had got up, blowing flurries of snow across the ruined terrace, whining over jagged edges of broken glass.

"He's gone," he said at last. "We'll look at satellite surveillance, of course, but it won't tell us anything. You could hide an army in those mountains. This will not please my father, but there it is. Have we secured the other buildings?"

"Yes, sir," the captain said. "It looks like they scrubbed all their records."

"Only to be expected. Bring in the specialists. They have a day to recover anything useful. We'll ship the prisoners out at dawn, and when the specialists are finished we will raze this place to the ground."

"And their families, sir?"

"Fuck, I forgot." Colonel Pessanha pinched the bridge of his nose between his thumb and forefinger, and closed his eyes. "Send out drones right now, and check their disposition. We'll confront them at dawn, issue orders to surrender. Even better, we'll get one of the scientists to do it. Tell him we'll kill them all if he doesn't cooperate. We'll take everyone back, turn them over to the Peixotos. Let them work out how to punish these people for their crimes. After all, this mess, this unholy research, it's all the fault of their famous gene wizard."

5

Sri Hong-Owen was walking a transect of the rim forest early one morning, collecting hand crabs for a population survey, when Euclides Peixoto called her out of the blue. He told her that there'd been a little trouble she should know about, back on Earth, and read out a brief official announcement about a successful action against a nest of criminals in Antarctica who had been in flagrant breach of the new regulations controlling scientific research. Survivors had been arrested and transported to Tierra del Fuego; their laboratories had been destroyed.

"I'm sorry to be the bearer of bad news but there it is," Euclides said, not sounding sorry at all.

"Alder. Is he one of the survivors?"

Sri was standing knee-deep in a ferny glade amongst tall sugar pines, a long pole fitted with a loop of smart wire in one hand, a catch net containing a big hand crab in the other, her spex showing Euclides Peixoto's face in a window of virtual light. Shock had scooped her hollow. She felt as cold and weightless as a ghost. She felt as if she was about to fall off the face of the world.

Euclides said, "I understand your son ran away before the fireworks began."

"Then he's alive."

"The soldiers looking for him think so."

"How many people were killed? Do you have a list of casualties?"

"I can't tell you offhand, but it looks like the place was very thoroughly trashed," Euclides said, and put up an inset showing an aerial view of the station, buildings burned-out in splashes of black along the snowy shoreline of the fjord.

It was bad, but it wasn't as bad as it could have been. Sri's shock was fading, displaced by cool, calm anger. She could have told Euclides Peixoto that innovations produced by the scientists in her Antarctic fastness had, over the years, earned his family more than ten billion reals, that their work had not been illegal in Greater Brazil until the new regulatory bill had been passed two months ago, and because it was not now nor had it ever been illegal in Antarctica the attack was a violation of at least three different international treaties. But nothing she could say would unmake the raid or help Alder, and if Euclides was hoping that she would break down or lose her temper, she wasn't about to give him any kind of satisfaction.

"OSS will probably want to talk to you," Euclides said. "It would save everyone a lot of trouble if you could give them some advice about where your son might be hiding."

"You can tell them I don't have the first idea where to find him," Sri said. She pulled off her spex and sat down amongst the ferns, absent-mindedly watching the hand crab-pick at the knotted mesh of the catch net with its strong black nails as she thought things through.

After Arvam Peixoto had been recalled to Earth, the garden habitat where he'd made his headquarters had fallen vacant—Euclides Peixoto had chosen to live in Paris, and the Air Defence Force had reassigned Arvam's people elsewhere. So Sri had moved in, setting up laboratories in a wing of the mansion, building a string of small tents containing experimental biomes on the icy plain south of the habitat's dome, planting fields of novel vacuum organisms. The hand crabs were the first of her experiments in bodymorph design, scuttling creatures with a bony carapace, four multijointed "fingers" and a peglike "thumb," and a cluster of simple compound eyes over a mouth equipped with flaps and feelers. A hundred days ago, she had released a batch into the forest that circled the rim of the habitat's tent and they had multiplied and spread with gratifying speed—the crab in the catch net was a fat and healthy specimen with a beard of translucent nymphs budding beneath its busy mouthparts.

She'd been planning to pull crabs from burrows along several transects, measure their age and size and reproductive health, and work up an estimate of population growth and health. A simple little nature study. A bit of fun. Well, there was no time for that now. She opened the catch net and tipped out the crab, which hitched around in a crooked circle before scampering away across a stretch of ground softly carpeted with pine needles and vanishing into a shrubbery of elderberry that marked the course of a stream at the edge of the glade. Then she called her assistants and gave them the news, explaining that it was obvious that the attack had been instigated by the radical green faction in the government.

"I want to find out why my contacts in the Senate failed to give any kind of warning, and why Euclides Peixoto had the news before me. I want to find out how many people were killed and injured and I want to know what has happened to the survivors. If they are being held prisoner, if charges are being brought against them, I want my lawyers in Brasília to provide legal representation as soon as possible. I want a collation of any news items about this atrocity, and reactions from the governments of the European Union, the Pacific Community, and the other signatories of the revised Antarctic treaty. But first of all, I need a gig. I have to go to Paris. I have to talk to Berry."

—●—

Sri had brought Berry with her when she'd taken charge of the habitat. She'd employed tutors to fill in the gaps of her son's patchwork education, indulged him by supplying animals and birds he could hunt in the rim forest, taken him on trips to the so-called free cities of Camelot, Mimas, and Athens and Spartica on Tethys, and done her best to give him some direction and shape to his life. Then, on his sixteenth birthday, Berry had tried to enlist in the Air Defence Force and had been turned down flat. He'd blamed Sri for that, and for everything else he believed had gone wrong in his life. After a series of epic rows and sulks he'd moved to Paris, and that was where Sri went now, still enveloped in her wintry calm, piloting a gig across the low-relief moonscape, landing at the outer edge of the spaceport on the floor of Romulus Crater, and hitching a ride to the city in a military rolligon.

The sergeant in charge of the garage next door to the freight yard's cluster of airlocks told Sri that all the trikes had been signed out. She could wait or walk, her choice. She tried to call Berry for the tenth or twelfth time, but he was still offline. So she walked, loping along in an efficient low-gravity gait she'd long ago perfected, past silent manufactories and warehouses, past untenanted apartment blocks whose walls were covered with graffiti scrawled by soldiers of the occupation force: mad, multicoloured galleries of regimental badges and mottos, belligerent boasts, and cartoon atrocities.

The streets were deserted. Apart from a few hundred essential workers, no

Outers were allowed to live inside the city limits, and the TPA's civil servants, private contractors, and military personnel lived and worked in the Green Zone at the centre of the city, or in offices and apartments built around the railway station at the top of the long slope of its park. The air under the latticed roof of the tent was cool and still and stale, as in a house that had been shut up and abandoned. The halflife grass that covered the avenue was newly laid and vividly green, but the palm trees that lined it on either side, planted after the war to replace the city's famous sweet chestnuts, were dying, the blades of their crowns yellowing or dry and brown. In the middle of a big intersection, a statue of an astronaut in an antique pressure suit lay where it had been toppled from its plinth; the park beyond was a basin of dry dust scored everywhere by tire tracks. An arcade of artisans' workshops, long ago smashed and looted, gaped like a row of caves. Off-duty soldiers lounged outside a corner café; several whistled at Sri when she went past. She circled the barricades of the Green Zone, passed a row of burned-out buildings, their roofs collapsed and walls slumped and blackened like blowtorched candle-wax, and tracked across another dead, dusty park toward the compound, a square, white structure at the foot of the park's sloping tracts of replanted forest.

Before the war, when Paris had been at the forefront of the resistance to the incursion of the Brazilian and European joint expedition, Avernus and her crew had taken up residence in the compound. Afterward, Arvam Peixoto had given it to Sri. One of his little jokes. Now Berry lived there.

Sri hadn't visited her son for more than a hundred days: the reeking squalor inside the compound was as shocking as a slap to her face. The formal plantings of the central courtyard had been trashed and several people were sleeping or had passed out amongst litter that lay everywhere. A young woman wearing fatigues with the sleeves torn off, displaying muscular arms glossy with military tattoos, sat cross-legged on the slender wing of a bench, forking up beans and rice from a ration pack; when Sri asked her if Berry was at home, she jerked a thumb toward the string of rooms on the other side of the courtyard.

Berry was sleeping in a dark and hot little room amongst half a dozen young men and women. He was naked and half drunk or drugged but docile enough, pulling on a pair of combat trousers and following Sri outside, yawning and scrubbing at his eyes with his fists. They sat down on the parched grass of the lawn and Sri told him straightaway that the research station in Antarctica had been attacked and Alder was missing.

"Don't worry," she said. "Alder and I knew it was likely to happen. We made extensive plans that covered every possibility. Right now he will be hunkered down in a shelter, waiting until his enemies stop searching for him. As soon as it's safe he'll send a message."

Berry thought for a moment. His complexion was blotchy; his eyes sore and red-rimmed. He'd put on weight—a fold of his belly bulged above the waistband of his combat pants as he sat tailorwise—and he had a tattoo on his arm, an animated red devil with horns and barbed tail that over and again jabbed splashes of fire with its pitchfork. He'd grown out his hair and tied it back in a tightly pleated pigtail that hung past his shoulder blades. The style in which Arvam Peixoto had once worn his hair, Sri realised. At last he said, in his slow, sleepy drawl, "My brother's smart. He can outwit the bad guys."

"Of course he can." Sri paused, then said, "These are dangerous times, Berry. I think you should come back to the habitat for a little while. You'll be safe there, and you can be a great help to me."

She knew that Berry liked the military, its discipline and order, its fetishism of violence, and planned to have him help out with the habitat's security. The seasoned ex-marine sergeant presently in command would look after him, teach him, set him straight. But when she started to explain it to him, he shrugged and said that he wanted to stay in Paris.

"I have friends here. I have work."

"I've just seen some of your friends. I won't ask who they are or why you have allowed them to trash the compound, but it breaks my heart to see you waste your life, Berry. You're so much better than this."

"I'm not wasting my life. I have work here. My own club. A place where soldiers can hang out and kick back. I like doing it, I'm good at it, *it's what I want to do*," Berry said, with the anxious look he always got when he thought that he was about to be punished, or something he treasured was going to be confiscated.

Sri tried to explain that because the new president lacked supporters in the Senate, he'd been forced to form a coalition with senators belonging to the radical green faction. And they had not only pushed through a great deal of hardline legislation, but were also using their power to remove or diminish everyone who disagreed with their policies. "That's why they targeted Alder. And that's why you should move back with me, Berry. Just for a little while. In case someone decides to make an example of you because of your brother's so-called crimes."

"*Your* crimes," Berry said. "That's what this is all about. The things *you* did. That you made Alder do."

"He was doing good and necessary work. As was everyone at the research station. People you knew, Berry. People who may well now be dead."

"It's all about you. It always is. I can't go back to Earth because of what you did there. I can't enlist. And now you want to ruin everything I've done here, like always."

"I should have taken better care of you," Sri said. "Paid a little more attention to you. I know that, and I apologise. And this club of yours, I'm pleased to hear that you've been able to find something you like. It shows initiative. Why not use that initiative to help me, and help Alder, too?"

They talked back and forth for half an hour, but it did no good. Berry went through his usual stages of denial—clumsy attempts to change the subject, irrational anger, finally a smoldering sulk. Sri lost her temper and told him to stop being so selfish, to think about where his brother might be now, the hardships he must be suffering; Berry said that he'd learned all he knew about selfishness from her. Nothing she said got through to him after that, and then, because her assistants hadn't been able to obtain any useful information about the raid on the research station, she had to endure a brief meeting with Euclides Peixoto, who presented her with a list of casualties and watched her study it with a sly and eager shine in his gaze, no doubt hoping to suck up any morsels of grief.

There were three people missing, including Alder, and fifteen confirmed dead—names she knew, men and women she had recruited and trained, who had accepted Alder's leadership without question after she had been forced to leave Earth, who had continued to do excellent and important work. Euclides said that the survivors would be held at an army camp in Tierra del Fuego until his family had decided what to do with them.

"Frankly, this is something of an embarrassment to us. A black eye, politically. So they'll probably have to sit in that camp until things are calmer and we can see a way forward. It might take some time. You should be prepared for that," Euclides said. "Oh, and I have been asked to ask you to forget about any legal maneuvers. It will only embarrass the family further. If you do, there will be blowback. And if that doesn't hurt you, it will certainly damage your people."

"In the end, 'my people' were working for the family. And if the family had protected them to begin with, it wouldn't be in this embarrassing position now."

"They were breaking the law. And the family can hardly condone that, can it?"

Euclides Peixoto, dressed in a tailored version of the blue tunic and trousers of the Air Defence Force, was standing in front of the floor-to-ceiling window of his office, his back to the view of the tree-clad slopes of the park and the river that cut through it. He was a handsome man mantled with the languid arrogance of someone who had never needed to exert himself to get what he wanted, vain and foolish but possessed of a weaselly cunning and proven to be a survivor blessed with no small amount of luck.

Before the war, Euclides had fallen in with the faction in his family that had opposed the attempts by the green saint Oscar Finnegan Ramos, Sri's mentor, Euclides's great-uncle, to promote peace and reconciliation with the Outers. Euclides had tried to use Sri in a plot to depose Oscar, but she had realised that she would almost certainly be killed afterward and had made her own move, killing the green saint, escaping from Earth, giving herself up to Arvam Peixoto. But now Arvam was dead, and Sri was once again at the mercy of Euclides. He couldn't punish her for Oscar's death because of his complicity in the wretched and sordid plot, but he never missed an opportunity to remind her of how much he enjoyed having power over her.

When she suggested that the scientists and technicians from the Antarctic facility could be brought out to Saturn, where they would be of immeasurable help in sorting through the treasure trove of the Library of the Commons, he said that she wasn't the only person doing research in that area, and besides, as he was sure she knew, the security of her position had been undermined by the recent unfortunate events in Antarctica.

"No point going to the trouble of shipping people all the way out here, only to send them straight back if you're recalled," he said, and changed the subject, stepping daintily across the room to a display case containing a pressure-suit chestplate decorated with an intricate painting. "It's one of Munk's *Seven Transformations of the Ring System*. The last in the series. You know him? Munk? He was one of the big artists out here, before the war."

"I don't know much about art," Sri said.

"Me neither. But this fellow Munk, I'd say he did a pretty good job on this. You'll never guess who presented this to me. An old friend of yours and mine from way back when."

"Loc Ifrahim."

"Either that's a good guess, or you know something I didn't know you knew."

"It was a reasoned deduction. We have few people in common, and Mr. Ifrahim is the only one who has ready access to looted works of art. I assume he is trying to ingratiate himself."

186

"I have to admit that he's been useful now and again. The fellow that owned this used to be the military commander over on Camelot, Mimas. Colonel Faustino Malarte. Remember him? He was tangled up in a scandal involving smuggling stuff like this and selling it back home."

"I'm not interested in politics."

"I know. You don't care about things that are important to other people; you only care about your work. That isn't a criticism, by the way. In fact, it's the one thing I like about you. It means I can talk to you about politics because I know you won't make any use of what I let slip. Anyhow, good old Malarte, he was the subject of an intensive investigation. Our friend Loc Ifrahim was part of it—he started it up in fact, although he did it in such a sly way that most people didn't notice. So Malarte was duly investigated and found guilty of abuse of his office. And then, while he was waiting to be sent back to Earth in disgrace, he was murdered by a couple of Outers. You really don't know any of this? I guess not. Well, it's a good story," Euclides said. "One of the killers was an associate of the member of Camelot's senate who'd been helping Malarte get hold of the stuff he was smuggling to Earth. The other was Malarte's mistress. Who'd started sleeping with him to save a couple of members of her family from prison, but they went to prison anyway. Anyhow, Malarte was in so much trouble that when they killed him, they did him a favour—saved him the embarrassment of a court-martial and the firing squad. Which I found kind of annoying, to be frank, since he was a scion of the Pessanha family, and we Peixotos don't agree with them about all kinds of things. A juicy court-martial would have been a nice black eye for them. Instead, they got a martyr. But that wasn't why I had the killers executed. It was because we can't have Outers killing our people, even if those happen to be liars and rapists and crooks."

"I suppose you are trying to make some point with this sordid little tale," Sri said.

"I'm coming to it," Euclides said. "This chestplate was one of the choicest items looted by Malarte. Loc Ifrahim liberated it, and he presented it to me. Naturally, I had it checked out. And you know what? Turns out it's a fake. See, Malarte's mistress, she was a pupil of Munk's. So either the Outers were swindling Malarte, selling him fakes, or Loc Ifrahim had the mistress cook up a fake in exchange for giving her the opportunity to get her revenge. Malarte was killed in the storage vault where he was keeping his loot before it was shipped out. The woman got hold of the code for its lock, and she and her accomplice ambushed him there. The investigation concluded that she had stolen the code, but I wouldn't put it past Loc Ifrahim to have slipped it to her. The sly son of a bitch gets rid of Malarte, he gets hold of a very valuable work of art, *and* he makes it look like he did me a personal favour. And aside from all that, he swung it so his very close friend Captain Neves was made chief of security over in Camelot. That Ifrahim, he's a player. But don't worry, I'm keeping a very close eye on him. One of these days he'll slip, and I'll be there. Ready to present him with his own head."

Sri was only mildly appalled by Euclides's story. She'd long ago become habituated to the intrigue, rivalry, and criminal behaviour amongst the senior members of the TPA. And while diplomats, civil servants, contractors, and senior officers of the armed forces systematically looted the cities and settlements of the Saturn System, Euclides Peixoto strutted and bullied like the worst kind of prison commandant.

Greater Brazil had played a major role in winning the Quiet War, but it had not been magnanimous in victory or charitable to those it had defeated. Cities whose governments had rolled over before the war and remained neutral still retained a degree of independence, but their citizens could not travel anywhere without first applying for permission that was hardly ever granted, they were constantly monitored and checked, access to the nets was limited, meetings of more than five people were banned, and so on and so forth. The situation was even worse on Dione, where almost all the Outers were by now penned in the prison camp of the so-called New City. Most of their possessions had been confiscated, they endured countless random inspections and interviews, and food and water and other essential supplies were strictly rationed. According to Euclides Peixoto, it was the most effective way of keeping them under control, but it was a constant source of friction between his administration and the governments of the free cities, and a pointless waste of the Outers' expertise and skills.

And the political climate was growing ever more hostile to the Outers. Plans were being drawn up to ship so-called high-risk prisoners, including surviving members of Paris's government, to a special camp on the Moon, and a full-scale test of a so-called zero-growth initiative had just been implemented in the New City, where everyone above the age of twelve had been injected with contraceptive implants. The radical green faction in Greater Brazil's government believed it was not enough to police and control the Outers: they should also be prevented from having children. There would be no death camps or mass executions, merely a slow, humanely controlled dwindling until the last genetically modified human being died and the antievolutionary threat posed by the Outers was ended forever. It would take at least a century, but it was vitally important for the survival of the human race.

If Greater Brazil had defeated the Outers by itself, then the zero-growth initiative might already have been rolled out on all the other inhabited moons of the Saturn and Jupiter systems. But the European Union had moral objections to an enforced mass-sterilisation programme, and the Pacific Community had not only entered into a working partnership with the population of Iapetus but was also shipping in colonists from Earth, expanding its base on Phoebe, and threatening to annex and settle several of the smaller moons whose few inhabitants had been forcibly removed after the war.

Disagreement between the three members of the TPA over the direction and aims of the occupation had developed into a kind of Cold War standoff, prickling with mistrust and paranoia. And so, despite the increasing power of the radical greens, Greater Brazil wasn't yet willing to give up exploitation of the Outers' scientific and technological knowledge; at least, not while the European Union and the Pacific Community were still plundering it and there was the chance that they might stumble on a fragment of exotic physics, mathematics, or genetic engineering that would become the cornerstone of a new technology as world changing as aeroplanes or antibiotics. Radical green legislation meant that scientific research in Greater Brazil was now licensed and controlled by a new and fanatically fierce regulatory body, but work on the Moon and in the Outer System remained unfettered because it was deemed necessary for state security. Nevertheless, even though Sri and her assistants were able to explore Avernus's gardens, reverse-engineer Outer biotechnology, and mine the great archives of the Library of the Commons with only minimal interference from review boards and oversight committees, she was driven by an increasing sense of urgency, of time running out.

By now, Sri believed that she had a firm grasp of the principles that underpinned the design of the exotic gardens created by Avernus. She had interviewed many people who had known the gene wizard or had worked with her, and although attempts to construct an expert AI simulation had so far proved disappointing she had not yet given up on the idea. More data was needed, and further integration of existing data. Sri was developing algorithms that mapped the possibilities of what she called "biological information space" and had learned a great deal about the way in which Avernus's many and varied gardens maintained homeostasis—some had been cycling through a variety of states without ever exhibiting population crashes or extinctions for fifty years or more. She had also devised many new wrinkles in the design, function, and propagation of vacuum organisms, and used them to create strains that exhibited pseudosexual recombination of their basic instructions and stochastic inheritance of varieties of the pseudoribosomes that transcribed instructions and the pseudomitochondria that underpinned their metabolic functions: features that allowed variation between individuals, and therefore the potential for evolution by Darwinian selection.

And in addition to all of this, her most recent row with Berry had stimulated a new interest in the development of the human brain and the fundamental neurological mechanisms that generated and regulated emotion. It proved to be a useful distraction from her anxiety about Alder, and in her usual fashion when dealing with a field in which she had only a little basic knowledge, Sri read widely and digested and summarised what was known and made lists of important questions that had not yet been answered. Discounting Freudian fairy tales and dubious socio-anthropological comparisons with young, subdominant male chimpanzees, there seemed to be a consensus that adolescent misbehaviour—tantrums and sulks, inchoate rages, all the rest—was caused by changes in the brain during its final maturation at puberty. The effects of this rewiring were more pronounced in boys than girls because the changes were not only driven by huge doses of testosterone surging through the bloodstream, but were also compressed into a shorter time frame, causing a radical disconnection between emotional states and higher consciousness.

At bottom, Sri thought, it was one of the side effects of the extremely conservative nature of brain evolution. Despite drastic modifications of body form, all vertebrates possessed the same basic structures—forebrain, midbrain, hindbrain—that carried out the same basic functions. Thus, although the neocortex had massively ballooned in mammals (and most especially in human beings), it was underpinned by a limbic system similar to those possessed by reptiles, amphibians, and fish. And it was in the limbic system that mechanisms regulating basic emotions such as joy, distress, anger, fear, surprise, and disgust were located.

These emotions, and the typical facial expressions associated with them, were universally recognised by every human culture. They were hardwired into the brain, they were often expressed within a few milliseconds of being triggered, and they were triggered via stimulation of the sensory thalamus without intervention of higher functions in the neocortex, so that people could be catapulted into states of fear or anger without first making a conscious, reasoned analysis of the trigger. In evolutionary terms this short circuit was a survival technique that made perfect sense. If a lion jumped out at you, you had to start running at once; if you paused to think about whether or not you needed to run, you'd be killed and eaten. But because people no longer lived in the African savannah, many of the situations that triggered basic emotions had nothing to do with immediate survival, which meant that many human cultures and individuals exhibited heightened responses to situations that did not require heightened responses. And this was most pronounced in adolescent males—they went from zero to a hundred with no stages in between, and there was no point trying to reason with them because their reactions did not proceed from reason: conscious thought only became involved afterward, producing *post hoc* justifications for irrational behaviour.

A second set of universal emotions—the blushings of love, guilt, shame, and embarrassment; the pricking thorns of pride, envy, and jealousy; the pleasurable feeling of acceptance by others that the Japanese called *amae*—were associated with higher cortical functions and took longer to build up and longer to die away than basic emotions. Some, like jealousy or shame, were shared by other primates, or even by other mammals. Others, like envy or guilt, appeared to be unique to human beings. There was much speculation about instances where primates or other mammals seemed to exhibit the latter emotions, but as far as Sri was concerned no one had ever produced any unimpeachable evidence. And all were fundamentally social, associated with interaction with peers rather than environmental stimuli, and because they took more time to develop than basic emotions, they were more amenable to the general background state or coloration of the brain—to mood—and could be altered by learned experience. Basic emotions like the fright/flight reflex differed from culture to culture by only a small degree, but higher cognitive emotions showed a great deal of variation.

So if you were going to make human beings more rational, Sri thought, you would have to suppress basic emotions, perhaps by making them harder to trigger, and enhance emotions associated with higher cognitive functions. Of these, *amae* was the most interesting. Even though there was no word for it in Portuguese, English, or any of the other major Western languages, it was definitely universal. Sri knew it as the feeling she had after making a successful presentation to her peers. Approval, belonging, being valued.

Evolutionary psychology provided a pat explanation: *amae* had been selected in hominids struggling to survive on the African plains because it was part of the social glue that bound together individuals in a tribe, and so made the tribe stronger, less prone to divisive squabbles, more prone to cooperation and swift agreement. But Sri wasn't interested in Just-so stories, however plausible. She was interested in utility. And she was especially interested in evidence that *amae* appeared to alter the threshold for triggering basic emotions, suppressing those that, while useful in preserving the life of the individual, were potentially destructive to group cohesion. If she could find some way of triggering or inducing *amae*, she thought, she could make Berry feel that he was part of something, that he was wanted, cared for, appreciated, then perhaps he would become less prone to tantrums and sulks. He could find it in himself to love her again.

Outers had done much useful work on *amae*, for it was a vital part of their various attempts to create scientific Utopias, and Sri had several interesting discussions about it with one of the leading researchers, Umm Said, in the prison camp of the New City.

Built by the Brazilian occupying force twenty kilometres north of Paris, Dione, the New City was a living demonstration of the benefits of cooperation, mutualism, and communal action that *amae* promoted and rewarded. Although the narrow wedge of its tent was jammed edge to edge with hopelessly overcrowded and shoddily constructed apartment blocks, it was by no means a slum. Tiny gardens flourished everywhere. Platforms had been cantilevered from the sides of the apartment blocks and fibrous netting spread over the rest of the walls, transforming utilitarian structures with spills and terraces of crop plants and herbs. Playgrounds, little cafés, and other social spaces had been built on the roofs, and all the roofs were linked by slides and ziplines. As with public areas, so with private spaces. Although Umm Said lived with her partner and their four children in a single small room, it was clean and bright and exceedingly neat. Their scant possessions were stowed in a couple of chests or hung from pegs, bamboo-fibre mats covered the floors, and cushions were set around a low table, the only piece of furniture—the family slept on thin mattresses that they unrolled every night.

A tall elegant black-skinned woman, Umm Said had a quick, sharp mind, and like all Outers was generous and unstinting when it came to sharing her ideas. She and Sri sipped green tea, nibbled sushi prepared from kelp and rice and fermented beans, or little dumplings or rolls fried on a tiny hotplate, and spent hours discussing higher emotional states.

According to Umm Said, the Outers' predisposition to behaviour that fostered feelings of *amae* was encouraged by exposure to all kinds of environmental cues, from city planning to the small change of social interaction, and was reinforced by positive feedback. Individuals whose behaviour enhanced the *amae* of others were also more receptive to cues that boosted their own *amae*. Outers also possessed a culturally specific emotion, wanderjahr, that was expressed most strongly in their teens and twenties, a yearning restlessness that drove them to leave home and travel from moon to moon. Supporting themselves with menial jobs, they discovered what excited and engaged them, experienced every variation of Outer culture, and learned how to get along with every kind of person. And because this taught them to be open-minded and tolerant, and made them feel that they belonged not to any single social subgroup or city but to the entire Outer System, they were predisposed to adopt *amae* as their primary or default emotional state.

Sri, a habitual contrarian, pointed out that the flip side of an emotion that promoted cohesion of a tribe or cohort was a heightened sensitivity to signals and signs denoting difference and otherness. In stressful situations, this sensitivity could direct hostility and intolerance toward outsiders, and the positive feedback of peer approval would amplify individual attacks into mob behaviour.

Umm Said said that this idea was very familiar to Outers. "That's why we have a system of carefully calibrated checks and balances. A kind of hydraulic mechanism that diverts collective emotion into secondary channels before it can build up into an unstoppable flood."

"It didn't work too well in Paris. It was under mob rule at the beginning of the war. Your 'hydraulic mechanism' was overtopped."

"That's because our mayor dismantled too many of the usual checks and balances. Of course, he was just one generation removed from Earth," Umm Said said. "His father was a diplomat from the European Union who made his home here."

"So Marisa Bassi was an outsider who lacked the ant pong of the mob. A bad seed who didn't understand the importance of *amae*."

"Perhaps he understood it too well, and used it for his own ends," Umm Said said. "The point has been extensively discussed, as you might imagine. Unfortunately, he was killed during the battle for Paris, so we'll never know the truth."

"His body was never found, and I've heard claims that he didn't die after all. That he is leading the deadenders—what you call the resistance," Sri said.

"Their methods are certainly as futile as Marisa Bassi's. And far less effective than the collective practice of nonviolent protest."

"I don't see any evidence that one is any better than the other," Sri said. "You've tried every kind of nonviolent tactic, from boycotts and sit-ins to hunger strikes. And yet here you all are, in this prison camp."

"Persuasion through enlightened discussion is also a form of nonviolent resistance," Umm Said said, and with a steady hand refilled Sri's bowl with green tea.

By now Sri was a long way from her original goal of finding a way to choke off Berry's tantrums and anxieties. The work had become an obsession, an end in itself, as her work so often did. She believed that Umm Said was wrong. That being born and raised as an Outer wasn't the only way to acquire a strong propensity toward *amae*; that it might be possible to reengineer the brain to make it less prone to behaviour driven by the basic emotions of the limbic system. If an emotion could be culturally acquired or reinforced, then the reentrant paths that process engraved within the brain could be mapped. And if they could be mapped, they could be synthesised.

She wrote a speculative paper, presented some of her work via avatar at various meetings of behavioural psychologists and neuroscientists in Greater Brazil, and received some encouraging feedback. The research had taken up much of her time since the attack on the Antarctic research facility, but she justified it to the oversight committees by talking up the insights gained into Outer behaviour and social control, and speculating about practical applications such as crowd control and media manipulation. She'd spent years pandering to factions within the Peixoto family, and knew exactly how to tickle the self-interest of civil servants and politicians.

In the middle of this, one hundred and sixty-three days after Alder disappeared, one of Sri's data miners flagged an anodyne comment on one of the science boards. *I hope you will continue to enlighten us with your excellent and uplifting work.* It was one of the blind messages that she and Alder had arranged to use in case of an emergency. It meant that he was alive and safe.

Sri spent the rest of the day floating on air. Alder had not been killed when the research facility had been raided. She did not know where he was, who he was with, or what he planned to do, but she knew that he was alive, that he had at last escaped from Antarctica, and he felt safe enough to have sent the message. She knew better than to attempt to send a reply or post an acknowledgement that she had received and understood his message. When he was ready, he would contact her again. He was brave and intelligent and capable. He would find a way that would allow him to emerge from hiding without being arrested. He would find a way to begin to rebuild his power base.

Meanwhile, Berry moved from Paris to Camelot, Mimas, and started up another club, this time in partnership with a crew of young Outers. It seemed that Outers who had grown up after the war and could no longer go on wanderjahrs because of the travel restrictions imposed by the TPA were growing ever more restless, like caged birds unable to begin their migration at the appropriate season. Their frustration was expressed in escalating social turmoil, from minor acts of vandalism and refusal to perform civic duties to increased use of psychotropics and a spew of antiestablishment artworks and texts. Some attempted to justify their rebellious attitude by cobbling together a nihilist philosophy based on twentieth-century Situationism and several flavours of anarchy; Berry and his new friends ran a club in Camelot's free zone, Club Blank, where the movers and shakers of this movement congregated and held court. They believed in the absolute extinction of hierarchy, in judging everything by its context rather than by categorical principles, and in metaphorical analysis of everything, from language to cultural identity, using an array of invented mathematical and pedagogical languages. There was a playful, pranksterish aspect to all this. If everything floated free, valued only for its utility within whichever context it happened to occupy, nothing much mattered: everything, including the movement itself, was a kind of elaborate in-joke. But Berry took it very seriously indeed, and he believed that the club's rituals—the pounding tribal rhythms of its music and the wild freestyle dancing of its denizens, its elaborate lightshows, the psychotropics that boosted serotonin production and produced analogues of the so-called oceanic feeling in which the self dissolved into its environment—were far more than a way of escaping the mundane world for a little while. No, as far as he was concerned, they were a religious experience: a true transformative ecstasy that brought you closer to God.

Sri had a violent falling-out with Berry after she suggested that she could help him to obtain the same emotional state by using forced MRI feedback, tailored viruses, and other carefully controlled protocols to manipulate the reentrant pathways of the brain. She told him that it would help him to control his mood swings; he said that she was trying to turn him into a docile zombie. They had a violent, lacerating argument, and Berry was also using a formidable battery of psychotropics by then. For a little while, he was utterly lost to her.

Sri worked. It was what she did. It was what she was. And then, a little over a year after the raid on the Antarctic facility, still no word from Alder apart from that one message, a sympathetic officer in the Titan base told her that one of Avernus's spiderholes had been found.

Sri quit Dione for Titan the same day. She didn't bother to ask permission of Euclides Peixoto or the military transport office. She appropriated a shuttle, powered straight out to Titan, and landed at the Brazilian base outside Tank Town, on the shore of the Lunine Sea. Four days later she was aboard a dirigible, approaching the northern edge of Xanadu, the continent-sized province that spanned Titan's equator.

The rough, rugged landscape was similar to the foothills of the Himalayas—rumpled ranges of hills cut by tectonic faulting and braided river channels—and like the Himalayas it had been created by collision between two land masses, although on Titan these floated on an underground ocean of ammonia-rich water rather than on partially molten rock. Avernus's hiding place was at the edge of a sinuous valley that wound between ranges of craggy hills. Before tectonic activity had uplifted the area, it had been part of a river system carved by flash floods of liquid methane and ethane during the infrequent but violent rainstorms at Titan's equator. Now it was a dry playa floored with hydrocarbon sand and bounded by cliffs of ammonia-water ice frozen hard as rock and fretted with canyons and gullies that originated in alcoves in the clifftops and ran downslope, ending in triangular fans of debris.

Sri insisted on walking around by herself. She wanted to get an idea of the place where Avernus had been hiding. She wanted to ground herself in its reality.

Tall cliffs loomed above her, carved with steep gullies so numerous that the fans of debris at their feet had merged into a continuous smooth apron that sloped down to a broad valley floor cut by sinuous channels and silted with black hydrocarbon sand. Much of the sand had drifted into low longitudinal dunes at right angles to the cliffs; the dirigible squatted like a giant quilted manta ray above one of these dunes, quivering against its tethers in a stiff breeze. Beyond it, on the far side of the valley, ripsaw hills rose into the omnipresent orange haze.

Black grit crunched like popcorn under the treads of Sri's insulated boots as she trudged up a gentle slope of consolidated debris toward the cliffs. She had grown used to living as light as a bird on Dione: Titan's pull of 0.2 g made her feel that her bones had turned to stone and a vengeful old woman had clamped herself onto her back. She was badly out of breath and sweating hard inside her pressure suit when she reached the edge of an area about the size of a soccer field that had been graded flat, stretching in front of the overhang where Avernus's little plane was garaged.

The original search party had stripped away the fullerene dropcloth that had camouflaged it. It was bright red, with a big propeller at its nose and stubby wings and a closed cockpit. It would not have seemed out of place on Earth.

Sri had seen it once before, passing above her when she'd been lying on her back on a ridge inside a volcanic caldera, immobilised by a tangle of threads fired by one of Avernus's creatures. She'd resolved then and there that she would never stop searching for Avernus, and although she was at the threshold of one of the gene wizard's hiding places she did not feel any triumph or excitement. After more than four years, her prey was as elusive and enigmatic as ever.

She climbed a steep path at the edge of a gully, hauling herself up roughly carved steps, muscles burning, pulse pounding, stopping every couple of minutes to get her breath. Near the top of the cliff, the path turned and dipped into a channel so narrow that the shoulders of her pressure suit brushed its smooth walls as she descended to a standard airlock. She cycled through and stepped out onto the top of a flight of steps fitted into a hollow, helical space like the inside of a nautilus shell. Light the warm colour of sunlight on Earth shone through a screen that, fretted with a random pattern of circles and ovals, stretched from top to bottom of the space. A little stream followed the sweep of the stairs, trickling between plantings of vegetables and herbs, down to a lawn of real grass and a little orchard of gnarled and dwarfed fruit trees.

Sri took off her helmet and closed her eyes and breathed in the cool air, the mingled odours of damp earth and green, growing plants, then walked down the broad curve of the staircase. A hammock was slung between two apple trees. One niche under the staircase contained a shower and a toilet; another an industrial foodmaker. Apparently, Avernus had been living on CHON food supplemented by whatever she could grow in her little garden. Power came from wind turbines hidden in a channel out on the surface and thermogenerators that tapped into the residual heat deep under the ice. Sri tried to imagine living alone in this burrow, buried under Titan's eternal ice, no one else within two thousand kilometres, nothing but her own thoughts for company. Growing vegetables. Maintaining the garden's simple life-support systems. Occasionally hiking out along the valley, or amongst the hills beyond the gullied clifftops.

It was like trying to think herself inside the daily habits of a ghost. She saw in her mind's eye the old woman turning away from her, walking off across a bleak landscape, dwindling into obscurity.

After examining everything in the habitat, Sri went back outside and clambered down the path and crossed the hillocky dunes to the dirigible. The lieutenant who'd led the search party steered the craft two kilometres down the valley, to the place where Avernus had parked her ship: an insulated landing pad set amongst a field of huge ice boulders on a lenticulate island raised above the black dunes that combed the valley floor.

The pad had been spotted by one of Sri's autonomous drones, and a high-resolution deep-radar survey of the surrounding area had revealed Avernus's little habitat. The shape and size of the camouflage shroud recovered nearby suggested that the ship had been one of the aeroshells used by Outers before the war to shuttle people and goods through Titan's atmosphere. No one knew when the ship had departed, or on what course. There was no radar or traffic control on Titan, the ship had most likely been stealthed, and after it had quit the moon it had probably flown a minimal free-energy trajectory requiring only brief burns of its motor.

Sri was convinced that Avernus was no longer in the Saturn System. Why would she risk discovery by moving from one moon to another? No, she must have rendezvoused with a ship that had taken her further out. Perhaps to Neptune. There were reports of increasing activity amongst Neptune's moons. Euclides Peixoto was making noises about sending a punitive expedition; there were rumours that the Pacific Community were in clandestine contact with rebel Outers.

The dirigible drifted low and fired off its anchors. Sri climbed down and walked around the landing platform. The house-sized boulders had been worn smooth as eggs by wind-blown hydrocarbon sand. Some stood on eroded pedestals. A garden of gigantic sculptures set on rippled black sand.

She looked for but failed to find any bootprints—no doubt the constant wind had smoothed them away—and walked out from beneath the dirigible's shadow and climbed to the prow of the island. A ladder of black dunes caught between gullied cliffs stretched away into orange haze. Wind seethed like static as it blew past the bowl of her pressure suit's helmet. Sri had resolved to never stop searching for Avernus, had dreamed of persuading her to work with her in a long and fruitful collaboration, but the thought of trying to follow the gene wizard into the outer dark at the edge of the Solar System filled her with a weary dismay.

Enough, she thought. She would put Gunter Lasky to the question—she was certain that the old pirate had known about this hiding place all along—and she would recommend that Tank Town should be shut down as soon as possible. And then she would abandon the chase. She had details of Avernus's gardens, interviews with her associates, a vast integrated database of her work. Enough. It was time to move on. Time to make use of what she knew.

She had been thinking about the phenotype jungle on Janus recently. There was a political problem with the little co-orbital moon right now. The Pacific Union had earmarked it as one of the places it wanted to secure by set-tling it with hardy pioneers, had made it clear that it would proceed without the approval of Greater Brazil and the European Community. Euclides Peixoto was furious about it; when Sri had last met with him, he'd spent half the time ranting about PacCom's recklessness. All right. She could suggest that he could preempt PacCom's plans by allowing her to move her labora-tory there. She would live in the phenotype jungle to begin with, and build a garden of her own. It was time she made something of everything she had learned, and she could promise to make Euclides rich by giving him a majority share in her discoveries. . . .

On the adamantine ice, under Titan's orange sky, Professor Doctor Sri Hong-Owen once again began to map out her future.

PART FOUR
REBEL REBEL

I

Five years into his sentence for first-degree murder, Felice Gottschalk was working as a trusty—a prisoner who guarded other prisoners. Before the war, ordinary criminals who had committed crimes of varying degrees of violence because of flaws or glitches in their brain chemistry would have been subjected to a battery of remedial therapies and interventions; now, they supervised and controlled hundreds of nonviolent protesters, refuseniks, former politicians, and leaders of the peace and reconciliation movement, all of them crammed into the reeking tunnels of the maximum-security prison built by the Europeans outside Xamba, Rhea. Apart from dealing with suicides and the occasional sit-down protest, the work wasn't difficult. Escape was impossible: all prisoners had a tiny capsule injected into their third cervical vertebra that not only continuously transmitted their location but also grew pseudo-axonal fibres that knitted into their dorsal root ganglion and induced paralysing migraines and muscular spasms if they took so much as one step outside the prison boundary. As for the daily routines of prison life, the prisoners had established a thoroughly democratic cooperative that reflected in miniature the life of the city before the war. Most refused out of principle to collaborate with their captors by working in the manufactories, farms, or vacuum-organism fields, but they were by no means idle. Crews of volunteers cleaned the dormitories and common spaces, and maintained the life-support systems. Groups wrote and staged operas, choral works, and theatrical events; there were madrasas and discussion groups about every kind of scientific and artistic discipline, endless debates about the inexhaustible topics of ethics and morality.

Felice Gottschalk made no friends, and because he had committed the rare and repugnant crime of murder he was mostly left alone. He didn't participate in the petty cruelties that his fellow trusties inflicted on the prisoners, but he did nothing to prevent them, either. And while many wasted hours in speculating about what they would do when they were released from prison—complex plans of revenge, fantasies about the fortunes that could be earned by working as civil police for the Three Powers Authority, or the paradises that might be constructed in one of the many abandoned oases and habitats that the TPA would surely give them to reward their cooperation—

as far as Felice Gottschalk was concerned, daydreams about the future had ended when his mission to find Zi Lei had gone so badly wrong. It had been a very comprehensive failure, and now he must atone for it. For the death of his brother, yes, and for his presumption, and his folly, and the grievous sins of selfishness and pride.

He worked day shifts one week; night shifts the next. This was the pattern of his life, turn and turn about, for five years. And then one day he was summoned to the administration block and told that he could either stay in Xamba and continue to work as a trusty for the rest of his life, or volunteer to go to the Moon, Earth's moon, and work in a new, experimental prison facility built by the European government and its allies in Brazil, the Peixoto and Nabuco families. And after ten years, he would be granted his freedom, and he could become a citizen of the European Union.

He asked the army captain where he could go after he'd been freed; the woman shrugged and said anywhere he chose.

"Could I go to Earth?"

"If you think you could survive it, why not?"

For the first time since he had been arrested, Felice Gottschalk felt a faint spark of hope. He had always dreamed of breathing the air of Earth, of walking under her blue skies, seeing with his own eyes her forests and oceans. Surely he would not have been offered this chance unless he deserved it. His murdered brother, Dave #27, had once told him that goodness could spring from evil, just as beautiful flowers could grow from filth. He had already spent five years attempting to atone for his wickedness. Perhaps in ten years more he might complete his penance and be absolved, and set out on a new life. Perhaps he could find some way of rededicating himself to the service of God and Gaia.

So he chose, and went to the Moon.

He travelled with three other trusties and several dozen prisoners selected by the Europeans: deposed representatives from Xamba's Senate, members of the former government of Baghdad, Enceladus, who had fled to Xamba at the outbreak of the war, and selected leaders of the nonviolent protests. Trusties and prisoners slept out the voyage in hibernation coffins stacked in the hold of a freighter, and after the freighter achieved orbit around Earth they were transferred to a shuttle and flown onward to the Moon, and the prison, where they were revived.

Felice Gottschalk woke in the prison clinic. He was weak and confused and his entire skin was on fire. It took him a little while to understand that he had suffered a violent and atypical adverse reaction during revival. That he had almost died. The next day, when he was more lucid, the medical technician, a small, birdlike old woman with glossy red hair cut in a kind of helmet that framed her pale face, and a brisk but kindly manner, told him the rest of the bad news: he was suffering from the early stages of an autoimmune disease that somewhat resembled systemic lupus.

"Your immune system is attacking the connective tissue in your joints and lungs, and also in your skin," she said. "Before you shipped out, did you ever suffer from skin rashes?"

"Everyone in the prison had some kind of skin problem. The air wasn't very clean, and we mostly ate CHON food."

"You are suffering from a very bad reaction right now, covering about eighty percent of your body. I've dosed you with steroids to reduce the inflammation. You also have a small reduction in your lung capacity due to scarring caused by minor bouts of inflammation. That will grow worse, over time. You will find it harder to breathe, and that will affect your heart because your blood will not be properly oxygenated and so your heart will have to pump harder to keep you alive. And you have incipient leukemia, because your immune system is beginning to attack the cells in your bone marrow that create new blood corpuscles—the cells that carry oxygen. I can treat that with whole-blood transfusions. I may even be able to cure it with injections of donated blood marrow, if I can find a volunteer whose tissue type matches yours. But that won't be easy," the medical technician said, looking straight at Felice Gottschalk. "You see, I ran your DNA through a sequencer and I discovered some novel tweaks."

The spy tried to sit up but he was very weak—the gravity was much stronger than Rhea's—and the impulse to kill the old woman quickly passed. He lay back, blood thumping in his skull, and asked her what she was going to do.

"If you think I'm going to betray you to the people who run this place, think again. As far as I am concerned we're all in this together. Even trusties. Even trusties who have been tweaked in a number of unusual ways. Muscle strands with very fast contraction times, for instance, and with unusually strong fibrils. Motor nerves that fire more quickly than the norm. Rod cells in the retina that detect infrared and near-ultraviolet light. And so on and so forth. I wonder, did the person who fixed you up want you to be a soldier?"

He looked away from her shrewd gaze.

"There are stories that the Ghosts were stretching the limits of human gene engineering, before the war," she said.

"I had an unusual childhood, but I am not a Ghost."

"You don't have to tell me anything if you don't want to. I won't pry. But anything you do tell me may help your treatment," the old woman said, and explained that she couldn't cure him because she didn't have access to the necessary retroviral treatments. He could throw himself on the mercy of the Europeans and Brazilians who ran the prison, but if they agreed to treat him, routine genome scans would flag his tweaks and he would be exposed.

"I can relieve the symptoms with blood transfusions and high doses of steroids and other treatments. Light therapy may sometimes be helpful, for instance. But I cannot do anything about the underlying cause of the symptoms, and they will grow worse, and more complicated, in time."

The spy said, "If there's no chance of a cure . . ."

"You want to know if it will kill you. Yes, I'm afraid it will. But not immediately."

"How much time do I have?"

"The truth is, I don't know," the old woman said. "The genes responsible for your condition are multilocus and multivariant, and they are triggered by a wide variety of environmental cues. Put simply, your condition is the result of a complicated and unpredictable interaction between your genetic make-up and your environment. Perhaps the people who tweaked you didn't know about it. Or perhaps they did, but thought it an unlikely side effect of the changes they needed to make. In any case, although it has some similarities to lupus, it has a different etiology, and its progress will be different, too. All I can say for certain is that you've been suffering from it for some time, and hibernation, or revival from hibernation, has definitely made it worse."

"Will I have ten years?"

"You want to know if you will live long enough to work out your sentence."

"I want to know the truth."

"It isn't likely, no. I'm sorry."

It hurt to laugh. Something sharp and heavy shifting in his lungs. The inflamed skin of his face cracking in a hundred paper cuts. Tears swelling in his eyes, stinging as they rolled down his cheeks—even tears hurt. But the laughter let out something that had been squatting inside him for a long time. He could feel it go.

"I thought I was being punished for daring to think that I was something I was not," he told the old woman. "But it wasn't that. It wasn't God, or fate. It was something far simpler. It was the people who made me—they didn't do their job properly."

2

Whenever it was her turn to put the twins to bed, Macy Minnot turned down the light in their sleeping niche to a starlight glow and told them a story about Earth. She had discovered that she was pretty good at storytelling; it came naturally to her, as easy as falling off a log. In fact, that was how she'd started off one of the bedtime stories—one of the stories about her fictional version of her own self.

"I was sitting on a log in a clearing in the woods, eating my lunch, and I fell off," she told the twins. Han and Hannah, six years old, blond head by blond head, sharing the same solemn, sleepy gaze. "Why? Because I'd seen a flash in the air and I toppled over backward as an arrow cut the air over my head and buried itself in a pine tree. The arrow was fletched with black feathers, and resin was running out of the bark around its shaft. It looked like the tree was bleeding. . . ."

Of course, it took longer than that to tell, because Macy had to explain just about everything. Han and Hannah knew what pine trees were, they'd helped Macy plant force-grown saplings in the habitat's parkland, but they'd never seen a fully grown one. And although they knew about woods in principle, they had a lot of trouble picturing a tree-filled park so big that you could walk through it for a day and not reach the end. And as for bows and arrows . . . But that was part of the fun, using the stories to teach them about life on the world that Macy had come from; where everyone had come from, once upon a time in the long ago.

Newt had his own ideas about what made for a good story, mostly involving pirates and breathless adventures in caverns under the surfaces of moons, or giant balloon cities sailing the azure ocean of Neptune's atmosphere. Strings of colourful scenes with no shape and no real ending. One damn thing after another.

"What you need to do," Macy said, "is find a few good characters and see where they take you. The story comes out of who they are and what they want, and the problems they have to overcome to get it. It isn't just a bunch of stuff that happens to them."

"The kids like my stories a lot, thanks very much," Newt said.

How she loved the way his smile crimped one corner of his mouth and his eyes narrowed in insouciant challenge. Loved it even when it exasperated her. Newt could take any amount of criticism because he didn't take any of it seriously.

Macy said, "My mother used to tell me stories from the Bible—the original Christian version. There are some good ones in the Old Testament. You should check it out."

"I already did," Newt said. "After you told me about it the first time. There are some good ones, all right, but most are pretty violent."

"Your pirate stories always end in a fight."

"They aren't real fights, and the pirates aren't real pirates. No one gets killed, like the giant soldier this kid knocks down with a pebble. Or the fellow who has his head cut off by two women out for revenge. I read that, and I thought, Macy's mother told her about stuff like this when she was little? Everyone trying to conquer everyone else, slaughtering their enemies or turning them into slaves? No wonder she turned out so tough."

"Life on Earth is tough. Red in tooth and claw."

"You ever miss her? Your mother? You hardly ever talk about her, so I can't help wondering."

"I hardly ever think of her. Does that make me a bad person?"

Newt shrugged.

"She wasn't really there for me, at the end," Macy said. "Before I ran away. She'd become very holy, spending eighteen hours a day immersed in virtual reality, searching the landscapes of pi for traces of the fingerprints of God. . . . My best memories of her are from back when I was very young, before she joined the Church of the Divine Regression. She used to play with me then, and read to me. But after she signed on to become a holy mathenaut, I had to go live with all the other kids in the Church. I missed her at first, sure, but I guess I got over it."

"My tough girl," Newt said tenderly, "from the rough, tough planet Earth. You've come a long way since you left."

"Yeah. But it turns out that no matter how far I go, I can't escape my past. Especially when it isn't even past."

When the Free Outers had arrived at Neptune, they'd discovered that the ice giant's biggest moon, Triton, had been claimed and colonised by Ghosts, the cult whose reclusive leader claimed to be guided by messages sent by his future self from an Earthlike planet around the star Beta Hydri. Macy had suffered a run-in with the Ghosts before: a little gang of them had kidnapped her just before the war because she had become one of the figureheads of the peace movement. It was a considerable shock to find that they had been squatting out here all along, in a city they were building under Triton's icy surface. They offered to help out the refugees from Uranus, but only if the Free Outers joined their so-called great enterprise. Only a few did, at first. The rest settled on Proteus, the next moon in.

Although Proteus is the second largest of Neptune's moons, it is a small, lumpy body with a mass just one quarter of one percent of Triton's, an average diameter of a little over four hundred kilometres, and a violent past. Four billion years ago, Triton and a binary companion wandered inward from the Kuiper Belt and encountered Neptune. As the pair swung around the ice giant, the companion was ejected, Triton was captured, and the orbits of Neptune's original suite of inner moons were severely disrupted. Unseated, tumbling erratically, they smashed and cannoned into each other, the collisions reduced them to a disc of rubble, and after Triton's orbit became circularised some of the rubble reaccreted and formed several new moons, including Proteus.

When they had first set down on Proteus, the Free Outers, low on construction materials and other resources, demoralised by the loss of four of their ships and sixteen of their friends, and by the immediate defection of several of their number to the Ghosts, had crowded into a hastily built cut-and-cover tunnel. But they were young and resilient, and soon began to make plans for a more ambitious settlement. They established a mining facility on Sao, an irregular outer moon rich in carbonaceous material, and used their surviving crew of construction robots to deepen a pit crater near Proteus's equator, terracing and insulating its sides, capping it with a canopy of construction-diamond panes and fullerene spars. It was hard and difficult work at first, everyone on short rations and working long shifts. Idriss Barr, always cheerful, seeming to thrive on adversity, became their leader by default. He even talked several people out of joining the Ghosts, although many more, about a third of their number, eventually defected.

There were other losses too. Galileo Alomar was killed when a temporary cabin at the mining facility on Sao lost pressure. Heideki Suso was crushed between two slabs of construction diamond while supervising the final phase of the fabrication of the canopy. And during the installation of the chandelier lights Anya Azimova slipped and fell, the clip of her safety harness snapped, and she plummeted more than five hundred metres, a fall that even in Proteus's vestigial gravity was instantly fatal.

The loss of Anya Azimova was especially hard. Her partner, Tor Hertz, had been piloting one of the unmodified ships attacked and destroyed by Brazilian drones during the flight from Uranus, and her death orphaned their twins, Hannah and Han, then two years old. After a great deal of communal discussion, Newt and Macy had volunteered to adopt them. A solemn and serious undertaking that precipitated their decision to formalise their relationship. Some Outers married according to the tenets of their various faiths or philosophies, but Macy had long ago lost the belief in which she'd been inculcated during her childhood in the Church of the Divine Regression, and Newt was wholly innocent of any kind of religion, so like the majority of Outers they pledged their love and allegiance to each other at a civil hand-fasting—a brief, simple ceremony attended by all the Free Outers—and afterward celebrated by a huge party.

Having children of their own had turned out to be problematical. Macy's genome was base stock, unmodified, while Newt, like all the other Outers, carried a number of artificial genes in his chromosomes. Some of these tweaks were adaptations to microgravity—the single-chambered hearts in the major veins of his arms and legs that stopped blood pooling at his extremities, altered rates of calcium reabsorption so his bones didn't become brittle, an enhanced spatial awareness. Others coded for cellular mechanisms that repaired radiation damage to chromosomes, an increase in the number of cones in his retinas, so that he could distinguish colours by the equivalent of moonlight on Earth, and the ability to enter into a form of hibernation. Also, he lacked an appendix and wisdom teeth, and possessed an additional set of tooth buds beneath his adult teeth. In short, he and Macy were genetically incompatible. And although it was possible to weave new genes into the chromosomes of Macy's eggs, the Free Outers' only gene wizard had defected to the Ghosts, and no one else possessed the necessary skill set. Macy and Newt had tried in vitro fertilisation, but several rounds had failed to yield any viable embryos. And so, unless they also defected to the Ghosts, they were stuck.

Macy wondered if she was a bad person for sometimes feeling relieved that the choice about whether or not to have children had, for the moment, been taken out of her hands. For she was still not yet reconciled to exile in the outer dark. Although the Free Outers had established a home on Proteus, they still faced every kind of uncertainty, threatened not only by their near neighbours but also by the possibility that the TPA might come after them again.

And now, some four years after arriving at the Neptune System, their vulnerability had been starkly underscored by news that a crew of Pacific Community diplomats was on its way from the Saturn System. The Ghosts made no secret of the fact that they had been in contact with the Pacific Community, just as they made no secret about having acquired the technical specifications of the fast-fusion motor from Free Outers who had defected to them. As far as they were concerned, they were the undisputed masters of the Neptune System; the squatters on Proteus had no voice or vote, and if they dared to protest or disagree they should be prepared to suffer the consequences.

In fact, many of the Free Outers welcomed the news. Whenever this was discussed at communal meetings Macy made it plain that she thought it more likely that the PacCom diplomats were coming here to probe the Ghosts' strengths and weaknesses or to deliver some kind of ultimatum than to make nice, but a majority believed that this might be the first step toward negotiating some kind of alliance with the Pacific Community and making peace with the Three Powers Alliance. They'd been so short of hope for the past seven years that they grasped at every scrap, no matter how exiguous.

And so everything was at hazard once again. More than ever it seemed to Macy that any children she and Newt might have together would be hostages to a bleak and uncertain future. Yet when it had come to taking responsibility for looking after the orphaned twins, she had stepped right up to the plate, and didn't regret it for a moment.

Han and Hannah had reached the point in their young lives where they had begun to develop in sudden leaps and bounds, gaining ten IQ points overnight, constantly surprising and challenging Macy and Newt with new insights and interests. Like all the children of the Free Outer community, the twins had been forced to grow up fast, and their education was haphazard and heavily emphasised practical skills. There was always work to be done, and now they were old enough they pitched in along with everyone else.

By now, the Free Outers' habitat had been capped and sealed, warmed to a habitable temperature, and pressurised. The bottom of the pit had been flooded and the circular lake filmed with a monomolecular halflife skin to tamp down fat waves that sloshed from side to side in Proteus's featherweight gravity, and stocked with tweaked kelps that quickly formed underwater forests that trailed slicks of fronds across its restless surface. The crew of construction robots had graded the sides with broad terraces in a variety of organic shapes and had erected clusters of small pressure tents—homes that could be pressure-sealed in the event of a catastrophic failure of the canopy roof. Emergency refuges had been constructed beneath the surface, too, and exit tunnels ran out to landing platforms east and west of the habitat. Vacuum-organism farms had been established on the surface, in shallow troughs scraped into the surface and illuminated and warmed by mirrors that focused the weak sunlight. And now the habitat's upper terraces were being planted out with rolling meadows and stands of white spruce, larch, Douglas fir, piñon pine, and white pine, all dwarfed and tweaked to grow in low gravity, creating a landscape like the mountain forests and alpine tundra found in high elevations of the great mountain ranges of the west coast of North America.

The Free Outers had named their habitat Endeavour. It would be beautiful when it was finished, but some believed that it was only a temporary home. Newt and other members of the motor crew were part of a group that was making plans to explore the inner fringes of the Kuiper Belt, and they were working up detailed strategies for constructing viable habitats; Macy had joined a small crew who had uncovered in the archives of the Library of the Commons plans for bubble habitats with skins of halflife polymers and aerogel insulation held rigid by internal pressure and a web of fullerene spars anchored in a central node. By making use of materials that had been developed since the plans had been drawn up, it might be possible to build habitats the size of Proteus, islands and archipelagos that could be set in orbit anywhere around the sun. While other members of the crew elaborated schematics for every kind of zero-gravity architecture, Macy devised a variety of simple and robust ecosystems. She told herself that it was just for fun, a pleasing theoretical exercise, but she couldn't help thinking that this might be a way of moving inward one day. Of creating a thousand floating gardens close to the hearthwarmth of the sun.

Meanwhile, the Free Outers still had plenty of work to do in their home on Proteus. One day, Macy was working with a gang of children on a terrace cantilevered out from the western side of the habitat, showing them how to plant out tree seedlings. The children bounced to and fro, dressed in padded coats and trousers, excited chatter and laughter chiming in the chill air as they lugged trowels and seedlings and watering cans from place to place, dug holes and dusted them with fertiliser granules, tamped soil around the seedlings and puddled them with liberal amounts of water. As always, Macy was infected by the children's unforced enthusiasm, and amused and comforted by their innocent, unquestioning acceptance of the bizarre circumstances of their lives, the strangeness of the place they called home. They made the extraordinary ordinary, and the ordinary extraordinary; gave you a fresh perspective on the relative importance of your own problems.

The soil factory Macy had designed and built was running very effectively now. The big kidney-shaped terrace had been covered with topsoil to a depth of about half a metre over a bed of crushed siderite and fullerene gravel, and conditioned with a catch crop of fast-growing grasses and clovers, a green carpet rich and lustrous in the diamond light of the chandelier lamps strung from the apex of the roof. When Idriss Barr called, Macy was showing Han and Hannah a soil sample she'd stuck under a magnifying screen. Han was rapt with solemn concentration as he studied wriggling nematodes, springtails like curious mechanical horses, delicate webs of fungal hyphae, and jewel-like strands of cyanobacteria; Hannah chattered away, naming the various minibeasts and getting about half of them right.

Macy's spex vibrated in her pocket. When she put them on, Idriss Barr said, "I think you call this sort of thing a heads-up. Sada Selene wants to have a word with you."

"I'm sure you can find a polite way of telling her I'm too busy."

"It's too late for that, I'm afraid. She's already on her way."

Macy turned and saw two figures gliding along one of the ziplines strung across the gulf of air beyond the tall transparent barrier at the edge of the terrace.

"She wants to put a proposal to you," Idriss said.

"What kind of proposal?"

"She wants you to meet with the Pacific Community representatives when they arrive."

"You're kidding."

The two people riding the zipline slanted in above the lip of the barrier and dropped neatly to the terminus set beyond a stand of young spruce.

Idriss said, "I told her about your objections, Macy. She said that you must set aside your prejudices because your experience could be crucial to the success of the negotiations."

"My experience? I've never met anyone from the Pacific Community."

"The fact that you're from Earth."

"Me and ten billion other people."

"Listen to what she has to say, Macy. We can all help you to decide what to do about it afterward."

Now the two people came around the edge of the trees and loped across the meadow. Sada Selene and her partner, Phoenix Lyle. They visited Endeavour three or four times a year, attending trade and policy meetings, but until now Macy had managed to keep out of their way. She didn't trust Ghosts in general, and trusted Sada Selene even less. Sada and her, they had a history. Immediately after Macy had defected to the Outers she'd been incarcerated in the city of East of Eden, Ganymede. Sada and Newt had helped her escape. Macy had ended up on Dione, in the habitat owned by Newt's family; Sada had joined the Ghosts and a couple of years later had been part of the little gang responsible for kidnapping Macy.

Sada didn't look much different from any other Outer. A tall, skinny young woman dressed in a figure-hugging suit-liner, her pale hair roughly cropped, a tattoo of the constellation Hydrus sprawled across her right cheek. But her partner was an extraordinary creature who might have stepped from the virtual landscapes of some fantasy saga or one of Newt's silly stories about pirates and monsters: a tall, powerfully built man with black mirrors for eyes and skin the colour of new copper and smooth as plastic and completely hair-less (he didn't even have eyelashes), dressed in a white suit-liner molded to his torso and cut low at the back to accommodate his tail. Rooted at the base of his spine, it was long and muscular, and divided at its end into clasping fronds like a fleshy orchid. Despite his imposing presence, he was no more than an escort, hanging back as Sada Selene stepped close to Macy with cool confidence.

"Here you are," she said. "Making mud pies as usual."

"Making a home," Macy said.

She was dressed in paper coveralls with a rip along one shoulder seam that had been mended with tape, auburn hair scraped back and held with a twist of plastic wire, dirt crested under her fingernails, a smear of mud on one cheek. Sada overtopped her by almost a metre, clean as new porcelain in her immaculate white suit-liner.

"I suppose you could call it nice enough, in an unevolved kind of way," Sada said. "But do you know what this reminds me of? This sunken chamber and its poor imitation of Earth? East of Eden. A place designed by people who liked to pretend that they were artists and scientists, that they lived the life of the mind, but who were really no more than farmers suffering a collec-tive failure of imagination. Perhaps it's good enough for you, Macy. But it isn't in any way acceptable for those of us who want to explore new ways of being human. These low-gravity architectures are no more than imitations of the African forests that our ancestors of the long ago quit for the savannahs and seashores. They force us to use our monkey muscles to get about in them, force us to think monkey thoughts. No, if we are going to explore entirely new ways of living, then our settlements and cities have to be entirely new. Unfettered by memories of Earth."

"This from someone whose boyfriend has a tail," Macy said.

"It looks good on him, doesn't it?"

Phoenix Lyle was swishing the fleshy tip of his tail back and forth to the general delight of the children gathered around him.

"Those are your wards," Sada said. "The blond boy and girl holding hands. Hannah and Ham."

"Han."

"They're cute, in an old-fashioned way," Sada said. "I expect Idriss told you why I'm here. I hope we can set aside our differences and discuss it sensibly."

"Everyone thinks I'm an expert on everything to do with Earth because I was born there," Macy said. "I'm not even an expert on Greater Brazil, let alone the Pacific Community."

"I never imagined that you were. But you might be able to contribute some useful insights."

"I suppose you've already discussed this with Idriss."

"At great length. Eventually, he agreed to agree with me."

"He should have told you that I hardly know anything about the Pacific Community, and most of what I do know is propaganda and black information put out by the Greater Brazilian government when they and the Pacific Community almost went to war, ten years back. I've never been there. I haven't even *met* anyone from there."

"Not yet. But you will."

"Are they coming here? To Endeavour?"

"Why would they want to do that? They want to talk to us," Sada said, with acid patience, "because we are the principal power in the Neptune System. But I have agreed that Idriss can attend the preliminary meetings. As long as he is accompanied by you."

"Because you think I might have some useful insights. I can give you one right now," Macy said. "You're trying to play the Pacific Community against its partners in the TPA. Have you given any thought to the possibility that the Pacific Community might be using you?"

She would have said more, told Sada that she and the rest of the Ghosts, and most of the Free Outers, were relying on good intentions that the Pacific Community almost certainly didn't possess, that a small band of refugees trying to make a favourable deal with the political giant—China, Japan, India, Southeast Asia, Australia, and parts of Africa: five billion people—was like hoping to lever the Moon out of orbit, if only they had a long-enough lever and a place to put a fulcrum, but she was distracted by children's squeals and cries. They'd been chasing the tip of Phoenix Lyle's tail as he lashed it from side to side, and he'd thrown a muscular coil around the waist of a small boy who'd gotten too close and lifted him wriggling and kicking into the air.

Macy stepped up, told Phoenix Lyle to pick on someone his own size, and took hold of the boy and pulled him free. He immediately began to cry, huge shuddering sobs, his face hot and wet against her shoulder. Phoenix Lyle smiled blandly and said that he was only having a bit of fun, and so were the kids.

"You took things too far," Macy said. She was angry, because of Phoenix Lyle's crassness, because of Sada's presumption. "You people always take things too far."

Sada told her that Phoenix hadn't meant any harm by it. She said, "The offer is genuine. You can help all of us, Macy. And in a funny way I look forward to working with you. After all, we had some fine fun in East of Eden, didn't we? Fooling the old fossils who thought the place was some kind of Shangri-la."

"As I recall, you didn't tell me what you were going to do until after you did it," Macy said. "That won't happen again."

"Talk it over with your partner, the heroic pilot. Talk with whoever you want. You have plenty of time. The PacCom ship isn't due to enter orbit around Neptune for thirty days. But for the sake of everyone in your funny little habitat," Sada Selene said, "I hope you make the right choice sooner rather than later."

3

The two men sat on weather-bleached canvas chairs in the shade of a big boxy hangar, off to one side of a runway aimed at a technicolor Texas sunset. Cash Baker working on his third Antarctica beer; Colonel Luiz Schwarcz drinking iced tea. They'd been playing catch-up, but after Cash had brought Luiz up to date, telling his old friend how he'd turned his life around by joining the Reclamation and Reconstruction Corps, there'd been a stretch of silence. At last, Luiz said, "Man, one of the things I miss most, up on the Moon, are sunsets."

"We have good ones here," Cash said. "Especially like now, when the wind blows from the northwest and hangs some desert dust in the air. And there's an awful lot of dust up there right now because we're in the middle of a drought. A real bad one. But I guess you don't hear about things like that, up on the Moon."

"Perhaps we don't pay as much attention as we should," Luiz said.

"I don't blame you, man. You have your work, and you have your family, too."

"I got lucky, I know."

"Hey, it's okay," Cash said. "I'm not trying to get in a pissing contest. I screwed the pooch, sure. But I got over it."

There was another stretch of silence.

Cash said, for something to say, "I still think the best sunsets I ever saw were the ones around Saturn. The sun dropping through the rings, burning down behind Saturn's limb."

"A glorious sight," Luiz said.

"Like a thousand H-bombs going off."

"Do you remember much of that stuff?"

"You mean before I had my ticket cancelled? I really can't tell anymore. It's like, I know me and Vera Jackson flew into Saturn's atmosphere on that operation. Deep Sounding. I know those pirates—the ones who called themselves Ghosts?—sent drones chasing after our singleships, and we escaped a close encounter by blasting straight up into space. But that's because I watched the video we shot over and over, hoping it would tickle some memory. Until one day I realised that I couldn't tell the difference between remembering watching the video and remembering actually being there. . . ."

"You were there. Most definitely."

"You ever run into her, these days?"

"Vera? I believe she went back to Europe. I don't even know if she's still flying." Luiz took a sip of his iced tea and said, "Did you ever have a close encounter with her?"

"There's something I'd definitely like to remember," Cash said.

"I bet you tried," Luiz said. "I know the rest of us did. She was a glorious piece of work. Beautiful, yet fierce. All business."

"From what I've seen, she was definitely some kind of flier."

"She was. Like many of us, I had my doubts, bringing the Europeans into the programme. It was a political move, which meant that it was born out of some kind of compromise. Neither side getting what they really wanted and ending up with a deal that was neither one thing nor the other. And that might be fine in politics, but it doesn't cut it when it comes to flying combat planes out in the real world—because as we know all too well there's no grey area when you're pushing at the very edge of the envelope. But although I wasn't prepared to say it then, I have to say now that some of those Europeans knew their way around the sky. And Vera Jackson was better than the rest of them. Almost as good as us."

"And we were pretty good, back in the day. I remember that much."

"And here you are, still flying."

"It's no J-2, but it goes where you aim it, and it's light and quick—built from those new composites we stole from the Outers. Like something made out of cobwebs. Drawback is, unloaded, it's so light you can forget about taking off in a strong headwind. And it has a pretty low absolute ceiling, around about four thousand metres. Which means you have to buck around in thermals when you fly over mountains, and if you run into a thunderstorm you have to fly under it and hope you don't hit a downburst gust that nails you to the ground. But yeah, it's still flying."

Cash finished his beer and slung the long-necked bottle toward the trash can, and smiled when it ticked the edge and rattled in. He was hanging loose, doing his best to think of this as purely a social visit, just another evening with the boys at the bar, kicking back and having a little fun. Telling stories of the long-gone. The long-lost. Nothing serious. Nothing that could come back and bite you.

He told Luiz, "The resupply work is mostly milk runs, but I do see a bit of action now and then. Like a couple of weeks back, I'm coming into this camp on the front line. Out at the edge of the desert, looks just like all the others. Trailers and tents pitched in the middle of nowhere, acres of bare soil sprayed with that halflife polymer they use to stop it blowing away, trees waiting to be planted, dew traps, new irrigation ditches. . . . You have to land on the access road because there's no airstrip. That's one reason why the Wreckers Corps use these little courier planes, we can land just about anywhere. The wind is blowing into the desert for a change, so I come around to land in the headwind because that will bring me up nice and short. And as I'm circling around, barely a hundred metres above the deck, heading back in toward the line of trees, I see these scudders below me, get this, *on horses*. Like something out of the good old days. And they raise up and start shooting at me."

"These are the famous rebels you have here?"

218

"The Freedom Riders? No, they don't bother the Wreckers Corps. Far as they're concerned, the men and women in the Corps are working stiffs like most everyone else. Doing good work too, reclaiming land from desert, making Texas and the rest of what we used to call the U.S. of A. what it once was. No, they don't have a quarrel with us." Cash realised he was talking about what he'd promised Howard he wouldn't talk about, and said, "To get back to my story, those scudders who shot at me, they were bandits plain and simple. I didn't realise that was what they were doing until a round went through the side window, right next to my head. They put some rounds through the starboard wing, too, and it made me so mad I circled back and shot at the sons of bitches. I carry a pistol, in case I have to put down somewhere in the back of beyond. It isn't just bandits you have to worry about, out in the wild. Fellow I know had to set down in hills south of here. He was flying a tiltrotor like yours, and the engine died on him. Instead of sitting by his bird and waiting to be picked up he tried to hike out, and got himself eaten by a bear."

"Rather ironic," Luiz said. "You bring back nature and nature bites you in the ass."

"I doubt the guy who was eaten saw the funny side," Cash said. "Anyway, I got on the radio and told the guys in the camp to break out their guns, they had bandits out beyond their perimeter, and then I came right back at the scudders who shot at me. I was about on the ground, so low I was flying in the middle of my own personal dust storm, and I held the yoke with my knees and I emptied the pistol out of the broken window. I knew I wasn't going to hit anything, but I wanted to show them I wasn't going to put up with shit like that. People in the camp started shooting at them too. Killed one and drove off the rest. The one they killed was just a kid. Fourteen, fifteen. Teeth filed to points, patterns of welts on his back, tattoos across his face. He was wearing a necklace of human ears, too, and he stank like a polecat."

Cash reached down and fished another bottle from the icewater in the cooler. His fourth, but what the hell, he was talking with an old buddy he hadn't seen for six, seven years. It was a special occasion.

"You still have the edge," Luiz said. "That's good."

"It was a dumb thing to do, but it felt like the right thing at the time," Cash said.

Man, the cold beer was fine going down, what with the heat and wind stripping the moisture right out of him.

"When I first saw you, you know, I was worried you had given up," Luiz said.

"How do you mean?"

"I mean your clothes."

"My clothes? This is how we are here, when we're off duty. R&R #669 is a pretty relaxed crew."

Cash was dressed in jeans and a T-shirt, and hand-tooled red leather boots—they were the most expensive things he owned, the boots. Luiz Schwarcz, who'd always been a piss-elegant little fucker, wore black silk trousers and a white, round-collared jacket under the cage of his exoskeleton—he'd spent most of the past six years on the Moon, and despite gene therapy and exercise regimes his muscles weren't able to cope with Earth's gravity. A pale yellow silk scarf was twisted around his neck; his moustache was waxed to sharp points and his head was shaved to a close stubble; his mirrored sunglasses reflected Cash and the sunset behind him.

"If I flew out to some camp in the ass-end of nowhere dressed like you," Cash said, "the roughnecks'd probably shoot me. After they'd picked themselves up from laughing so hard."

Luiz smiled. "I was worried that you might have let yourself go. Now I see that you have gone native."

Cash set his bottle of beer on the picnic table and pinched the bridge of his nose between thumb and forefinger. He was getting the first pangs of a headache. He had a lot of headaches these days, and there didn't seem to be anything he could do about them.

He said, "I'm a working man, Luiz. I wear my uniform on the job, and afterward I kick back with everyone else. Besides, I was born here. This is what I am. This is what I do."

"You are still a pilot. Vera Jackson was good, but you were better. As I should know, having flown with both of you."

Here it was, the thing they'd been circling around since Luiz had touched down. Hell, since he'd gotten in contact, two weeks ago. Telling Cash he was coming back to Earth for his father's funeral, he could jog over to Bastrop one day and they could catch up. . . .

Cash said, "Vera didn't get hit. And you didn't get hit either. I did. You both had what I didn't have: luck. And luck is what you need plenty of if you want to be the best there is."

"Some people say that a man makes his own luck," Luiz said. "But as far as I am concerned luck is just what happens to you, out in the world. For no one can control the world, and they are crazy if they think they can."

"I always thought you had your shit together," Cash said. "I mean, here

I am with my funny little plane made of cobwebs, and there you are, still flying singleships."

"These days I most often fly a desk. I want to tell you," Luiz said, "that the charges they brought against you, attacking a ship against orders and all the rest, were the purest kind of bullshit. You were gone, man. You and Vera were dealing with the automatic defences planted on that chunk of ice, while I was hanging back, waiting to come in and lay my egg. I saw it all. You were attacked by drones, you took them down, but one blew up very close to your bird. You were hit, you lost control, you lost your comms, you went shearing off. I couldn't raise you, and I couldn't chase after you because by then Vera had dealt with the last of the defences and I had to get in close to the slab and set down the H-bomb. And after the bomb blew, Vera and I were busy chasing fragments and blowing them to dust before they hit Phoebe, and you were still veering off at something like four percent maximum thrust. I put in a call for retrieval, gave them your delta vee and vector, and I assumed that's why they knew where to pick you up. All of this, it is in the deposition I made when you were charged."

"I wish I could remember it," Cash said. "They told me the retrograde amnesia might wear off, but it never has. I guess that can happen when you have a hole bored right through your head."

He meant it as a joke, but it didn't seem to come out right. He pinched the bridge of his nose again, trying to snuff out the red pulse of his headache.

"I know you got hit by shrapnel from that drone," Luiz said. "I *saw* it. And they say you managed to fix your bird and join in the war and then get hit again, by some ring fragment? It seems very unlikely to me."

"I guess I was having a shitty day."

"Well, you survived it," Luiz said. "Your real bad luck, that was when they decided to go after General Peixoto and wanted to use you as part of their case."

"They had a record of the messages he sent, Luiz. Telling me to back off from attacking that Outer tug. They had the flight recorder of my bird, too, showing that I brought it in from the edge of the Saturn system. And the fleck of basalt they recovered, it definitely wasn't part of any drone. Oh, sure, they could have planted it. Made the whole thing up. But before you accept that, you have to ask one simple question—why would they bother? They had plenty of other stuff to use against the general. They didn't *need* to make anything up. They didn't need to fake up shit to show that I wasn't the hero the general claimed I was. That he'd suppressed the real facts about how I was killed and brought back to life. No, it's easier to believe it really happened."

"All I know is what I saw," Luiz said. "And if the action that took down that chunk of ice doesn't make you a hero I don't know what would. I was ready to speak for you, man. I would have done it. Vera would have done it too."

"I thank you for it," Cash said. "But you want to talk about luck, they never used my testimony because the general took the honourable way out. A room with a locked door, a bottle of brandy, a revolver. He knew his family would lose everything if he was disgraced by a court martial, so he killed himself to save them. And after he killed himself the whole thing fell apart. They were going to throw me to the wolves, and suddenly it didn't matter. So after a while, they just let me go."

"He was a good man," Luiz said. "And a good soldier."

"Yeah. And he won the war, too. They can't ever take that away from him."

"They tell us there's another war coming. Maybe against the PacCom. For real, not like the last time."

Cash and Luiz talked about that for a little while. They watched the wreckage of the sunset fade. Venus following the sun down to the west; the sickle of the Moon cocked eastward; the first stars pricking the wide sky as it darkened toward night. Cash found the steady yellow star of Saturn and asked Luiz if he thought he might ever go back there.

"I don't think so. We beat them, didn't we?"

"Yeah."

"Here on Earth, this is where the next war will be. The Outer System, it's history," Luiz said. "Right now we're building a prison on the far side of the Moon to accommodate the worst of the Outers—the ones who fought back. Word is that there are plans to ship all of them to the Moon eventually. No, they're irrelevant. What is important now, the Pacific Community is pushing hard to assert itself. I've been hearing that those Freedom Riders and all the other rebel groups, they've been receiving clandestine help from PacCom infiltrators. Weapons, money, you name it. Sooner or later, we're going to have to push back. We're going to have us a real war."

"I'm ready for it," Cash said. "Think they'd take me back then?"

"If they have any sense. I guess I better get going. I have many klicks to go before I sleep."

They walked to Luiz's tiltrotor, the little motors in Luiz's exoskeleton tick-tocking, Cash's bootheels clicking on slab concrete. Embraced each other, told each other to take care.

"I can get you a full medical at Monterey if you want it," Luiz said. "They owe you that."

"I'm doing fine," Cash said. "Don't be a stranger, you hear?"

Luiz climbed stiffly into the tiltrotor. The wash of its cruciform blades blew over Cash as it rose up, and then it put its nose down and buzzed away southward.

Cash watched until the blink of the tiltrotor's green and red running lights had dwindled into the twilight, then walked back to the hangar, stepped through the half-open door into the cool dark inside, and said, "Well, that's that."

Two men emerged from the shadows. Cash's cousin, Billy Dupree, and his uncle, Howard Baker. Billy scratched a match alight on his thumbnail and cupped its little flame to his face and lit the jay, its end glowing bright as he pulled in smoke and said in a pinched voice, "I didn't know whether to shit or run when you started talking about the Riders."

"He called them bandits. I felt I should qualify it," Cash said.

"It wasn't wise," Howard Baker said.

He was in his late sixties but still strong and straightbacked, in blue jeans, scuffed work boots, and a leather vest over a broad chest thick with white hair. He'd taken Cash in hand after Cash had agreed to quit the smuggling racket, and fast-tracked him into R&R Corps #669, a small transport unit that worked out of a base outside their home city of Bastrop. Sergeant Howard Baker had half his family working in the unit, and passed a cut of the profits from his various schemes to the base commander to make sure the man looked the other way.

Cash was carrying a beer bottle by its neck, his fifth. He took a long drink and wiped his lips on the back of his hand and said, "It was just like I said it—he wanted to see how I was, and to shoot the shit about old times. No more, no less."

"Colonel Schwarcz may be your friend, and maybe he did come out here just to catch up and talk about old times, no other reason," Howard said. "But you can't ever trust him. Not one hundred percent. Not because he's in the military, but because he isn't blood. That's the one thing we have in common with the great families. We trust blood before everything else."

"If someone wanted to find out, am I connected to anything bad," Cash said, "they wouldn't send Luiz. It isn't the kind of errand they give to someone of his rank. No, what they'd do is pull me in, start asking me hard and direct questions."

Howard shook his head. "It's always good policy to believe that your enemy is at least as smart as you are. To put yourself in their place and think

223

of what you'd do, and then assume that they'll do it. If I were them? I wouldn't arrest you. Maybe I'd get something out of you if I did, maybe not. But I'd definitely learn a lot more if I let you run around, see who you met, who you talked to."

"If this was something more than a visit from an old service buddy I'd agree," Cash said.

"Even if we could be sure that's all it was, we still have to believe it wasn't," Howard said. "How we turn a tidy profit without getting into trouble? We keep one step ahead of trouble, all the time. But in this case, I reckon you did all right. Apart from that little slip, bringing up the Riders, you were about note perfect."

Cash took another drink of beer. "You heard what he said about the Riders, and PacCom infiltrators?"

"That's the line they're using now," Howard said. "They put it about that the Riders are in cahoots with the enemy so the military, if they're ordered to go after them, won't have any qualms about attacking their fellow citizens."

Billy exhaled a big cloud of sweet rank smoke. "That goes for your service buddy the colonel, too."

"The military isn't the real enemy," Cash said. "Most of the people in the armed services, they're just like us, come from the same places we do. I should know. No, it's the politicians feeding them lies are the problem."

"Listen to your cousin," Howard told Billy. "He's beginning to figure out how things work."

"I still reckon we should have snatched him," Billy said. "A full colonel? The man in charge of some secret training programme up on the Moon? We could have named our price."

"That's not even funny," Cash said.

"That's good to know, because I'm deadly serious." Billy drew on his jay and said, "I got to ask, Cash. Were you two ever sweethearts? The way he dresses, the way you were talking together . . . and I know it must get lonely, out there in outer space."

"You're thinking of your time in jail," Cash said.

Billy smiled through wreaths of exhaled smoke, and Howard told them to knock it off. "You two squabble so much I swear you must of been married in former lives. How about you exercise more than your jaw muscles? We need to get the shit on board so Cash can get going at first light."

Cash drained his beer and tossed the bottle, Billy snuffed out his jay on the doorpost, and the two cousins followed Howard inside. The old man switched on the hangar's lights, the hard glare shining off the dull green fuselage of Cash's T-20 courier plane. Off to one side were pallets stacked with cardboard boxes and wooden crates, everything stencilled with red crosses. Some really did contain medical supplies; others were packed with munitions. Rifles and power packs and ammunition, two kinds of plastic explosive, and sidewinder mines—smart, deadly little things that could be keyed to home in on a particular location or to chase down a person's heat signature or scent.

Early tomorrow morning, flying a milk run to an R&R plantation, Cash would be making an unscheduled stopover a couple of klicks west of what was left of the town of Odessa. Back in the twentieth century they'd pumped oil from the Permian shale all around Odessa. Long after the Overturn and the civil war that had ended with incorporation of what was left of the United States of America into Greater Brazil, descendants of some of those oilmen were still living out there. Wildsiders. Ordinary men and women who'd clung stubbornly to their birthright, who'd joined the Freedom Riders because they wanted to win back the legitimacy and dignity that had been snatched from them. Cash would have liked to have explained it properly to Luiz, but they were on different sides, and now Luiz was on his way back to the Moon. He probably wouldn't ever see his old friend again, Cash thought, and was struck by a brief pang of regret. That part of his life was well and truly over.

4

The dead girl lay in the middle of the apartment's single room, near the sunken and padded sleeping niche. Sprawled carelessly on her back on tawny halflife grass, arms outflung. She was naked and her pale breasts and stomach and flanks were smeared and ribboned with dried blood. Her dry eyes stared sightlessly past Loc Ifrahim as he leaned over her. Rigor had come and gone. She had relaxed into death, beyond help, beyond all human plight.

Captain Neves said, "The kid told me there wasn't anyone else involved. That this was a private party. I had a forensic drone give this place a thorough work-over and it looks like he was telling the truth. Which should make this easier to deal with, don't you think?"

"Did he tell you why he killed her?"

They were standing on either side of the dead girl, both dressed in long padded coats, their hands in their pockets, their breath smoking. Captain Neves had dialled down the apartment's temperature to preserve the scene.

Captain Neves shook her head. "At first he said that he didn't know what had happened. That he'd blacked out and found her like that. Then he said it was an accident. That they were playing around with the knife and she somehow fell on it."

Loc counted the bloody little mouths in the girl's skin. He'd popped two patches of pandorph before coming here and everything seemed bright and clear and remote. He said, "Some accident. It looks like she fell on that knife eleven times."

"More than that. He cut up her back pretty badly, too. It's what they call perseveration," Captain Neves said. "He started, and he couldn't stop. I found only his fingerprints on the knife, and although he washed himself afterward, there were traces of her blood under his nails. Also scraps of his skin under her nails, no doubt from the scratches on his forearms. It looks like she put up a struggle. There's nothing linking anyone else to the scene, no evidence that he was set up."

"Do we have any video from spyware?"

"In here? No. The fellow he pays to run security for him knows his job. The place is clean. But I culled video from the city's net, and tracked him and the girl back to the club he runs. They left at two sixteen, entered this building about thirty minutes later. Just the two of them."

"Where is he now?"

"Safe and secure. No one can get at him, and he can't do himself any harm."

"He finally went and did it." Loc watched his thoughts flicker to and fro as he calculated the angles. He said, "You're absolutely certain none of the locals know about this?"

"No one knows about this but you and me, and the trooper who's looking after him," Captain Neves said. "The kid called me. I came over and secured the scene. And then I called you."

"What about Cândido's people?"

Joel Cândido, a greyly efficient career soldier, had replaced the unfortunate and unlamented Faustino Malarte as governor of Camelot. He was very keen on meetings and endlessly finessing protocols and regulations, and left the day-to-day running of the city to a cadre of civil servants and Captain Neves's police.

226

"I didn't want to trouble Lieutenant Colonel Cândido with a silly little domestic incident," Captain Neves said.

"You have a plan," Loc said. "Don't deny it. I can see that you've been dying to tell me ever since I arrived."

"And I can see that you're flying on that stuff again."

"Almost high enough to see into your mind. Almost, but not quite. So, tell me what you want to do."

"It's very simple. We help the kid get past this, and then find out how much it's worth to Sri Hong-Owen," Captain Neves said. "That's why I haven't told Cândido, or anyone else."

"Except that trooper. Can he be trusted to keep his mouth shut?"

"She. And I trust her more than I trust you," Captain Neves said.

"You should smile when you say that. Then it would be almost funny."

"It's funnier if I don't smile."

"It isn't a bad plan, and it might work. Although not in quite the way you think it will. Who is she?"

"The girl? No one in particular. A refugee from Paris, Dione, living here with her two fathers. But she does have an interesting connection," Captain Neves said. "One I think we can make use of, if we want to help the kid."

"The so-called resistance," Loc said.

"Tell me you already knew this."

"She's the right age, she's from Paris, probably feeling resentment because of what we did, probably feeling resentment because she and her fairy godfathers can't go home. . . . Was she active or a fellow traveller?"

"She's never been arrested for anything, but I have files on several of her friends, so she has a file too."

"It's easy to see what might have happened here, instead of what did," Loc said. "She came back here with the kid. One of her friends from the resistance was waiting for them, they got into an argument. Perhaps she was going to do the right thing and go to the authorities, tell them everything. Her friend found out, tried to persuade her to keep quiet, flew into a murderous rage when she refused. Knocked out the kid, killed the girl."

"Something like that," Captain Neves said.

"Exactly like that. All we need now, to complete our little story, is a fall guy."

"Oh, I already have someone in mind," Captain Neves said.

"You bitch," Loc said affectionately. "You're enjoying this."

"Don't tell me you aren't having fun too," Captain Neves said, and leaned into Loc's kiss across the dead girl and bit his lip, hard enough to bruise.

The young man Captain Neves had measured for the fall was the youngest of the dead girl's angry little friends, like her a refugee from Paris, Dione. All Captain Neves had to do was snatch and drug him, have him wake up in the room with a bad hangover and blood all over him, the dead girl on the floor, troopers pounding on the door, demanding to be let in. . . . It would be dealt with as a security matter, because the boy was associated with the resistance (strictly speaking he was a wannabe who'd gone to a couple of meetings and tagged a few walls, but Captain Neves planned to pin several unsolved acts of sabotage on him), so the locals wouldn't be allowed to get near the scene or the suspect. It was too easy, really, Captain Neves said. Like shooting fish in a barrel. While she was setting it up, Loc went to talk with the repentant murderer.

Captain Neves had stashed him in the apartment pod she used for her private interrogations. It hung from a high branch of a banyan tree at the western edge of the forest that filled the tent taken over by the city's Provisional Authority. Loc dismissed the trooper who'd been babysitting the prisoner and stood with his back to the door. The pod was floored with the usual halflife grass. A rack of fullerene bars had been bolted to one wall; a pair of steel handcuffs hung by one loop from the topmost bar. The only piece of furniture was a scarred plastic table. The tools that usually littered it had been cleared away, replaced by flasks of tea and coffee and icewater, a tray of candied fruit and savoury pastries.

Berry Hong-Owen sat on the floor by the window that capped the far end of the pod. He was dressed in paper coveralls and a blanket was draped shawl-like around his shoulders. Staring at the patch of floor between his bare feet, a shroud of lank hair half obscuring his face. The window at his back was fully polarised and darkly mirrored everything in the pod. Loc saw himself reflected there, trim and elegant in his dark grey tunic and trousers, moving forward to stand above the kid, who shrugged when Loc asked him how he was.

"I did it," he said. "Okay? I told that policewoman I didn't, but I did."

Captain Neves had shot him full of tranquilliser. His voice was an uninflected drone, like that of a very simple AI.

"You don't have to worry about that anymore, Berry," Loc said. "It's gone away. It's as if it never happened."

"Does my mother know? Did she pay you to help me?"

"She doesn't know a thing," Loc said. "This is our secret. You and me against the world."

"If she was paying you to look after me, that's exactly what you would say," Berry said. "She spies on me. Did you know that? Not because she cares for me. Because she doesn't want me to have any fun."

"Did you have fun, with the girl?" The thought slipped out, became words before Loc could catch it, so he hurried on: "You're not the only person to get into trouble like this, Berry. We are all under tremendous stress. This is an unfamiliar and dangerous place, and the natives are by no means as friendly as they appear to be. And in any case, the girl was part of the resistance. She didn't get close to you because she liked you. She did it because she wanted to find out what you knew, and because her friends thought you might be useful to them. She was using you. So there's no need to feel guilty about what you did. Let's be clear about that. She was nothing. A spy. A whore. And she's gone."

"She was nice to me."

"Of course she was. It was her job." Jesus and Gaia, it was hard work getting through. Like speaking to someone at the bottom of a well.

"I don't remember anything. I must have done it, but I don't remember," Berry said, looking up at Loc through his greasy fringe.

He'd put on a lot of weight since Loc had last seen him. He'd been partying hard with a group of spoiled kids with fashionably nihilist attitudes who'd battened on to him because he had a line of credit and a small but useful amount of influence with the occupying force. He'd been doing a lot of tailored drugs, too, more than enough to make an elephant psychotic. Drinking heavily, as well. And according to Captain Neves he was also bulimic, bolting down ice cream a litre at a time and then throwing it up. His eyes were sunk in fat pillows of flesh, bloodshot oysters shining with unshed tears. He stank of fear: rancid butter with metallic overtones.

"She probably drugged you," Loc said. "They do that. Give you drugs to make you talk. She drugged you, and tried to find out your secrets, and you had a reaction. What happened, Berry, it was self-defence."

"I liked her," Berry said, after a long pause.

"You'll get over it," Loc said.

Berry turned his head away. "What are you going to do now? Take me to my mother? Tell her what I've done?"

"Is that what you want?"

Berry shrugged. "She doesn't care about me. What she'll do, is have someone tell me off, and give me more credit and send me somewhere else. Where I'll have to make a bunch of new friends all over again."

He was feeling remorse, but not for what he had done. Not for the girl. No, he was wallowing in self-pity, worried that it would cause him all kinds of inconvenience, stop him from having more of his kind of fun.

"If you want to stay here, with your friends, I can help you with that," Loc said. "I can help you get over this little problem, help you get on with your life. And then, in time, perhaps you can help me."

He said more, variations on a theme to make sure that the idea sank into the mud of Berry's brain, told him to think it over and left the sullen man-child in Captain Neves's care, and commandeered a tug and went to Janus to confront Professor Doctor Sri Hong-Owen in her lair. Not to demand any form of payment for his services. As he'd explained to Captain Neves, a demand of quid pro quo was a blunt tool you could only use once. It would be far better to tell the Professor Doctor that her son's mess had been tidied up as a matter of simple courtesy. Perhaps it would make her more disposed to do them a favour later on, perhaps not, but it would definitely give Loc the chance to see for himself what she had been doing ever since she'd shut her-self away.

Her laboratories, run by a small crew of fanatically loyal assistants, trickled out enough marvels to placate Euclides Peixoto and the oversight committees, but only her assistants knew exactly what she was doing on Janus. Loc had informants in every city in the Saturn System, men and women who called themselves his friends as long as he kept them sweet with bribes and backhanders, but they'd been unable to penetrate the fog of rumour and counterrumour that swirled around Professor Doctor Sri Hong-Owen. He was pretty sure that Euclides Peixoto didn't know any more than he did. And perhaps Euclides didn't care, as long as royalties from the gene wizard's discoveries and inventions continued to fatten his coffers. But Loc cared. Information was power: the only power he presently possessed.

Euclides Peixoto had rewarded Loc's candour about the crimes of General Arvam Peixoto with the position of chief of the Office of Special Affairs, a small crew of troubleshooters who investigated every kind of problem in the interface between the TPA and the Outers, dealing with compromising or embarrassing situations, generally making sure that no scandals ever reached the light of day. It was good, necessary work, and it had enabled Loc to insinuate himself into all kinds of interesting nooks and crannies. He reported directly to Euclides Peixoto, could travel anywhere on the moons controlled by Greater Brazil. But it did not satisfy him because he knew that he was no more than an instrument of Euclides Peixoto's will. A useful but minor servant.

He wanted to be so much more than that.

Five hundred klicks out from Janus, a security drone intercepted and challenged the tug. Loc dealt with its impertinent questions and told the tug's pilot to surrender control, and the drone guided the tug toward the anti-saturnian side of the little moon. Drifting in above a lumpy plain overgrown with tracts of vacuum organisms, Loc spotted a fan of bright material, presumably excavated debris, but saw no other sign of the biomes and biofactories that the gene wizard was rumoured to be constructing deep beneath Janus's icy rind.

The tug touched down neatly and lightly on a platform perched on the inner rim of a large impact crater. Loc sealed up his pressure suit and climbed out, moving with edgy care in the vestigial gravity, and one of Sri Hong-Owen's assistants escorted him along a cableway to a dome filled with jungly greenery—not something made by Sri Hong-Owen, this, but one of Avernus's weird gardens, abandoned long before the war. Inside, he was met by a second assistant, the androgyne neuter Raphael, who told him that the Professor Doctor was too busy to see him.

"Anything you wish to tell her, Mr. Ifrahim, you can tell me. Or perhaps you would rather make an appointment. I should warn you, though, that it may take some time to set up a meeting."

"I need to talk to her face to face about a highly confidential matter concerning her son," Loc said. "Tell her that, and then let's see what happens."

Raphael was very tall and very thin, with honey-coloured skin, a cloud of hair like spun gold wire, and a face like one of those optical illusions which switch between two perspectives. Not quite male, not quite female, a little of both but adding up to something completely different and impossible to read. It—yo—steepled yo's long fingers before yo's face and studied Loc with what might be sly amusement, or calculation, or artfully disguised dislike, take your pick. They were seated on fat cushion seats in a balcony office with a view across a green sea of puffy treetops draped with catenaries of flowering vines, chandelier lights burning at the apex of the tent's dome like a shattered star and black sky beyond. The air was hot and packed with humidity. Loc was sweating in his suit-liner, but his head, washed clean by a fresh patch of pandorph, felt cool and clear. He was registering everything around him with dispassionate precision. Storing it away for later analysis. He hadn't even flinched when, as he'd been led along a high path to this office, something that looked like the severed hand of a long-dead corpse had scuttled off into the lush undergrowth.

Raphael said, "Berry has achieved majority. He is responsible for his own actions. However, in unusual circumstances, I am authorised to act, as it were, *in loco parentis*. If you care to discuss his problem with me, perhaps I can be of some help in dealing with it."

"I've already dealt with it," Loc said. "And that is why I must insist on speaking with his mother. We both know that Professor Doctor Hong-Owen has many enemies. That she has survived one scandal, but may not survive another. So it is imperative that I speak with her as soon as possible, to discuss the best way forward."

"If this is a matter of reimbursing your expenses—"

"This isn't about money," Loc said. "I want to be very clear about that. This isn't in any way about money. This is about helping a confused and lonely young man who has lost his way. I rescued him after he fell in with some dangerous people. He isn't physically hurt, but mentally . . . he is very distressed. Anguished. I have done my best to help him, but he needs his mother now," Loc said, but he knew, with a falling feeling that had nothing to do with the lack of gravity, that he wasn't going anywhere, the neuter shaking yo's head, yo's expression so cool, so carefully composed as yo told him that Sri Hong-Owen was not speaking with anyone at present.

"She has much work to do, and does not want to be disturbed."

Loc summoned up a show of outrage. "I'm sure that many people would be shocked to hear that she values her work more highly than her son's well-being."

"Tell me something, Mr. Ifrahim. Would you be as shocked as you pretend to be if we were talking about Berry's father?"

"The father in question died a long time ago, on Earth."

"Nevertheless, I believe that there is a kind of double standard here," Raphael said. "A symptom, no doubt, of a regrettable imbalance in your culture. As for Berry, I will say only this. Professor Doctor Hong-Owen has tried several times to find him gainful employment. He has always refused her help. I will repeat my offer of help in this matter, but I doubt if Berry will pay any more attention to me than to his mother."

"What's it like, knowing you'll never have sex again?" Loc said.

The thought slipping out of his teeming head, hanging there in the hot, humid air. Fortunately, Raphael took it seriously.

"It's calming. It gives you a useful perspective on human foolishness. One you might appreciate, Mr. Ifrahim. Thank you again for your concern. And good luck with Berry. I hope you can do the right thing by him."

5

A majority of the Free Outers agreed that Idriss Barr and Macy Minnot should accept Sada Selene's invitation—that taking part in the negotiations between the Ghosts and the Pacific Community diplomats was vital for their security and survival. But there was a long and contentious meeting about how Idriss and Macy should present themselves and what they should and shouldn't say; no one was especially satisfied with the various compromises that Idriss had engineered; all kinds of rifts in the little community were exposed. Afterward, Mary Jeanrenaud intercepted Macy and told her that she had to set aside her hatred of the Ghosts in general and Sada Selene in particular. "You must remember at all times that this is not about you. It is about the survival of our entire community."

"I couldn't agree more," Macy told the old woman. "I take everything that has anything to do with the Ghosts very seriously."

Mary Jeanrenaud, clearly spoiling for an argument, adopted a tone of wintry condescension. "You may think that you understand us, Macy, but you never will. Not really. But if you can find it in yourself to do this service gladly, for the greater good, there may be some hope that you can come to an accommodation with our way of life."

"Oh, I'm learning all kinds of stuff all the time," Macy said. "For instance, I think I've finally figured out this democracy thing of yours. For a long time I thought it was about making the best choices that satisfy most of the people most of the time. But now I see that it's a way of getting along with people you have to get along with in order to survive. Even if you don't like them."

Twenty-eight days later, the Pacific Community ship settled into the quarantine of an isolated orbit some two million kilometres from Neptune. A Ghost shuttle set out to collect the PacCom diplomats, and Macy and Idriss Barr boarded a tug that took them from Proteus to the Ghosts' colony, grandly named the City of the New Horizon, on Triton.

The Ghosts had begun to settle Triton in secret more than a decade ago. According to their unseen guru, Levi, they were the chosen people. He claimed to have received messages from his future self: proof that his followers would throw off Earth's chains and develop faster-than-light technology that would allow them to reach out to planets around other stars.

They'd been preparing to fulfill this destiny for some time, recruiting young people from every city and settlement in the Jupiter and Saturn systems, stockpiling supplies and dispatching them to their beachhead on Triton in robot carriers. And they'd also jacked up the level of aggression and hostile posturing between Earth and the Outers before the Quiet War: attacking a pair of singleships from the Brazilian-European joint expedition when they'd penetrated deep inside Saturn's atmosphere for a propaganda exercise; encouraging and supporting the promises of Paris's renegade mayor, Marisa Bassi, to counter any attack on his city with swift and deadly force; firing a chunk of ice at the Pacific Community's base on one of Saturn's outer moons.

The confusion of the Quiet War had provided the Ghosts with the opportunity to steal ships, make their mass exodus from the moons of Jupiter and Saturn, and begin the next stage of their long-term plan to fulfill Levi's prophesies. The City of the New Horizon was spread across a wide area beneath cantaloupe terrain at Triton's equator: a series of chambers excavated with dismounted fusion motors, linked by monorails that ran through tubes bored by powerful and indefatigable construction robots, and invulnerable to all but multiple strikes by high-yield hydrogen bombs. The Ghosts were using vacuum organisms to mine and transform deposits of complex organic material found everywhere beneath the nitrogen and methane frosts on the moon's surface, and had also drilled boreholes forty kilometres down to the ocean wrapped around its rocky core. Robot refineries had begun to process minerals and metals from the ammonia-rich water, and the Ghosts had grandiose schemes to build electrolytic plants that would oxygenate the upper layer of the ocean, and to establish an entire ecosystem there. They planned to float cities in Neptune's atmosphere, too. In a hundred years, they boasted, the Neptune System would be inhabited by clades of posthumans adapted to every possible habitat, a thriving, buzzing commonwealth that would drive and shape the future of the human race.

The team of negotiators from the City of the New Horizon and the diplomats of the Pacific Community met in a recently built chamber more than a hundred kilometres north of the city's centre: a nest of large, spherical spaces surrounding a central axis, each divided into irregular terraces linked by the usual low-gravity drop shafts, ziplines, and chutes, everything the stark white of freshly fallen snow, with no decoration or attempts at landscaping apart from clusters of tweaked bromeliads that grew here and there from the walls, removing potentially harmful trace gases from the air, and the halflife mosses in the toilet blocks that absorbed and purified urine and feces.

The Ghosts slept in dormitories, ate in refectories, worked wherever they were needed. There were spaces dedicated to manufactories and workshops on the lower levels, but everywhere else could be configured to suit every requirement, from kindergartens to hospitals. These stark live/work spaces possessed the chilly elegance of unadorned functionality, and there was an admirable purity to the collective will of the city's inhabitants, but Macy thought that it was about as homely as an anthill, utterly lacking in privacy, bustling with constant and purposeful activity twenty-four hours a day. And yet the Ghosts were not glassy-eyed and humourless fanatics. Most were under the age of fourteen, generally reckoned to be the age of majority in Outer communities, nurtured and born in ectogenetic tanks, and tweaked so that they matured quickly, reaching puberty at age ten and passing through adolescence in a couple of years but seemingly none the worse for it except that they knew nothing but the city, and the teachings of Levi and his mad, glorious dreams. They were cheerful and energetic, played all kinds of sports, took part in musical groups, theatrical pieces, and long philosophical debates, and commonly sang while they worked, lusty hymns to the grand future they were building and the great victories they would win. They called each other *brother* or *sister*, and often held hands while they talked or walked about together. They were not organised into families (they honoured their parents but did not live with them or defer to them) but into cadres, and members of each cadre worked and trained and spent their scant leisure hours together, and held group criticism sessions in which each in turn would confess what they called thought crimes, were gently rebuked by the others, and gratefully accepted small punishments.

Macy had expected to meet a parade of grotesques, but it turned out that most of the Ghosts were no different from other Outers—Phoenix Lyle, with his black-on-black eyes and his copper skin and serpentine tail, and a few others like him, had changed themselves before they'd joined the Ghosts. According to Levi, tweaks that altered physical appearance were useful only if they were adaptations to new environments, but otherwise they were affectations, wasteful, neither novel nor particularly radical. They were, in short, hands for feet—an old Outer joke about misguided ideas concerning adaptation for microgravity. First you exchange your feet for another pair of hands. And then you have to grow another head out of your ass, because you won't know which way is up. No, Levi and his Ghosts believed that the real frontier of human evolution was not the body, but the mind. The human species was defined by its big brain, but like all evolutionary artefacts the human brain was scaffolded onto and extended from older structures, so the limits of the human mind and human imagination were constrained by random compromises. To really explore what it means to be human, Levi had said, human beings must reengineer the organ that defined them as a species: improving memory, enhancing neuronal transmission and increasing the bit rate of thought, paring away or modifying redundant emotions, and making dozens of other tweaks and modifications.

Of Levi himself there was no sign. Macy Minnot, Idriss Barr, and the diplomatic representatives from the Pacific Community were told that he was watching them with great interest, but would take no direct part in the negotiations; like God, he was often referred to but never seen. No one who was not a Ghost had ever met him; no one knew anything of his history, not even his original name, before he had assumed leadership of his cult. One rumour had it that he had died years before, and lived on only as an expert system. Another claimed that he was a true AI, a self-aware, supernally intelligent digital consciousness out of the fantasies and nightmares of the long ago. Or that he suffered from an exotic cancer which had so bloated him that he was confined to a life-support vat. Or that he had entered cryosuspension, leaving behind a series of prophetic pronouncements, and would not be awakened until the end of the so-called years of crisis, when the faster-than-light drive was finally made ready and he could lead his children to their promised lands amongst the stars.

Macy was pretty sure that, like the Ghosts, the PacCom diplomats must have been cut for enhanced intelligence and fast-track maturity, for most of them were young, smart, and irrepressibly cheerful. Chinese, Indian, Filipino, Malay . . . a rainbow coalition of teenage ambassadors led by an aged Australian, Tommy Tabagee. Apart from a war-gaming exercise staged inside the city's chambers and monorail tubes to demonstrate the Ghosts' willingness to defend their home to the death, and tours of the ocean mining facility and the great vacuum-organism farms on the surface, there were few formal meetings. The PacCom diplomats explained that they could best understand the aims and needs of the Ghosts by participating in every aspect of their ordinary lives, and the Ghosts surprised Macy by being completely candid about their philosophy and plans.

This openness was all very well, but she found it impossible to keep track of the unstructured and informal interactions between the Ghosts and their guests. The PacCom team roamed unchecked throughout the chamber, talking to anyone and everyone, working alongside their hosts in manufactories and workshops, taking part in discussion and self-criticism groups, and in musical and theatrical events. Drones recorded everything they said and did, but Sada Selene refused to give Macy access to the surveillance data.

"I can't do my job if you won't let me do my job," Macy said.

"Do as they do," Sada said. "Talk to them. Work with them. Play with them. How they react and interact with the famous defector from Greater Brazil will tell us a lot more than a few subjective opinions."

So that was how it was. The Ghosts didn't really want Macy to be an observer after all; they wanted to use her as a stalking horse. The revelation didn't especially anger or upset her because she'd been expecting some kind of trickery, but her frustration mounted as the days passed and she failed to discover what lay beneath the PacCom diplomats' boundless enthusiasm, or to determine whether they genuinely hoped to reach some kind of reconciliation between the TPA and the Outers. And while she picked up hints that the diplomats and the Ghosts were talking about trading the secrets of the Brazilian fusion motor for refined metals and other raw materials in short supply in the Neptune System, she was kept out of the loop by both sides, and so was Idriss Barr.

Idriss was sanguine about it, telling Macy that it was only to be expected. "The Ghosts did a lot of hard work to entice the Pacific Community out here," he said. "We shouldn't expect to be given a free ride. But if they enter into any kind of an agreement with the Ghosts, then we will benefit by association. And I've had some useful conversations with the representatives. It's far too early to trust them, but the signs are very hopeful. We will have much to talk about when this is over. And everyone will want to know what you think."

The problem was, Macy didn't know what to think. All she knew for certain was that she wasn't cut out for diplomacy. Dealing with two sets of people who spent all their time lit up with fake friendliness, pretending to be straightforward and candid while sharpening knives behind their smiles, was exhausting and depressing.

About the only person she had time for was the leader of the PacCom delegation, Tommy Tabagee. A grandfatherly fellow, dignified and witty, with black skin and a mass of dreadlocked grey hair, he behaved as if the negotiations were an amusing bit of theatre especially devised for his benefit, entertained Macy with an endless fund of anecdotes and cautionary tales about the rewilding of Australia, and pumped her for stories about her adventures in the Outer System. He told her that the Pacific Community had taken part in the Quiet War because the consequences of allowing Greater Brazil and the

European Union free rein in the Jupiter and Saturn systems would have been disastrous for the rest of Earth as well as for the Outers, and explained that his people had very quickly come to an accommodation with the inhabitants of Iapetus by taxing them very lightly, occupying only a small part of the moon, and otherwise allowing them to get on with their lives.

"Of course, we want what the Brazilians and Europeans want, namely, access to the technology and expertise of your adopted people. But unlike the Brazilians and Europeans, we prefer trade and cooperation to full-scale looting. It's more expensive, to be sure, but the benefits amply repay the investment. We are, you see, a pragmatic and practical people. We share with the Brazilians and Europeans a desire to repair the damage done to Gaia by the industrial age, and to live lightly on the land. We've done our very best to make Australia an exemplar of our intentions, and to return the land to the Dreamtime. A very serious and costly enterprise! And yet we've been accused by radical greens in the European Union and Greater Brazil of failing to be true to Gaia because we embrace technologies they would like to ban for no other reason than misguided fanaticism. Perhaps one day, when all this foolishness and bad blood is settled, you could visit Australia, and I'll walk with you along one of the Songlines of my people, and I can show you exactly what I mean."

Macy thanked him for his invitation and told him that she wished she could take him up on it, but it was more likely that she would be heading further out than returning to Earth.

"Then perhaps I can visit you, on Pluto or Charon or whichever worldlet you choose to make your home," Tommy Tabagee said. "Every world has its own Songlines, you know. That's one of the things we learned from the good people of Iapetus. A good example of how cooperation benefits both sides."

"Is it really cooperation? I mean, the Iapetans didn't ask you to take over their moon."

"Nor have we. Well, no more than a very small portion of it. A small footprint in a wide wilderness. As on Earth, so here. And if you spoke to the Iapetans, I bet they'd tell you they're happy for us to be there, rather than the Brazilians or the Europeans. The point is, Macy, we believe that winning the peace is far more important than winning the war. And that's what we're trying to do. That's why we're here."

Macy knew that he was spinning her a neat line of propaganda, but she didn't mind because she knew that he knew she knew. It was all part of the game.

One day, when she was feeling especially bruised after Sada Selene had intercepted her in the refectory and asked her to eat elsewhere because the Ghosts and the PacCom diplomats had become embroiled in a confidential bit of business, Tommy Tabagee found her sitting alone in a niche at the waist of one of the big spherical spaces. Open tiers stepped away below. Work spaces, dormitories, communal areas, all white and bright and clean, displayed like a section through an architectural model. Voices and the small change of human activity rising in the cold air. Tommy Tabagee sat beside Macy, dangling his feet out over the void, and said that if it had been up to him she would have been quite welcome to sit in on the talks.

"We're all in this together and we all more or less want the same thing, after all."

"Really? What's that?"

"Why, some kind of reconciliation, of course. Some way of patching up the differences between Earth and the Outer System."

"So it isn't just about getting hold of the secrets behind the fast-fusion motor. That is what they're talking about back there, isn't it?"

Macy had been building up toward asking him about that for some time. Her anger encouraged her to forget all caution and just go ahead and do it.

Tommy Tabagee's smile didn't waver. "I figured you would have heard about that by now. And I don't blame you for being angry. I know you have a proprietorial interest, because you and your partner stole the specifications from the Brazilians in the first place. I heard how you saved Avernus, too, and helped to make a fool of Professor Doctor Sri Hong-Owen. Did I ever tell you that I met her? An interesting woman. Frighteningly clever, but barely human, if you ask me. A curiously vulnerable mixture of arrogance and naïveté."

"Are you changing the subject, Mr. Tabagee?"

"I do tend to ramble, don't I? All right, I'll try to be as straight as possible: of course we want the bloody fusion motor. Without it, we're very badly disadvantaged out here. I should know, having spent so long in hibernation on the voyage from Saturn to Neptune. If we had the same capability as our allies, it would give us more influence. We might just be able to push history in the right direction. Toward peace and reconciliation. Otherwise there may well be some sorrowful days ahead." Tommy Tabagee said this with some passion. He was very serious, for once. "And besides all that, information wants to be free. As I've told our hosts, my job is to hasten the inevitable. If they won't give us what we need, we'll get it another way."

Macy looked at him. "Are you making me an offer? If you are, you must know that the Ghosts are listening to us. They listen to everything."

"I hope I'm giving you something to think about. Them too, if they're eavesdropping," Tommy Tabagee said, raising his voice. "I don't have anything to hide."

"And I don't have anything to give you, Mr. Tabagee."

"Don't underestimate yourself, Macy. I may have known you for only a brief time, but I'm sure you can handle the responsibility of making a hard and difficult decision like this."

"It isn't mine to take."

"I don't see why we should involve anyone else in this. After all, you stole the specs in the first place. I reckon that gives you the right to make an independent deal."

"My partner and I stole the specs. And we gave them away to our friends. So before we could even consider giving or trading them to you, we'd have to discuss it with our friends. And I hope very much that they wouldn't agree to it."

"Because you're afraid of what the Ghosts might do?"

"They outnumber and outgun us, so that's definitely a consideration. Also, we can't trust you."

"Of course you can't. But you can think about this little conversation. And talk about it with your friends."

"They'll say no, Mr. Tabagee. No amount of talk will change that."

"Then what harm will talking about it do?"

Two days later, the negotiations broke up with nothing settled. The Pacific Community diplomats returned to their ship, and it quit its orbit around Triton to begin its long, slow journey back to Saturn; Macy and Idriss returned to Proteus. Macy carried a data needle that Tommy Tabagee had passed to her when they'd said goodbye. "It contains a military-grade encryption key," he'd said. "You can use it to talk to me without worrying about the Ghosts listening in. I know you'll have to talk to your friends about it first. That's fine. Take your time. I have a long voyage ahead of me, and I'll be spending most of it asleep. When I wake up, I hope to hear what you have to say."

Macy told the other Free Outers about Tommy Tabagee's overtures during the long meeting in which she and Idriss Barr gave accounts of their talks with the Ghosts and the PacCom representatives. Idriss was cautiously optimistic. The PacCom diplomats had left empty-handed because they had failed to reach any kind of agreement with the Ghosts, and the Free Outers now had the chance of opening a separate line of communication with the Pacific Community. It would not commit them to anything—certainly not to trading the specifications of the fast-fusion motor for vague promises about a future alliance. But simply showing that they were willing to talk might give them some influence; perhaps even some protection.

A minority, led by Mary Jeanrenaud, disagreed loudly and vehemently. They wanted nothing further to do with the Pacific Community because it was too dangerous: if the Ghosts discovered that the Free Outers were talking with the Pacific Community, they might decide to put an end to the Free Outers' independence. Macy was happy to sit back and let Idriss deal with these points, and with many other suggestions and objections. He loved debates like this, was lively and eloquent, and radiated charm and good humour; a good deal of his persuasive power stemmed from the fact that it was very hard to dislike him. In the end, the Free Outers could only agree that they disagreed. They would not reach out to the Pacific Community, but they would not reject out of hand the possibility of beginning a conversation if the Pacific Community reached out to them.

Idriss and Macy had been gone for twenty days, and she'd been out of contact with Newt and the twins for all that time because the Ghosts had refused to allow what they called unnecessary use of their communications system. After the meeting broke up, she and Newt took a long rambling walk along the terraces of their habitat, led by Han and Hannah. She saw with pride and nostalgia that while she'd been away the children had changed in a hundred tiny and marvellous ways. They were eager to show Macy the new rows of tree seedlings they had planted, extending the line of the new forest along the edge of a vibrant meadow. Han had appropriated a watering can and pretended to douse the feet of his favourite trees and talked to them in soothing tones as if they were pets. Hannah held Macy's fingers in her hot little fist, naming the trees by species, explaining how much they had grown and how tall they would soon be.

The children had already forgotten that she had been away, and didn't question what she had been doing. She was happy to wander with them wherever they chose, luxuriating in their artless talk, chasing after them and allowing herself to be chased. The spare copses of spindly trees and the soft green swathes of clover and catch grass might be poor imitations of forests and meadows on Earth, but it seemed to Macy that she had come home for the first time.

Later, after they had fed the twins and put them to bed and Newt had told them another episode of one of his pirate stories, after he and Macy had made love, quick and hungry, another homecoming, they lay in each other's arms and she told him about the offer that Sada had made just before Macy and Idriss had left. To tweak Macy's eggs so that they would be compatible with Outer sperm. So that she and Newt could have children of their own.

She watched him while he thought about this. Their faces centimetres apart, his gaze sharpening as he said, "Did you say no straight away? Or did you say you'd think about it?"

"I said that I'd have to talk to you. And I asked her how she knew about our problem. She refused to tell me, of course."

"It was probably one of the defectors," Newt said.

"Or Mary Jeanrenaud. She loves gossip, and she hates me."

"Gossip is the glue that holds us together," Newt said. "And she doesn't exactly hate you."

"Well, I don't know what else to call it."

"Sada could have made this offer at any time," Newt said. "Why make it now?"

Macy felt as if a cramped muscle had relaxed. Newt understood. He saw the problem, just as she did. She said, "She knew that Tommy Tabagee asked me about the fusion motor, but she never even mentioned it."

"Because she knows you turned him down."

"Because she knew I would have to talk to the rest of the Free Outers about it, and she knew they would turn it down."

"As they did."

"As they did. But she must be wondering what else he might have asked or offered me. I doubt if she expects us to tell her, even if we accept her offer, but she hopes that it will keep us close."

"Did you want to say yes?"

"Of course I did."

"But we can't owe her, can we? So we'll have to work things out by ourselves," Newt said.

The voyage back to Proteus and the long contentious meeting had exhausted Macy, but sleep eluded her. While Newt slept beside her, her thoughts turned in futile circles. She remembered a virtual model of a possible adaptation for life in Triton's ocean that Sada had shown the PacCom diplomats: a human-sized tadpole with a thick tail formed from its fused legs, small arms clasped across its narrow chest, a neckless head with a band of electrical sensors instead of eyes, a tiny pouting mouth, a feathery collar of bloodred gills. While it slept, Sada had said, a membranous caul rich in blood vessels and colonies of symbiotic bacteria would extrude from its anus, absorbing nutrients from the water and turning them into sugars and fats. A true posthuman species, the first of many.

Macy had long ago come to terms with the changes that had been made to the genomes of Newt and the other Outers. But the Ghosts had changed the way their children thought because they believed it would bring about the future that was their rightful destiny, and they were willing to turn their grandchildren into fishpeople or batpeople for the same reason. Yes, they would do anything to fulfill Levi's prophesies and they would not let anyone stand in their way. For long sleepless hours, Macy wondered how she and Newt and the twins would be changed if the Ghosts ever decided that it was necessary to end the Free Outers' vestigial independence.

6

Cash Baker belonged to a floating pool of pilots who operated out of the depot at Bastrop with no fixed routes or duties. He spent half his time making front-line deliveries, and the rest on milk runs—flying officers between bases as required, ferrying small loads to other R&R depots or to the regional administration headquarters in Austin. It was common knowledge that much of the stuff was luxury goods for high-ranking officers, but Cash could care less. He flew every place he was told to fly. It suited him personally because he loved flying and hated routine, and it suited his uncle's business because he was able to make unscheduled stopovers and drop off all kinds of clandestine cargo.

The drought didn't let up. It hadn't rained since early spring. Summer stretched out hot and dry and endless. Rivers shrank into their channels. Dust storms extended the desert's edge east and south, erasing decades of R&R work. Fire ripped through ten thousand hectares of rewilded forest north of Bastrop and hot winds blew smoke and soot across the city. Productivity in city farms was at an all-time low because of power and water shortages. Food rationing was strictly enforced. There were several serious clashes when police tried to stop people leaving Bastrop and other cities around and about to forage in the countryside. Freedom Riders claimed responsibility for numerous acts of sabotage. East of Dallas, a group hijacked trucks carrying military provisions and distributed them to hungry citizens.

Half the personnel of R&R Corps #669 were seconded to security detail, standing guard at roadblocks or patrolling hot spots. Howard Baker suspended the smuggling operation because there were too many strangers on the base and every load going in or out was being checked.

"We'll hunker down and wait this out," he told Cash. "When it's over our friends will be begging to be resupplied with more of our good stuff."

"Assuming they don't bring on their revolution," Cash said.

"They've been talking about revolution since forever, but it won't ever happen. Sure, they're taking advantage of the unrest right now, but it'll pass. Things will get back to normal before you know it."

Flying into Austin from Columbus River early one evening, carrying iceboxes full of crabs and shrimp for a reception for senior R&R officers and the region's governor, Cash saw threads of smoke rising from the western quarter of the city—the low tree-clad hills where the rich and powerful had their homes. Fires were burning along the culvert of the Hondo River and a hood of smoke was creeping over half the city, making the sunset even more apocalyptic than usual.

Traffic control instructed him to divert away from the area and make a dogleg south and then east to reach the R&R base. He landed and taxied up to the hangars, and the sergeant who took delivery of the seafood told him that people had tried to march up the Hondo's bare channel, a big demonstration led by the archbishop of Austin against use of water in the gardens of the rich.

Cash, thinking of how the lush green quilt of the rich quarter contrasted with the scorched and dusty browns of the rest of the city, allowed that they might have a point.

The sergeant was a veteran who wore a patch over the empty socket of his right eye and had three fingers missing from his left hand, the kind of bluff no-nonsense soldier who always knew exactly where to fix the blame. Telling Cash, "Used to be the families would have been the first to make sacrifices. I can remember the time, must have been thirty years ago, when we had food shortages worse than this. And the families, they dug up their gardens and parks to grow corn and such. They all ate dole yeast like the rest of us, too. But these days, they seem to feel entitled to do whatever they want. People are on rations, they're starving, and the young blades are throwing extravagant parties or they're driving around town looking for prole girls to pick up, throwing bread at passersby. And they keep their swimming pools filled and their fountains working while ordinary folk have to queue at bowsers for a drink of water. So it isn't any wonder that something like this has happened. And it isn't any one-day wonder, either. Most every one of my people has been drafted for riot control."

"It's that bad?"

"They even took my clerks. Everyone bar base security. You stick around, flyboy, they'll take you, too."

"I don't think so. Someone has to truck in their seafood."

"Point," the sergeant said, and spat dryly.

Cash told Howard Baker about it the next day. "I borrowed a jitney and drove out of the base, tried to get as close to the action as I could. I wasn't in uniform and the jitney wasn't an official R&R vehicle, but more than a few people threw rocks at it anyhow. You know the big square they have, where the old railroad station is? It had been turned into a field hospital. There must have been a couple hundred wounded people there, and more turning up all the time. There were dead outside, too. Elements of the Fourth Battalion had been deployed by then and they were using live rounds."

"How many dead, do you reckon?" Howard said.

"I counted twenty-eight bodies. Men and women, and two children. Then a bunch of police turned up to try to clear everyone out of there and I left. I couldn't get close to the river, but I saw plenty of smashed storefronts. One block was on fire and no one was doing anything to put it out. All the fire trucks were probably on the other side of the river, protecting those mansions."

Cash took a pull on his bottle of beer. It was his first, ten in the morning. He knew his uncle disapproved, but he needed it to ease the tremor in his hands and the pressure in his head. They were up on the roof of the accommodation block where members of the Baker clan bunked down. Howard Baker kept his pigeons in wire-mesh cages there, and grew tomato plants and herbs in tubs. He was pinching out side shoots from a trough of young tomato plants and using a spray bottle to wash dust from their leaves, working calmly and slowly as always. The city of Bastrop stretched out beyond the camp perimeter and the elevated section of the ring road, hundreds of identical ten-storey blocks laid out across the valley in a grid that simmered under a haze of smog. Tree-clad hills rose to the north, fresh and green against the hard blue sky.

Howard said, "From what I heard, it had been brewing for some time in the blocks, and Austin's archbishop is a young firebrand wants to make a name for hisself. Well, the OSS has him under house arrest right now. They say it's for his own protection, but you can bet we won't be hearing from him again."

"At least he took a shot at the status quo," Cash said.

"What happened in Austin, the status quo got pushed and it pushed right back," Howard Baker said, squirting water methodically over leaves, working from top to bottom. "You saw those wounded people, and the dead. You want to see that happen here? I know I don't. The way you change people's minds, it isn't by burning down their houses. Let me know if I'm wasting my breath, by the way."

"I'm not about to do anything stupid," Cash said.

"I hope not, because there's a strong strain of stupidity runs through our family. You may not appreciate me telling you this, but you are a valuable asset to our business. It may not be as glamorous as flying spaceships around the rings of Saturn, but it's a hell of a lot more useful as far as we are concerned. Stick with it. We Bakers have fought enough wars for other people's causes. It's past time we looked after ourselves."

Cash Baker's family were Scottish-Irish stock who'd moved from Virginia to Texas while Texas was still a Republic. A goodly number had fallen in the Confederate War, and many more in the wars of the twentieth and twenty-first centuries. They'd clung on through the bad years of climate change and the Overturn, when rising ocean levels had overcome every attempt at defending the coastal plain along the Gulf of Mexico against inundation and had driven millions of refugees inland, and Bastrop had swollen from a sleepy county seat to a city crammed with block housing and high-rise farms. They were proud and stubborn, governed by kinship and ancient unwritten codes of honour rather than common law, prone to addiction to every kind of drug, and to violent deaths. Most lived and died unremarked, but every other generation threw up someone who distinguished themselves in the outside world, including a boxing champion, a football star, a country-music singer who'd blown a fortune on a blizzard of crack cocaine and crystal meth, and a couple of handfuls of war heroes.

Cash had definitely inherited a good dose of his family's wild side. He'd been smart enough to join the Air Defence Force and get the hell out of Bastrop, but he'd been cocksure and reckless too, and eventually his luck had given out. He'd been a hero, and then he'd fallen from grace. He knew there was no way back to what he'd once been, he was grateful for his uncle's help, and he was down with the smuggling racket, he really was, but he also knew that running guns to the Freedom Riders wasn't enough. The injustice thrown into stark relief by the drought and the food shortages mirrored his own smoldering grievances. Like the ordinary people who had taken to the streets, he'd also been held in contempt by the powers that ruled the land. Picked up and used and cast aside.

There were riots in many of the cities on either side of the Rio Grande that summer. They were put down with brutal force and their ringleaders were given show trials and executed. Cash stood shoulder to shoulder with other members of R&R Corps #669 at roadblocks and barricades, patrolled the streets. All the while thinking that he was on the wrong side, upholding the rule of people who'd done him wrong against people who deserved better.

When the rains finally came in late November, more than three thousand people had been killed in riots and ten times that number were in prison camps. Cash spent some time helping distribute food aid in Bastrop and Columbus River, and then went back to flying, mostly between R&R Corps #669's depot and the territory to the west, where the R&R Corps were cleaning up old pump-jack oil wells and the remains of wind farms and erasing the ruins of small towns and roads. The land there had mostly healed itself. Rewilded territories stretching vast and quiet and empty under the big sky. Candelilla and scrub catclaw, creosote bush and dry grassland. Some new kind of engineered tree that seemed able to grow where nothing else could. Antelope and bighorn sheep and deer, mountain lions and wolves and black bears, descendants of animals bred and released by the R&R Corps half a century ago.

One day, early in April, Cash was flying over tawny hills when he saw a flash like broken glass winking amongst trees crowded into a ravine. He circled around and saw a white house tucked amongst the trees near the top of the ravine, hung out over a dry river bed. His comm beeped and a robotic voice told him that he had entered a restricted airspace. He made a wide turn and flew on to his destination, the ruin of a town near an ancient nuclear test site that the R&R Corps had recently begun to clean up, thinking about the house on the ridge looking out over the playa and thinking about another house, in the Venezuelan jungle, puzzling over an idea that had come to him.

He turned it over in his head, studied it from every angle, and at last mentioned it to his cousin. Billy thought it was a joke at first, but when Cash pressed on he grew quiet and serious, saying at last, "You have any notion about how much trouble you'll get yourself into?"

"I've been in places like that, Billy. I know how they're fixed for security, and I reckon I know how to take that security down. And if they do catch me, then at least I can say I stood up for something. Besides, I've done jail before. I can do it again, no problem."

Billy shook his head. "Something like this, they won't keep you in jail long. Pretty soon you'll be taking that short walk to the long drop. And that ain't nothing to what old Howard will do to you, if he hears of this. He'll tear off your hide and nail it to the hangar door and use it for target practice. Just to start with."

"I appreciate the advice."

"But you aren't going to take any notice of it, are you? Well, when they stretch your neck, at least I can say that I tried to stop you."

"I'd also appreciate a little help."

"Oh man. Don't even *think* of getting me involved in this."

"It isn't anything. I've met plenty of foot soldiers, dropping off loads, but I reckon I need to get close to people higher up. People who can make things happen."

"You think I know anyone who'd help you with a crazy-ass scheme like this?"

"I just want to talk to someone about it, is all. If they don't like it, fine. I'll give it up there and then."

"They'll most probably think you're some kind of double agent and kill you."

"That's why I came to you first. You know the right people, and they know you and they trust you. All I want is an introduction. Nothing else."

Billy shook his head again, but he was smiling now. "You really think you can sell it to them?"

Cash smiled back. "I sold it to you, didn't I?

—●—

It took a while to set things up: it was close to the end of June when Cash and half a dozen Freedom Riders rode out into the desert on tough little horses, travelling east and then south, crossing a playa into low hills where early in the evening they camped under a stand of young trees with smooth pale trunks and umbrella canopies of hand-shaped leaves. They ate army rations from self-heating pouches, passed around a pipe of marijuana and a flask of pulque, and finalised their plan of action.

248

The leader of the little group, Arnie Echols, told Cash that the trees under which they'd camped were a variation on the people trees found in just about every city in Greater Brazil, from Detroit to Punta Arenas. Designed by the famous old gene wizard Avernus before she and the rest of the Outers had quit the Moon for Mars and points south, people trees had sugary sap, produced protein-rich nodules and pods that yielded cooking fuel, bark that could be stripped off in layers that could be used to make paper or clothes, and leaves that could be eaten raw or boiled up into a tasty porridge. These tough variants were just as useful, and had been tweaked so that they could grow in every kind of habitat—the salt marshes of what was left of the coastal plain, the dry pine hills, the desert. Everywhere they went, Freedom Riders planted packages containing people-tree seeds, starter cultures of the symbiotic fungus that would help them find water, and fertiliser to kick-start their growth. The trees grew very quickly; stands of them were scattered all over the Southwest.

"We make little gardens where nothing else will grow," Arnie Echols said. "And I can tell you that they make living out here much easier."

One of the men said that they were God's gift. Another said no, they were from the mind and hand of a gene wizard who had modified Avernus's design. But where did the inspiration come from, if not from God, the first man said, and they talked seriously about this for some time. Cash learned that the Freedom Riders had no compunction about using every kind of technology to survive in the wilderness. They had stills that pulled moisture from air, featherweight sleeping bags, slates and comms equipment that ran on artificial photosynthesis and plugged into what they called a dark net. A clandestine tribe living in places where men where forbidden to live by law, but not, as one of the Freedom Riders said, by nature.

Cash lay awake most of the night, sore and tired from the long day's ride. The horses staked out nearby made a tearing sound as they cropped dry grass. The desert spread dark and quiet beyond the hills, under a moonless night sky full of stars. He watched several bright stars moving steadily east to west: satellites and ships in orbit. He felt that he hung suspended between worlds.

Late in the afternoon of the next day, Cash and the Freedom Riders were laid up amongst rocks on a hilltop, in sight of the white house that stood at the head of the ravine, some five klicks away. Two of them went out on foot, carrying explosive charges and an aluminium case containing six dragonfly drones that Cash had liberated from the big R&R base at Loma del Arena with a fake requisition order. The drones would locate cameras and sensors, hack into their radio chips, and insert demons that would take down the house's security net. The two men returned a couple of hours later and told Cash and Arnie Echols that there were just four guards at the house, but there were wolves, too.

"That's a bad complication," Arnie Echols said. "Those things will be better armed than we are, and they can outrun a car, let alone a horse."

"They patrolled every airbase I flew from, back in the day," Cash said. "They're smart and fierce, sure, but they're only machines. They'll be linked to the AI that controls the security net. Once the drones have done their work, they'll go down like the cameras and everything else. You'll see."

Weeks later, Cash told Billy Dupree that the raid had been like a scene from one of those old cowboy movies of the long ago, with Indians raiding a homestead. After the drones had taken down the security and communications systems, and knocked out the wolves, explosive charges planted to the west of the house went up in a showy and distracting column of red fire, and the Freedom Riders rode up the dry creek to the east and fired canisters of riot gas through the windows. The guards had come stumbling out, coughing and choking, and had immediately surrendered.

"The news had it that you tortured and killed the guards," Billy said.

"We winged one, is all. The youngest. He came out with his pistol drawn and started firing at random. Nearly hit me," Cash said, remembering how the guard had staggered across the dark terrace, weeping and snorting and firing his gun at shadows. "A couple of rounds went whooping past my head, I fell flat on my ass, and one of my friends shot the guy. It busted his arm and knocked him down, and that was that."

"And then you blew up the house."

"Then I took pictures of the house, which I know you've seen."

It had been a hunting lodge owned by a senior member of the Montoya family, a simple but beautiful place with fieldstone fireplaces and old wooden furniture, rugs and the skins of wolves and a bear on the flagstone floors, and heads of deer, pronghorn antelope, and mountain lions on the walls. Cash had taken plenty of pictures of the heads and the skins, documenting how Carlos Montoya and his sons spent their time out in the desert, hunting animals reintroduced by the R&R Corps, treating the rewilded land as if it was their own private kingdom.

"When I was done, we walked the guards down the creek a ways, and then blew it all to hell," Cash said. "And rode straight out as fast as we could."

"You just went right ahead and did it, didn't you? Walked away from us and everything we did for you without so much as a goodbye. And now you're back, and I have to wonder what it is you want," Billy said.

"I know you and Uncle Howard and everyone else must be pretty mad at me. I don't blame you. As to why I'm here, I want you to know what's been going on. What I learned."

"I've half a mind to rat you out," Billy said. "The reward would come in handy, and it would get the police and the OSS off our backs."

"I didn't think they'd go after anyone but me. I apologise for that."

"They turned everything in the base upside down, looking for you."

"Then it's a good thing I didn't tell you what I was planning to do."

"You have balls of steel even coming here," Billy said.

They were sitting knee to knee in the storeroom of a café at the edge of Bastrop, with two friends of Billy's keeping watch outside. Cash was travelling under a fake ID.

"If you came here because you need more plastic explosive," Billy said, "then count me out. How many places have you done now? Seven?"

"Just two. The rest were down to parties unknown who I guess just flat-out liked my idea. We have enough munitions to knock down every hunting lodge and holiday home in the entire region if we wanted to," Cash said. "But there's too much security around them now, and too many army patrols in the desert. Why I'm here, one reason anyhow, is I want you to know I'm moving on."

"You still haven't told me why you're doing this," Billy said. "Wasn't smuggling illegal shit exciting enough?"

"What I was doing, it couldn't ever satisfy me, after the kind of flying I used to do."

"That friend of yours got you stirred up, didn't he? I saw it at the time, and I should have done something about it."

"You know those people trees that grow out in the desert, and in the marshes along the coast?"

"Yeah. There's a couple of crews dedicated to ripping them out."

"Good luck to them. The Freedom Riders have been planting them for about four years now. They grow real fast and they're all over the place. Here's a funny thing. Anywhere you dig around one of the trees, you find these black threads. They grow through soil or sand or even through rock, all the way down to the water table, no matter how deep it is. And if the water is salty, the black stuff filters out the salt, brings up pure clean fresh stuff for the tree. The Freedom Riders claim those black threads are some kind of fungus, but

I've seen stuff on the Moon looks just like it. Vacuum organisms. They grow out on the surface, or under tents with funny atmospheric mixes that people can't breathe. And they aren't really organisms—they aren't really alive. Organisms are made up of cells. Vacuum organisms are made up of tiny machines that behave like cells, what's called bound nanotech."

"So they're regular miracles of modern science," Billy said. "What does this have to do with you and me and this whole mess?"

"I met with one of the people who are involved with this whole tree thing, and also with passing on information about leaving the cities, and how to live lightly on the land. I got his attention, and he wants me to go work with him."

"So I guess this is goodbye."

"I know if I asked you to join me you'd laugh in my face—"

"Or maybe punch you upside the head, if I thought it would knock any sense into you."

"Just take a look at this," Cash said, and held out a data needle. "There's information about all the places we dealt with. It shows you what our so-called masters get up to out in the wild, where ordinary folk aren't allowed to go. And there's stuff about how to live out in the wild, too. Take a look, make copies, pass them around."

Billy Dupree studied Cash and said, "You've changed."

"I found something to be serious about. I haven't been drinking, either," Cash said. "That's why my hands are shaking, in case you thought it was because I had the fear."

Billy reached out and took the data needle. "I'll look at this, but don't think it'll change anything."

"Things are going to change whether you like it or not," Cash said. "This might help you see which side is the right side, when it does."

Two weeks later, Cash Baker was sitting with Arnie Echols in a ruined one-and-a-half storey house on the outskirts of Albuquerque, at the western edge of an old exurb. Streets and streets of houses half drowned by sand, standing forlorn and roofless amongst thorny scrub. It was close to midnight. No light but the stars and a sickle moon, the vast desert quiet stretched all around.

"Here he comes," Arnie Echols said, and a moment later Cash heard the faint drone of tires on sand. He put on his night-vision goggles and followed Arnie out into the middle of the street.

Three trikes cut around a stand of mesquite and drew up a few metres away. A tall, lithe man swung off the lead trike and came toward them. Even in the false greens of the night-vision goggles, Cash could see that he was young and handsome, long pale hair framing a face with high cheekbones and slightly slanted eyes. Holding out a hand and telling Cash, "It's good to meet you at last, Captain Baker. I'm Alder Hong-Owen."

1

After his overture to Sri Hong-Owen was so rudely rebuffed, Loc moved her son to Paris, Dione. Partly because the family of the young man who had been framed for the girl's murder by Captain Neves refused to accept the official story and were spreading rumours and causing Berry all kinds of trouble; partly because Loc would be able keep a close personal watch on him in Paris, and would know at once if his mother ever reached out to him. But she never did. Berry took up with his old friends, drinking hard and doing every kind of psychotropic; Loc sent a few choice clips of Berry's more embarrassing moments to Sri's lieutenant, Raphael, but received no reply. The gene wizard had cut herself off from her son as completely as she had cut herself off from the rest of the Saturn System.

Loc kept an eye on Berry, just in case, and turned to his other special projects. He was finally beginning to make some money from the Quiet War: a steady income from the art-smuggling business that he and Captain Neves had taken over after Colonel Faustino Malarte had been removed from the scene; shares in licensing various scraps of Outer technology he'd passed on to a minor member of the Gamaliel family; fees paid by businesses that needed advice on and access to the Saturn System. But he did not yet have enough to set himself up in the style he deserved when he at last returned to Earth, and besides, money was only a means to an end. The ambition that had driven him to study relentlessly for the civil service exams when he'd been a ragged kid in the slums of Caraccas drove him still. He was not yet forty. He had another century ahead of him; perhaps more. He did not want to spend it running some minor consultancy business or growing roses in a gated arcology. He wanted to leave his mark on the world. He wanted to change history. He wanted to found a dynasty that would rival the greatest of the great families.

Loc had considerable autonomy as head of the Office of Special Affairs, but his plans were conditional on the whims of his superiors and the vagaries of the political climate, and the latter had begun to exhibit some alarming shifts of late. President Nabuco had used emergency powers granted by one of his puppet committees to suspend elections and extend the reach of the Office for Strategic Services, which had recently arrested on conspiracy charges several senior members of the Fonseca and Fontaine families who had been his most vocal critics. There was growing unrest in almost every territory in Greater Brazil, especially the north, which had suffered a year of droughts and food shortages. And the Pacific Community was slowly but surely strengthening its presence in the Saturn System: constructing a small city on Iapetus and expanding its base on Phoebe; taking control of previously unoccupied oases built by Outers before the war on two moons of the inner system, Atlas and Pandora; claiming several of the small irregular moons that orbited at the outer edge of the Saturn System by emplacing a few settlers in crude cut-and-cover habitats. The PacCom government was also campaigning for some form of reconciliation with the Outers, arguing that the Brazilian policy of control and segregation was proving too difficult and costly to sustain, suggesting that a managed retreat and a client-state relationship with the Outers was the best way forward. That the future was not in empire and dominion, but in commonwealth and partnership.

Greater Brazil and the European Union had their own plans for the Outer System. They were constructing a facility on the Moon that would house their most important political prisoners, a trial run for a grand scheme to transport the inhabitants of every Outer city and settlement to lunar camps. The Outers would enjoy a certain degree of self-government, might even be allowed to trade their skills and knowledge for credit, but they would not be permitted to travel outside their camps and would be subjected to the zero-growth initiative. As for the Pacific Community, its ships were not only outnumbered, but they were also much slower. If it ever came to a confrontation, the Brazilians and Europeans were confident that they could easily shut down the PacCom presence in the Saturn System.

But then a PacCom freighter returned to Iapetus after a two-year round-trip to Neptune, and the PacCom government told its allies in the Three Powers Authority that it had made contact with two communities of Outers in the Neptune System, the Ghosts and the Free Outers, and hoped to establish full diplomatic relations and negotiate trade agreements with both of them.

It was a shrewd and provocative move. The Ghosts had been troublesome allies of the city of Paris, Dione, before the Quiet War. Fierce opponents of the Brazilians and Europeans then, and no doubt equally fiercely opposed to the TPA's occupation of the Jupiter and Saturn systems now. As for the Free Outers, when Arvam Peixoto had routed them from their nests around Uranus, they'd fled outward in ships equipped with the fast-fusion drive; either they'd developed it independently or, more likely, they'd somehow stolen or acquired the schematics of the Brazilian model. The possibility that the Pacific Community might make an alliance with these factions and purchase information that would enable them to build their own version of the drive and eliminate at a stroke their major handicap when it came to defending their possessions in the Saturn System was a serious threat to the balance of power, and to the survival of the TPA. Many in the Brazilian military, especially the ambitious young blades from the great families, believed that war wasn't far off. A real war this time. A good old-fashioned war with armies and navies squaring up to each other, bombing missions and air combat, battles in space. Give them a wing of singleships, they said, and they could clear the Pacific Community from the Saturn System inside a week.

Loc Ifrahim knew that it wouldn't be as simple as that. Oh, there was no doubt that Greater Brazil outgunned the Pacific Community in the Saturn System, but her military forces on Earth were overstretched, and the government was distracted by serious domestic issues. The president had lost a lot of support after the OSS began to arrest members of the government, there was open warfare between factions in the Senate, and almost every territory was troubled by nationalist and pro-democracy rebels. Loc's good friend Yota McDonald, recently returned from Earth, said that in the four weeks he'd spent in Brasília there had been more than two dozen car bombings and numerous acts of so-called nonviolent protest, including an attempt to contaminate the water supply of the Senate with a psychotropic drug. The rebels, once isolated pockets of malcontents at the borders of remote territories, were now a mainstream movement with considerable support amongst the general population. Clandestine videos and literature about democracy and human rights were circulating throughout every city in Greater Brazil. The OSS was making mass arrests and transporting trainloads of people to camps in the far south every day, but this was having little effect on rebel activity, and was providing all kinds of ammunition for the pro-democracy movement.

So Loc wasn't surprised by the announcement that senior politicians from Greater Brazil, the European Union, and the Pacific Community would be attending an extraordinary summit about the future of the Outer System, convened in the neutral territory of South Africa. Despite the sabre rattling and dire rumours and black propaganda, it was clear that the government of Greater Brazil wanted to explore every alternative to war, if only to prolong the peace until they had crushed internal resistance and built up the strength of their armed forces. A couple of days after the announcement, Loc was summoned to a meeting with Euclides Peixoto. The man shuffled across his big office and grasped Loc's hand in both of his, holding on after the official video shot, asking him about Berry Hong-Owen.

"I hear he's partying like there's no tomorrow. Keeping up the troops' morale with that bar of his. You did good, cleaning up his act and bringing him back to Paris," Euclides Peixoto said. "Yes, there's no doubt that you have a talent for solving tricky problems, and that's why I thought of you for this special assignment that's just now come up."

"I am at your service, as ever," Loc said, feeling that his doom was looming at his back, a black wave about smash into him and carry him away. That was the downside of pandorph. It sharpened your perceptions, but it also amplified your emotional states. And Loc was suddenly feeling very paranoid. Euclides Peixoto clearly knew all about the murder that he and Captain Neves had covered up—why else would he have mentioned Berry? And if he knew about that, what else did he know?

"I like to reward my best people," Euclides Peixoto said. His smile was warm and wide but his dark gaze was cold and flat. "Give them what's coming to them. And when it comes to handling the Outers, there are few better than you, Mr. Ifrahim. My secretary has all the details, but because it's such a delicate and tricky matter I believe it's only right I explain things to you. Man to man."

They sat in sling chairs in front of a big window with a stunning view down the long slope of Paris's tent. Trees fresh and green in bright chandelier light, water sparkling in the river's rocky chute. Euclides explained that the Brazilian and European governments had decided to send a diplomatic mission to Neptune, to gather as much intelligence as possible about the strength and disposition of both communities, to discover whether or not the Free Outers had already sold the secrets of the fast-fusion motor, and to lay the groundwork for a peace treaty that would grant the Ghosts and Free Outers sovereignty of the Neptune System in exchange for a promise that they would acknowledge the TPA's right to govern the Jupiter and Saturn systems, and keep the Uranus System neutral territory unoccupied by either side. It was a pragmatic strategy that would neutralise the Pacific Commu-

256

nity's unilateral plans for some kind of alliance. Containment and control instead of conciliation. Neptune was a long way from anywhere else. As long as the Outers didn't attempt to interfere with the TPA's affairs, they would be allowed to do what they wanted until the TPA—or at least, the Brazilians and Europeans—were in a position to mount an overwhelming attack.

"The diplomatic service is in charge, needless to say, but I have the power to appoint an expert to their team," Euclides told Loc. "And I can think of no one better than you."

Loc hadn't taken the bullet he'd been expecting, but even though things could have been much worse, this—a dangerous and pointless foray to a nest of rebels at the edge of the Solar System which had no chance of any real success—was still pretty bad. He began to demur, saying that he was of course tremendously flattered, mentioning several investigations that needed his personal attention, suggesting one of his own staff who could take his place, but Euclides Peixoto cut him short.

"You have more experience of the Outers than anyone else on my staff. As for your team, it's time to see if they can manage without your immediate supervision. After all, you won't be here forever, will you? Also—here's the capper—you have a personal connection with one of the Outers who will be taking part in the talks."

Loc knew at once who Euclides Peixoto meant: Macy Minnot, the traitor who had defected to the Outer System before the Quiet War. Loc, who'd suffered several bruising encounters with her, had hoped that he would never see her again after she fled to Uranus with the Free Outers. But now she had reached up from the past like a drowning sailor grabbing hold of a shipmate, clinging to him, threatening to pull him under.

Euclides Peixoto was nailing him with his dark stare, waiting for an answer. Loc smiled and said yes. Yes, of course he would go.

"Of course you will," Euclides Peixoto said. "Step over here. We'll get a few more shots for posterity. How about in front of this magnificent chestplate you gave me? Oh, and there's one other thing. I have to appoint someone to look after the security of the team. I think, since you two work so well together, that Captain Neves would be ideal."

"Are you sure he's doing it to punish us?" Captain Neves said, the next day.

"His mention of Berry—that was no accident. Putting us both on the team, that's no accident either. He knows about that murder, my attempt to talk to Sri Hong-Owen, God knows what else."

"Then he's going to look very stupid if we succeed, and come back heroes."

"There's no chance that will happen," Loc said. They were in the pod that Captain Neves used for her special interrogation sessions. It was one of the few places in Camelot, Mimas, where they could talk without worrying about being overheard by spyware. Captain Neves sat by the black mirror of the window while Loc ankled up and down, possessed by a restless agitation no amount of pandorph could ease, saying, "The Outers will almost certainly guess that this isn't really anything to do with negotiating a settlement. And they can't be trusted to honour diplomatic immunity, either. The best we can hope is to get back from this alive."

"I know you don't care what I think, but I'm going to tell you anyway," Captain Neves said. "If Euclides Peixoto wanted to get rid of you, he would have done it already. Sent you home in disgrace, or put you on trial right here."

"It isn't just Euclides Peixoto. I have enemies. So many enemies."

"Come here," Captain Neves said, her voice sharp and crisp. Commanding him. She drew him to her when he sat down, pressing his head against her breasts, running her fingers through his beaded braids, telling them click by click like a clerk working an old-fashioned abacus. She said, "You've been overdoing the pandorph again."

"It helps me think."

"It makes you think too much. The wheels are spinning and throwing off plenty of sparks, but they aren't gaining any traction. This trip will give you a chance to get clean. I'll help you do it. We'll survive this and we'll go on together," Captain Neves said.

"You and me against the world," Loc said.

"Any world you care to mention," Captain Neves said, feeling her lover's pulse slow and his trembling stop, listening as he told her how fine it would be when they returned to Earth, how they would live the high life together, on the far side of their crimes.

◆

Two days later, Loc Ifrahim and Captain Neves were aboard a freighter heading out from the Saturn System toward Neptune. It was a long trip. Neptune was three times as far from the sun as Saturn, and the two planets were some forty degrees away from opposition, Saturn at half past eight to

Neptune's six o'clock. They were separated by over four billion kilometres. Although Loc could send encrypted messages to his office via a tightly focused laser, he grew increasingly anxious as the time lag ticked up from seconds to minutes to hours, worrying that Euclides Peixoto was interfering with his people or, even worse, having his files forensically analysed. It didn't help that the leader of the Peixoto family's negotiators, Sara St Estabal Póvoas, had helmed the diplomatic crew back at Rainbow Bridge, Callisto, when Loc had been involved in a plot that had very nearly blown up in his face. She made it clear that as far as she was concerned he and Captain Neves were surplus to requirements, and told him that she couldn't stop him attending the briefing meetings and training sessions, but he must remember at all times that he was no more than an observer and would not be allowed to have any input.

Loc didn't care. He knew that everything important would be discussed and decided behind his back, and besides, for most of the voyage he was in no condition to make any kind of meaningful contribution. Despite Captain Neves's help, coming off the pandorph was no walk in the park.

There were no physical symptoms of withdrawal, but psychologically it was like falling to the bottom of the ocean. His mind growing sluggish and cold. His thoughts moving through lightless depths under tremendous pressures. Everything around him leached of colour and significance. He slept much of the time, ate only when Captain Neves forced him to eat. If there had been any pandorph on the ship he would have raged and begged for a taste, but she had found the patches he'd tried to smuggle aboard and thrown them away. He cursed her, accused her of being a heartless bitch who wanted to hurt and humiliate him, and much more. She let him rant until his anger turned to remorse and self-disgust and shame, and he wept and begged forgiveness, told her that he knew she was doing this for his own good, that she was strong and he was weak.

Loc confessed all his grievous sins, his thefts and betrayals and murders. How he'd arranged the death of Emmanuel Vargo, the designer of the Rainbow Bridge biome, by bribing a medical technician to give the man a drug that would kill him when he was revived from hibernation at the end of the voyage from Earth to Jupiter. How he'd conspired with Euclides Peixoto's security chief to murder Emmanuel Vargo's lover when she'd come dangerously close to the truth; how he'd conspired with dissident Outers to get rid of the security chief when things had begun to unravel. How he had fatally assaulted a Ghost who had insulted him at a meeting on Dione, and then had killed the Air Defence Force scientist he'd been escorting because the man had tried to prevent him from escaping. How he'd shot an Outer and a Brazilian marine during the battle for Paris.

And then there were the murders she already knew about, because she'd been a party to them. The assassination of Colonel Faustino Malarte. The deaths of the two Outers who had tried to swindle them in a business deal. The boy who had been executed for the murder committed by Berry Hong-Owen.

Captain Neves held him as he choked out his secrets, told him that none of it mattered.

"So much blood," he said. He had a wretched, empty look. "Once you start killing, it's hard to stop. Because it makes things so simple. It gets rid of the problem. It clears a path. I've waded in blood. Swum in it. And as long as I got what I wanted I didn't care. But all of it, everything I have, is soaked in blood. . . ."

"Hush," Captain Neves said. She was cradling him in her lap, stroking his braids as he sobbed and snuffled. As she had held hurt and unhappy children when she had been no more than a child herself, in the dusty camps in the great desert of the American Midwest. "It doesn't matter. It's all gone now. We'll buy ourselves out after this, just like we agreed, and go to Earth, and start over. We'll have such fine times together. You'll see."

Slowly, Loc began to recover, ascending day by day from the depths of his depression like a diver returning to the sunlit surface of the ocean. He and Captain Neves found an observation blister where they could avoid the rest of the people on the ship, play their little games, talk hour after hour. Stars scattered everywhere in the black sky wrapped around them: stars of every colour and brightness everywhere they looked. Captain Neves pointed out and named constellations, something she'd learned as a kid out on the ruined prairies. They made love after their fashion, and afterward blotted floating droplets of blood from the air. They talked about everything they wanted to do when they returned to Earth. Loc said that they could be on their way almost as soon as they had returned to Saturn. He would find a way of getting her a posting in Greater Brazil. They wouldn't be detained by debriefings or discussions about following up the negotiations with the Outers because the negotiations would come to nothing.

Captain Neves was happy to listen to his plans about the future, his fluent and cynical contempt for his superiors. He was healing.

Slowly, Neptune resolved from a bright star to a minute blue disc. The freighter fired up its motor and spent several hours decelerating at 0.5 g—after all the time they'd spent in the various microgravities of Saturn's moons, this was a crushing force that more or less immobilised Loc and Captain Neves—slowing so that it could be captured by Neptune's gravity, entering into a wide orbit and creeping toward the outermost moon, Neso, where the Outers were waiting for them.

It was a dark, irregular rock just sixty kilometres across, a fragment of a moon that had been broken up by tidal forces when Triton had been captured: one face an undulating cratered plain that had once been part of the surface of its parent body, the rest cut by shear planes and deep fractures, like the broken roots of a rotten tooth. It traced a retrograde orbit that took twenty-five years to complete a single circuit around Neptune, with a semimajor axis of more than forty-eight million kilometres—a distance that the Ghosts and Free Outers considered to be a just and adequate quarantine for their contentious visitors.

The conference venue was a bubble habitat that had been especially constructed and set in orbit around Neso. A sphere five hundred metres across blown from insulating layers of aerogel interleaved with tough halflife polymers, given rigidity by the pressure of its atmosphere, an internal skeleton of fullerene struts, and bands set at ninety degrees to each other, running from pole to pole and around the equator. A toy globe. A bright little sphere of air and warmth and light afloat in an infinite cold black ocean. Two shuttles of Outer design stood a little way off, lines linking them to airlocks on the surface of the habitat. After the Brazilian freighter nosed close, a pair of Outers zipped across the gap in a scooter, dragging a line which the delegates used to cross over.

Loc was stricken with delirious vertigo as he was carried in a sling across a black gulf as deep as the universe. An Outer in a pristine white pressure suit received him at the far end and brusquely shoved him into the airlock, a hemispherical bubble on the outer curve of the habitat that opened into another, bigger bubble stuck to the habitat's inner wall. When Captain Neves cycled through, Loc was still in his pressure suit, helpless and trembling, loathing his weakness and longing for a cleansing jolt of pandorph. She helped him strip off his suit and calmed him down, and together they swam out into the habitat's dimly lit, roomy interior.

It was crisscrossed with the three-dimensional web of its internal skeleton and a kind of spherical tree or bush hung like the nucleus of a cell at its centre, a rigid tangle of forking branches scaled with stiff black leaves.

Sleeping pods hung like giant fruit on the struts, glowing in shades of pink or orange, and motile lights swam everywhere, a small galaxy of wandering fireflies. Rayleigh scattering in the aerogel layers of the habitat's wall diffused their light to a deep twilight blue like a ghost of Earth's sky; it took an effort to remember that the skin of this bubble was less than a metre thick, with an infinity of freezing vacuum beyond.

This spooky fairyland was inhabited by a gang of young men and women in their twenties and early thirties, tall and fiercely bright and quick, a group of heroes at the height of their physical powers. Barefoot, equipped with opposable big toes, they maneuvered around the web of struts like a troop of monkeys, used handheld reaction jets to zip through gulfs of thin air. Feral human beings, space and zero gravity their native domain.

They were evenly split between the two factions that had colonised the Neptune System. Ten members of the Ghost cult, all dressed in white, severe and reserved, pale faces marked with tattoos of the constellation Hydrus; ten Free Outers. Sada Selene, a fierce young woman who had once helped to kidnap Loc but ignored him now, was amongst the former; Macy Minnot was amongst the latter, looking tired and careworn.

During the round of introductions, Loc managed to avoid Sada Selene and brought himself close to Macy Minnot and exchanged a few words, expressing his pleasure at seeing her again, saying how strange it was that they should meet after all this time, at such a distance from their home.

"Some might call it fate," he said.

"Or bad luck," Macy Minnot said. "I hope you aren't planning any of your usual mischief."

Her gaze was as pinched and suspicious as ever. Her skin grainy, dark smudges under her eyes, her auburn hair cropped unflatteringly short. Despite her years in exile she was nowhere near as adept at maneuvering in free fall as her companions. Loc could almost feel sorry for her, exiled out here, living an unnatural life with unnatural creatures.

"I'm here to observe the proceedings," he told her. "And to give advice, as required. And you? Despite being an outsider, you must have risen high in your little society."

"I guess you could call me an observer too. I know I'll definitely be keeping an eye on you."

"We're going to be stuck here with each other for a while, Ms. Minnot. Given the circumstances," Loc said, "it wouldn't hurt to be candid with each other."

"If we're being candid, you can tell me who your woman friend is."

"Captain Neves is in charge of our security. Where is your good friend Newton Jones?"

"At home. Looking after our kids."

"Home being Proteus. It can't be easy, living on a barren chunk of ice so far from anything you could call civilisation."

"We've made the best of it."

"And you have multiplied. Begun a dynasty."

"We don't have children of our own yet. The twins, they were orphaned. Their father was killed by your people back at Uranus, when they attacked his unarmed ship," Macy Minnot said, with a fierce direct look that Loc remembered very well.

"Not *my* people," he said. "That would have been Arvam Peixoto's expeditionary force. And the good general, as you may have heard, received his just deserts for that and other careless actions."

"Yet you survived."

"We have both survived, Ms. Minnot. Despite everything. Let's hope that we can survive this."

"Let's hope we can make something of it," Macy Minnot said.

After the introductory session, everyone sat down for a meal in the largest of the habitat's pods. A primal ritual: two tribes meeting and breaking bread together, sizing up each other's differences and strengths and weaknesses.

Both the Ghosts and the Free Outers were supposedly democratic collectives in which everyone had equal rank and authority, but it quickly became clear that Idriss Barr, charismatic and tirelessly enthusiastic, was the primary interlocutor for the Free Outers, while the Ghost delegation was led by Sada Selene, who immediately made a point of protesting about Loc's presence. He'd been part of the diplomatic mission in the Saturn System before the war and was therefore, quite obviously, a spy. And he'd murdered one of her people at a scientific conference on Dione. It was not right that he should be here now. She wanted him to leave.

Sara Póvoas was prepared for this. She said that Loc was an important member of her team, personally appointed by Euclides Peixoto, but since the Ghosts had genuine reservations about him she would make sure that he would have no active role in the negotiations. It was a clever ploy that used

Loc's presence to unsettle and provoke the Ghosts, and pretended to withdraw privileges he'd never possessed as a sop to their pride. The Ghosts fell for it at once, with Sada Selene taking obvious pleasure at having scored a point. Loc, amused by her naïveté, told Captain Neves that the Ghosts' leader would have done better to hold that card in reserve and use it to disrupt the proceedings if things had started to go against her.

"She's too aggressive. And she believes that aggression is a virtue, so she's also arrogant. A fatal combination. Póvoas and her team will play her easily."

The next day, the negotiations began in earnest.

To begin with, Sara Póvoas and the other diplomats cleaved to a conciliatory line, asking the Outers what they wanted to do out here, how they saw their future, what they needed or didn't need from the TPA. . . . Vaguely phrased questions that gently probed the Outers' outlook and convictions and attitude. Nonspecific replies to the Outers' list of demands. Soothing generalities. Bland assurances.

Sada Selene responded to this exactly as Loc had predicted, making it clear that she and her associates were not interested in any kind of treaty or trade mission, or anything else that would compromise their autonomy. The Ghosts had no need of anything the TPA had to offer, she said, and they had nothing to fear from the TPA either. She conjured up views of the Ghosts' city on Triton—chambers and manufactories bustling with all kinds of activity, refineries that produced metals and minerals from water drawn from Triton's deeply buried ocean, work crews swarming over the frames of ships in a vast hangar, racks of pods in which masked operators lay, flying swarms of attack drones by remote control. She said that the Ghosts commanded the volume of space around Neptune, claimed that they would have no trouble taking control of the Uranus System if they wanted to, and reminded the Brazilians and Europeans that the cities on the moons of Saturn and Jupiter were as vulnerable to attack now as they had been before the Quiet War. As was Earth, if it came to it.

"If you hit us, we'll hit back ten times harder," she said. "I'm sure you haven't forgotten the attack we mounted on the squatters on Phoebe, at the beginning of the last war."

Loc thought that was a nice touch: *the last war*. The Ghosts were ready to go at it again, and they wanted the TPA to know it.

While Sada Selene was all razor-blade sarcasm and barbed aggression, the spokesperson for the Free Outers, Idriss Barr, was genial and relaxed, although no less serious. He spoke for several minutes at the end of that first session, telling the Brazilians and Europeans that although the Free Outers cared passionately about the Jupiter and Saturn systems and the fates of their friends and relations, they had made a fresh start out here. The war had given them the opportunity to light out for new territory, and they weren't going back. This was their home, and although they would resist every attempt to bring it under the jurisdiction of the Three Powers Authority, they were willing to talk with the TPA as equals. To make sure that the terrible mistake of the Quiet War was not repeated. To begin to explore some way of moving forward.

After that speech, Idriss Barr was content for the most part to sit back and let others talk things through, although he displayed a knack for intervening at crucial moments, usually when both sides were exhausted and uncertain about where to take the discussion next. Loc studied him with grudging respect; Captain Neves agreed that he was trouble. A true alpha male. Kingly. Someone who could cause serious problems if he could ever reach out to the Outers in the Jupiter and Saturn systems.

"Killing him right now would save us a lot of trouble later on," Captain Neves said, and Loc believed that she was only half kidding.

That evening, he saw Idriss Barr drop out of a game that involved a lot of shouting and flying to and fro, Free Outers rebounding from the walls of the habitat in the big space above the equatorial web in every direction, and he made his way toward the young Outer, sat down beside him, and asked if he had lost or won.

"I was tagged," Idriss Barr said. "So I get to sit out and catch my breath for ten minutes before I can rejoin the fun."

"It isn't about winning or losing," Loc said. "It's how you play the game."

"Exactly."

Idriss Barr was barefoot in a cut-down suit-liner. His skin glowed with ruddy health and he was blotting sweat from his face and arms with a bunched towel. A big happy human animal. Loc, swaddled in a sweater, a fleece jerkin, leggings, and a pair of thick sockshoes against the frosty cold, could feel the heat radiating off him.

"I've lived amongst Outers for a long time now," Loc said. "More years than I care to count. But there are still many things I don't understand. I try, of course. It's my job. But it isn't easy. I see that the Ghosts aren't playing with you, for instance. And I have to wonder why that is."

"Perhaps you should ask the Ghosts."

"They take themselves very seriously, don't they?"

"I thought you were supposed to be an impartial observer, Mr. Ifrahim."

"I believe I just made an observation."

Idriss Barr laughed. Those candid golden eyes. Lion's eyes. An easy smile in a face that wasn't especially handsome but had an appealing openness. It was easy to like him. To want him to like you, to be your friend. Pure alpha through and through. Like Arvam Peixoto, but without the streak of chilly cruelty.

"And I'm sure that you've seen that the Ghosts have very different ambitions from us. But you are mistaken if you think that can be used against us."

"Because you are united against a common enemy?"

"Because there's room enough for a hundred different ways of life out here. A thousand. We have our differences with the Ghosts, but we're both engaged in the same grand adventure. A broadening of possibilities and potential that, far from being a threat to the people of Earth, promises a glorious and harmonious future."

"Alas, there's nothing inevitable about the future," Loc said. "Except for the hard fact that in the long run none of us will be there to see it. You should put the future behind you, Mr. Barr, and think about how you are going to survive the realities of the present."

Idriss Barr slung his towel around his neck and studied Loc for a moment. "You're thirty-five."

"Something like that," Loc said. He didn't want to admit that the man was dead on the nose.

"You're the same generation as me and my friends. You aren't part of the gerontocracy. The old people who run everything. Your new president—how old is he? A hundred and ten, a hundred and twenty? And he replaced a woman who died at the age of a hundred and ninety."

"A hundred and ninety-seven. But why should age matter? Longevity treatments—"

Idriss Barr clapped his hands together. It was like a gun going off in Loc's face: he couldn't help flinching.

"Of course it matters! On Earth, the old grabbed all the power long ago. And although the cities of Saturn and Jupiter liked to boast that they were the last redoubts of democracy, the old always outvoted the young. And they had more kudos too! They had longer to acquire it, and they traded it amongst themselves, so the young had great problems getting favours done or organising projects because they lacked the necessary kudos. You see, Mr. Ifrahim, both sides in the Quiet War were dominated by old men and women who were refighting a war of a hundred years ago. The same rivalries over the same things. Throughout history, it's been the same. Old people going to war against each other over long-held grievances.

"Well, my friends and I have left all that behind. And so have the Ghosts. We have travelled out to the edge of human experience, where there are so many new worlds to explore and experience, where we are trying to create something different. Something new. And I think you have some sympathy with that. I think you're like us. I think you also hunger for change."

"Let's say for the sake of argument that's true," Loc said. "What do you need from me? What do you think I need from you?"

"Those are good questions, but they're the *wrong* questions. Your friends talk about peace treaties and trade, but there's really nothing we need from you. We can source from local materials everything we need to survive and work, and we have no need for superfluous stuff collected to signify status, as birds or fish make bowers to attract a mate. Oh, it's true that Outer society was founded by people who fled from the Earth to a haven on the Moon because they were frightened of losing their wealth and power. But everything changed when the governments of Earth came to take their city from them, and they had to flee again. The worst of them went to Mars, but the majority, including all the people who had kept their lunar city running, the scientists and technicians and all the rest, they went to Jupiter and then spread further out still, to Saturn. And they founded a new kind of society, where people owned only what they needed and status was measured not by what people owned but by what they could do, their research and their arts, their work for the common good. We still cleave to those principles. Of course we do. It's the only logical way to live. The best way to live. And that means that as long as we can live off the land and enjoy the freedom to pursue our artistic and scientific work, we don't need anything else," Idriss Barr said, and pushed away from the spar and flew across the wide space, shouting and jostling with his friends in a game that Loc couldn't begin to understand.

"He's wrong," he told Captain Neves later, as they lay fully clothed in each other's arms, cloudy breath mingling, in their little pod. "The kind of society he describes, where everyone shares the same ideals and is driven by the same kind of dreams and hopes, only works in special circumstances like this. Somewhere cut off from the rest of human society. Somewhere where it takes a lot of work to survive, so that everyone must work together to provide basic needs. It's like one of the old research stations in Antarctica, or on the Moon. A place where people have volunteered to live because they want to be there, not because they happened to be born there. Because they have a mission.

"Once upon a time the Outer System really was like that. A marginal society of niche clingers. Every day, every hour, taken up with the struggle to survive. But as life became easier Outer society began to differentiate. Different people wanted different things. And so they began to trade with each other. For kudos rather than money, but the principle was exactly the same: gratification of desire. And then they began to need things that only we could supply, and they began to trade with us. Idriss Barr does not realise it, but it will happen here, if there is no war. It's the human condition. He says that his people need nothing from us. But they will. They will. And the first person able to exploit that need will make a fortune."

Captain Neves was staring into Loc's face, her eyes serious and intent under the unplucked hedge of her eyebrows, which met in a faint tangle above the bridge of her broad nose. Loc could see himself reflected in the inky wells of her pupils, the darkness where she lived. He could feel her breath on his cheek when she said, "I think you've let Idriss Barr get inside your head. He's made you believe that his people can make a go of it out here."

"They've been out here for less than ten years, and they are already building cities. They spun this little habitat in only a few weeks. What else will they do, given enough time?"

"It doesn't matter what they can do, or what they might want or need. Either they'll fail because there aren't enough of them and they don't have enough resources, or they'll be taken down because it looks like they might be making a go of it."

"As I told Idriss Barr, nothing about the future is inevitable."

"We already know what we want to do," Captain Neves said. "Go back to Earth as soon as we can. Use our experience and our contacts to make a real fortune, when the war comes. That's the plan."

"And it's a good plan," Loc said. "It'll set us up for life. But you're not the kind of person who will be able to settle into retirement. Neither am I. We'll want to do something else. This might be it."

"Is this something serious, or are you causing trouble because you're bored?"

"Machiavelli taught us long ago that if you want to control a territory, you support the weaker powers in it without increasing their strength, and crush the strongest."

"We studied Machiavelli in officer school," Captain Neves said. "He also said that you can't avoid war; you can only postpone it."

Loc shrugged inside her loose embrace. "It's just an idea at the moment.

A possibility. The Ghosts, there's no point in talking to them. They're fanatics with no interest in making a deal, as they've made plain from the outset. They only agreed to this meeting because they want to find out about us, and make vain threats and boasts. The talks will fail in a day or two, you wait and see. But Idriss Barr and his people aren't Ghosts. They are something else."

"You've fallen in love," Captain Neves said, smiling.

Loc smiled too. "All I'm going to do is talk. What harm can it do?"

Over the next two days, as Loc had predicted, the negotiations began to stall. The Ghosts sat in frosty silence as the Brazilian and European diplomats set out their proposals, and then spent hours picking apart every detail and making outrageous demands until nothing was left. And while they continued to ignore Loc, they engaged the other diplomats in intense conversations about their lives and work, no doubt hoping to add the information to socioeconomic and political models of Greater Brazil and the various cities on the various moons of Jupiter and Saturn. Of course, the Brazilians and Europeans were attempting to do exactly the same thing, but although the Ghosts boasted freely about the defensive and offensive capabilities of their cadres and ships, and their willingness to sacrifice everything to protect the future that their leader and guru had entrusted to them, they yielded only scant details about their city and the lives of their people.

Somehow, Sara Póvoas's expertise and the energetic optimism of Idriss Barr and the Free Outers kept things together. Loc watched everything, analysing every player's strengths and weaknesses and habits of thought, noting how everyone interacted with everyone else, feeling out the cross currents of power and influence. He tried his best to explain some of it to Captain Neves, who was growing increasingly bored and impatient with talks that went around and around without any movement forward or back. She saw a hopeless knot; Loc saw a web taut with intrigue and alive with possibility.

The Free Outers were growing increasing frustrated with the Ghosts' tactics, yet dared not challenge them openly. Partly out of solidarity, no doubt, Outers standing shoulder to shoulder with Outers. Partly because they were clearly intimidated by the Ghosts: because they were a small band of refugees living in the shadow of a kind of death cult. Yet it was clear that they hoped to persuade the Brazilians and Europeans of their legitimacy, and wanted to define some measure of common ground in which they could, at some later date, sink the foundations for a peace treaty. Loc was increasingly confident that he would be able to work on their hopes and fears, and persuade them to open a clandestine back channel so that they could continue talks with the TPA without the knowledge or interference of the Ghosts. That he might gain some personal prestige from this farrago, and later, maybe, just maybe, be able to profit from it.

And anyway, it wasn't as if he had anything better to do.

He couldn't approach Idriss Barr, of course; both Sara Póvoas and the Ghosts would suspect he was up to something. But everyone knew that Macy Minnot disliked and distrusted him because he'd once tried to have her killed, so he believed that he could talk to her without arousing any suspicion or accusation of double dealing. After the communal dinner on the third night, he found her sitting on a platform near one of the poles of the habitat, looking down at the gulf where the Free Outers flew about in the perpetual blue twilight. Shouting and laughing as they chased after a small ball and each other, rebounding from walls and swinging around spars and rocketing off in different directions.

"I still don't understand the rules of that game," he said.

"The person with the ball has to pass it to someone else as quickly as possible," Macy Minnot said, without looking at him.

"That's it?"

"That's it."

"I notice that you don't play."

"I've played. But I'm not quick enough. I slow the game down."

"As the Ghosts slow down the negotiations."

"That isn't very subtle, Mr. Ifrahim. You're losing your touch."

"I think we've reached a stage where we can safely abandon subtlety and nuance."

Macy Minnot looked at him, her face as usual clenched as a fist. "If you want to find out why the Ghosts are doing what they are doing, you should ask them."

"It's clear that they want only to advertise their strength and determination, and to make sure that your friends gain no advantage from these talks. It hurts, doesn't it?"

"Excuse me?"

"To think that this will come to nothing. I understand. After all, you have more to lose than anyone else."

"Is that what you think?"

"Your friends are here because they want to be here. Because they believe that they are the cutting edge of human evolution. The seed from which a thousand Utopias will flower. But you are here by accident. You managed to make a kind of life for yourself. And I'm impressed, I really am. You are tougher and more resourceful than I thought. But is it really what you want?"

"Do we ever get what we really want? How about you, Mr. Ifrahim? After all you've done, do you think you've been properly rewarded?"

"After this, I'm going to retire. Captain Neves and I will go back to Earth. We'll marry, and set up a consultation business in Brasília. Have you ever been to Brasília, Ms. Minnot? Some people don't like the climate—they say it's too hot, too dry. Others say that it is too crowded. But if you have enough money, it is a fine place to live."

"I'm sure you'll be very happy."

"I haven't been back to Earth since the war. I look forward to returning very much."

"Why don't you tell me what you want from me, Mr. Ifrahim? Or did you come simply to gloat?"

"You think I have some kind of nefarious plan."

"I'm going by past experience."

Loc smiled at this sally, feeling something akin to affection. Sri Hong-Owen had once asked him if he'd believed in fate. He certainly believed that you couldn't choose where and when you were born; perhaps that was fate or perhaps it was nothing more than chance, but after that, your life was what you made of it. Still, it was hard not to imagine that fate, or something like it, had twisted his life and the life of Macy Minnot around each other. A spiral like DNA's double helix. Complementary pairs. She his dark half. The shadow to his light.

He said, "I didn't want to come here. I was ordered to accompany the diplomatic team because Euclides Peixoto, who I am sure you remember, wanted someone to observe their work, and also wanted to punish me. So here I am. An observer. I have no part in the negotiations. No influence on Ms. Póvoas, or the people to whom she reports. But that doesn't mean that I want these talks to come to nothing. Let me share something with you, if I may. Officially, the TPA does not differentiate between you and the Ghosts. Unofficially, there are some people who appreciate your difficult and delicate relationship with neighbours who are more numerous, better equipped, and highly aggressive."

"And they care why?"

"You have every reason to mistrust the TPA, of course. But times change. The attack on the Uranus System was the initiative of an egomaniac who suffered the ultimate punishment for his intemperate action. And there are some of us who believe that it isn't in our interests to go to war against the Ghosts, let alone you. If we can take one thing away from this meeting, it's the opportunity to continue a conversation."

"Go back to Earth, Mr. Ifrahim. Have a nice life there—why not? But stop trying to play God."

"I'm sharing a few observations with you, Ms. Minnot. I mean no harm by them."

They stared at each other like lovers seeing each other naked for the first time. Then Macy Minnot shrugged. "Talk doesn't mean anything anyway," she said. "We talked to Tommy Tabagee, and it got us nowhere."

"Oh, I don't think that's true. You invested considerable time and effort setting up this habitat so that you could talk with the TPA."

"We want to find a way of making peace with the TPA. That means something more than just talking about it."

"If you don't talk, you'll never reach any kind of agreement," Loc said, and pushed off from the platform and sculled away down a long spar, heading toward the pod he shared with Captain Neves.

Halfway there, Sada Selene stooped down on him, falling out of thin air, checking her momentum by catching hold of one of the nylon loops strung along the spar, swinging around in a somersault and landing on her feet in front of him like a pirate boarding a captive vessel. Tall and slim and imperious in her clean white suit-liner, her smile knife thin.

"I really wouldn't count on Macy Minnot, if I were you," she said. "I don't think she's forgiven you for what happened at Rainbow Bridge."

"And has she forgiven you for kidnapping her?"

"She's learned to live with it. All the Free Outers have had to learn to live with us. We're all there is out here."

"Yet they are equal partners in these talks."

"They have their uses. You talk more readily with them than with us, for one thing. And you probably wouldn't have come all the way out here to meet only with us."

"If who we can and cannot meet was ever up to you, I'm sure you'd be right."

"You told Idriss Barr that there was nothing inevitable about the future," she said. "Yes, of course we were listening to your conversation. We listen to everything."

"I had never thought otherwise."

"You're wrong about the future. It is what it is. And we will do whatever we have to do to make it come out right. Remember that," Sada Selene said, and kicked away, arrowing past Loc toward the spherical black tangle of the tree at the heart of the little world, where the Ghosts had made their camp.

Loc thought that it was only an idle threat, one of many such that Sada Selene had made. He should have known better.

Loc was woken by Captain Neves in the small hours of the night. She told him that the Ghosts were gone. They'd disabled the spyware sown by the diplomats, stuck portable airlocks to the wall of the habitat, and bailed. Most had crossed to their ship; two had tried to sneak aboard the Brazilian freighter and they'd blown themselves up when marines intercepted them, damaging the hull. Part of the life system was in vacuum. Emergency repairs were being made and the ship was preparing to get under way.

"We're leaving right now, before anything else happens," Captain Neves said. Her face, set in a grim expression, looked ashen in the greenish light of the little pod. The spike of a short-range radio was jammed in her right ear.

"Something has already happened to the ship. Shouldn't we stay here until it's fixed?"

"It's an order, not a suggestion," Captain Neves said, and pushed Loc through the slit in the pod's wall.

The habitat's constellations of wandering lights had been switched off; the volume of airy darkness was defined by the faint pastel glow of the pods scattered along the spars and pools of bright light playing across the outer skin as maintenance drones searched for evidence of sabotage. Captain Neves kicked away from the pod, towing Loc toward the big net strung in front of the main airlock, where a squad of marines suited up in battle armour were watching the Free Outers pull on their pressure suits.

Loc grabbed a line at the edge of the net, hauled himself along it to the marine captain, and asked him what was going on.

The captain stared at Loc through the gold-tinted faceplate of his helmet and said through the suit's external speaker, "We're keeping them for your protection, sir."

"As hostages? That's not a good idea, Captain. They had nothing to do with this incredibly stupid action of the Ghosts," Loc said, speaking loudly so that the Free Outers could hear him. "What's more, the Ghosts care as much for these people as they care for us. Or for themselves, for that matter. Which is to say, they care not one whit if they live or die."

"Get your suit, sir. We're evacuating the habitat now."

"Let them go, Captain. We don't need hostages, but we may need their goodwill."

"Get inside with the other civilians. We're about to evacuate all of you."

Loc barged through the people crowded into the bubble of the airlock's antechamber and confronted Sara Póvoas, asking her if she approved of taking the Free Outers prisoner.

"I might have known you'd take their side," she said.

"I'm trying to make sure we do the right thing," Loc said.

"You're trying to salvage some kind of deal with them, so that you can line your pockets," Sara Póvoas said. "Don't think I haven't seen what you've been up to, Mr. Ifrahim."

"Perhaps I can succeed where you have failed, Ms. Póvoas."

Loc would have said more, but Captain Neves grabbed hold of him, spun him around, and shoved him toward the rack where his pressure suit hung, forked open down the chest by its big double zip like a man split by an axe, and told him to put it on.

"They're making a bad mistake," Loc said.

"No need to make it worse," Captain Neves said.

Braced against each other, they stripped down to their suit-liners, fastened up their pressure suits, and checked their lifepacks. Marines started to call out names and escorted the diplomats through the airlock one by one. Loc and Captain Neves were being left to last—deliberately, in Loc's opinion. Dread congealed in his belly, thick and heavy as nausea.

Through the transparent wall of the antechamber, the Free Outers in their variously coloured pressure suits were balancing like acrobats on the rippling net, while marines turtled up in heavy black battle armour clutched lines and tried to keep their pulse rifles trained on them. Loc thought to switch on the common band and heard Idriss Barr explaining to the marine captain that his people would not leave except in their own ship.

The captain cut him off, told him his people were all prisoners of war, and said that if they didn't line up now and obey orders he'd shoot one of them as an example to the rest.

"I cannot permit that," Idriss Barr said.

"You have no choice," the captain said.

Idriss Barr laughed. "Of course I do."

All around, above and below and around its equator, panels blew away from the habitat's skin. The spiderweb framework flexed and shuddered and the spherical volume was filled with whirlpools of mist that spun and thinned and vanished, sucked through the open panels into the vacuum of space. The powerful lights of the drones tumbled away, leaving only the dim glow of the pods, dabs of pink and orange in a vast black volume.

Inside the airlock's antechamber, Loc clung to Captain Neves, his breath rattling inside his helmet, watching with stark disbelief as the marines shone lights wildly all around, catching glimpses of the Free Outers as they flew through empty space, moving fast and straight as arrows, flashing into existence as light caught them for a moment, vanishing into the general darkness. Some of the marines chased after the Outers; others braced against spars or lines and took aim with their pulse rifles. An Outer caught in two overlapping pools of light plunged through a black gap and vanished a moment before a bolt struck the lip of the hole and that part of the wall exploded outward like a flower, long rips extending away in every direction.

Then one of the marines in the antechamber grabbed Captain Neves and Loc, hauled them through the open inner hatch of the airlock, and slammed it shut behind them. The airlock decompressed with a sharp crack, the outer door swung open, and the marine waiting outside helped them one after the other into the rigid triangle of a sling and clipped the utility belts of their suits to tethers and triggered the sling's motor.

"Don't worry," Captain Neves said, as the sling pulled away from the airlock. "We're going to be all right."

The dark curve of the habitat receded as the sling hauled them along a line stretched toward the freighter, which hung small and sharply detailed in faint sunlight—a little over three kilometres away according to the radar package of Loc's suit's, and growing closer at a steady eighteen kph. All around, vast black emptiness spangled with stars. Loc clung to the sling's frame, his fingers cramping inside heavy gloves. The surf of his breathing was loud inside his helmet; cold dry air feathered across his face. For several minutes, nothing happened apart from the slow expansion of the freighter. He began to believe that they would make it. Then something flashed at the edge of his vision and he turned, clumsy and stiff inside his suit, and saw a second flash light up the habitat from inside. A frozen glimpse of ragged flaps of the habitat's skin peeling away, the web of internal spars etched in stark shadow against a fading red blossom, and then darkness again.

"They blew up the habitat," Loc said. "Someone blew up the habitat."

"Ghosts. It's on the military band. They launched a bunch of drones," Captain Neves said, and the sling jolted to a stop and the stars began to wheel around them.

Loc cried out. He couldn't help it. Beside him, Captain Neves unclipped her tether from the sling's frame and attached the end to his utility belt. She was reaching past him, trying to unclip his tether, when the line they were travelling along snapped outward in a great curve, as fast and sudden as a cracked whip. Captain Neves swore and Loc was flung against her so hard that his head jarred inside the padding of his helmet. Everything revolved around him. He glimpsed a blindingly bright star—the freighter, its fusion motor lit, moving through a shoal of red flashes that blinked and faded in random patterns. And then there was another tremendous jolt and he and Captain Neves went spinning away from the sling. His tether had broken loose and Captain Neves's tether was stretched between them. Stars wheeled all around. Loc felt his gorge rise and sweat pop all over his skin. He closed his eyes, scared that he'd throw up and futz his suit or choke on his own vomit. . . .

He felt the tether slacken. A moment later Captain Neves slammed into him and he grabbed hold of her and a series of short, sharp jolts buffeted him in different directions. Captain Neves was using her reaction pistol to counter their spin.

"All right," she said, and wrapped one arm around his waist. "That's the best I can do. . . ."

Loc risked opening his eyes. The stars were still revolving, but at a slow and regular pace now. A stately waltz. Captain Neves was talking, asking for help over and over. Trying different channels, Loc realised. He pulled up his suit's comms package and began to ask for help too. No reply. Maybe the freighter had moved out of range. . . . He looked all around, searching for its star of fusion light, and Captain Neves pulled him close and told him to quit moving about or he'd start them tumbling again.

"They killed the ship," Loc said. He felt that he was at the centre of a great ringing calm.

"I don't know. Maybe. Or maybe it shut down its comms when it was attacked," Captain Neves said.

There was a sobbing catch in her voice, and Loc saw then that her left arm was hanging limp at her side. It was twisted oddly at the elbow and there was stuff bulging out, black against the yellow of the suit's fabric.

"You're hurt," he said.

"The line pinched my arm against the sling. Cracked the suit's elbow joint. But it's okay. The suit sealed itself, at the shoulder."

"Oh Christ."

"It's all right. I'm not going to die. Not today."

"Are you bleeding?"

"Some. Not much now. The arm's mostly frozen, I think. I'll be all right. They'll patch me up on the ship."

"Tell me we're going to survive this."

"It looks a lot worse than it really is."

"How can it get any worse!"

"Loc! Loc! Look at me. All right. You have to stay calm," Captain Neves said. Her face was centimetres away from his, separated by the faceplates of their helmets. She told him to take a deep breath and hold it and let it out slowly. "And again. Like this."

For a couple of minutes they didn't do anything but breathe together.

"You're going to be fine," Captain Neves said.

"I know we're in trouble because you never called me by my first name before," Loc said. It was supposed to be a joke but it came out wrong.

"The Ghosts attacked the habitat and our ship. Sent in a swarm of drones. That's why the ship took off. It jettisoned the line, and the line whiplashed. I saw it coming. Tried to get us free. . . ."

"It wasn't your fault," Loc said.

"We have to stay calm and alert. The ship will come back. For us. For the marines."

"We could try to reach the habitat. What's left of it. The marines can help us."

The idea of being inside something, even if it had no air, was unbelievably attractive. Anything was better than endlessly falling through nothing at all.

"The habitat took a bad hit," Captain Neves said. "A drone detonated right inside it. Maybe the marines survived it, maybe not. I don't know. I do know they're not talking on any of the channels. . . . Anyway, we're too far away. And moving too fast. Stay still. Stay calm. Take slow deep breaths. We'll get through this together. I promise."

"Don't die," Loc said. "Please don't die."

"I'm doing my best."

The stars revolved around them. The sun's brilliant star crossed the black sky from left to right every few minutes. Captain Neves said that she couldn't find the freighter, and told Loc it didn't mean anything. It was stealthed and her suit's radar only worked over short distances. The Free Outers' ship was nowhere to be seen either, but Captain Neves got a fix on the tiny moon, Neso, and said that the Outers might be squatting down there.

"If the Ghosts didn't attack it too," Loc said.

"If I was them, I'd sit tight until I could be sure it was safe to head for home," Captain Neves said. "But before I did that, I'd sweep the area, look for survivors. So as soon as we're pinged by radar, we light up our emergency beacons and we start calling, on every channel. Okay?"

"It might be the Ghosts' radar."

"That's a risk we'll have to take."

There was a growing tightness in her voice but she was quite calm, as if this was a training exercise. Loc looked into her face, her dark brown eyes. Locked behind the faceplate of her helmet. Unreachable. He talked about what they would do when they got back to Earth until she told him to be quiet, he should save his air. They clung to each other, and he watched her eyes lose focus and told her to stay awake. Then he told himself that she was only sleeping.

He kept talking to her. His mouth was dry and although he kept sucking water from the helmet's nipple it did not slake his thirst and at last he stopped, worried that he would run out of water before he ran out of air. He tried using the radio but no one answered. He held Captain Neves as the rigid patterns of the stars wheeled slowly around. He knew that he was going to die and he did not much care. At any time he could switch off the rebreather in his lifepack and he would pass out when the partial pressure of carbon dioxide passed a critical level and he would not wake up. It wouldn't be so bad.

Loc could no longer see the habitat. The sun was the brightest star of all the stars sliding past, chased by Neptune's tiny blue crescent. Swinging up on his left side past his knees, his hips, his shoulders, vanishing overhead, swinging down on his right side . . . he must have fallen asleep, because without a beat of time a voice was in his ears. His first thought, rising on a surge of relief, was that it was Captain Neves, that she'd only passed out. . . . No, it was someone else, calling his name. Calling Captain Neves's name.

Something flared to one side, a pale jet blinking on and off, and Loc suddenly realised that a shadow hung between him and Neso, growing larger and acquiring three dimensions. A ship. The freighter had come back. . . .

But then he saw that it was not the freighter's razorshell but a squat boxy thing, an Outer tug sidling up, suddenly very close. He switched on his suit's emergency strobe and switched on his helmet light too, aiming it straight at the tug. He saw the rack of its cargo frame and the blister of its lifesystem. It was very close now, close enough to see that its black paint had flaked away in places to show pink underneath.

A light blinked under his chin. Someone was trying to talk to him on the common channel. Loc switched over to it and said that he was alive but his friend was hurt, she needed help. "Hurry. Please hurry."

"We'll be right there," the voice said.

It was Macy Minnot.

PART FIVE

CHIMES OF FREEDOM

T he Free Outers fled inward, toward the sun. Eight ships carrying a little over three hundred souls. The survivors of the delegation, and those who had escaped from Endeavour in the scant hour allowed by the Ghosts, whose ships had landed outside the Free Outers' habitat just before the attack on the Brazilian freighter. Drones armed with thermal lances had immediately begun to trash the vacuum-organism fields on the cratered plain around Endeavour, and banner messages projected through the diamond panes of its roof had announced in black lettering ten metres tall that a holy war of liberation had been declared against the occupiers of the Outer System, the Free Outers could either join it or leave the Neptune System at once. When the Free Outers tried to contact the Ghosts, they discovered that this same message looped on every channel. Then, directly beneath the apex of the spiderweb roof, a block of giant numbers appeared: minutes counting backward from sixty to zero. Newt told Macy that he'd snatched up the go bag they'd packed for emergencies and grabbed the twins and bolted through one of the escape tunnels, priming *Elephant* and taking off just before the deadline expired.

"It wasn't anything like the drills. Han and Hannah knew it was for real, but they did good. They didn't argue. They came right along. When we got to *Elephant*, Hannah asked me if we were going to die. She looked so frightened. Han was scared and excited, but Hannah *knew*. She knew what it was all about. That was the hardest thing. Dealing with that. They didn't have to do it that way," Newt said, rigid with anger. "They could have asked us politely."

"It's not in their nature," Macy said. "I guess, in some odd way, giving us the chance to join them was a sign of respect. But they didn't want to discuss it with us because, as far as they're concerned, whether or not any of us chose to join them was a matter of faith. And you don't question faith."

"A lot of people stayed behind," Newt said. "Too many."

"Maybe they thought the Ghosts were doing the right thing," Macy said. "Or maybe they just couldn't face lighting out and starting over someplace else."

"You're taking this very calmly, considering they tried to kill you."

"I can't see any other way of dealing with it. After we agreed to meet with the diplomats from Greater Brazil and the European Union, Sada told me that we'd made the right choice. She didn't mean it was the best thing to do as far as our interests were concerned, or that it was morally right. She meant that it fitted into the great plan they're working toward. The Ghosts do what they do because they believe it's necessary—to make sure history is steered in the right direction. So there's no point arguing with them; there's not even any point getting mad at them. Besides, they could have killed us if they wanted to, but they didn't. They're crazy, but they're not bad to the bone."

"They're bad enough."

"What did you say to Hannah?"

"When she asked if we were going to die?"

"Yes."

"I told her we were going to find you."

"And you did."

"Yes, I did."

"We survived."

"We survived."

"And we'll go on."

"We'd better."

Everyone aboard the refugee ships was numb and exhausted. When Newt and Idriss Barr proposed a possible destination it was accepted almost at once, with very little debate. They could not return to the Uranus System because they feared that it would be guarded and watched by Brazilian drones, and because it had already proven to be of no worth as a hiding place. But although their morale was at its lowest ebb, they were not yet ready to return to Saturn or Jupiter and surrender to the TPA. And so their small mismatched fleet angled up out of the plane of the ecliptic toward a rendezvous with Nephele, one of the class of objects known as centaurs that follow wandering orbits between Jupiter and Uranus.

Some centaurs are planetoids; others are the nuclei of spent or semiactive comets; all have been ejected from the Kuiper Belt after encounters with one of its dwarf planets. Nephele was one of the largest, a rough ovoid of water ice with a semimajor axis of a little over two hundred kilometres and a dark red surface rich in thiolins, olivine grains, methanol ice, and sooty carbon. It orbited the sun with a period of some ninety-one years, with an aphelion that swung inside the orbit of Saturn and a perihelion that grazed the edge of the orbit of Uranus. Currently, it had just passed perihelion. Heading sunward, it was roughly 1.4 billion kilometres from Saturn, a little over nine times the distance between Earth and the sun.

The Free Outers matched orbit with Nephele fifty-eight days after quitting the Neptune System, and started work at once. Pleased to be engaged in practical matters. Salving their sorely wounded pride by engaging with straightforward problems of material science and engineering. Spinning useful materials from ancient ices and tars. Living off the land.

They'd had to leave behind their crew of construction robots, but had brought with them the modified units which had spun the temporary bubble habitat where the ill-fated negotiations had taken place. They set up a mining and refinery system that processed the organics that coated Nephele's surface, melted and purified water ice, and used these materials to create a new habitat just two hundred metres across, with a water-filled bubble forming an anchoring point at its centre and platforms strung above and below the main internal struts, some for hydroponic farms, others for general living space.

Their dreams of exploring human limits, building cities on the moons of Uranus and Neptune, and expanding into the Kuiper Belt had been abandoned. Left behind with almost everything else when the Ghosts had evicted them from their home on Proteus. Nevertheless, when it was finished, Nephele's tiny new moon, with its racks of lights, greening gardens, and watery nucleus, had a fragile, precious beauty. A teardrop jewel hung amongst the little fleet of ships as they swung around the dark and misshapen centaur.

The Free Outers agreed that they had done the best they could in the circumstances, and began to plan improvements as soon as they had moved into their new home. Water ice could be used to weave a shell around the bubble habitat; strengthened by a pseudofungal vacuum organism from Avernus's great catalogue that would grow through the ice and extrude a fine but incredibly strong web of fullerene threads, it would provide protection from the perpetual sleet of cosmic radiation and occasional micrometeorites. Aerogel insulation on the inside of the water-ice shell would reduce the habitat's infrared signature, and a radar-reflective coat and a layer of bound soot on the outside would make it even harder to spot. The tarry surface of Nephele could be planted out with vacuum-organism farms. Borrowing a trick from the Ghosts, a dismounted fusion motor could be used to melt deep pits into its surface, and these could be insulated and capped to create microgravity biomes. Every ton of meltwater would yield several grams of tritium and deuterium fuel. In time, the Free Outers might even be able to construct a linear particle accelerator and use it to synthesise antiprotons.

But these and other plans could not be realised until they had first survived the unclear and hazardous reefs of the immediate future. Meanwhile, they were short of just about every kind of consumable, and had to strictly enforce food rationing until the refinery ramped up production of CHON food and the catch crops planted by the farm crew matured. And they were low on fuel, too, with only enough for less than half their little fleet to be able to reach either Saturn or Uranus. All they could do was hunker down and hope that they would be overlooked when the war between the Ghosts and the TPA began.

That there would be a war was, at present, their only certainty.

2

The prison was set inside the great basin of Korolev Crater, on the Moon's far side, just south of the equator. Its domed tent, built by construction robots confiscated from the Outers, spanned the rim of a crater some four kilometres across. Inside, a thin atmosphere, two hundred millibars of carbon dioxide leavened with a little sulphur dioxide and water vapour, was maintained at a balmy 18° Celsius. Most of the floor was patched with fields of photosynthetic vacuum organisms that fixed carbon dioxide and drew up minerals from the lunar soil and synthesised plastics and exotic biochemicals. A quilt of autumn colours that stretched in every direction. During the long lunar night the fields were lit by rows of suspensor lamps, but during the day the sun produced light enough. Felice Gottschalk had forgotten how bright the sun was, on the Moon. Bright enough to blind you, if you looked at it long enough. He'd forgotten how big and hot it was, too. He could feel its heat through the thin material of the close-fitting bodysuit that he wore when out in the fields, supervising the stoop labour of his stick of prisoners under a high roof that glowed gold with diffused sunlight.

The prisoners, former politicians and leaders of the peace and reconciliation movement, and the trusties who supervised them, were mostly left to their own devices. The prison was an experimental facility, set up to find out if Outers could be safely quarantined in self-sufficient, self-policing communities. The Brazilian and European guards used a panoptic surveillance

system to monitor the prisoners, and rarely entered the tent or directly intervened in ordinary prison life; Felice Gottschalk and the other trusties were
responsible for keeping order, allocating work, and enforcing rules and
instructions issued by the prison administration; the prisoners grew CHON
foods and dole yeast, harvested and processed plastics and biochemicals produced by the vacuum organisms, which could be traded for fresh food and
other luxuries, and spent their free time as they pleased.

Felice lived with the other trusties from Rhea in a two-storey flat-roofed
apartment building in Trusty Town, one of ten identical white cubes scattered
amongst lawns and spindly young trees under a secondary dome at the edge of
the prison tent. The acknowledged king of Trusty Town was a vigorous young
psychopath named Edz Jealott. He'd had himself tweaked to develop a car-
toonishly exaggerated musculature, and spent a great deal of his free time
exercising to maintain the tone and definition of his massive arms and legs, his
broad shoulders and the gleaming shield of his chest. He liked to parade
around naked or mostly naked, accompanied by a posse of lieutenants and girlfriends. He had been in remedial treatment ever since, at age fourteen, he'd
fatally stabbed his younger sister. Now, with the tacit approval of the prison
administration, he ruled the trusties with arbitrary and brutal authority.

Soon after Felice was discharged from the prison clinic, two of Edz
Jealott's lieutenants tried to ambush him, a ritual hazing all trusties had to
endure. Felice broke the arm of one man and knocked out the other. After
that he was mostly left alone, and did his best to ignore Edz Jealott's regime.

Trusties had access to every part of the prison tent. They jogged or cycled
around its circumference, and rambled amongst the cliffs and boulderfields of
the rim. Felice discovered a talent for freestyle climbing. He soloed several
new routes, and had a favourite spot near the top of the western rim, close to
the skirt of the tent, where he could sit and look out across pieced fields of
vacuum organisms to the comb of salt-white barracks that housed the prisoners and the blue-tinted dome of Trusty Town perched above it, in a low
saddle in the rim wall. Groups of prisoners small as insects worked here and
there in the fields and the black flecks of surveillance drones hung above them
in the bright air. His world entire. The only world he had now. Perhaps the
last world he would ever have.

Despite regular exercise and strong doses of steroids, he was troubled by
a persistent stiffness in his limbs and a numbness that came and went in his
fingers and toes, and he was sometimes a little clumsy, dropping things or
knocking them over. The medical technician, Amy Ma Coulibaly, assured

him that his condition was developing more slowly than she had expected, and he tried not to think of it as a death sentence, but it was always there, even at moments when he was happiest. Like the shadow of a rock under the surface of a sunlit lake.

During his long convalescence after the trauma of revival from hibernation, Amy Ma Coulibaly had taught Felice the rudiments of chess; he visited her at the clinic three or four times a week to play a game or two. He lost most of the time: the old woman was a fierce and agile tactician. She made her moves swiftly and decisively, altering the position of a piece on the slate's virtual board with a flick of her forefinger, leaning back while Felice agonised over his response. He was fascinated by the way in which a few simple opening moves so quickly developed into a complex web of possibilities, how lines of power and influence switched in strange and unexpected configurations as the game developed. It was so very like battle calculus that he had to wonder why he and his brothers hadn't been taught to play chess during their training. Perhaps it was because of the fierce intellectual pleasure that immersion in the game generated. His childhood and his training had been strictly utilitarian, and the lectors had roundly denounced every kind of pleasure.

Felice and Amy Ma Coulibaly talked about the small change of prison life while they played—the rivalries, intrigues, and romances amongst the prisoners and the trusties, Edz Jealott's excesses, the significance of the latest tweaks made by the prison administration to the rules and regulations. Amy did most of the talking. She loved to gossip, and had sharp and vividly expressed opinions about everyone and everything in the prison. She was one of the pioneering generation of Outers, a century and a half old, born into a wealthy family in New Zealand, where many of the richest and most powerful people on Earth had moved to escape the worst effects of climate change, food riots, energy shortages, terrorism, and the general breakdown of civilisation at the back end of the twenty-first century. But even refuges like New Zealand had become unstable, and when she had been just five years old Amy's family had decided to buy shares in a settlement, Athena, that was being built near Archimedes Crater in the northwest quadrant of the Moon. A year after they had quit Earth, the violent release of millions of tons of methane gas from clathrate fields in the Antarctic had triggered a chaotic and comprehensive climatic disaster—the Overturn—that had caused the deaths of several billion people and had radically and permanently altered global politics. Twenty years later, the powerful military and criminal families who'd taken control of most of the countries of Earth had turned their attention to the refugees on the Moon, who had fled outward before the threats of annexing Athena could be realised. They had possessed considerable experience in building habitats by then, settling on Mars and on Jupiter's second-largest moon, Callisto, colonising other moons of Jupiter and Saturn. And then Earth had moved against Mars.

Felice Gottschalk believed that he knew some of this story—how a treacherous plan by the colonists on Mars to nudge an asteroid into a collision course with Earth had been foiled, how heroes from the Chinese Democratic Republic had sacrificed their lives by H-bombing the settlements on Mars and diverting a comet and breaking it up so that it had stitched a string of impacts around Mars's equator and killed every last Martian. This was the version of history drilled into him during his strange childhood, but according to Amy Ma Coulibaly the Chinese had struck the first blow after the Martians had refused to cede their independence, a sneak attack that had destroyed the settlements at Ares Valles and Hellas Planitia. A few of the surviving Martians had attempted to avenge this atrocity by altering the orbit of a Trojan asteroid so that it would intersect the orbit of Earth, but their plan had failed, and the Chinese had wiped out the survivors of the sneak attack with the cometary impact. Amy said that if the Chinese hadn't lost more than half of their small fleet of ships in this effort they might have gone on to destroy the nascent colonies of the Jupiter and Saturn systems, too. Instead, both sides had recoiled from the enormity of the Martian holocaust and a peace treaty had been hastily drawn up and ratified. Amy had been present at the signing ceremony that had taken place in the ruined city of her childhood, Athena. This was a solemn and important moment in human history from which no one seemed to have learned anything lasting. It was true that the fragile peace between Earth and the Outers had lasted a century, but only because the chief political powers on Earth had been preoccupied with making good the damage caused by the Overturn and centuries of industrialisation and global warming.

Amy had raised a family with her partner and had helped to build the city of Rainbow Bridge, Callisto. After her partner died, she had moved to Athens, Tethys, and had taken up a new career as a medical technician. She'd been a friend and occasional collaborator with the gene wizard Avernus, and had also been involved with the peace and reconciliation movement, and that was why she had been put in jail by the TPA after the war.

"But I was never a refusenik," she said. "I'm too old and cowardly to take part in the nonviolent protests. So I was sent here, with all the other old crocks."

Felice Gottschalk gave her a bowdlerised account of his search for Zi Lei, the year he'd spent helping to repair and rebuild Paris, Dione, and his adventures on Iapetus with the gypsy prospector Karyl Mezhidov. He couldn't bring himself to tell Amy that they had something in common, that they'd both lived on the Moon in former lives, that he'd been born here, tweaked to resemble an Outer and grown to maturity in only two and a half thousand days, trained as a spy and saboteur. And if Amy suspected his true nature, she never mentioned it, and never asked who had designed his tweaks, or where he had come from, or what he'd been doing before the war. She seemed to like him for what he had become, and as far as he was concerned the past was past. The daily routines of the prison were his life now, a chain of beads told one by one, each a minuscule measure of atonement for his sins.

A little over two hundred and fifty days after Felice had woken in Amy's prison clinic, a new batch of prisoners arrived. Gene wizards, engineers, experts in every area of science and technology. They were housed in Trusty Town rather than in the barracks of the ordinary prisoners, and were put to work collaborating with scientists in the European Union and the territories of the Peixoto and Nabuco families. One of them, Bel Glise, was an old friend of Amy Ma Coulibaly, and she often sat with Amy and Felice while they played chess and gossiped. A rake-thin, edgy woman of some sixty years, she was a mathematician and a poet—famous for her poetry on every inhabited moon of the Outer System, according to Amy—but she never talked about her work, or much else, either.

"Now is not the time," she said, with a thin smile, on the only occasion when Felice's curiosity got the better of him and he asked her if she had written anything in the prison.

He didn't much like the woman. Most Outers kept themselves scrupulously clean, but Bel Glise had a faint persistent sour odour, her long pale hair hung lank and dull around her thin face, and she bit her nails to the quick. Sitting hunched and forlorn like some admonitory revenant, she watched the games of chess with unnerving concentration, saying hardly a word.

Amy told Felice that he should try to understand Bel Glise a little more and criticise her a little less. She had lost several members of her immediate family in the war; she'd been arrested on a trumped-up charge so that the Europeans and Brazilians could exploit her expertise in a branch of mathematics useful in data mining; and she was finding it hard to adjust to life in prison.

"She's the most intelligent person I know," Amy said. "Her mind operates on very abstract levels, and her interrogators have difficulty understanding her even when she is doing her best to explain her ideas. So they hurt and threaten her. They treat her with massive doses of veridical drugs and use her implant to give her brief jolts of intense pain to punish her when they feel that she's being especially uncooperative. And that makes it even harder for her to give them what they want, and so they hurt her more. A nasty little positive feedback loop. I'm trying to help her with cognitive therapy, and sitting with us is part of that."

Amy was a good friend—the only friend Felice had—and he needed her medical expertise and the drugs she gave him to ameliorate the symptoms of his condition. And that meant that he had to try to be a friend to Bel Glise. The mathematician cut a lonely figure in Trusty Town. She sat by herself in the commissary or wandered alone between the accommodation blocks, twisting her hands over one another as if trying to wash off some indelible stain, her lips moving and her eyes focused elsewhere. She could often be found on the promenade where Trusty Town's dome abutted the flank of the main tent and a long, flat panel of construction diamond gave an unobstructed view out across the lunar surface. There was nothing much to see— an undulating plain littered with small craters and fans of ejecta and a few larger rocks, stretching away toward a low hill at the horizon, the rim of another crater—but the panorama seemed to fascinate and calm her.

Felice Gottschalk liked it, too. Liked to watch the way shadows changed shape and the colours of the landscape slowly transmuted from every shade of grey to bronze and golden tans as the sun tracked across the black sky. It reminded him of the last days of his training, when he and his brothers had been allowed out onto the surface, when he had been full of happy anticipation, dreaming of the missions he might be given, the victories he would help win. And yes, sometimes of escape. Even then, he'd dreamed of escaping what he was, of finding his own true self. Sometimes, as he stood staring out at the lunar panorama, his mind ticked through a simple calculation. The Moon was about eleven thousand kilometres in circumference and Korolev Crater was off to one side of the meridian. If he walked about two thousand kilometres eastward, he would be able to see Earth rise above the horizon. It would take him about two hundred hours, a little over eight days. . . .

He was standing there one day, lost in contemplation, when he became aware of a disturbance behind him. On the far side of a broad stretch of parched and threadbare grass, two of Edz Jealott's lieutenants were circling Bel Glise, taunting her, blocking her attempts to walk away. As Felice Gottschalk approached, he saw that the taller of the two men was Zhang Hilton, the man whose arm he'd broken in the brief fight six months ago, after he'd been discharged from the clinic. Zhang Hilton was trying, half seriously, to pull down the zipper of Bel Glise's coveralls, and she was trying with furious and silent concentration to preserve her modesty, shielding the zipper with one hand and with the other batting at Zhang Hilton as he pried and prodded, and his companion made coarse suggestions.

A drone floated high above, sharply silhouetted against the blue of the dome. Felice could hear the faint whisper of its fans as he loped across the grass, Zhang Hilton turning to him, smiling, asking him if he wanted a piece of the action.

Felice ignored the man and asked Bel Glise if she was all right. She nodded once, straight up and down, her bloodless lips clamped tight.

"I'll walk you back to your room," Felice said.

"We just got her warmed up and you step in?" Zhang Hilton said. He was still smiling, but his gaze was deadly serious. "Man, I don't think so."

"How is your arm?" Felice said.

"I heal quick," Zhang Hilton said. "How about you?"

"If you want to fight me, don't involve anyone else. Just walk up and ask," Felice said.

He was staring into Zhang Hilton's face, watching for the cues that would give away the man's intentions, but he was also aware of Zhang Hilton's friend in his peripheral vision, turning now to look at something. He glanced around, a half-second jerk of his head. Two men were coming across the plaza from the west and a man and a woman were advancing from the east, all moving with the jaunty bouncing stroll that marked out Edz Jealott's lieutenants. Felice saw Zhang Hilton's expression change slightly, caught the man's wrist when he began to reach inside his jerkin and body-checked him and threw him to the ground and kicked him hard below the angle of his jaw, at the spot where nerves clustered, then pulled his shock stick from his belt and flicked it on and turned to face the other man, who'd conjured a three-ball flail from somewhere. The man held it low and swished it to and fro as he sidled to the left. Felice turned to follow him, aware of the other lieutenants closing on either side, armed with various of the nonlethal weapons permitted by the prison administration.

The drone hung unmoving high above. No help there. In the early days, the guards had put a stop to every kind of trouble by zapping everyone involved, but now they intervened only if it looked like someone was going to be killed.

Felice stepped toward the man with the flail, drawing circles in the air with his shock stick. The man swung at him and he drew himself in, the three iron balls at the ends of their taut chains whirring past his belly, and jammed the shock stick against the man's ear. The man howled and fell to his knees and dropped the flail; before Felice could snatch it up, the other lieutenants charged in on either side. A man jabbed a shock stick at Felice's face and Felice kicked him in the kneecap and put him straight down, spun in a half-circle, and broke the woman's nose with his elbow. Another man moved in from the left, swinging a cosh fabricated from a flexible sleeve of plastic stuffed with gravel and sand. Felice fended off the first blow with his left arm, the shock numbing it from elbow to shoulder; the second caught him on the side of the head and drove him to his knees. He saw the bloody-nosed woman wrestling with Bel Glise, saw Zhang Hilton staggering toward him with a cudgel gripped loosely in one hand, saw the cosh come down again and ducked away and felt air part above his head. Then the fourth lieutenant stepped in and kicked Felice hard in the small of his back and laid him out flat and breathless.

That wasn't what knocked him out. The drone did that, zapping everyone in the vicinity with bolts of white-hot pain before Zhang Hilton could smash Felice's skull.

When Felice Gottschalk regained consciousness, he was lying on his back, looking up at Edz Jealott and the blue curve of the dome. The light hurt his eyes. His head felt as if it had been split open and his left arm was hot and swollen. When he pushed to his knees, his sight pulsed black and red and the world revolved around him at a tilt and he almost fell down again.

"You started a fight," Edz Jealott said. "I won't have that in my town."

Men and women stood in a wide and loose circle around the two of them. Edz Jealott's girlfriends and lieutenants, other trusties, scientists. The young giant wore only a bodysuit rolled down to his waist, white elastomer molded to his muscular legs and bulging over the bullybag of his genitals. On the broad shield of his chest a nest of tattooed snakes composed entirely of flame writhed around each other in slow motion. His skin was milkily translucent and his mane of black hair hung in oily ringlets to his shoulders.

"If you want to fight anyone, fight me," he said, and struck the knot of flame-snakes with a hand big enough to wrap around Felice's head. "I'll even let you take the first shot."

Felice didn't reply. There was no point. Besides, it was taking most of his concentration to stay on his feet. The ground was pitching to and fro and Edz Jealott's face kept doubling and sliding back together, the man making a speech now about the need to stick together, why it was dangerous for anyone to think that they could do what they wanted and ignore the common good. There was a commotion amongst the people loosely gathered around them— it was Amy Ma Coulibaly, intercepted by one of Edz Jealott's lieutenants as she pushed through the watchers, the man twisting her arm up behind her back. Felice stepped toward her, and Edz Jealott caught his arm, swung him around, and swept him up in an implacable embrace. For a moment, they stared at each other; then Edz Jealott reared back and slammed his head forward and with the stony prow of his forehead broke Felice's nose. Felice fell flat on his back, dazed and half blinded by the hot knot of pain. He rolled over and pushed to his knees, and Edz Jealott's kick caught him square in his chest and sent him flying backward. The Moon slammed into him with all its unforgiving mass, and he didn't feel anything else.

Waking once more in Amy Ma Coulibaly's clinic, staring up at the pale glow of its ceiling, Felice felt as if he had reached without passing through any intermediate stages the terminal point of his illness. His torso and his left arm were badly bruised, he could feel his ribs creak every time he took a breath, and his nose was swollen and splinted. Amy told him that he had a concussion, and insisted on subjecting him to a battery of neurological tests. Rather more, he suspected, than was strictly necessary, but he was too confused and too weak to put up any resistance. He asked about Bel Glise. Amy told him that she had suffered nothing more than a few bruises and a mild case of shock.

"I'm glad."

"You should be ashamed," Amy said, jabbing her slate with her forefinger, flipping through the false-colour representations of his brain's neuro-dynamic activity. "Causing trouble like this. Is it pride, Felice? Or is it because you don't really understand other people?"

"I couldn't walk away from it. I had to try to help her."

"You knew it was a show, didn't you?"

"When I saw the others, yes. Not at first."

"You knew that they were using Bel to lure you into some sort of trap. And you knew that they wouldn't have done anything really bad to her because the guards would have punished them. You should have walked away."

"I was angry. Because they were using her. Because I had put her in danger."

"And now?"

"How do I feel now? Ashamed. Confused. I poison everything I touch. I put your friend in danger, and you must be in danger too. I should go. . . ."

But when he tried to sit up his head ripped wide open and muscles across his chest seized up with pain, so he lay back and watched the ceiling tiles slide apart through fat lenses of self-pitying tears.

"This isn't in any way a normal society," Amy said. "It's more like a tribe of wild primates. Ruled by an alpha male with the help of a circle of men and women who behave like him because they are frightened of being exploited and threatened like the rest. And because Edz Jealott is at the head of the tribe, it reflects the way he thinks, and the way he thinks is crippled. You challenged his authority by acting as though it had nothing to do with you. He couldn't ignore that because it was damaging his reputation, and reputation is all he has. Hence this."

"If he wanted to fight me, he could have called me out."

"He wanted to humiliate you. Hopefully, he thinks that he's succeeded," Amy said. "Otherwise he'll come after you again. Now, not another word. Let me finish up here, so you can rest."

Felice slept for a while, and woke to find Amy sitting straightbacked beside his hospital bed, hands folded prayerwise in her lap. She asked him how he was feeling, and he said that he felt that she had something to tell him.

"The bruising and cracked ribs are healing amazingly quickly. And your nose won't look quite as noble as it once did, but it's healing too," Amy said. "But I need to ask—have you been experiencing any numbness or dizziness recently?"

"It's my condition, isn't it?"

"The tests show an impairment to your peripheral nervous system. It's a natural progression. Neither faster nor slower than I expected."

"This is why Edz Jealott could beat me up."

"That's exactly the attitude that got you in so much trouble," Amy said, and he shrivelled from her look of severe reproof.

Because he knew that she was right. He'd thought that he was different from the other prisoners and trusties. A nation of one, a secret king harbouring the secret wound of his illness, aloof and invulnerable, noble and virtuous. Edz Jealott had proved him wrong, had shown him that he was as human as everyone else. He supposed that he should be grateful, that he shouldn't hate the man, but he couldn't quite manage it. Perhaps that was part of being human too.

3

The front-line camp of R&R Corps #897 was a row of Quonset huts hunched at the foot of the tanks and towers of a soil factory. To the south, gleaming like steel under the darkening sky, the Platte River ribboned away through a patchwork of restored reed beds and grassland. Everywhere else was a desert stripped of topsoil by a century of megastorms. A vast and tumbled waste fretted with gullies and crevasses and sinkholes, haunted by strong and restless winds that prowled writhing ridges of rock and winnowed tufts of tough catchgrass that clung amongst broken stones and blew swirls of sand past the posse of riders heading toward the camp, hunched on their horses in flapping dusters or serapes like road agents escaped from the myths of the long ago, the red blaze of a sunset foundering on the low and level horizon behind them.

An advance party had ridden into the camp several hours before. As the riders came down the ancient blacktop a small crowd surged through the gate in the security fence, whooping and cheering. Cash Baker checked his horse and thumbed back his broad-brimmed hat and looked around. Men and women dressed in green denim shirts and blue jeans; a jostle of upturned faces pale in the glare of the arc lights strung along the fence. This was the part he liked the least. An assassin could step forward, face cold and pitiless as a snake's, and aim a revolver or trigger a satchel bomb. Soldiers could jog out from the shadows under the soil factory's towers. . . .

People raised their hands toward him and he reached down and shook a few. The other riders were shaking hands too, and their leader was halted in the middle of the crowd, leaning on the horn of his saddle and talking with an officer who had caught the bridle of his horse. After a few moments he sat up, blond hair shining in the arc lights, and lifted his hands over his head. The crowd grew quiet. Every face turned toward him as he thanked them for their hospitality. "We've ridden a long way to be here, so I hope you'll excuse us if we take an hour to tend to our horses and freshen up. But I look forward to talking to you. We have much to discuss!"

Cash Baker had been riding with Alder Hong-Owen and his crew for six months now. At first they'd worked their way north along the Rocky Mountains, visiting with fugitive groups of so-called wildsiders—people who refused to quit the land and lived as nomads, a thousand small groups with a thousand names. Some of them native Americans, fiercely proud and independent. Others the descendants of refugees from the great shipwreck of civilisation. Sheep-herders and goat-herders in their temporary camps in summer pasturage high in the mountains. Bands of hunter-gatherers who pitched their smart-fabric tents here and there for a few days or a few weeks, tending little gardens hidden amongst rocks, in clearings in forests of pine and birch and alder, moving on. There was a village of houses built into ledges in the side of a steep canyon, with gardens strung along the canyon floor and wind-powered turbines hidden in tunnels carved through the ridge-rock. A group of rabbit farmers who presented everyone in Alder's crew with patchwork gilets stitched from black and white pelts. A group that had colonised a nuclear shelter from the long ago, tending a hydroelectric plant, a farm of ancient mainframe computers, and a communications network that stretched along the backbone of the Rockies.

Everywhere they went, Alder Hong-Owen's pilgrims distributed people-tree seeds, talked about revolution, and discussed the latest news from the rest of Greater Brazil and the moons of Jupiter and Saturn.

Bandits, criminals, and the like who'd gone feral were rare in the mountains. Most had been hunted down by the wildsiders, who either killed them in firefights or captured them and dumped them bound and naked and tattooed with lists of their crimes at the edges of the ant-heap cities. But when Alder's crew of pilgrims quit the mountains ahead of the winter snows and cut around the northern end of the Great Desert, they were twice attacked by bandit crews. The first time a sneak raid at night, two guards left dead with their throats cut, five horses stolen amidst a wild stampede in the pitch dark. The second time, one snowy day early in December, a woman was shot out of her saddle by a rifleman as they rode through the ruins of Coleharbor, south of the great salt pan of what had once been Lake Sakakawea. They were pinned down by desultory gunfire until, as dusk began to fall, Cash led a counterattack. They engaged several indistinct figures in running gunfights amongst wrecked houses, lost their only drone, and pressed on until they reached a position the bandits had abandoned only minutes before, a horse-shoe of stones amongst a stand of leafless sycamores, bloody bandages, and clothes scattered around a smoldering fire, tracks trampled into the snow heading toward the hills to the north. The next morning, riding out of the ruins, they passed poles alongside the road, leaning into the blizzard and topped with grisly heads wearing caps of bloody snow, eyes rolled back, ears sheared away. Whether meant as threat or tribute they never knew nor cared to discuss.

They celebrated Christmas with a community of wildsiders in a village of shipping containers buried in the raddled plains just south of the Missouri River, in what had once been North Dakota, left on New Year's Day, and rode on south along the edge of the Great Desert in a meandering path that some-times doubled back on itself or looped out to the east or west. By now, they were beginning to talk to members of the R&R Corps. To individuals or small groups that came out to meet them at first, and then to entire camps.

There had been food shortages and riots in the cities that winter. Martial law in most of the territories of the former United States. In Panama City, soldiers opened fire on starving people who marched on the mansion of one of the scions of the Escobar family. More than seven hundred people were killed that day, and thousands more died in riots that laid waste to half the city. The bishop of Manaus led a prayer vigil for peace; on the third day, in the middle of the service, an assassin walked through the congregation that packed the cathedral and shot the bishop dead as he raised the host for Mass, and in the square outside soldiers shot into the crowds as they fled. The gov-ernment declared that the martyred bishop had been an agent of the Pacific Community, there were mass arrests of priests and other dissidents across Greater Brazil, and trials and executions of the most prominent so-called trai-tors were broadcast across the nets.

A number of brigades of the R&R Corps refused to leave their barracks when they were ordered to help the army put down riots. Army units fought their way into camps, rounded up everyone, selected men and women at random, and executed them. When the Commander in Chief of the R&R Corps protested, she and many of her senior officers were placed under arrest and transported to the notorious military prison outside São Paulo. The rank and file of the R&R Corps were in a mutinous mood, but had lacked direction and leadership until Alder Hong-Owen, son of the famous gene wizard Sri Hong-Owen, rode through the camps along the front line at the western edge of the Great Desert to speak amongst them.

The stopover in the camp of R&R Corps #897 was little different from all the others. Cash spoke first, drawing on the tricks and techniques he'd been taught when shilling for the Air Defence Force. Standing on a table at one end of the crowded mess hut, he told the story of how he'd been made into a hero by General Arvam Peixoto and then disgraced as part of a plot to bring the general down, explained that his elevation and fall from grace was just one example of how the great families used and discarded ordinary people, and then asked Alder Hong-Owen to step up and talk, raising his voice to be heard over the crowd's whoops and applause.

Alder spoke with an easy and engaging confidence. His pale hands shaping the air, his mellifluous voice floating above the packed heads of his audience. He spoke of how gangsters, arms dealers, pirates, and plutocrats had seized power during the confusion after the Overturn and had founded new dynasties. How these so-called great families had co-opted certain ideas of the green movement—restitution and rewilding, ecological stewardship, living lightly on the land and all the rest—and used them to gain and hold on to power. How the great and good work to reclaim and restore Earth's damaged ecosystems had been turned into a tyrannical creed. How people had been herded into cities that were prison camps in all but name, or forced to toil on pharaonic projects. How enemies had been invented to keep the population under control, for as long as the population feared those enemies they would not question those in power. The Pacific Community, and then the Outers, and now the Pacific Community again. And always the wildsiders and bandits on the borders. How the sacrifices endured by the many were not shared by the few who ruled them.

"Ordinary men and women have suffered every kind of deprivation and hardship in the name of Gaia, yet this is how the so-called great families of Greater Brazil live," Alder said, and conjured images of the houses of the rich in a memo space. Some from his own files, some taken by Cash Baker, some from surveillance satellites. Mansions and hunting lodges. Great estates walled off from the world. Islands made over into private paradises.

He answered every question put to him, and it was long past midnight when he and his crew distributed people-tree seeds amongst the R&R crew and explained where to plant them and how they would grow.

Early the next morning, the small party rode out in a mist of thin rain blown by the cold March wind in drifts and billows across fields of cotton-wood and willow saplings. They rode across the pontoon bridge that floated on the broad, shallow flood of the river, rode on down a dirt road that cut straight through rewilded grassland, and just two kilometres south of the river they were ambushed.

The three men riding point ahead of the rest of the party disappeared in an eruption of red flame and black smoke and a harsh thunderclap that rolled out across the grassland as dirt and pieces of horses and men rained down. The other riders checked their startled mounts and circled round, shouting to each other as men rose up from the waist-high grass on either side of the road, two on the left, three on the right. They were armed with automatic rifles and began firing at once from distances of less than twenty metres. Rounds snapped through the air and knocked spouts of mud and water from the road as Cash crawled behind his foundered horse. He'd lost his hat and his ears were ringing. His horse had been shot through the neck and kept trying to lift its head. Its eyes were rolling and it was blowing bloody foam through its nostrils. Cash drew his pistol, but his hands were shaking badly and the gunsight wove and jittered as he tried to take aim at the nearest of the bushwhackers and his shots went wide. A burst of gunfire struck the road close by and spattered him with wet dirt. He thumbed mud from his eyes and braced his pistol against the worn leather of the saddle's seat, but the harder he tried to keep it steady the more it shook. One of the bushwhackers collapsed as if someone had cut him off at the knees and the other ducked away, bent low as he ran off into the windblown sea of grass. Cash rolled over, pointed his wavering pistol at the other side of the road, and saw that the three other bushwhackers were down. One was crawling like a broken-backed snake along the ditch, and Cash got up and limped after Arnie Echols and caught hold of Arnie's arm as he raised his pistol.

"He can tell us who set us up," Cash said.

But the man had been shot through both lungs and when Cash turned him over he coughed a spray of blood and died. His halflife camo gear pulsed with dark irregular patches as it tried to match the blood seeping through the ditch's mud.

"Who are they?" Arnie said. "Army?"

"The Army would have surrounded the camp with tanks. These are bounty hunters I reckon," Cash said. "And amateurs at that, luckily for us. Anyone who knew what they were about would have hit us as we were crossing the bridge."

He searched the dead man but failed to find any ID, just three clips of steel-jacketed rounds, a pair of handcuffs, and a packet of chewing resin in his pockets, a hunting knife sheathed at his belt, the spike of a short-range phone in his ear. Cash washed blood from his hands in cold ditchwater, then stood up and followed Arnie back along the road. Two bodies covered with dusters, horses lying dead or gravely wounded, horses standing in the rain with their reins trailing. People were kneeling around wounded men and women, cutting off clothes, breaking open medical kits. One of the wounded sat against the belly of a dead horse, the shoulder of his green nylon serape wet with blood, blond hair plastered in rat-tails, face pale as chalk: Alder Hong-Owen.

They agreed that they couldn't ride back to the R&R camp because it was very likely that someone there had betrayed them. Arnie Echols used the phone that connected to the clandestine communications network to arrange a rendezvous, and they buried the dead by the road, fixed up hammocks between pairs of horses, and walked their wounded through the grassland and out into the desert beyond. Late that night they met up with a group of wildsiders camped in a deep ravine, and the wildsiders led them east. They crossed the river at a series of fords strung between low islands and as the stars began to fade from the sky they reached a camp in the hills beyond.

Alder Hong-Owen's left shoulder had been shattered by a high-velocity round and he'd developed pneumonia during the journey to the camp. A medical technician brought in from the big R&R depot outside Omaha did what he could, but said that Alder needed the kind of surgical intervention and postoperative treatment that only a hospital could supply. Alder refused to leave the camp, and Cash and the others backed him up when the technician appealed to them.

"He'll lose the use of his arm," the technician said.

"Better that than lose his life," Cash said.

The medical technician was affronted by this slight on his honour, and said so. Cash told him that he shouldn't take it personally. "One of those bushwhackers got away, and we have to assume he has friends, or maybe told the Army about us, hoping to get a share of the reward. And that means we can't show our faces anywhere people might be looking for us."

Alder was young and strong. Within a few days he was using the wildsiders' communications network to keep track of the growing political and civil disturbances and to talk with leaders of Freedom Rider cells in cities scattered the length and breadth of Greater Brazil. A week later he was out of bed and hobbling around the camp, wincing and sweating, sitting down to rest at frequent intervals; two weeks after that he quit using painkillers and declared that he was fit enough to travel.

The next day, he and Cash rode through the sandy hills beyond the camp with two wildsiders trailing them. Alder's arm was strapped to his chest in a sling of black cloth, but he handled his horse well enough and if he was in any pain he didn't show it. They stopped at a grove of people trees growing green and vigorous in a shallow basin below a ridge top, sat in the shade amongst knobby roots and black ropes of symbiotic nanomachinery clutching at rocks, and shared a lunch of cheese and bread and pickled tomatoes while Alder explained that he wanted Cash to travel east and meet one of his contacts in Indianapolis.

"They need a pilot," he said.

Cash held up his hands to show the tremor in his fingers. "I'd have to get a load on to be able to fly. I don't see what good that would do anyone."

"Maybe my friend can help you with that. And we're short on people who can fly shuttles, and you're about the only one I trust."

"You mean space shuttles?"

"To the Moon, when the time comes," Alder said.

4

News about growing unrest in Greater Brazil seeped into Trusty Town via a sympathetic European scientist who was collaborating with one of the gene wizards. Most of the trusties said that it would never amount to anything. The great families were too powerful. Every form of dissent would be ruthlessly suppressed and in the end nothing would be changed.

"The trusties have to believe that the revolution will fail because they have a personal stake in the survival of the status quo," Amy Ma Coulibaly told Felice Gottschalk. "They may not realise it, but they've become as politicised as any of the prisoners."

"It isn't a revolution," Felice said. "That's the point. Some of those agitators might want to *start* a revolution, but they haven't managed it yet. And they probably never will."

They were playing chess, and as usual Felice's endgame was a hopeless position. Yet he persevered, hoping that Amy would make a mistake, even though experience had long ago taught him that she would not.

While she waited for Felice to make his next move, Amy said, "As I understand it, ordinary people in Greater Brazil have had to pay for the Quiet War and the occupation of the Jupiter and Saturn systems, while the great families have grown fat on profits from looted technology. And now their government wants to go to war against the Pacific Community, over who should govern some distant balls of ice. Their sons and daughters will be drafted into the military; they'll lose what little freedom they have left; their cities will become targets for enemy missiles. They've had enough. They want things to change."

Felice moved a pawn to the sixth rank, threatening Amy's remaining knight. "But you can't change things simply by wanting them to change, can you?"

"Are you speaking from personal experience?" Amy said, with a dry look. She'd cut her hair short and dyed it jet black a couple of weeks ago, and was wearing dark purple lipstick and black eyeliner that heightened the papery paleness of her skin.

"You have to know *how* you want to change."

Amy moved her rook one step sideways. "Perhaps they want what we used to have, before the war. All they lack is a leader to point them in the right direction."

Felice saw that if he took the knight he'd be checkmated when the rook took the pawn, so he moved his other surviving pawn a step past his king. Amy moved the threatened knight, checking his king and forcing him to move it back, then moved her other rook into the same row and declared checkmate.

"I lost some time ago," Felice said, rubbing the numb and stiff fingers of his left hand. He was taking doses of steroids by intramuscular injection now, but they weren't making much difference.

"You always fight to the very end," Amy said.

"As I was taught."

"Your nose doesn't look so bad now. In this light, at least."

"I believe I began to change long before Edz Jealott broke my nose. I hope I'm still changing."

"Except for your endgame."

"If I don't play every game to the end, how can I ever hope to win?"

"What would you do if the government fell?"

"If there was a revolution?"

"If it succeeded."

"I don't know. It doesn't mean that we would be freed, does it?"

"If we were."

"Go to Earth, if I could."

"Don't you want to be fixed up first?"

"I can get fixed up on Earth, can't I?"

Amy smiled. "Perhaps we could go together."

"To New Zealand?"

"Why not? I'm sure it's still there."

A military ship touched down at the prison's landing field, and robots unloaded construction materials, transported them into the tent, and fabricated a geodesic dome close to the western flank of the rim wall. Two days after the dome had been completed and pressure-tested, a second ship arrived and disgorged a batch of prisoners from Earth. They were marched straight to the new dome and put to work, constructing a barracks inside it. There were rumours that they were renegade scientists and scions of the great families who had shown sympathy with the agitators in Greater Brazil, but no one knew for sure because the new prisoners were kept entirely separate from everyone else.

Amy said that it was a sign that the government of Greater Brazil was weakening. "If President Nabuco was confident that he could crush the revolution, he would have killed those prisoners instead of sending them here."

"They are hostages," Felice said.

"Exactly so. If the government falls, the president will use them to bargain for clemency."

"What about us?"

"Let's hope we also have some value. To one side or the other."

Soon after the new prisoners arrived, one of the Outer prisoners disappeared. Goether Lyle, an expert in n-dimensional topology. When he didn't turn up for his daily session with his collaborators in Greater Brazil, trusties were ordered by the prison administration to search the barracks and the vacuum-organism fields; later that day, his body was discovered a few hundred metres from the new geodesic dome. It appeared to be a straightforward suicide. Goether Lyle had been found sitting cross-legged, head bowed, his face mask, air tank, and harness rig lying nearby.

That evening, Felice asked Amy if Goether Lyle had ever talked about killing himself.

"I didn't really know him."

"He was from Athens, like you."

"So are many other people in this place."

"Well, did he ever talk to you about it during one of his health checks?"

"If he did, it would have been in confidence. Between patient and doctor."

"That doesn't matter now, does it?"

"It matters to me. Why don't you tell me what's on your mind, Felice?"

"It wasn't suicide," Felice said.

"It wasn't?"

Felice cupped the back of his neck with his palm. "The surveillance system tracks our implants every minute of the day, everywhere in the prison. But it took several hours to find Goether Lyle's body. Either his implant had been turned off, or it had been removed."

"You know that isn't possible."

"I was thinking that one of the guards could have switched off Goether Lyle's implant via the surveillance system before luring him out into the fields and killing him."

"If one of the guards happens to be listening to us right now, that kind of talk could get you into trouble."

"They don't much care what we think."

Amy studied him. "You haven't really changed, have you? You're still looking for someone to save."

"I can't save Goether Lyle."

"You think someone killed him. You want to save other people from the same fate."

"You could talk to your friend. The European doctor. Ask him whether there was any unusual bruising on Goether Lyle's body. Any indication of a struggle."

"Goether killed himself, Felice," Amy said, with uncharacteristic asperity. "He found a dead spot in the surveillance system and took off his face mask. As suicides go, it would have been more or less painless. The high concentration of carbon dioxide would have rendered him unconscious before the low pressure could cause internal haemorrhaging. People have killed themselves before, in here. And they'll do it again. So let this go. Don't do anything stupid."

"When someone else dies," Felice said, "you'll know that I'm right."

5

Cash Baker rode out of Omaha in an R&R truck driven by a cheerful middle-aged woman who told him to take good care of himself when he swung down from the cab at the depot on the outskirts of St. Louis. He hitched a ride on a freight train that headed north and east out of St. Louis and stopped at every station along the line to Indianapolis. It was raining in Indianapolis. Seven in the evening, the sky sheeted with low cloud, flood-lights burning along the tracks in the freight yard, rain falling on the strings of boxcars. Cash followed the instructions he'd been given and caught a bus that would take him to the east side of the city. Two men sat behind him and when the bus started moving again one of the men leaned forward and told Cash that they were there to help him.

"Who am I talking to?"

Cash had his hand in his slingbag, holding the grip of his pistol. But there was no point pulling it because the men could be armed too, and if he caused any kind of trouble the bus's AI would lock the doors and call the police.

"Friends who want to keep you out of the hands of state security," the first man said.

"Your contact in Tower Twenty-Eight is compromised," the other said. "You're lucky we spotted you before the OSS did."

"We'll get off at the next stop," the first man said.

They got off at the next stop. A banana-yellow electric car was parked at the curb under the dripping foliage of a big people tree. Gouts of rain drove across the deserted plaza beyond. The tiered lights of a residential tower rose into the wet black night.

Cash climbed into the back of the car and one of the men got behind the wheel and the other sat beside Cash and insisted on shaking his hand. A simple human gesture that made Cash feel slightly better, although the men wouldn't tell him where they were going. They drove for an hour or so along a twisty route, at last turning off the road and gliding down an avenue of trees and pulling up in front of a big white-porticoed house that looked as old as the United States, rain spearing down out of the night all around.

A burly dark-skinned old man with a trimmed white beard stood in the big, double-height doorway, framed by yellow light, calling out to Cash as he unpacked himself from the little car, telling him to come on in out of the goddamn weather.

That was how he met Colonel Bear Stamford.

The two men drove off in their little yellow car and Cash followed the colonel into a hallway, dripping on the tiled floor, taking in the wooden staircase and the wooden panelling on the walls.

"We'll get you dry, and then we'll talk," the old man said.

A house robot floated out of the shadows beyond the staircase and led Cash to a bedroom where he showered and put on the sweater and jeans laid out on the bed. He spent a moment thinking about whether or not to tuck the pistol in the waistband of the jeans, decided it wouldn't make any difference, and followed the robot downstairs to a large room where ladders of old books crowded real wood shelves and a memo space showed a view of Earth from geosynchronous orbit.

Colonel Stamford rose to greet him from one of the leather wing chairs that stood on either side of a carved stone fireplace in which real wood logs burned, and asked him if he preferred whiskey or brandy. Cash said he'd settle for coffee. Another robot, smaller than the first, poured him a small cup from a silver pot while Colonel Stamford asked Cash about his adventures with Alder Hong-Owen and the houses and hunting lodges of the rich that he'd attacked last year. They used the memo space to check them out. The view was live, patched from surveillance satellites, tracking in to show the ruins of buildings blackened and burnt in their various wildernesses.

"You stopped after four actions," Colonel Stamford said.

"The point wasn't to destroy every one of those places, but to make folk aware of them. That's why I took the photos and made the movies," Cash said. "I think it worked, because I wouldn't be here otherwise, would I?"

"Perhaps you didn't expect to meet someone like me. Someone who is quite obviously of the establishment, such as it is."

"This past year I've learned we have all kinds of friends, Colonel."

"When did you last eat, Captain Baker?"

"I've mostly been travelling today. I had me a good breakfast before I started out."

"I would be honoured if you would stay and have dinner," Colonel Stamford said.

They ate in a room that seemed to have been furnished solely for that purpose, with a long oak table and oak chairs with carved backs and seats cushioned with cracked red leather. The small robot glided back and forth on its ball drive between the room and a kitchen somewhere else in the house, serving onion soup and fresh bread, a rice dish with bits of vegetable in it, and three kinds of sauce in silver pitchers. The colonel drank blood-dark wine; Cash, wanting to keep a clear head, stuck to water.

The dining room, like the hallway, was panelled with dark wood. Life-sized oil paintings of men and women in military uniform hung along one wall. Three of them in pressure suits of antique design. One, Colonel Stamford told Cash, had been the first woman to step onto the surface of Mars; somewhere in the house was one of the rocks she had brought back.

"My family has a long history of serving the United States of America. As has yours. Those days are part of the long ago of course, but we still maintain some of the old traditions."

At last Cash dared to ask the question he'd been itching to ask ever since he had arrived. "Are you in charge of this thing I joined?"

"I don't think you could say that anyone in particular is in charge of anything."

"That's what they say. I've always found it hard to believe, though."

"Because of your military background. I quite understand. But we are not in the military now. We are part of a horizontal and highly distributed organisation, and it's very important that it stays that way. First, because it means that it cannot be destroyed by cutting off its head. Second, because it means that it belongs to everyone. For my part, I have connections with people who are interested in what you and your friends have been doing this past year. They supported the peace and reconciliation movement before the Quiet War, and they are very much against the idea of going to war against the Pacific Community."

"You mean the Fontaine family. This is their territory, right? And I know they've always voted against military spending. Even though we fought for them. *I* fought for them, back when. Around Chicago.

"Would you like to speak with the Fontaines?"

"How are you connected?"

"I served as a soldier for Greater Brazil for thirty years, Captain Baker. Fighting against so-called bandits and wildsiders to consolidate the Fontaine family's grip on this territory. To make it safe for the R&R Corps to move in and begin to clean up the Great Lakes region. I am retired now. This house is my family's house. My great-great-great-grandfather bought it in 1948. We held on to it through the Overturn, the civil war, and cession to Greater Brazil. As I believe your family held on, in Bastrop."

"It wasn't a matter of holding on. It was more like we just kind of never left," Cash said.

"My family has a military tradition," Colonel Stamford said. "We fought in every major war and most of the minor ones. I number two congressmen and a senator amongst my ancestors, as well as the woman who was in charge of the Indianapolis militia when things went bad during the Overturn. But I am the last of my line. My wife died a year after our son was killed in a firefight in the ruins of Detroit. I retired soon after that, and I became interested in history. I was spending most of my time writing a history of my family that no one would ever read, and then I fell in with the Freedom Riders after I was asked by a friend to make contact with them. And I came to believe that I could still make a contribution. That I could help to right the wrongs done in the name of Gaia. Oh, much good has been done, of course, but it is despite the so-called great families, not because of them.

"I dare say that you know all about the way the great families have traduced the holy project of restoring and renewing Gaia for their own purposes, so I won't rehearse those arguments here. We have been trying to help people understand that. We have learnt from the Outers about communitarianism and nonviolent resistance, and we have helped those hungry for change to form a democratic movement. We have made alliances with wildsiders who have more in common with ordinary people than any in the great families. In short, Captain Baker, we have sown a harvest that we will soon gather in. I'm ready to make my own small contribution to that, and I hope you are, too."

Cash told the colonel that he believed he was here because someone needed him to fly a space shuttle, told him that he wasn't sure he was up to it.

"Because of what happened to you in the Quiet War."

"Yes, sir."

"You've been frank with me, Captain. That takes courage. As for your peripheral nerve damage, we may be able to do something about that, by and by."

"The Air Defence doctors told me it was permanent, sir."

"I think you should get a second opinion," the colonel said. He poured the last of the wine into his glass, gave Cash a wry look across the table, and said, "I drink too much. And I also talk too much. A failing of the old, who can no longer do much of anything *but* talk. Still, I hope my company will prove tolerable to you for a few days. My friends need to verify your credentials. Despite your long association with our mutual friend, despite his assurances, they must be certain that you are not a double agent. *I* do not think you are. But I have nothing to lose, and they stand to lose everything if I am wrong, and so they must be very careful. I hope you understand."

"Are you saying I'm a prisoner here?"

"You are my guest, Captain. You can come and go as you please in the house and in the grounds. Beyond that, you are on Fontaine family territory. Their police force could keep you in custody while you were checked out. But that would risk getting the attention of the OSS. Who would disappear you so thoroughly that no one would know you had ever been born. So here you are. It's a compromise, but not, I hope, an unhappy one."

"I guess I walked into something bigger than I thought it was."

"It's bigger than any one person can imagine, Captain Baker."

Cash was caged in the house and its grounds for three days. It didn't let up raining and the low skies and gloomy light didn't help his growing mood of edgy paranoia. He played with the whole Earth view in the memo space, zooming in on places he knew and places he didn't, careful to keep well away from anywhere he'd visited during the past year. He talked with Colonel Stamford about the history of the colonel's family, and learned a lot about the history of the United States. He tried to talk to the house robots but most of them weren't very bright, and the two or three able to hold a conversation were clever enough to dissemble. He took long walks around the grounds in the rain. It was the kind of place he would have firebombed, once upon a time. Long lawns soft with moss. Magnolias lifting their candles in the rain. Tracts of rhododendrons with packed buds about to burst into flower. Trees coming into leaf. Its footprint was bigger than the block in Bastrop where Cash had been born and raised and upward of five thousand people lived, but only the colonel and an old woman who worked as his gardener lived there.

Cash came across the gardener on the second day, in a far corner of the grounds. An old woman bundled up in a dark green hooded slicker and waterproof overtrousers spattered with mud, watching a pair of construction robots that were building an earth mound over a stone chamber inside a circle of newly planted birch trees. The place where the colonel would be buried when he died, the gardener said.

"So all this will become a graveyard for just the one guy?" Cash said.

"He is leaving his house and garden to the people of Indianapolis. A gift from the past to the future. And I am giving him this," the gardener said.

She was short and broad-hipped and slightly stooped. The hood of her slicker was cinched around her brown and deeply lined face, a few stray strands of white woolly hair caught around the margins. She was so very old that it was hard to tell how old she was. She reminded Cash of a schoolteacher he'd once had. Her gaze level and wise and patient. Her voice low and smoky. She explained that the mound was modelled on an ancient burial site in England, where several of the colonel's ancestors had come from in the long ago.

"When it's finished, I'm going to turf it with prairie grasses and wild flowers. June grass and bottlebrush grass and fox sage. Butterfly milkweed and black-eyed Susans and yellow coneflowers, and so on and so forth."

"You might want to try bluebonnets, too."

"You're from Texas, I believe."

"Yes, ma'am. East Texas. The city of Bastrop."

"They're having a hard time of it there."

"I believe they could do with some of this rain we're enjoying."

They were standing under a tree, on a wet mulch of last year's leaves. Rain dripped through the fresh green canopy and fell on the grass and the bare white tines of the young birch trees and danced on the yellow shells of the robots as they backed to and fro in the mud. Water beaded and dripped from the rim of Cash's hat. His fists were stuffed deep in the pockets of his duster to hide their palsy. It was pretty bad that morning.

The gardener asked him if they had gardens in Bastrop.

"Rich folk do. Most of the rest live in apartment blocks. My uncle, he grows stuff up on the roof. Tomatoes and chillies, mostly."

"A sensible man."

"I'd say he knows what he wants and what he doesn't."

"Do you have any other family in Bastrop? A wife, perhaps?"

"I was married one time, but it didn't take. And it was a long way from Bastrop. Most of my family live there. Hell, all of them, I guess. We settled there long ago and were just too plain dumb or stubborn to move on. Are you from around here, ma'am?"

"I was born in San Diego."

"I don't know it."

"It's on the west coast, what used to be called California. Or it was. It isn't there any more. The rise in the oceans took some of it, and a couple of big quakes levelled the rest."

"I'm sorry."

"Don't be. It happened long before you were born."

"I've heard of California."

"It's called North Tijuana now. The southern part, anyway, where San Diego used to be. The territory of the Guzman family. You still call Texas Texas."

"Well I guess we don't know what else to call it."

The gardener asked him about Texas, and the places he'd travelled through, and his part in the Quiet War; he asked her how long she had been working as a gardener. She considered the question seriously and said that she supposed she had been a gardener all her life.

"You must like it a lot."

"What would be the point of doing work you did not like?"

"I guess some people don't have a choice."

"Then there is something wrong with them. Or with the society in which they live."

"A little of both, I reckon."

"My work is my life; my life is my work. I have made many gardens in many places, but there's nowhere I can call home. Not anymore." The old woman paused, then said, "I had a daughter. We separated in difficult and dangerous circumstances, and later on she died. She was killed."

Cash said that he was sorry to hear it.

"You were in the Air Defence Force. So no doubt you have heard of General Arvam Peixoto."

"Yes, ma'am. I even met him a couple of times."

"He captured my daughter. He was interrogating her. She put out his eye, and in the confusion attempted to escape. She was . . . unsuccessful. I didn't hear about it for some time. Not until General Peixoto was disgraced. It was leaked out then, by his enemies. Put on the net—the official news channel. That's where I saw it. On the news. I made her what she was, you know. As I made so many other things. She resented that. She said that I'd made her a monster. As perhaps I had. She was my companion and my assistant, but she was never really my daughter, as I was never really her mother.

And yet we loved each other, in our fashion. Can you tell me—what kind of man was Arvam Peixoto?"

"I can't really say, ma'am. I served under him, but I didn't know him."

"Was he a kind man? A wise man? Or was he as cruel and capricious as his enemies claim?"

"I'd say he knew his own mind. He knew what he wanted, and knew how to get it. I heard he had a temper, but I never saw it myself."

"Was he capable of murder?"

"He was a good officer, ma'am. I know that."

"A good officer. Yes. He won the war, after all."

The gardener said this without bitterness. A simple statement of fact. They stood in silence while the rain fell down everywhere beyond the shelter of the tree. The robots working unceasingly, one backing to and fro with loads of earth and gravel that the other spread and tamped down.

At last the gardener said, "After I heard about my daughter's death, I decided to come back to Earth. I am glad that I did. I spent a long time making gardens in bottles. Hermetic ecosystems perfectly circumscribed by their boundaries, unable to become anything other than what they already were. Fixed patterns. Complex, yes, sometimes. But fixed. I had forgotten how dynamic Earth's gardens are. Subject to weather and to invasion from the land all around. To every kind of random influence. I could make a fairly accurate guess at what this garden might look like in five years, if it was left untended. But in a hundred? It might be a wild wood, or a briar patch, or a swamp."

Cash, relieved to be talking about something else, said, "I guess you have to keep fighting back nature to make sure something like this stays the way it's supposed to be."

"That suggests that a garden is separate from nature. It is not. No more than we are. No, a garden is simply a small part of the natural world on which we have imposed our own ideal of beauty. And where does that ideal proceed from if not from nature in the first place? All we do, then, is seek to improve on nature. The tree that's sheltering us. Do you know what it is?"

"I'm sorry to say I don't know much about trees and the like. I've seen a lot of the wild in the past six months, and liked an awful lot of what I saw. But I haven't yet gotten around to understanding it."

"It's a Chinese tallow tree. First introduced to this country—to what was once the United States of America, and still is, according to our friend the colonel—by Benjamin Franklin. One of our first scientists. He brought the tallow tree to the United States at the end of the eighteenth century because it provided oil for candles and lamps. Gardeners planted it because its foliage makes a fine display in autumn. But although it is useful and beautiful, it is also invasive. It grows quickly, and when its leaves fall they release chemicals that alter the soil and make it inhospitable to other plants. That's why nothing grows under it. Should we condemn it for that? Or should we improve it, make it a little less invasive, a little more beautiful?

"Some think that we are like the tallow tree. That after we moved out of Africa, we became as invasive and destructive as any animal or plant on the planet. That we changed the world as irrevocably as the Chicxulub impact or the Deccan Traps. As I once thought. But now I think we are far more than mere agents of destruction. That we have more of goodness than evil in ourselves. That we are not enemies of nature, nor are we separate from it. We are at our best agents who drive evolution in ways that are both useful and beautiful. Gardeners who could make a garden of the Earth, and of many worlds besides," the old woman said, and excused herself and went off to shout at one of the robots, which had managed to get itself bogged down in the mire on the far side of the mound.

On the evening of the third day, while Cash was in the study playing with the memo space, there was a commotion outside the house. Vehicles pulling up, the voices of men and women. Cash snuck into the reception room at the front, with its stacks of obsolete electronic equipment and furniture covered in white sheets, and twitched back the dusty curtains. He saw cops in slickers and with plastic bags over their visored caps milling around cruisers and a limo, the scene starkly lit by spotlights that had come on along the eaves of the house, rain falling though the blades of white light and falling around the cops and the vehicles.

Cash had a bad panicky feeling and headed toward the kitchen, planning to bug out through the back door, but one of the robots intercepted him and told him the colonel requested his presence in the hall.

"What's this about? Why the cops?"

"No one tells me anything, sir," the robot said, and led him to the big entrance hallway where Colonel Stamford was talking to a burly man in a black suit while half a dozen men and women hung back. The gardener was there too, her green slicker dripping water on the marble floor. The man turned as Cash came up and flashed a smile, very white in his neatly trimmed black beard, and held out a hand and said, "I'm Louis Fontaine. Good to meet you, Captain Baker. I've heard a lot of good things about you."

Cash shook his hand and said that he hoped a few of them might be true, looking sidelong at the gardener.

Colonel Stamford said to Cash, "I believe you have already met Avernus."

The gardener shook Cash's hand and held on to it, studying his face, saying, "I think it's time we talked about how I can help you."

6

Six days after the death of Goether Lyle, Felice Gottschalk was roused from his bed by a squad of prison guards. There had been another murder; the victim was a member of his stick, Jael Li Lee. The former leader of the Senate of Athens, Tethys, deposed on trumped-up charges by the Brazilian occupying force and replaced with someone more tractable. His body had been found in the washroom of his barracks some time after the night's lockdown. He had been strangled, and Edz Jealott's name had been written on the wall of the washroom in his blood. Every prisoner in the barracks was put to the question, along with Edz Jealott and Felice Gottschalk. They shot Felice full of a hypnotic, fitted him with an MRI cap, and interrogated him for two hours. He told them truthfully that he knew nothing about the latest murder, and at last he was returned to Trusty Town.

Several members of Edz Jealott's gang were waiting outside the main airlock. As Felice walked past they called out and asked him who he was going to kill next.

He went straight to the clinic, and found Amy Ma Coulibaly and Bel Glise waiting for him.

"I need to talk to you alone," he said to Amy. "Some place where we won't be overheard."

"And Bel and I need to talk to you," Amy said, "and this is as safe a place as any to do it. Bel dealt with the spyware."

"We want you to help us find the person who killed our friends," Bel Glise said.

"You told me that Goether Lyle killed himself," Felice said to Amy.

"All of us are under tremendous pressure, and Goether felt it more than most," Amy said. "He was convinced that the prison administration knew what he was doing. So when his body was found out in the fields, I thought— no, I hoped—that it was suicide. Jael's death proved me wrong."

The two women explained that before the war Goether Lyle had done much scholarly research into the so-called libertarian warez used by activists to subvert the surveillance and monitoring systems of late-stage capitalist regimes of the long ago. He and several of his friends, allowed access to memo spaces because of their work, had used the principles developed by those long-dead activists to create a simple AI that had infiltrated the prison's net. The AI could switch prisoners' implants on and off and create blind spots in the surveillance system, and had also opened a back door into the stock system that supplied prisoners with goods in exchange for the biochemicals and plastics harvested from the vacuum-organism fields, enabling Goether Lyle and his friends to order pressure suits and other items, and falsify the inventory and tracking data to hide the true nature of the contraband.

"In short," Amy said, "we were planning to escape."

"To Earth," Bel Glise said.

"To Greater Brazil," Amy said. "They need us."

"The agitators," Felice said.

"The Freedom Riders," Amy said. "We have been in contact with them for several weeks now. They need our help. They know about democracy in theory, but in practice . . . We have been advising them as best we can, but the bit rate of our transmissions is very low and we can't do it very often because of the danger of being discovered."

"You're planning to walk out of here," Felice said. "And then what? Steal a ship?"

"We plan to take control of the tent, and wait here until a ship comes to pick us up," Amy said.

"The prison administration will cut off the tent's power," Felice said. "And its air and water."

"We have taken care of that," Bel Glise said.

"It isn't just the four of you," Felice said. "You two, and Goether Lyle and Jael Li Lee. The four Athenians. It's bigger than that, isn't it?"

"I hope you understand why we can't tell you," Amy said.

"After Goether died, Jael checked his account," Bel Glise said. "As a precaution. It took a little while, but at last he discovered a discrepancy in the look-up tables. It seems that a second party has been hacking into the surveillance system."

316

"Whoever it was, they traced Jael and killed him," Amy said. "Just as they killed Goether."

"Someone in the prison," Felice said. "One of us."

"We think so," Amy said.

"Edz Jealott isn't clever enough to work up something like this," Bel Glise said. "But he may have forced someone to do it for him."

"It could be anyone," Amy said. "It might even be one of the new prisoners."

"How do you know it isn't me?" Felice said.

Amy took the question seriously. "If you were the murderer, and if you knew about us, you would have killed me first."

"Amy says that you have certain skills that may be useful," Bel Glise said. "I saw something of them, I think, when you helped me."

"That didn't work out too well, did it?" Felice said.

"You were outnumbered," Bel Glise said. "This time, you will have to deal with only one person."

The two ill-matched women, Amy slight and fiercely vivid, Bel Glise pale and willowy, were anxious but determined. United in common purpose. Felice wondered how deep their conspiracy went, briefly wondered whether Amy had cultivated her friendship with him because she'd thought that one day he might be useful, and realised that he didn't care. He was on the inside now. Eager to do whatever he could. Eager to serve.

"You want me to be bait for a trap," he said. "I check Goether Lyle's account, and follow the trail that Jael Li Lee uncovered. And then I wait for whoever is watching it to come after me. Someone who has already killed two men."

The women looked at each other. Amy said, "You don't have to do this if you don't want to."

"Of course I want to do it," Felice said. "It's what I was made to do."

Felice knew that Amy Ma Coulibaly and Bel Glise wanted his help because of what he was, not who he was. He knew that he was being used, but after six years of taking each day as it came, each day no different from any other that preceded it, he had a mission again. He would have done it even if Amy hadn't offered to take him to Earth afterward, to try to find a cure for his condition.

Bel Glise had modified the clinic's blood sniffer so that he could use its link to the prison's net—which enabled it to upload diagnostic data directly to prisoners' files—to access Goether Lyle's account. Felice worked all night, resurrecting a simple demon and tailoring it to the virtual environment of the prison net. Then, with the feeling that he was stepping off a cliff, he opened Goether Lyle's account and spent a little time flipping through the objects stored there. A notepad space filled with tracts of scribblings about some kind of metatopology, written in notation as compact and baffling as Egyptian hieroglyphics. Several small and simple virtualities that modelled various n-dimensional universes. Long Q&A sessions with Brazilian mathematicians. The draft of a research presentation. The back door to the surveillance system was hidden somewhere amongst this commonplace clutter, but Felice didn't bother to look for it. He uploaded his demon, a simple, dumb, very reliable gatekeeper that would flash a question to anyone who opened Goether Lyle's account or checked the user log, and would run a tag-and-trace routine. Then he turned himself off and slept the last two hours of the night. He had made himself into a target. All he had to do now was wait.

The next morning, in the refectory, Edz Jealott and a posse of lieutenants walked over to the table where he was eating. He sat back and looked straight at them. He didn't move when one of the lieutenants leaned over and with two fingers dredged up a dollop of porridge and put the fingers in his mouth and sucked noisily.

Edz Jealott, rubbing one hand over the knot of flame-snakes writhing on his bare chest, smiled down at Felice. His fingernails were smoothly buffed and tinted with something that gave them a pearly sheen. "We had a nice little talk about Jael's death, me and the guards," he said.

"Despite that, they let you go," Felice said.

"They knew I didn't have anything to do with it because I was with this fine thing last night," Edz Jealott said, and swung a slender young woman into a tight embrace and kissed her slowly and luxuriously, moving his hands up and down her body as his lieutenants laughed and clapped. Edz Jealott pushing the woman away, smiling at Felice, saying, "The guards asked me to help them find the killer. That's why we're watching you, dead man. I thought it only fair to let you know."

"If I was the killer, you'd already be dead," Felice said, and stood and walked out, laughter and taunts trailing after him.

He took his stick out into the fields. They worked desultorily, talking about the latest rumours about Greater Brazil.

One of them, Rothco Yang, told Felice, "Don't worry, my friend. When this place is shut down I will give you a good reference."

Rothco Yang believed that civil war in Greater Brazil was not only inevitable but would also soon free them. Others in the stick weren't so sure. The Quiet War and its aftermath had made it clear that the Brazilians were capable of anything, and it was doubtful that their European allies would be a moderating influence. And so on and so on, no end to the back and forth of discussion and argument until the shift was over and Felice marched the stick back to the barracks.

He went straight to his room and checked the gatekeeper demon. Nothing. That evening, Edz Jealott was sitting at the table nearest the door of the refectory, surrounded by his lieutenants. Everyone but Edz Jealott was staring at Felice as he went past.

"Killer," a tall young man said in a high mocking falsetto. Another man made a gun shape with finger and thumb and pointed it at him; a third said that they were watching him.

"Everywhere you go, we'll be there."

Felice thought about that as he ate his meal. Then he went to see Amy Ma Coulibaly, told her that Edz Jealott was planning to frame him for the murder of Jael Li Lee, and explained what he wanted her to do.

"One of his lieutenants followed me here," he said. "I expect that one of them will be following me everywhere from now on. It's going to make it very difficult for me when the time comes to act."

"Can't you find a way to lose them?"

"Perhaps. Perhaps not. Do you want to take the risk?"

"I don't want to risk revealing what we can do before it is time to do it."

"You already took that risk, when you set me against the killer."

Felice watched the old woman think about that. Her face was shuttered and expressionless, her eyes focused on something far beyond him. They were sitting on fat cushions in the little side room, the slate with its chessboard glowing between them.

At last she said, "I can't let you control it."

"As long as someone takes them down, when I need it."

"I'll see what I can do. Meanwhile, I think we should play at least one game, for the sake of your friend outside," she said, and touched the slate with her forefinger, moving the queen's bishop's pawn two steps, the first move in the English Opening.

Felice pretended to take no notice of the man who trailed him back to his apartment block. Back in his room, he used the blood sniffer to connect to Goether Lyle's account, and saw with only a faint sense of shock that something had attached itself to the dumb little gatekeeper demon. A simple communication program. He checked it out, excised a few lines of code that would have revealed his location, and fired it up. It immediately presented him with a blank two-dimensional space in which words began to appear, emerging letter by letter, travelling from right to left and fading away.

>>*why do you ask if i was born in a vat on the moon.*

>*i thought i had found one of my brothers*, Felice typed, hunt-and-peck on the blood sniffer's keypad.

>> *i found you. you did not find me. and i am no ones brother. if you want to know who i am meet me and find out.*

Whoever was at the other end of the program wanted to get straight down to business. A string of letters and numbers unravelled. A grid reference.

>>*do you know where that is?*

>*i can find it.*

>>*come alone.*

>*of course.*

>>*or else i will find you later on and deal with you.*

>*i understand.*

>>*in two hours. i have a little business to take care of first.*

>*please don't do anything until we have talked.*

His words faded left to right, like a wave collapsing on a beach. There was no reply.

It was a little after midnight. Trusty Town's dome was polarised to black; its street lights dimmed to a residual glow that showed only the shapes of things. The whole place seemed to be asleep, quiet and still apart from the whirr of a drone high in the dark air and the gliding whisper of Felice Gottschalk's slippers as he walked across the big plaza, stopping when men and women stepped out of the shadows on either side of the entrance of the tunnel that led down to the main airlock.

The soft slap as a man thumped his palm with a weighted sap.

The snap as a shock stick sparked a sudden star.

A woman's nervous giggle.

A teasing falsetto: "Killer killer killer . . ."

There were people behind Felice, too, but he pretended to pay no attention to them, standing with one hand in the pocket of his blouson as the light over the tunnel entrance grew brighter and Edz Jealott stepped forward, bare-foot and bare-chested in baggy white trousers. He smiled at Felice and said, "We know where you're going. The barracks, right? And we know what you're planning to do."

"Killer killer," came the falsetto from the shadowy figures on the left.

A murmur of agreement all around. Edz Jealott snapped his fingers. Zhang Hilton stepped up to him, handed him two pairs of red work gloves, and stepped back into the shadows.

"We could kill you where you stand," Edz Jealott said. "But that would be no fun at all. Our kind of justice is not just about dealing with the bad guys. It's about style. Here. Take a pair. We'll get it on, just you and me."

Felice was completely calm. Living in the moment. "Do you really think the guards will let you do this?"

"I'm not going to kill you. I'm going to put you down in a fair fight. And then I'll turn you over to the guards. After that," Edz Jealott said, "you'll very definitely wish I'd given you an honourable death. A manly death."

"Which he doesn't deserve," Zhang Hilton said.

"My friend is pissed off because you put the hurt on him the last couple of go-rounds," Edz Jealott told Felice. "But he has nothing to worry about. I'll beat you down, but I promise I'll do it very scientifically."

Felice said, "Did someone tell you I was coming here? Was it an anony-mous tip?"

He was wondering if the killer had set him up.

Edz Jealott laughed, looking around at his lieutenants. "We've been watching you. We said we would—weren't you paying attention? And it's obvious where you're going, and why."

"All of this is your idea."

"What did I just say?" Edz Jealott tossed a pair of gloves at Felice's feet. When Felice didn't pick them up, the big man shook his head and said through his smile, all teeth and clenched muscle, no emotion in it or in his dead gaze, "We can do it bare-knuckle if that's how you want it, killer. But we're going to do it."

"No, we're not."

All the time Felice's left hand had been inside his blouson pocket, grip-ping the keypad and comms package he'd dismounted from the blood sniffer. A crude phone, set to send a signal as soon as he pressed any key. He mashed one now, with his thumb.

For a moment, nothing happened. Then everyone around him fell down, muscles locked, shuddering and shivering like so many clubbed fish. Felice had phoned Bel Glise, and she had used the back door into the prison's surveillance system to send signals to the implants of Edz Jarrett and his lieutenants, informing them that they had strayed beyond the tent's perimeter.

Felice stepped amongst the stricken men and women, picking up a cosh and a couple of shock sticks, waiting until the implants had run through their thirty-second cycle and everyone around him relaxed and drew in sobbing breaths and groaned and swore, as if they had smashed down from a great height and found themselves dazed and badly hurt but still alive.

Edz Jealott was trying to push to his knees. Felice swung the cosh in a short swift arc that connected with the big man's temple with a hard pop. Edz Jealott pitched forward on his face. Felice straddled his shoulders and put a foot between his shoulder blades and grabbed his jaw with one hand, fitted the palm of the other over his ear, and twisted his head up and around and broke his neck.

He knew that Amy Ma Coulibaly would think he had killed Edz Jealott out of revenge, but he'd done it for her. To help her realise her dream of securing the prison until the revolutionaries came and freed everyone.

Zhang Hilton and several others had managed to get to their feet. Zhang Hilton spat a mouthful of blood, wiped his chin with a shaking hand, and told Felice that he was a dead man.

"I'm a ghost," Felice said.

He turned his back to the man and walked away down the tunnel. Ten minutes later he was outside, riding a trike down the switchback road to the vacuum-organism fields.

—◆—

The grid reference was at the centre of a small eroded crater close to the edge of the tent, four kilometres south of Trusty Town. Felice felt foolishly confident, his head filled with a fat, contented hum, as he drove along the perimeter road. He was free, just for a little while. Off the grid. Bel Glise had explained that it was a little like blind sight. The drones and cameras of the surveillance system saw him but the tracking AIs didn't register his presence, and a demon painted him out of every visual feed, so the guards couldn't see him either.

It wouldn't last, of course. The guards must have discovered that their system had been hacked by now, and despite Bel Glise's reassurances they might set up a work-around at any moment. Or armed squads might be sent into the tent to search for the trusty who had killed a man, then walked into the airlock complex and apparently vanished. And even if they didn't find him, he couldn't return to Trusty Town unless it was to surrender to the prison administration. His only hope was to try to live out on the farm. A ghost. An invisible man. Sneaking into the barracks for food and water and fresh air tanks every night; hiding out along the cliffs and rock slides of the rim for the rest of the time, hoping that the revolution would come good. But it was a pretty threadbare hope, and Felice didn't have much faith in it.

Meanwhile, it was good to be in action, doing what he had been trained to do. If the killer hadn't lied about the rendezvous, he would have plenty of time to familiarise himself with the terrain and make his preparations.

It was almost one a.m. by the clock, but the sun was above the western horizon and laid a hazy golden glow across the wide expanse of the brown and black and deep purple fields that stretched under the tent. The road ran across flat terrain blanketed in vacuum-cemented grey-brown dust and pitted everywhere with craters from the size of pinpricks to plates and littered with stony ejecta eroded into soft shapes by aeons of micrometeoritic impacts. The bare slope of the crater rim to Felice's left, steep cones and rounded hills of mass-wasted talus fringing its base; rough ground sloping away to his right to the boundary with one of the huge vacuum-organism fields.

He was less than a klick from the rendezvous point, the road dropping steeply to meet a gap cut into a slump of mass-wasted material, when he glimpsed a hitch of movement high in a corner of his vision. Before he could react, a taser dart struck his trike and shorted its motor. A second later, a catch net fell on him, slithering over his torso as muscular threads of myoelectric plastic tightened in constricting folds around his arms and chest. He struggled to free himself as the trike piddled to a halt, but his arms were pinned to his sides by the net and he couldn't even unfasten the safety harness. He could only sit and watch as a figure in the black bodysuit and black face mask of a prison guard—a woman, slim enough to be an Outer but only a hundred and seventy centimetres tall—descended the steep side of the gap in three huge bounds and reached him in two more.

The guard ripped the shock stick and the cosh and the comms pack and keypad from Felice's utility belt, then punched the release of his harness, dragged him out of the low-slung seat, and hauled him off the road.

He was dumped on his back near a trike parked in the shadow of a house-sized block. There was an explosive hiss at his back as most of his air supply was vented; then the guard stepped away, aiming a rail pistol at him, and said, "Are you alone?"

"Absolutely."

"Don't hope for rescue. We're in a dead zone here. No one can see us. Who are you?"

The guard's voice was muffled by her face mask and the low atmospheric pressure, but Felice could hear the lilt, half amusement, half eagerness, that coloured it. She was excited. Aroused. Ready to kill. And she felt that she was completely in control, which meant that she might be careless—that he might survive this.

Felice said, "I was born here, on the Moon, and given a number rather than a name. I was trained here, and inserted in Paris, Dione, before the beginning of the Quiet War. I defected afterward, and then I killed someone in Xamba, Rhea. One of my brothers. I killed him because he found me and wanted to bring me back. I was arrested and put in prison by the Europeans. And then I came here, as a trusty, to guard the political prisoners. Why am I telling you this? Because I think you are much like me. Because I don't want you to make the mistakes I made."

"You're one of the Peixotos' vat creatures. A spy cut to look like an Outer."

"Yes."

"And after all these years living amongst them, you miss your own kind. You think I'm like you. You want to be my friend."

"You knew what my message meant."

"The Peixotos weren't the only family to make spies. You're old and used up. And I'm the latest model, faster and stronger than you and your brothers ever were."

"You work for another family, then."

"Didn't I just say that? But don't expect me to tell you anything else, old man. What's so funny?"

"I thought the revolution would have no chance of succeeding, but I was wrong. Because the great families aren't united. Because they're squabbling over the spoils of war instead of doing what's right by their country. Are you here to assassinate key workers, or to kidnap them?"

The guard stared at him through the round lenses of her face mask. Dark brown eyes, an unflinching and unforgiving gaze.

Felice dropped his own gaze, as if submitting to her dominance. "Let me ask you this, then. Why give your loyalty to people who consider you expendable? You have many years of life ahead of you, and it isn't as hard to disobey your orders as you might think. You disobeyed them when you reached out to me. All you have to do is take one more step, and let me help you. If we work together, we'll survive this. We'll find a way to escape."

"Do you really think you can talk your way out of this?"

"I'm telling you what you can do, if you choose to do it. I've lived amongst ordinary people a long time. Perhaps I don't know them as well as I should, but I do know that they are very afraid of us. Not because we're different, but because we're so very much like a part of them that they don't want to acknowledge. Because we're their dark half. I've survived this long only because I have been very careful to hide what I really am. I can teach you how to do that, if you'll let me."

"It doesn't sound like much of a life to me," the guard said. "Besides, I have a job to finish. Which reminds me."

She took a long step sideways to her trike, lifted something the size of a basketball from the box behind its seat, and bowled it toward the spy.

It bounced slowly over the dusty ground and he recognised it and scrambled to his feet, struggling against the net that bound his arms, crying out in horror and despair. It was the severed head of Amy Ma Coulibaly.

"I left the body in her clinic," the guard said. "With an amusing little message written on a wall in her blood."

"You didn't have to kill her. I already know what you can do."

"No. No, you don't. And you won't live to find out, either."

Felice was finding it hard to think clearly. Great waves of raw emotion were crashing through his head. Hate and sorrow and pity and anger. He was staring straight at the guard, forgetting to pretend to be cowed by her, stepping hard on the impulse to simply run at her and end it all there and then. But at the same time some cold part of him that was never touched by any emotion, the last of what he had once been, was studying the ground and the walls of the gap on either side, making a crucial triangulation.

He said as calmly as he could, "Your mission has failed."

The guard shook her head. "Not from where I'm standing."

"You failed when you killed my friend. You didn't kill her because it was necessary for the success of your mission. No, you killed her to show me that you were better than me, to prove that I couldn't protect her from you."

"Well, you couldn't," the guard said.

Raw red anger surged through Felice then, stronger than anything he had ever felt before. As if he was being born all over again. His pulse thumped like a drum in his skull. The effort to keep still left him trembling and soaked in sweat.

"You did not have to kill Amy and you did not have to kill Goether Lyle or Jael Li Lee either. Goether Lyle didn't know who you were; neither did Jael Li Lee. And even if they had uncovered your identity, they would not have been able to tell the prison administration. You made a mistake when you murdered Goether and you compounded that mistake when you murdered Jael. It led me directly to you, and it convinced the prisoners that it was time to free themselves."

"Bullshit."

"I know you know my implant isn't online—you will have tried to use it against me. And if you take a look, you'll see that the implants of all the other prisoners aren't online either."

The guard didn't reply, but Felice saw a subtle change in the tilt of her head and knew that she was accessing the surveillance system. She was smart and quick, it would only take her a couple of seconds, but it was all he needed.

He sprang sideways and at the same time discharged the superconducting loop he'd extracted from the battery of one of the shock sticks and glued to the palm of one of his gloves. He'd been intending to use it against the guard; instead, with a sharp snap that left his whole skin numb, it shorted out every thread of myoelectric plastic that bound his arms. He shrugged free of the net as he came down and kicked off again, a grasshopper leap to the top of the cut's wall. And then he was pelting along up the slope toward the bulging face of a cliff wall and a narrow chimney pinched between two folds of grey rock.

Felice was halfway there when a kinetic round smashed into his left leg and knocked him tumbling head over heels across the dusty ground. He tried to get to his feet, but his femur was broken and he fell flat on his face. It saved his life: a second round whooped past his head and smashed a spray of shards from a pitted block of stone. Like a crippled ape he scuttled on knuckles and his one good leg into the shelter of the chimney, and started to climb.

The chimney lay back at a sharp angle within the folds of rock. When the guard reached the base and tried to shoot him, she succeeded only in knocking splinters from a fold of rock below him. Despite his broken leg he soon outdistanced her. The chimney gave out after a couple of hundred metres and he flopped over the edge of a narrow setback.

Above him the ground sloped gently up to the skirt of the tent and a massive abutment that was the baseplate of one of the huge struts that supported the tent's canopy. The strut itself arched up and out in a massive parabola and big panes stretched away on either side of it, burning with the sun's golden glow, looming over bare pockmarked slopes with no hiding place that he could see.

Felice's left leg was slick with blood, swollen and blackened around the bloody crater that the round had punched into his thigh. He blocked off the pain and pushed up, balanced on his right foot and the knuckles of his hands, his broken leg skewed so that his left foot lay sideways on the ground, yes, just like a crippled ape, swaying slightly, waiting with patience and stillness learned long ago under the discipline of Father Solomon's shock stick.

He saw the shadows at the top of the chimney shift fractionally and threw himself forward as the guard launched herself upward in a graceful arc, taser in one hand, rail pistol in the other. He corkscrewed into her and locked his arms around her thighs, and then they were tumbling down the chimney's steep chute. He almost lost his grip when his back smashed against an outcrop of rock; then, as they spun out into thin air, he managed to hook his fingers around her utility belt and jack himself up so that in the scant moments of their fall they were locked face to face. The guard had lost her pistol but was trying to jam her taser against Felice's side. He chopped the blade of his palm into the nerve cluster at her elbow and the taser dropped from her numbed grip, and as the broken ground rushed up at them he clamped the glove of his left hand over the diagnostic port of her lifepack and discharged his second and last battery.

Enough current passed through the port to stun her for a moment. And then they smashed into the ground and tumbled away from each other in commingling clouds of dust. Felice curled in a ball and let himself roll and bounce, arms wrapped tight around his knees, head tucked in and down. Something hard and fist-sized clouted him in the ribs and drove breath from his lungs; smaller stones rattled and bounced down through curdy clouds of dust settling around him as he pushed to knuckles and his good knee. His left leg was a distant country under siege. His right ankle throbbed steadily—he'd twisted it somehow in the smashing tumble of the fall. A knife slid under his bruised ribs every time he took a breath. Under his bodysuit every square centimetre of his skin felt bruised and pummelled.

The guard lay in an untidy tangle at the base of the slope. When Felice tried to put weight on his right ankle it gave way and pain speared his leg to the hip, so he sat down and slid down on his behind toward her. One of the lenses of her face mask had cracked and there was a puffy black mass of swollen pressure-bruised flesh behind it. Her good eye tracked him, and she tried to strike him with a fist-sized stone when he reached her, but she had no strength left and he caught her wrist and prised the stone free and tossed it away. He pinned her arms with one hand and with the other unlatched and stripped off her face mask. She coughed and writhed and tried to hold her breath, lips going blue, her face blackening, blood and mucus frothing from her nostrils. He held her wrists and met her furious gaze, and then she drew in a gasping gulp of the thin carbon dioxide atmosphere and shuddered and lay still.

Felice rolled the guard's body on its side and switched off the manifold valve that was bleeding air through the face mask; she had vented most of his own supply, but he reckoned that he would be able to survive on what was left in her tank. He tried to stand up again but his ankle gave way and he sat straight down. He wondered if he could crawl to the trike, wondered if he could climb onto it, wondered if the killer had disabled it. . . .

However it fell out, there was only a slender chance that Bel Glise or one of her friends would think to search for him. Yet he wasn't ready to die. He had enough air for six hours if he stayed awake; much longer if he willed himself into the deep sleep that slowed his metabolism to a crawl. And if he was never found, at least his death would be more merciful than he deserved.

7

Newt and the other members of the motor crew had built from spare and scavenged parts a couple of dozen small satellites equipped with optical and radio arrays, and had strung them in orbit around Nephele's trailing Lagrangian point so that they could keep watch on Neptune and Saturn. The bubble habitat was more or less complete, but everyone slept on board the ships and took part in weekly evacuation drills. When war came they'd be a soft target for either the Ghosts or the TPA; they had to be ready to bug out at a moment's notice. But for a long time nothing happened. The Ghosts broadcast messages warning the TPA to quit the Saturn and Jupiter systems or face the consequences, but did not appear in any hurry to carry out their threat of mounting a war of liberation, while the TPA had not yet launched a counterstrike against the Ghosts to avenge the loss of its ship.

Loc Ifrahim said that this wasn't surprising: it look a long time to organise a long-range campaign, and required detailed planning and the accumulation of a great deal of intelligence. Not only that, but relationships between Greater Brazil and the Pacific Community had greatly deteriorated and it was widely expected that war would break out between them before too long. And that meant that Greater Brazil could not spare any ships of the line, especially as the Pacific Community had built up a considerable presence on Iapetus since the end of the Quiet War.

Few of the Free Outers took any notice of Loc's opinions. After all, not only was he Brazilian, but he'd also been some kind of spy before the Quiet War. He was their guest, so they treated him with consideration and courtesy, but they also made it clear that he wasn't especially welcome and couldn't be trusted. Several people suggested that he ought to be exiled to a tent on Nephele, but the majority thought this was a repugnant and barbaric idea, and so it fell to Macy Minnot to take care of him. She had insisted on rescuing him, so she was responsible for his welfare.

She almost felt sorry for the poor guy. He was homesick and heartsick. He'd lost the woman he loved and couldn't even mourn her properly. The bodies of the two Free Outers who'd been killed during the breakout from the habitat at Neso, and that of a grievously wounded marine who'd died before he could be placed in hibernation, had been resomated with due and proper ceremony, and their nutrients had been incorporated into the hydroponic gardens of the bubble habitat, but Loc Ifrahim refused to give up Captain Neves's body: it was still in deep-freeze, waiting to be somehow returned to Earth. Which almost certainly would never happen. And meanwhile Loc was marooned in the outer reaches of the Solar System with a bunch of Outer refugees, and he refused to take part in housekeeping chores and other communal activities because, according to him, he was a prisoner of war, with rights that he expected his captors to respect.

"You can't be a prisoner of war," Macy told him. "Because we aren't at war."

"That's what you think."

"If you really want to be a prisoner of war, we could send you back to Neptune, let the Ghosts take care of you."

"Or you could send me home."

"I'd do it, if it was possible. I'd do it in an instant, just to get rid of you."

That was mostly how their conversations went. At least Loc was much calmer now. Immediately after he'd been rescued, he'd alternated between sulky silences, flights of self-hating sarcasm, and rages at everything and nothing. Now he skulked around like a ghost, spending most of his time on his own, watching the panoramas transmitted by Newt's array of surveillance satellites or studying the Ghosts' crude propaganda.

Macy, who knew all about the deep ache of homesickness, had some sympathy for Loc's plight, and was pleased when one day he volunteered to help with the hydroponic gardens. She believed that he might be coming to terms with his situation, as she had long ago come to terms with hers. That he was finally showing some backbone.

She taught him how to prick out seedlings. Tomatoes, cucumbers, peas, lettuce, spinach: strains cut to grow quickly and crop within a couple of weeks. He wasn't much good at it, but he persisted, working alone, slowly and clumsily, while the children and the rest of the farm crew made a game of their work. After a few days he began to unbend a little, and told Macy that he had been thinking about how the Free Outers could make the best of their situation.

"I was listening to your partner and his friends discuss how to stealth habitats like this with shells of water ice and radar-reflective skins," Loc said. "I admire their ingenuity, but it seems to me that it would be a dismal and desperate kind of life. And in any case, it hasn't worked very well for you so far, has it? You were driven from the Uranus System, and then from the Neptune System, and now, in greatly reduced circumstances and numbers, you are huddled around a frozen chunk of debris, living hand to mouth and hoping that somehow history will pass you by."

"We know that it won't," Macy said. "That's why we're making plans. Some of us, anyhow."

They were resting side by side at the root of one of the main spars, just above the big bubble of the central nucleus. An array of hydroponic platforms dwindled away down the length of the spar, orientated toward lights fixed to the habitat's equatorial girdle. Other spars were splayed at different angles above and below and all around, nets strung here and there like cobwebs in an attic, arenas where the Free Outers played or held meetings, or simply basked in warmth and light. A flock of children were chasing each other through this maze, screaming with laughter and delight as they swung from spar to spar like a troop of monkeys, Han and Hannah amongst them.

"I know all about your plans," Loc said. He wore a suit-liner like everyone else, had taken all the beads out of his hair and cut it back to a thin stubble, and seemed to have aged about ten years. "Some of you think that you can hide out here, replenish your strength, and move on to some other godforsaken snowball. Others hope that the Ghosts will make good their promise to drive the TPA from the Jupiter and Saturn systems. And that simply isn't going to happen."

"Or maybe the TPA will tear itself apart first," Macy said.

"Greater Brazil goes to war with the Pacific Community, and the winner of that mighty conflict is so weakened that the Ghosts can easily defeat it."

"Or it sues for peace."

"A pretty little fantasy, spun by people with no experience of war. You see, Macy, war is never entered into lightly. A nation preparing for war builds manufactories to stamp out weapons and tanks and planes. It builds fleets of ships and spaceships. It drafts and trains tens of thousands of people to serve in its armed forces, and many times that number are indirectly involved. Its scientists and technicians are drafted, too, and spend every waking hour devising ingenious methods of mass destruction. All its resources, every gram of its political will, is poured into the war effort. So if there is a war between Greater Brazil and the Pacific Community, the victor will be stronger at the end of it, not weaker. And besides, how many Ghosts are there? Five thousand? Ten thousand? There are more than *two billion* people in Greater Brazil. Twice that number in the Pacific Community. I'd say that those were pretty hopeless odds, however you cut it."

Macy said, because she knew otherwise he would take forever to come to the point, "If we can't hide, if we can't rely on the Ghosts, what should we do?"

"Why did Greater Brazil send a diplomatic mission to Neptune?"

"You're going to tell me it wasn't anything to do with negotiating a peace treaty."

"The negotiations were important, inasmuch as the possibility of a peace treaty with Greater Brazil would have compromised the Ghosts' dealings with the Pacific Community. But it was also an intelligence-gathering operation. It's always useful to know as much as possible about your enemies. Even if they are as insignificant as the Ghosts."

Macy thought about that for a moment. "You think we should tell the Brazilians everything we know about the Ghosts? Then what? They'll be so grateful that they'll leave us alone?"

"No, Macy, I do not think that you should talk to the Brazilians," Loc said, as if to a small child. "It would mean trying to strike a bargain with

Euclides Peixoto, and I know very well that he cannot be trusted. But haven't you ever thought that the Pacific Community might be of some help to us?"

"You have to admit, it's a good point," Macy told Newt. "We even have someone we could contact. Tommy Tabagee wasn't such a bad guy, for a diplomat. A straight talker. Plus, if even half of what he told me about Pacific Community's dealings with the people of Iapetus is true, it will give us a fair hearing."

"I see all that," Newt said. "But what can we tell this guy that he doesn't already know? After all, he and his crew visited with the Ghosts. He spent more time on Triton than I ever did."

They were sitting in the control blister of *Elephant*. They'd put the twins to bed and were sharing a pouch of vodka that someone had distilled from fermented CHON and flavoured with a cocktail of congeners, passing it back and forth over the memo space, which was displaying a fuzzily enlarged view of the Saturn System.

"He probably doesn't know very much about the attack on the Brazilian ship. And he doesn't know what the Ghosts did to us, either. And we lived next door to the Ghosts for five years," Macy said. "We know how they think, what they want. . . ."

"They aren't making any secret of what they want," Newt said, holding out the pouch. "There's just a sip left."

"You can finish it for me. Loc says that it doesn't matter what we know as long as the Pacific Community believes we know stuff that will be useful to them."

Newt sucked the pouch flat and said, "So this is Mr. Loc Ifrahim's big idea. We rat out the Ghosts to the Pacific Community, and hope that buys us some protection."

"That's putting it crudely."

"It's how everyone will see it," Newt said.

"Including you?" Macy said.

"What I don't get," Newt said, sidestepping her question, "is why he wants to help the Pacific Community. Wouldn't that make him a traitor? Especially as the Pacific Community is about to go to war against Greater Brazil."

"He says that he can't go back to Greater Brazil because no one would believe that he *isn't* a traitor or a double agent, after he survived the Ghosts' attack," Macy said. "If he ever returns, he says, there'll be a show trial and afterward he'll be hung in front of the Memorial dos Povos Indigenas in the Eixo Monumental, the big park in the centre of Brasília. That's what they do to people they don't like, in Greater Brazil. Kill them and leave their bodies for the crows and vultures, so they are returned to Gaia in the worst possible way."

"He wants to save his skin by trading information with the enemy."

"I know it sounds bad. But I think it would help us, too."

"And how would he trade this information? We can't aim transmissions at Saturn. It would give us away to the TPA."

"We could move one of your satellites further out, use it as a relay. Make it look like the transmission was coming from somewhere else. Better still, we could take him to Iapetus."

"So that's what this is really about. Getting Loc Ifrahim back to what he likes to call civilisation."

"As far as he's concerned, yes. But it could help us, too. And besides, do you want to keep him here for the rest of his life?"

"It's a bold move," Newt said. "But I don't think that you have any chance of making it fly."

"Because I'm still an outsider, even after all this time. But if someone else made the case . . ."

"Hey, don't put me in the middle of this."

"Why are we out here? Because you took a stand. You supported the idea of expansion and exploration and driving human evolution forward, all of that, and I came along with you. Well, now *I'm* taking a stand."

"Things are different now. We can't just go chasing off after some wild idea. We have to work out what's best for all of us. You can ask for a debate about this, but if you do, it'll be put to a vote. And if the majority decide against it, well, that's that."

"Sometimes the majority gets it wrong. I know you know that, or we wouldn't be here in the first place," Macy said.

She couldn't stand being in the cramped confines of *Elephant* any longer, and crossed over to the habitat, put on her flippers and scuba gear, and went for a long swim inside the bubble of water at its core, amongst long strands of red and black kelp that grew from racks strung through the clear water. She couldn't run in zero gravity and she'd never really mastered the knack of flying, but swimming to and fro and around and around in the giant goldfish bowl was almost as good as running for calming her down and getting her thoughts unknotted.

At last she went back to *Elephant* and made up with Newt. But the tension between Macy's support for Loc's idea and Newt's reluctance to challenge the status quo quickly became knotted at the centre of their lives, and there didn't seem to be any way of untangling it.

"You've changed," Macy said. "You've become just like everyone else."

"Well, maybe I've grown up a little," Newt said. "Maybe I'm being realistic."

"And I'm being—what? Crazy?"

"I agree that we're in a chancy place right now. But we're dealing with it, and things will change, in time."

"In time? Suppose we don't have any more time?"

The twins picked up on this of course, and were too often solemn and quiet. Whispering to each other as they played. Clinging to Newt and asking him if he still liked Macy. Or clinging to Macy and asking her if she and Newt were going to split up. Macy told them that she and Newt loved each other very much and that was why they were arguing. And then she and Newt would argue about the effect their arguments were having on their children.

Macy spent much of her time organising the hydroponic gardens; Newt disappeared for hours with his friends from the motor crew. They were attempting to analyse radio traffic picked up from the Saturn System, filtering key words and phrases from the jumble of faint transmissions, using stochastic models to try to work up meaningful intelligence. So far they had failed to find anything except scraps of routine chatter between civilian ships and traffic control: military comms used tight-beam transmissions that were not only impossible to intercept at any distance but were also deeply encrypted. Macy had long ago lost faith in the monitoring programme, but then Newt came to find her one day, breathless, lit up with excitement, full of impossibly wonderful news.

Macy and the twins were harvesting the first coffee buds from strands of tweaked moss that floated and tangled across one of the hydroponic shelves. Hannah and Han were as adept in zero gravity as fish in water, sculling effortlessly on their fingertips, quickly filling their pouches even though they spent most of their time playing a complicated game of tag whose rules Macy couldn't understand no matter how many times they tried to explain. They shot out to intercept Newt when they saw him coming, colliding with him and knocking him off course, so that he had to let himself fall sideways to a neighbouring spar, with the twins clinging around his neck, before he could shove off again and arrow toward Macy. Shouting to her that he'd picked up a transmission from the Pacific Community settlement on Iapetus.

"It's about Greater Brazil. There's been a revolution."

"A revolution? Like a shooting war?"

"Not yet. The family that ran the territory where you used to live, the Fontaines, are part of it. So is most of your old outfit, the R&R Corps. And it gets even better. Avernus is on Earth. And she's right in the middle of everything."

8

Afterward, it was generally agreed that the revolution began when the archbishop of Brasília gave a sermon at the Catedral Metropolitana Nossa Senhora Aparecida that called for an end to preparations for war against the Pacific Community, and then led more than two thousand citizens down the Eixo Monumental to the Esplanada dos Ministérios, where they held a silent vigil. Officers of the OSS, backed by army units, ordered the crowd to disperse. When the people stood firm, soldiers moved against them with shock batons, kinetic weapons, grasers, and knockdown gas, killing more than thirty and injuring many more. The next night, ten thousand people gathered for a second vigil, led by a phalanx of the walking wounded from the night before and dissident senators and members of the Peixoto, Fonesca, and Fontaine families. They held up candles and pictures of the dead, and women stepped forward and placed wreaths on stones still stained with the blood of innocent protesters and taped flowers to the riot shields of the soldiers ranked along the east side of the Esplanada dos Ministérios. The vigil passed off peacefully, and on the third night peace protesters gathered outside major public buildings in cities across Greater Brazil. They carried candles and flowers, and laser pens projected luminous images of Gaia in all Her aspects in the nightblue air above their packed heads as they sang the century-old hymn to Her, set to the tune of Beethoven's *Ode to Joy*:

All on Earth must join together,
Strive to save our Mother's grace . . .

Two days later, crews of the Reclamation and Reconstruction Corps in every territory of Greater Brazil left their barracks and took control of public buildings and communication and transport centres and began distributing food from warehouse stocks. Armed only with rifles and spades and stout hearts, as a historian later put it, outnumbering the military and police three to one, within twenty-four hours they had seized control of more than half the cities of Greater Brazil.

After that, there was no turning back. Sittings of the Senate were suspended. Martial law was declared in Brasília and fourteen major cities. The president fled to his family's territory and established a so-called emergency government in Georgetown. All over the country, mobs swirled through cities in a delirium of looting. They stormed jails and OSS prison camps, freed every inmate, and set fire to the buildings or systematically demolished them. The branches of people trees along avenues or in squares or plazas were hung with strange and grisly fruit: OSS officers and government officials; men and women accused of being government informers. A thousand committees, councils, and panels tried to talk to each other all at once. Senior members of the Peixoto family were arrested at Brasília's spaceport when they tried to board a shuttle. Others made alliances with the Fontaine and Fonesca families and issued a joint statement declaring that they would establish Citizens' Parliaments and hold free and fair elections in their territories, based on the democratic principles developed by Rainbow Bridge, Callisto.

Revolution had come to Greater Brazil.

When everything kicked off, Cash Baker was recovering from the nanotech and viral treatments that Avernus had used to repair and modify his artificial neural network. Interfaces between the network and his motor neurons had accumulated the equivalent of tissue scarring while compensating for the brain damage he'd suffered during the Quiet War. Cash was put in a deep coma while bush robots cleaned and reengineered the interfaces, and tailored viruses inserted artificial genes that tweaked action and resting potentials. He spent a week more or less immobilised while the changes bedded in, had just been allowed up, and was undergoing every kind of neurological test when soldiers in Brasília opened fire on people who had marched from the cathedral to the Esplanada dos Ministérios.

Eight days later Cash reported for duty at the R&R Corps base on the outskirts of Indianapolis. Colonel Stamford advised him to wait, saying that he would be needed as soon as the spaceport at Brasília had been liberated, but Cash said that he wasn't about to take charge of any kind of spaceship until he had been tested out with regular flying, and since there was a shortage of pilots of every description he might as well help the cause while he was doing it. He'd passed every neurological test; his tremors were gone; it was the first time in years that he'd been completely dry and sober; he wanted to get back in the saddle.

The territory controlled by the Fontaine family had been largely untroubled by the revolution because Louis Fontaine had persuaded senior military officers to confine troops to their bases and had invited representatives from every city to help him oversee an orderly handover of power. But in the neighbouring territory, a square chunk that stretched south from North Virginia down to Florida and west to the Mississippi River, every member of the Pessanha family and most of the senior politicians and officials had fled, leaving the armed forces to battle with citizens. There was serious unrest in Atlanta, Birmingham, Huntsville, Jackson, Nashville, Memphis, Montgomery, Raleigh, and a score of minor cities. Soldiers loyal to the Pessanhas had set fire to warehouses before they'd fled, stores had been stripped, and workers armed with agricultural implements and a few rifles were having a hard time keeping people from ransacking the farm towers.

The day after he reported for duty, Cash Baker flew an R&R skycrane loaded with medical supplies into Atlanta, the capital of the Pessanha family's territory. A mob had stormed the headquarters of the state police, overwhelming the troopers left to guard it and beating them to death before hanging their bodies from windows, liberating prisoners, trashing the stacks that had held cross-referenced data on every man, woman, and child in the territory, and setting the compound on fire. Buildings in the downtown area and many mansions and houses in Cascade Heights, formerly the preserve of the rich and the political elite, were also burning. Smoke formed a general haze over the city, like one of the smogs of the long ago.

Cash landed his cumbersome bird on an apron in the military section of Dekalb-Peachtree airport, which had been secured by R&R Crew #45 and elements of the Ninety-second Armoured Brigade. On the other side of the main runway, civilians were climbing out of army trucks and hauling their suitcases toward hangars where government officials and their families were being kept for their own safety. Cash barely had time to drink a cup of coffee before his bird was unloaded, and then he was in the air again, this time heading for Chattanooga, where a distribution depot had been set up. As he cleared the city limits something big blew up to the south, sending a massive column of black smoke into the blue summer sky, with secondary explosions flaring at its base—the munitions dump at the Hartsfield army barracks, according to Dekalb-Peachtree air traffic control.

"Looks like you might have another civil war on your hands," Cash said.

"I do hope not," the air traffic controller said. "The last two we had, Atlanta was burned to the ground."

Out over the replanted forest north of the city everything looked peaceful, apart from the columns of army vehicles heading south down the main highway. Helicopters were rising from or falling toward the military base at Fort Oglethorpe like bees at a hive; Cash had to circle twice in a holding pattern before he could come in. He ate a quick meal while the skycrane was refuelled and reloaded, and then he was off again. So it went. He slept the first night in Atlanta; the second in Memphis, where R&R #12 was building a pontoon crossing because every bridge across the Mississippi had been cut by retreating army units. The ruins of major government buildings were still smoldering, but the riots had died out. Anger and reckless exuberance had given way to anxieties about the future, and to more immediate concerns about finding food, and restoring power and water and communications.

Louis Fontaine made a broadcast that went out across every functioning city net. He announced that the government had lost control of fourteen territories of Greater Brazil, urged soldiers and security police in regions secured by the people for the people to remain in their barracks and depots, and asked citizens to practise restraint and curb their impulse to attack symbols of authority or officials employed by the government. The Fontaine family and other families controlling the liberated areas would hold to their promise to organise elections as soon as possible. Meanwhile, everyone should work together to restore order and to ensure an equitable distribution of food. Every block of apartments in the cities should elect or appoint a representative and each representative would coordinate the efforts of volunteers to maintain order, and would also liaise with ad hoc authorities set up to run essential services in the cities and take stock of food and medical supplies.

"The revolution is over and the country is in the hands of the people," Louis Fontaine said. "They must not let it slip from their grasp."

The next day Cash was back in Atlanta, ferrying in a crew of negotiators. The munitions dump to the south of the city was still smoldering, but most of the fires across the city had been put out. At the airport the negotiators were whisked away in APTs, heading for the Capitol Building, where the city comptroller and other civil servants of the former administration were holed up, and Cash was told to head on up to Indianapolis.

After he'd brought the skycrane down in the centre of its appointed apron in the loading area, Cash found Colonel Bear Stamford and the old gene wizard, Avernus, waiting for him, accompanied by a handsome young man dressed in denim jeans and a rabbit-skin gilet. It was Alder Hong-Owen, his long blond hair pulled back in a ponytail, his left arm still strapped in a sling. He and Cash fell into each other's embrace, pounding each other's backs amidst the bustle of trucks moving in supplies and the roar and hot winds of helicopters and tiltrotors and flitters taking off and landing.

"I hear you've been fixed up," Alder said.

"Avernus did some good work on me, but I believe I have to thank you for the push," Cash said.

"Are you ready to give me a ride?"

"Anywhere you want to go, I'm your man. You know that."

"How about the Moon?"

"There is a prison on the far side of the Moon," Avernus said. As usual, she was dressed in a plain grey shift tunic and trousers. An old, old woman with a brown face as wrinkled and crazed as sun-baked earth, a woolly cap of white hair, and a calm and modest manner, nothing but her shrewd dark gaze to mark her as anything out of the ordinary. "Many citizens from the cities of Saturn and Jupiter are being kept there. Scientists and artists, and leaders of the peace and reconciliation movement."

"Also many of my people," Alder said. "They moved them up there from Tierra del Fuego. Either because they are an important resource, or as hostages."

"I'm told that I may still have influence over them," Avernus said. "I myself doubt it, but I will do what I can."

"They have extensive experience of democracy in action, and we need their help and advice," Alder said. "At the moment, the prisoners are in control of the prison itself but the guards and administrators are still on site. The situation is very fluid, with a strong risk that the Europeans may use the present confusion to attempt to take control. So we need to secure the place as soon as possible."

Colonel Stamford told Cash that Brasília's spaceport was now in the hands of the revolution, but there was a dire shortage of qualified pilots sympathetic to the cause. "Many fled into orbit when the revolution started," he said. "And those who refused to cooperate were dealt with by the OSS. We have six ships that can make the trip, but we lack pilots with combat experience."

"How about it?" Alder said.

"I'm already there," Cash said.

———◆———

He studied the mission profile while he flew with Alder and Avernus to Brasília in a little ramjet formerly owned by the governor of the Pessanha Territory. A suborbital lob took them high above the Caribbean and the vast green wilderness of central Greater Brazil, and then they were down, gliding toward the main runway of the military airbase at the edge of the spaceport's pits and gantries and rows of square salt-white hangars.

Cash was given charge of a civilian shuttle more than fifty years old. Its hull was indelibly stained by the heat of a thousand reentries and its controls were antiquated, but it was sturdy and had been scrupulously maintained, and was fitted with the new fusion motor. Cash did what he could about arming it, met with the crews of the other ships, then went up for the first time in more than seven years, grinning fiercely as acceleration pinned him against his couch and his bird shot through the top of the sky.

After a single orbit in which they assembled their formation and received confirmation that no one would challenge them, the six ships ignited their fusion motors and flew out toward the Moon's lean crescent, passing above the nearside some seven hours later. Cash didn't trust the safe-passage agreement: he ignored messages from traffic control at Athena and pings from the European and Pacific Community bases, and opened the doors of his shuttle's cargo bay. A battery of rail guns hastily welded to the rear pallet were primed with charges of smart gravel, and he controlled by a dead man's switch a one-shot x-ray laser cannon; if anything showed itself on the radar he'd have a bare second to evaluate the intruder and decide whether or not to let go of the switch and let the cannon's AI take care of it.

Cash was back in the catbird seat of combat, but he was painfully aware that he was operating at only ordinary human speed, that he wasn't merged with the shuttle's systems and senses, inhabiting every corner of them, but was locked in the bone box of his skull, peering at displays painted with virtual light in front of his eyes, fumbling and jerking at a control yoke that introduced annoying lags and imprecisions. It was like trying to perform a delicate surgical procedure using a marionette equipped with forks and spoons. A singleship flown by a goddamn rookie could pop up and take him out before he knew it was there.

But nothing challenged the convoy as it slid eastward through the lunar night. Cash felt a throb of nostalgia as he passed above landmarks familiar from the many exercises he'd flown while testing J-1 and J-2 singleships. Everything softened by Earthlight and drenched in shadow. The sooty plain of Oceanus Procellarum. The great ray system radiating from Copernicus Crater like a snowball spattered on a black windshield. Rumpled highland terrain around the dark lava seas of Mare Tranquillitatis and Mare Fecunditas. . . .

As they passed over Mare Tranquillitatis, Avernus said, "That's where it all began." The only time she spoke during the entire flight.

High above Mare Smythii, at the eastern edge of the nearside, Cash fired up the shuttle's motor to put it in lunar orbit. The other ships followed in close formation, travelling with a velocity of 0.8 kilometres per second and an altitude of two hundred kilometres amidst a cloud of proxies that broadcast bogus IDs and electronic chatter to confuse any potential attackers. Earth set behind them and the sun shot up above the curved horizon, starkly illuminating the ancient battlefield of the farside. There were no dark seas here, no highland plains. Just the unmodified remnant of an inhumanly vast and unyielding bombardment that had left the surface smashed and riven with craters of every size. Strings and chains of craters, craters overlapping craters, smaller craters punched into the floors of larger craters or lancing their lips. A pitiless and trackless waste lacking any human scale and failing every definition of beauty.

Alder talked briefly with someone in the prison facility, then told Cash that it was safe to make his approach. Cash sent several proxies speeding ahead, just in case. They glittered like fugitive stars as they diminished into the black sky, and after they had passed directly above the facility without being challenged or attacked, Cash's shuttle and the other ships briefly fired their motors and committed themselves to descent trajectories.

As the slumped and battered rim of Korolev Crater drifted beneath the shuttle's keel, Cash assumed manual control, ready to punch out if the defence system so much as squinted at him. He was falling in a long arc, passing over terraced slumping and lobate sheets of mass-wasted material on the inner side of the wall and sliding out across the floor of the crater, which was as pockmarked and riven as everywhere else on the farside. He used attitude jets to bump above over contours, concentrating fiercely, trying to compensate for the annoying lag between thought and action. The navigation system lit up with flight-guidance arrows and lines as it synchronised with the facility's traffic control, and then he saw a gleam like ice at the horizon, the facility's tent like a faceted insect eye socketed in a small and perfectly circular crater.

Alder was talking to someone on the ground again. Cash and the other pilots waited for go/no-go, balancing their ships on attitude jets, letting them drift as sideways, until Alder said that it was safe to land. Cash told the other pilots he'd go in first, notched up his velocity, overshot the dome of the tent, spun his bird around, and stooped toward the landing field in a flare of retrojets that blew long windrows of dust from the ground.

Forty minutes later, wearing paper coveralls over their suit-liners, Cash Baker, Alder Hong-Owen, and Avernus were sitting at a table in a conference room in the administration blockhouse, facing the European governor of the facility, Ella Lindeberg, and the acting head of security, Colonel Carlos Hondo-Ibargüen. Ella Lindeberg, a pale, slim, austere woman, did most of the talking. Explaining that the prison had been set up as an experiment in self-government: trusties overseen by guards employed by the Brazilian and European administration had policed the prisoners, who'd grown their own food and maintained facilities within the prison's tent. Shortly after the revolution had begun in Greater Brazil, the governors from the Peixoto and Nabuco families and other senior Brazilian officials had taken off for Athena. The prisoners had subdued the trusties, seized control of the airlocks, shut down the surveillance system and the system that controlled their security implants, and locked the administration out of the controls for the prison's fission pile and the life-support systems of both the prison tent and the administration blockhouse. Threatened with loss of power and air, and with more than twenty guards held hostage inside the prison, the administration had come to an agreement with the prisoners. The prisoners would be allowed to control everything inside the tent, and the administration would not attempt to regain it by main force. The standoff had lasted for almost two weeks now. The prisoners couldn't escape because they lacked pressure suits; Ella Lindeberg had been instructed by her superiors to maintain order until a peaceful transition could be negotiated.

"My government was always a minor partner in this enterprise," she said. "It is happy to cede authority to you so long as you guarantee safe passage for all personnel."

"I don't have any kind of authority," Alder said, "but you're certainly welcome to leave."

"I thought you represented the Brazilian government," Ella Lindeberg said.

Alder laughed. "There isn't any government at present. But I suppose I can put you in contact with someone senior to the colonel. Will that do?"

"There is one problem," Colonel Hondo-Ibargüen said. A burly man with dark brown skin and black hair trimmed in a square topknot of the kind favoured by marines. Clasping his big hands tightly on the table in front of him, clearly embarrassed. "It concerns the OSS detachment and a modification to the prison's air plant that the prisoners uncovered. If activated, it would have increased the partial pressure of carbon dioxide in the air of their living quarters to a lethal level. The OSS had sealed orders instructing them to use it if they lost control of the prison. The prisoners introduced a work-around, and informed us about it after the negotiations were successfully concluded."

"I want you to know that I knew nothing about this," Ella Lindeberg said. "Nor did the colonel, or any of the people under his direct command."

"I arrested all the members of the OSS detachment," Colonel Hondo-Ibargüen said. "Confined them to quarters. The problem is this: what do you want to do with them?"

Alder said, "Did they try to use this modification against the prisoners?"

"The logs show that they didn't," Colonel Hondo-Ibargüen said. "Although logs can of course be altered."

"But you have no evidence that they were altered?"

"No, sir. We lack the necessary forensic expertise."

"And no one in the OSS has confessed."

"Every one of them claims to know nothing about it."

"The orders were still sealed?"

"They seemed to be."

"Then they are free to go," Alder said. "It isn't for us to judge what people may or may not have done under orders from the old regime. Before we're through, we're going to have to forgive many things. Either that, or turn a large portion of the country into a prison camp."

"Things have changed, of course," Colonel Hondo-Ibargüen said. "I'm happy to accept that."

"Things have changed and will continue to change for some time yet," Alder said.

Alder, Avernus, Cash Baker, and the crews of the other shuttles walked in through the main airlock of the prison tent unescorted, dressed in pressure suits and carrying their fishbowl helmets, stepping out into a loading area with a small crowd waiting in front of flimsy-looking storage sheds. Cash had gone toe-to-toe against the Outers in the Quiet War, but this was the first time he'd met any of them. Tall, seriously skinny men and women dressed in grey coveralls with numbers stencilled across chests and backs, dignified and calm and polite, moving forward and shaking hands with their rescuers. Avernus and Alder went off with a dozen of them to negotiate terms of surrender.

By now, the crews had begun to bring in sleds carrying pressure suits and other supplies. Cash was helping to unload them when Avernus returned and told him that she needed his assistance. "A man is gravely ill. He must be evacuated as soon as possible."

"Someone you know?"

"My daughter and I once encountered him. Please. If I am to have any chance of saving him we must do this now."

In among the racks of pressure suits and other supplies were several of the fat clamshells used for moving injured people: coffins with lifepacks. Cash wheeled one alongside Avernus as she led him to Trusty Town's clinic. She asked him if he knew anything of spies disguised as Outers and planted by the Brazilians in Outer cities before the war.

"I don't remember everything that happened around then," Cash said. "I have holes in my memory. I guess I always will."

"They were creations of Alder's mother. Trained to infiltrate and sabotage our cities."

"If this guy is one of them, what's he doing here?"

"He told me that he was working for the Brazilians, but he defected. He also told me that he planted some kind of spyware in the place where my daughter and I lived," Avernus said. "And that later on he tried to kidnap us. This was in Paris, Dione, just before the war. The city's mayor had arrested us, and many others involved in the peace and reconciliation movement. We were being held in a prison outside the city. When the war began and Paris was attacked, someone broke in and knocked out the guards. My daughter overpowered him, and we freed the rest of the prisoners and left him there. This man says that he remembers her. That she was very quick and strong, and stabbed him with a tranquilliser dart. That's certainly what happened, and only a few people saw it, and most of them are dead. . . .

"Well, he meant us harm, once upon a time. Myself and my daughter. And now I am going to do my best to save his life. What would you call that?"

"Mercy, I guess."

"Mercy. Yes. Why not?"

The guy was in a bad way. Feverish and barely conscious, deep bruises mottling the pale skin of his torso, his left leg encased from ankle to thigh in an inflatable cast. The woman who'd been caring for him, Bel Glise, helped Cash load him into the clamshell, and trotted alongside it as Cash and Avernus wheeled it back to the airlock, telling a long and complicated story about the murder of two mathematicians who had created a back door into the security system as part of an escape plot, the death of a trusty ("The beast Jealott"), and the murder of Trusty Town's medical technician, the sick man's only friend. It seemed that the sick man had been badly injured when he'd confronted the killer, who had been one of the guards and also some kind of spy.

Cash didn't know what to believe. While he was waiting for transportation to his shuttle, he told Alder Hong-Owen that the injured man, Felice Gottschalk, could just as easily be the killer. "He could have murdered those two guys because he wanted to use their escape plan. And then he murdered the trusty and the guard because they got in his way."

Alder grew thoughtful, saying, "My mother was involved with at least two secret projects before the war. Both were located on the Moon, and both had something to do with ectogenic breeding programmes. She grew babies in artificial wombs, and tweaked them. She didn't give me many details, but I know that one led to the development of the fusion motor that gave us such an advantage."

"I flew her here once," Cash said, startled by the memory. "A long, long time ago. Picked her up from some place in the Antarctic."

Alder gave him a strange look. "About a year before the war?"

"Something like that. Yeah, just before I went out to the Saturn System. Funny how I can remember some things and not others."

"There was some kind of crisis with one of her projects on the Moon," Alder said. "She returned in a foul temper. Something had badly frightened her, but she never talked about it."

"So this guy, he really could be some kind of monster?"

"He could be my brother," Alder said. "My mother is a brilliant woman, but she has a monstrous ego. She would have found it amusing to use her own eggs or somatic cells to produce her ectogenes. . . . In any case, we can't let him fall into the hands of the Europeans, can we? Take him, and take Avernus too. She's too preoccupied at present to be of much help."

"I think all this reminds her of what happened to her daughter," Cash said.

"I think so, too. I'll stay behind and deal with the evacuation of the guards and the prison administrators. It's going to involve much delicate negotiation, but fortunately my mother gifted me with the ability to charm people into doing the right thing. Strange, isn't it, how things work out?"

"It's a small world," Cash said, "but I wouldn't like to be the guy who had to paint it."

He flew east and north, crossing the northern edge of Hertzsprung Crater. Earth, half full, rising ahead of him as he came around the near side. Above the western margin of Oceanus Procellarum he fired up the fusion motor, a brief hard burn to take the shuttle out of lunar orbit, then throttled back to a steady 0.2 g.

A few minutes later there was a commotion in the passenger compartment. Cash switched to internal video and saw Felice Gottschalk hauling himself along the ladder strung along what was usually the ceiling of the compartment but was presently, because of the axis established by the thrust of acceleration, one of its walls. Felice Gottschalk moved quickly, dragging the stiff post of his injured leg, and Avernus was climbing after him, above the heads of the first batch of Outer evacuees, who were sitting upright in two short rows of acceleration couches.

The shuttle was flying itself. Cash retracted the restraint webbing of his couch and reached up and swung around, bracing himself on the bulkhead beside the hatchway. Felice Gottschalk looked straight up at him. His face was the colour of paper and beaded with sweat, and he held himself awkwardly against the ladder because the thumb and two fingers of his left hand were dislocated; he must have hurt himself when he'd pulled free from his restraints.

"I mean no harm," he said. "I just wanted to see Earth."

Below him, Avernus told Cash that it was all right.

Felice Gottschalk, staring past Cash at the narrow window on the left-hand side of the cabin, said, "I didn't know she was so beautiful. I wanted to see her one time before I died."

"So did I," Avernus said, her voice soft and strange.

She persuaded Cash to help Felice Gottschalk settle in the spare acceleration couch. He sat awkwardly because of his broken leg, but seemed immune or oblivious to any discomfort as he gazed with rapt and mute wonder at Earth's half-globe. He was smiling. Earthshine set sparks in his eyes.

Avernus told him that everything would be all right. "I don't care who you are or what you did on Dione. The past is the past. All that matters to me is that you saved the prisoners from someone who meant them harm. You did the right thing by them, and I'll try to do the right thing by you."

Cash saw that Felice Gottschalk's head had tilted toward his chest. "There isn't anything you can do for him now," he said, and reached over and gently closed the dead man's eyes.

9

As far as most of the Free Outers were concerned, the revolution in Greater Brazil changed nothing. The Jupiter and Saturn systems were still controlled by the TPA, and both General Nabuco at Jupiter and Euclides Peixoto at Saturn had refused to acknowledge the authority of the revolutionary government. Then the Free Outers received a message from Tommy Tabagee, inviting them to send representatives to Iapetus, guaranteeing free passage and a voice in a debate on the future of the Outer System organised by the PacCom government.

At the meeting held to discuss this news, Loc Ifrahim argued eloquently and with great force in favour of sending representatives. He said that this was a hinge point in history. The chains of power had been broken and reforged in Greater Brazil, and her people had gladly taken up the burden of their own destiny. For it was a burden. Freedom was a burden. It was not something that could be taken for granted. It had to be fought for, and protected with unsleeping vigilance. The Free Outers had been presented with the opportunity to take part in that great struggle. They could agree to accept the Pacific Community's invitation, take part in the great task of making history, and help the people of Earth and the people of the Outer System reconcile their differences and forge a common future. Or they could refuse it, and relegate themselves and their children to the margins of human civilisation and human history.

This was greeted with a hostile silence. After a few moments, Idriss Barr said that fine talk about forging the future was all very well, but the future meant nothing if they did not survive to see it; before plunging headlong into the unknown, they should wait and see whether or not this revolution was permanent, and what it meant for Greater Brazil and for the Jupiter and Saturn systems. Mary Jeanrenaud vigorously agreed. They had come out here to make new worlds and new ways of living, she said. They should not be dragged back into the old ways, and they should certainly not be influenced by outsiders. More than a dozen other people expressed similar views, and by a simple show of hands it was decided that the Free Outers would wait to see how things fell out on Earth and whether it had any effect on the occupation of the Jupiter and Saturn systems before they committed to any kind of negotiations or discussions with outsiders.

Two days later Newt's surveillance satellites picked up activity around Neptune: the Ghosts had launched four ships toward the Saturn System. A message sent from Triton, aimed at the Jupiter and Saturn systems and relayed to the Free Outers by the PacCom settlement on Iapetus, made it clear that the Ghosts hadn't accepted the invitation to talk. A long lecture about history and destiny laced with vicious diatribes against the sins of the TPA and the corruption and weakness of Earth and its peoples, it boiled down to a single warning: *Quit our worlds or suffer the consequences.* Either the Ghosts believed that the TPA was in disarray and might be defeated by a swift and bold attack, or this was some kind of suicide mission by fanatic martyrs, the first shot in a long war of attrition.

The Free Outers held another interminable debate and decided once again that they couldn't risk sending anyone to Iapetus. Afterward, Macy went for a swim in the tank at the heart of the habitat and hung at its pellucid centre for a long, long time. Only the sound of her breathing in her face mask, and the slosh of currents. Red and black fronds stirring to and fro like drowned fright wigs.

Loc Ifrahim had spoken of a hinge point in history. She could feel it turning inside her, a slow but irresistible tide.

That night she told Newt what she planned to do. He heard her out quietly and soberly, then asked why she felt she had to do it. They were lying side by side on conjoined crash couches in *Elephant*'s command blister. Talking quietly, faces just a few centimetres apart, the twins asleep in the main part of the cabin.

"Because it's the right thing to do," Macy said. "Because Loc Ifrahim is right, and everybody else is wrong. I know I'm an outsider. I know that I still don't understand everything about Outer society, but there isn't any kind of Outer society right now. It's been shattered. And this is our best chance to start to put it back together. I know a lot of people hope that the Ghosts are going to war against the TPA on behalf of all of the Outers, but it's pretty obvious that this war fleet is part of that manifest destiny thing of theirs. Trying to make the future come out the way it's supposed to, according to the so-called prophesies of their leader."

"You know that. I know that," Newt said. "But most people won't be happy if you go against a decision arrived at democratically. It could give you a short ride to a world of trouble. It got *me* in trouble more than once, back in the day."

"I don't want this to get you into trouble now. I'll make it clear that it's on me. But I have to do it."

Newt smiled. "There's no way of talking you out of this, is there?"

"None that I can think of."

"You better let me work up a flight profile."

"I got one from the navigation AI. It says it's doable."

"It'll say anything you want it to say, if you ask it the wrong questions."

They talked about what they needed to do, what to tell the twins, what might happen if Macy was declared an outcast. They didn't talk about whether or not Macy had made the right decision. They didn't need to.

Like all the ships, *Elephant* had been kept topped up with fuel and consumables, ready to take off at a moment's notice. And kidnapping Loc Ifrahim turned out to be amazingly easy. Macy told him that she had some more news about the rebellion in Greater Brazil—he needed to see it before she showed everyone else. When he came aboard *Elephant* and began to strip off his pressure suit, Macy slapped an air mask over her face and flushed a dose of sevofluorane into the lifesystem's atmosphere, putting Loc under before he could begin to ask what she was doing. She kept him under with an anaesthetic patch, prepped him for hibernation, and packed him into a coffin. The difficult part was saying goodbye to the twins, who got it into their heads that she would be back in a day or so. Untangling that notion would be another hard task for Newt, after he'd explained to the rest of the Free Outers what Macy had done, and why.

She'd flown *Elephant* many times by now, but never before solo. Newt stayed in constant contact for the first hour and just finished helping her finesse the parameters of the burn that would put her on course for Saturn when Idriss Barr cut in, asking with anger and incredulity what she thought she was doing.

"Making history," Macy said, and said goodbye to Newt and shut down the comms.

Elephant took sixty-three days to fall from Nephele to Saturn. Macy kept busy with housekeeping tasks, building up her muscle tone by exercising assiduously with intertial weights and on the stationary bicycle, and teaching herself basic navigation and practising landings and every other kind of maneuver in the tug's virtual reality system. She routinely checked Loc Ifrahim's hibernation coffin, and talked to Newt and the twins at least twice a day, morning and evening, sometimes more. As *Elephant* left Nephele behind, the lag in communications grew so great that they were forced to default to text messages and video blips.

Newt forwarded news transmitted by the PacCom base on Iapetus. The People's Revolutionary Committee had established itself in Brasília and had announced a date for elections, but did not yet have authority over the entire country. Armand Nabuco and the remains of his government were holed up in Georgetown and controlled a swathe of territory between the Cuara River in the north and the Amazon in the south; six territories loyal to the former president had not yet surrendered; there was considerable insurgent activity everywhere else, led by former members of the OSS. More than a million people were living in refugee camps, there were food shortages and thousands were dying of disease every day, and it was the beginning of the hurricane season in those territories adjacent to the Caribbean. The only good news was that the European Union had refused to come to the aid of the deposed government, and the Pacific Community had declared that it was ready to supply aid if it was asked to do so, but would otherwise respect Greater Brazil's sovereignty.

The People's Revolutionary Committee and a group of Outer politicians who'd been imprisoned on the Moon had asked the TPA to engage in immediate talks aimed at finding a peaceful end to the occupation of the Outer System. The Brazilian authorities in the Jupiter System had not yet responded. In the Saturn System, the Europeans and the Pacific Community had indicated that they were willing to participate, but Euclides Peixoto had declared that he wouldn't enter into any kind of talks until the Ghost ships currently heading toward Saturn turned back. If the Saturn System came under attack from any quarter, he said, he would retaliate with swift and deadly force.

As for the Free Outers, the majority wanted to wait and see what happened when the Ghosts reached the Saturn System.

"There's a vague and unfocused hope that it will solve itself somehow," Newt told Macy, reporting on the latest debate about the crisis.

The twins were creating a garden on one of the hydroponic shelves. Macy did her best to encourage them. She gazed wistfully at videos of their enthusiastic work and energetic play. They sent her scans of paintings and drawings and she printed them out and stuck them around the lifesystem. She recorded stories that Newt could play back to them, but it wasn't the same as telling them stories in person. She missed them dreadfully and thought about them and Newt all the time, and kept herself busy so that she would not have time to regret leaving them.

It was the first time in many years that she had been so alone (Loc Ifrahim, sealed in his hibernation coffin, hardly counted as company). And she had never before been aboard *Elephant* without Newt. She remembered the long, languorous voyage after they'd fled from the Saturn System to Uranus at the end of the Quiet War. How they had made love everywhere, in every conceivable position. Newt teaching her the delights of free-fall sex after the motor had been switched off. Naked to each other for the first time. Learning each other's bodies, alive with all five senses. Newt's presence was imprinted everywhere inside the little ship but he was growing ever more distant as it fell through vast volumes of black vacuum.

Back when she'd been working in the R&R Corps at the northern edge of the Fontaine Territory, Macy, caught in a full-on winter storm, had spent nine days in a line hut out of radio contact with base, hunched in all her clothes over a convector heater or lying in the bunk under a mountain of blankets, living on MRE packs and instant coffee while everything beyond the hut's frosted window was erased by a blur of falling whiteness. She felt the same lonely anxiety now—although back then she hadn't had to worry about running out of air or water, and although she'd been entirely cut off from the civilised world, the base had been just thirty klicks away, half a day's ride in the snowcat once the blizzard had blown itself out, snow-covered pine trees standing under a flawless blue sky, sunlight sparkling on the crests of crystalline white drifts.

But she was such a very long way from everywhere else now, and despite her housekeeping routines and the daily contact with Newt and Han and Hannah, she never forgot that she was caught inside a fragile bubble of heat and light and air. A spark rising in an infinite flue. A mote of dust floating in a cathedral. The old airplane fear would seize her at odd moments and she had trouble sleeping, would wake with a sudden jolt, convinced there was something badly wrong, her pulse hammering in her ears for long moments before she felt the steady subsonic rumble of the motor through the pad of the sleeping niche, the whirr and sigh of the fans and pumps that circulated and refreshed the air.

At last she reached turnover. Although she'd practised assiduously for the moment, and Newt was in constant contact throughout, the business of shutting down *Elephant*'s motor and swinging the little tug end for end and reigniting the motor to begin deceleration was a blur of nightmare anxiety. When it was over Macy stripped off her suit-liner, sponged stale cold sweat from her skin, and crawled into the sleeping niche and slept for twelve hours straight.

One day Newt sent her shots of the Ghosts' little fleet, taken at the closest approach to Nephele, which wasn't very close at all, a gulf of several billion kilometres. The four ships were strung out in a line like broken fragments of a comet, each no more than a handful of pixels across. Tiny clusters of bright squares. Macy knew that it was impossible to resolve any meaningful detail, but all the same she stared long and hard at them. They had a high albedo, perhaps because they were painted white, the Ghosts' totemic colour, and they were far bigger than any ships that the Ghosts were known to possess.

—The spectra of their exhausts is weird too, Newt sent. The standard signature of the fast-fusion drive plus absorption lines corresponding to hydrogen and oxygen. It looks like they're augmenting thrust with mass drivers that are shoving out water so fast it splits into its atomic constituents. It's hard to get a red shift with the equipment I have, but my best guess is that they're throwing off a plume at around nine thousand klicks per second. About three percent the speed of light.

—If they have this extra boost why aren't they accelerating faster than *Elephant*? Macy sent back.

—Their ships are bigger. Greater mass needs greater thrust. I checked the archives. There are plans for half a dozen kinds of mass driver. I guess they made one of them work.

—We didn't know much about what they were doing, when it comes down to it.

—Like what else they've been building.

—I guess I'll see soon enough.

—Promise me again you won't get too close.

—I promise I won't do anything stupid on purpose.

A few days later, Newt called and told Macy that the Ghost ships hadn't gone into turnover. They were still accelerating.

—It looks like they're going to be flying straight through the Saturn System, he sent. Probably using a gravity-assist maneuver to bend their course so they head somewhere else. Jupiter or Earth. I think Jupiter. That's where many of them came from.

—They could hit targets in the Saturn System on their way through, couldn't they? Macy sent back. And then go on to cause trouble at Jupiter, or maybe even Earth. But I can't turn back. We need more than ever to figure out a way of working out a deal with the TPA.

She ate her lunch while waiting for Newt's reply. Curd cheese smeared on a gritty biscuit, a handful of small sour tomatoes from the cold store. She was eating sparingly, knew it was because she had the irrational fear of running out of food, couldn't help it.

A telescopic image of Saturn hung in the memo space. Just three hundred and forty million kilometres away now. A minuscule half-disc that looked slightly deformed because of the rings. Like the fuzzy image of a broken teacup. In nine days she'd be there, and her problems would really begin. The prospect filled her with a grinding dread. She might not be able to convince the right people to do the right thing. She might be thrown in prison, or worse. She might never see the twins or Newt again: an unbearable thought.

The comms pinged. Newt's reply had arrived.

—When it comes to making a deal, you're going to have to do some fast talking. You're slowing down so you can make orbit around Saturn, but the Ghosts are coming on faster and faster. . . . It means you don't have three weeks' grace after all. It means that the Ghosts will arrive at Saturn a little over five days after you do.

Macy and Newt spent the rest of the day discussing her options. There weren't many, and none of them were good. She could begin to accelerate again, but she would have to get rid of the excess velocity when she reached Saturn. *Elephant* was a true space vehicle and lacked a heat shield, so she couldn't brake by ploughing though the upper atmosphere of either Saturn or Titan. At best, she could fire up the motor for a day or so and add a couple of hours to the gap between *Elephant*'s arrival and that of the Ghosts, but then she'd have to slow down by performing a complex series of flybys past Saturn and Titan, which would waste more time than she saved. Or she could start accelerating again and keep going, swing straight past Saturn as the Ghosts were evidently planning to do, but she didn't yet know whether they were heading on to Jupiter or Earth or someplace else, and she couldn't be sure of their final destination until after *Elephant* had encountered Saturn. For all she knew, they could be heading for Mars, planning to reclaim the planet lost to the Outers more than a century ago.

And in any case, her options were limited by the amount of fuel she was carrying.

In the end, Macy and Newt decided that they'd stick with the plan. Continue to slow down, then swing around Saturn in a reverse gravity-assist and enter orbit and get to Paris, Dione, as quickly as possible. They also agreed that it was time to wake up Loc Ifrahim.

●

The coffin did most of the work. Macy fed Loc sips of fruit juice, swabbed his face and torso with wet wipes, and helped him to the head. She'd twice been through revival after long periods of hibernation and knew how bad it was. He picked at a small helping of boiled rice, chewing every grain, saying in his post-hibernation croak, "I've been ready to return to Saturn ever since you picked me up, Macy. There was no need for this drama. All you had to do was ask."

"We needed to save on consumables."

"And spending nine weeks in this little ship with me was not a pleasing prospect. I quite understand—the feeling is mutual," Loc said, with a ghost of his old crooked smile.

"We make quite a team, don't we?" Macy said. "They wouldn't believe me alone, or you. But both of us together . . ."

"May I ask, did you also bring aboard the body of Captain Neves?"

"There wasn't time."

"Ah."

"If this all works out," Macy said, with a deep pang of guilt, "you can take her back to Earth."

"Of course. Well, what has been happening while I have been asleep?"

Macy told him about the refusal by the Brazilian forces at Jupiter and Saturn to surrender control, told him that the Ghost ships were still accelerating toward the Saturn System, and explained what it might mean.

He thought for a while, then said, "You have not yet talked to the TPA. Or to the PacCom authority on Iapetus."

"We thought it best to keep radio silence."

"But now you think otherwise. Which is why you woke me. And not before time," Loc said. "Let's see what I can do, shall we?"

After some to-and-fro with Newt, Macy managed to aim *Elephant*'s main antenna at Dione. She turned the comms over to Loc Ifrahim and watched as he engaged in a text conversation with someone called Yota McDonald. An old friend in the diplomatic service, he said.

Yota McDonald explained that the revolution in Greater Brazil had caused a seismic shift in the balance of power at Saturn. A sizeable faction in the Brazilian contingent of the TPA, including the diplomatic, police, and civil services, and four of the five governors and their staff of the Brazilian-controlled cities, wanted to come to an accommodation with the Outers, but Euclides Peixoto and senior officers in the Army and the Air Defence Force refused to countenance any such move. It seemed that Euclides Peixoto was determined to stick it out at Saturn; not so much out of loyalty to the old regime, but because he did not want to relinquish power over his little empire. But he lacked the backing of the Europeans and the Pacific Community, and without their support the only way he could keep power was by main force. There had already been a long series of strikes and nonviolent protests in Camelot, Mimas, and Baghdad, Enceladus, and Athens and Sparta, Tethys. The governors of those cities had refused to challenge the protesters, and Euclides Peixoto had threatened to send in troops if nothing was done, a standoff that had not yet been resolved, mainly because the approach of the Ghost fleet was a menace overshadowing every kind of domestic problem. There could be no doubt about its hostile intent now. Euclides Peixoto claimed to be planning a spectacular counterstrike, and he wanted to attack their city on Triton, too. If Loc Ifrahim and Macy really did have useful intelligence about the Ghosts, Yota McDonald sent, Euclides Peixoto would certainly want to talk with them.

—We don't plan to sell anything to anyone, Loc sent back. This is too important. We will talk to the TPA security council.

—Euclides won't like that.

—He'll have to put up with it, if he wants to know what we know.

Loc Ifrahim and Yota McDonald discussed ways and means of contacting the various administrations, and of obtaining a firm promise that the TPA would issue a guarantee of safe passage. When Loc finally broke contact with his friend, Macy said that it was time they talked to Tommy Tabagee.

"We're going to land at the PacCom base on Iapetus. Unless you can convince me that you have a better idea."

"Oh, I have no objections," Loc said. "But let's not do everything in a rush. Before everything else, we need that guarantee of safe passage. It shouldn't be a problem as long as we can convince the TPA security council that we have valuable information about the Ghosts. Then, and only then, should we begin to negotiate the terms of our surrender. I think we can survive this, but don't expect cheering crowds when we arrive."

"I'll be happy just to stay out of jail."

"For what it is worth, I believe that you made the right choice," Loc said.

His smile was a true work of art. For once, Macy decided to take him at his word.

"I think we had better go through everything we know about the Ghosts," she said.

"An excellent idea. We will rehearse until you are letter-perfect. Although we must try to retain a few of your rough edges, I think. People so often mistake that kind of thing for honesty."

"Not something you could ever be accused of."

Loc smiled. "It's true that my talents lie elsewhere. Which is why we're going to make such a convincing team."

<hr>

Apart from tedious coaching sessions and long and tangled discussions with Tommy Tabagee, the Brazilian ambassador, and various members of the TPA security council, Macy Minnot and Loc Ifrahim spent as much time as possible out of sight of each other. Macy in the command blister; Loc in the living space. They had established a wary mutual respect, but it by no means resembled any species of friendship. More like a business partnership between two people who trusted each other against their better judgement.

Saturn and its retinue of moons swelled astern of *Elephant*. The Ghost ships stood off to one side of the gas giant—because of the different positions of Neptune and Nephele relative to Saturn they were approaching at another angle. At first, *Elephant's* telescope showed only the tiny spear of mingled light emitted by their fusion drives and mass drivers. Then, at maximum magnification, Macy could make out long fingers of shadow within the glow—shadows cast by the ships. And at last she could see the ships themselves, but even as *Elephant* entered the outer edge of the Saturn System she still couldn't resolve any real detail.

On that last day, *Elephant* swept in past the eccentric orbits of Saturn's retinue of small outer moons: the four moons of the Gallic group; the Norse group of some thirty moons in retrograde orbits, including Phoebe, the largest of all the outer moons; the five moons of the Inuit group. The rest of the system lay beyond. Two-faced Iapetus; tumbling, cavern-riddled Hyperion; smoggy Titan; battered Rhea. The smaller inner moons: Dione, Tethys, Enceladus, Mimas. A greater variety of moons here than around all the other planets in the Solar System, arrayed outward from the banded globe of Saturn and the Ring System, with its retinue of co-orbital moons and ring shepherds, and swarming moonlets embedded in the A Ring.

Iapetus's traffic control contacted Macy via tightbeam laser and she downloaded her flight plan for approval. It was purely a formality: she was already committed. As *Elephant* fell inward, she banished Loc to the passenger compartment, checked and rechecked the flight parameters, and kept an eye on the thin traffic between the various moons. Remembering how, when she and Newt and Avernus had fled Dione during the Quiet War, a singleship and its proxies had chased them across the rings. Aware that at any moment a missile or proxy could slam toward her out of the darkness. A speck of smart gravel travelling at hyperkinetic relative velocity could pierce *Elephant*'s hull and its fusion-motor chamber, and turn the tug into a sudden fireball and an expanding shell of tumbling debris within a microsecond. She'd never know what hit her and couldn't do anything to prevent it, but still.

But passage around Saturn was unremarkable. *Elephant* more or less flew itself, following the course that Newt had plotted and laid in. All Macy had to do was lie back and keep watch. The minuscule comet tail of the Ghost ships sank toward Saturn's ringed crescent and the nightside of the gas giant swung at her, expanding, blotting out more and more of the starry sky. *Elephant* juddered briefly, making the insertion burn, and then they were racing around the dark side of Saturn, faintly illuminated by the ghost light of ringshine. The pearl of the sun blistered the joint between black space and the planet's chthonic arc, sweeping upward above the pastel bands of day. And the sweeping bands of the rings lay dead ahead like heaven's bridge as *Elephant* soared outward toward Iapetus.

Beyond the outer edge of the ring system, Iapetus's traffic control warned Macy to stand by for interception. Less than an hour later, she picked up the radar trace of a ship closing behind her. A ground-to-orbit shuttle, a flattened oval like a pumpkin seed with the green star of the Pacific Community splashed across its tail assembly, matching *Elephant*'s velocity, laying off three kilometres to starboard.

Macy opened a channel and surrendered control of *Elephant*. The shuttle fired tethers that clamped to *Elephant*'s hull and the two ships reeled close. Three marines in pressure suits cycled one after the other through the airlock, big men bulked out by black battle armour, smoking with cold in the fuggy air of the lifesystem, taking up most of the cramped space. One immediately took control of *Elephant*; the other two escorted Loc and Macy across the gap to the bright cave of an airlock cut into the black shadow of the shuttle's hull. Macy was thoroughly disorientated by the arrival of strangers and the noise and unfamiliar surroundings of the shuttle's spacious passenger compartment. Her pressure suit seemed flimsy and shabby compared with the armoured bulk of the marines; she felt like a runaway child taken into custody by concerned adults.

Loc was already deploying his charm, chatting with the officer in charge all the way down to Iapetus and the small city that the Pacific Community had built in Othon Crater, on the dark northern plains of the sub-saturnian hemisphere. Macy and Loc were decanted into a pressurised APC and driven from the spaceport down a straight highway to the main habitat. A phalanx of officials from the three member states of the TPA and delegates from the five free cities greeted them at the transport hub, chief amongst them Tommy Tabagee. The venerable diplomat pumped their hands and welcomed them to Heaven's Gate. He wore a dark high-collared suit, and his grey dreadlocks were caught up in a gold net, but his manner was as breezily informal as ever and he was in high good humour.

"If we can put an end to this nonsense before it becomes something serious, then we can be satisfied with lives well lived, I reckon," he said, and explained that his aides would escort Macy and Loc to their quarters, where they would have a good hour to freshen up and get ready for their first meeting with members of the Tactical Group. "I've told them to go easy on you—that you need to rest up before the reception. Don't worry, nothing formal. A meet-and-greet session with everyone involved in this great enterprise of ours. Now, you'll excuse me if I cut and run, but I have some business of my own. We'll talk later. We've much to discuss, and little time."

—◆—

After the long hours of Loc Ifrahim's coaching, after imagining every possible way it might go wrong, Macy found the preliminary interview with the panel of TPA diplomats and military officers something of a relief. She had reached her destination; her worst fears had proven to be unfounded; she could at last begin the work she'd come to do.

As a token of what the chairperson of the panel called "a policy of openness and full cooperation" a Brazilian Air Defence captain walked Macy through the latest data on the Ghosts' little fleet. Throwaway drones had shot past them several days ago and returned pictures showing that each was encased in a sculpted shell of ice fifty metres thick and shaped like a spear-head—a very effective armour against kinetic weapons, high explosives, and ablation by high-energy weapons, according to the captain. The surfaces of the shells were coated with reflective material and inlaid with intricate grooves, and contained layers of superconducting mesh to protect the ships from the effects of EMP mines, and their shape meant that they could be used as aeroshields: it was possible that the Ghost ships could shed a considerable proportion of their velocity by ploughing through Saturn's atmosphere, and then they could loop around Titan and the other moons, picking off targets at will. The initial deceleration forces would exceed 15 g, but were survivable if the crews were packed in acceleration gel, with air in their lungs and body cavities displaced by oxygenated fluorocarbon fluid.

"But even if they pass through the Saturn System on a slingshot maneuver, they could cause considerable damage with missiles, proxies, and kinetic weapons," the captain said. "There is much that is still unquantifiable."

That last pretty much summed up everything about the Ghosts, as far as Macy was concerned.

After the captain's presentation the panel began to fire questions at her. She told them that she didn't know the extent or exact population of the City of the New Horizon, described what she had seen during her single visit, and outlined the experience of other Free Outers who had visited the Ghosts. She had never met the Ghosts' leader, Levi, she said, and didn't know if he was alive or dead, but she supposed that the Ghosts believed that he was alive, for how else could his future self send prophesies into the past? She confirmed that the Ghosts had obtained the specifications of the fast-fusion drive from Free Outers who had defected to their cause and said that she didn't know exactly how many ships the Ghosts possessed or where or when they had built the ships that were approaching Saturn: the Ghosts had begun to settle Triton a decade before the Quiet War and they planned for the long term. The ships could have been constructed well before the Free Outers arrived in the Neptune System, or they might have been built within the last year, in graving docks deep under Triton's surface.

The panel asked her about the attack on the Brazilian ship at Neptune, and she gave a brief account of the negotiations, the sudden exit of the Ghosts, and the attack on the Brazilian ship, and explained how some but not all of the Free Outers had managed to escape and meet up with those who'd fled from their settlement on Proteus.

Every so often the strangeness of all this hit Macy: she had come all this way to give sworn testimony about ships set on mounting some kind of attack on another planet. And then she'd think of the Ghosts' comet-smear setting behind the misty limb of Saturn, and get a chill.

One of the members of the panel, a European Navy second lieutenant, was a psychologist. He asked a number of perceptive questions about Sada's part in Macy's escape from the city of East of Eden, where she'd been more or less held prisoner after defecting from the Rainbow Bridge construction crew, and after the panel's chairperson had thanked Macy for her help, she had a long conversation with the psychologist about Sada and tried her best to answer as fully as she could a series of questions about how she thought Sada might react to a variety of hypothetical situations.

Macy said, "You think she's leading this attack, don't you?"

The psychologist had an annoying habit, probably a professional tic, of answering a question with another question. Saying now, "Is that what you think?"

"I know she would want to be part of it."

"We have AI models of the most prominent members of the Ghosts," the psychologist said. "Worked up from interviews with people who knew them before they joined the cult, from the meetings with Mr. Tabagee and his crew, and from the partial notes that our diplomats were able to transmit before the Ghosts murdered them. Sada Selene is a very dominant figure, strongly embodying characteristics idealised by other members of the cult. She is their Joan of Arc."

"One thing you should take aboard," Macy said. "They don't think of themselves as a cult."

"What, then?"

"They think they're a new species. The latest best new thing. And they believe that the future is theirs, because their leader's future self told them so."

One of Tommy Tabagee's aides, a slender, extremely polite young woman named Gita Lo Jindal, escorted Macy to a pod in one of the residential blocks that were scattered amongst the forested landscaping of the habitat's cut-and-cover tube. Ankling along a road of crimson halflife turf, breathing in chill air edged with the clean odour of the tall pines standing on either side, bright spangles of light shining through chinks in the dense green boughs, Macy felt a plangent note of nostalgia, remembering the forests along the northern boundary of the Fontaine Territory where she had been working when she'd been co-opted for a prestigious position on the construction crew sent out to quicken the new biome at Rainbow Bridge, Callisto. Where her life had changed forever, and she'd embarked on a long and strange journey that had taken her to the beginning of the edge of the Solar System and back again.

Before attending the interview with the panel Macy had sent a message to Newt, telling him she had arrived safely on Iapetus, that if she'd been arrested it had been so subtle she hadn't noticed. When she got back to her pod, she found a reply waiting for her: a brief video of Newt and the twins crowding close to the camera, telling her that they were rooting for her. Han had sent a drawing too, showing a stocky red-haired figure in a blue space-suit straddling the joint of Iapetus's white-black ying-yang disc. Macy had Gita Lo Jindal print off a copy and tacked it to one of the walls, where she could see it while she dozed for a few hours in the pod's sleeping niche.

When the aide returned, Macy asked her if she could find someone who could do something about the bird's nest she liked to call her hair. Gita Lo Jindal told her that someone would come to take care of it right away. "Mean-while, can I suggest a few touches of makeup, too?"

"What kind of reception is this, anyway?"

"Oh, just the usual mix of everyone who's anyone. But you don't have to worry about a thing," Gita Lo Jindal said. "You're one of the stars, which means you can't do anything wrong."

The reception was held on top of the largest of the habitat's buildings, a helix of platforms, offices, and meeting rooms twisted around a central core. It was already in full swing when Macy and Gita Lo Jindal arrived, people clumped and knotted across a broad terrace with a view across treetops toward the end wall, where silky waterfalls plunged between spires and pillars of black rock. Loc Ifrahim intercepted them, bowed to Gita Lo Jindal, and told her that he would like to borrow Ms. Minnot for a little while—there were people she needed to meet. He had shaved off his beard and his hair was trimmed and woven into many small braids that gleamed as if oiled, and he was dressed in a silvery suit, a white shirt, and white slippers. He had recovered much of his old poise and was clearly excited by the buzz of the crowd. In his element. Back home.

"I have been talking to my old friend Yota, and I have some news," he told Macy, as he escorted her down the length of the terrace. "There's going to be an announcement tonight. Euclides Peixoto has finally decided to take part in the talks."

"That's good, isn't it?"

"It means he thinks they're important; it doesn't mean that he agrees with what we're trying to do. Yota thinks that he'll try to wreck them, and I'm inclined to agree, but we'll see soon enough. Meanwhile, we must make nice with our hosts and pretend we don't know."

"What am I supposed to say to them?" Macy said.

"All you have to do is be yourself," Loc said, and introduced her to the Brazilian ambassador, Paulinho Fontaine, several of her senior aides and civil servants, and an androgyne neuter dressed in a white jumpsuit who told Macy that they had something in common.

"You once worked for Professor Doctor Sri Hong-Owen, at Rainbow Bridge. And I have the honour of working for her now."

It seemed that Sri Hong-Owen was living with a small crew on the co-orbital moon Janus, building a habitat and working on some kind of secret project—a simple gift that would, according to the neuter, Raphael, transform the way people lived in the outer system.

"The Ghosts know that the Professor Doctor is a great gene wizard—and a great prize," Raphael said. "They have contacted her several times, offering to help her defect. She turned them down, of course, and they did not take it well. And now they are coming here. Everything is at hazard, and we are offering to help in any way we can."

The talk turned to the latest news about the Ghost fleet. There had been no response to the cycle of messages that the TPA was transmitting to the fleet and to Triton, and time was beginning to run out: very soon the TPA would have to decide whether or not to stage an all-out attack on the Ghost ships, and how best to do it. Everyone wanted to know Loc and Macy's opinions; Macy was happy to let Loc deal with their questions. She was tired, and felt intimidated by the crowd of strangers. Her attention was beginning to drift away from the conversation, which had the stale flavour of opinions rehashed for the fourth or fifth time, when a tall old man with papery skin and a snow white spade-shaped beard interposed himself between her and the rest of the group, introducing himself as Tariq Amir Tagore-Mittal, the mayor of Camelot, Mimas. He wanted to know why the Free Outers had not returned with the fleet of ships that they had, according to him, stolen. Macy started to explain that some had been abandoned on Miranda when the Brazilians had invaded the Uranus System and others had been lost when the Ghosts had mounted their coup against the Brazilian delegation, but the old man cut in, telling her that those ships were needed to protect the Saturn System right now: it had been left exposed because of the Free Outers' selfishness.

Macy, fired up by a flash of righteous anger, told the old prig that she wasn't about to be lectured by a member of the administration that had allowed Brazilian and European ships to orbit Mimas unhindered and unchallenged before the Quiet War. "You want to talk about selfishness, I can't think of a better example."

She would have said more, but Loc Ifrahim smoothly intervened, telling the mayor that Ms. Minnot was tired and not quite herself.

It was true. She *was* tired. So tired that she didn't even mind Loc Ifrahim's presumption. She wanted to go back to the pod and see if Newt and the twins had sent another message. She wanted to sleep. She raised up on tiptoe, looking around for Gita Lo Jindal, and saw a wedge of senior diplomats and military officers moving across the far side of the big space, led by Tommy Tabagee and the white man-shape of an avatar.

The face floating in the screen set in the front of the avatar's head was the face of Euclides Peixoto.

"This will be interesting," Loc Ifrahim said to Macy.

"He didn't dare come in person."

"Whatever else he is, Euclides is not a coward. He is up to something."

"You should know."

"Because I worked for him, once upon a time? Well, I don't work for him now, and I have every reason to mistrust him."

Macy felt a pang of guilt for having touched on the raw wound of Loc's loss. She started to apologise, but he put his hand on her arm and told her it didn't matter.

"I still shouldn't—"

"Hush. Let's hear what the great scion has to say."

The avatar and Tommy Tabagee took up a position in the middle of the terrace. A little drone floated down in front of Tommy Tabagee's face, acting as a microphone. He said that he had the pleasure of introducing a man who needed no introduction to this distinguished company, so he would simply stand aside and let Mr. Peixoto make his announcement.

A hush spread as the avatar turned to study the people circled around, the white plastic of its man-shaped shell throwing off oily glints from the lights floating above the crowd. It paused when it faced Macy Minnot and Loc Ifrahim. Euclides Peixoto's face was expressionless, his gaze stony, moving past them as the avatar completed its circle. Drones aimed avid camera-eyes at it, the whir of their fans for a moment the only sound.

"I will not take much of your time," Euclides Peixoto said. "I will tell you straightaway that I have not come to join your enterprise. You've wasted too much time in debate. You're all infected with the pernicious virus of democracy. The idea of fairness. The idea that everyone deserves an opinion about everything, and everyone's opinion is worth the same as everyone else's. That kind of stupidity was wiped out years ago in Greater Brazil. Its hosts were killed by the Overturn, and it was unable to find a foothold in those who survived. For only the strong survive. Because they are able to withstand everything the universe can throw at them. Because they have proved themselves strong by defeating the weak, not by treating them as equals.

"That's what you ladies and gentlemen, gathered here in your pomp, have forgotten. Life isn't about cooperation. It's about struggle. The struggle of the strong to survive. And that's why everything will be lost if you have your way. You have already wasted time on talk when every second the enemy grows closer, and every second he grows closer he gets faster, too. He isn't slowing down for debate and votes. He knows what he has to do and he is by God and Gaia doing it.

"Well, I also know what has to be done and that's why I came here to say farewell. I'm ready to go out and face down the enemy on your behalf. Oh, don't thank me now. I neither need nor want your praise. I will defeat the enemy, and I will go on to Jupiter, and meet with General Nabuco and decide with him what must be done to restore the strength and honour of our families. And then I will return here. But not to be thanked. The strong don't need the gratitude of the weak, as you will find out, by and by.

"One more thing before I go," Euclides Peixoto said. The avatar stepped sideways to a buffet table, raised its left arm, and smashed it against the edge, shattering it at the elbow. "A little matter of a bad deed that has so far has gone unpunished. A gift that turned out to be fake. Yes, Mr. Ifrahim, I see you know just what I mean."

And the avatar put down its head and charged at Loc Ifrahim in a blur of bright motion and with the jagged stump of its truncated arm stabbed him in the throat and clung to him as he fell, stabbing him over and over in the throat and face and chest, blood spraying and spattering its white shell. Macy caught at its bloody, broken arm and tried to pull it off, but it shrugged her away. She flew backward, landed smack on her can, and bounced back to her feet, anger and fright singing in her head. A man was shouting, asking someone to shoot the fucking thing, but no one was armed. An Air Defence officer snatched silverware from a buffet table and stabbed at the ball joint of the avatar's neck; Macy grabbed a tray carried by a floating drone and hammered at the avatar's head until the screen cracked and went dark and the avatar shut down, whether because it had been mortally damaged or because Euclides Peixoto had cut the connection she would never know.

She helped the officer haul the avatar's limp and surprisingly light shell off Loc Ifrahim's body. He lay sprawled in a widening pool of his own blood. His eyes were turned up, he wasn't breathing, and Macy couldn't find a pulse in his wrist. She prised his lips apart and placed her mouth over his, tasting his blood, breathing her breath into him, pumping his chest with locked hands, one, two, three, breathing into his mouth again. She was still working on him when a pair of meditechs arrived, but there was nothing they could do then or later to revive him.

10

—For once in his life the poor guy was trying to do good, Macy wrote. But some silly little trick he'd played on Euclides Peixoto came back at him, and it killed him. I disliked him from the first time we met, but I truly feel sorry that he's dead. I think, at the end, he really had reformed. He really wanted to help out. There was an element of ego in it, he wanted to be in on what he called the hinge point of history so that he could win some kind of power or influence. But still. I'm sorry he's dead. And I never thought I'd say that.

—Meanwhile, Euclides Peixoto is chasing after his own version of glory. He's heading toward the edge of the system at the head of a small fleet. Ready to confront the Ghosts. We don't know what his battle plan is, but he's taken a large chunk of the TPA's assets. All the Brazilian ships, of course, plus the European singleships operating out of the *Flower of the Forest*. So he has two ships of the line and two wings of singleships, also a little fleet of converted Outer ships. And he has a small arsenal of hydrogen bombs too.

—If he does defeat the Ghosts, and if he wasn't lying—and we still aren't sure what was true and what was flat-out boasting or fantasy in that little speech I told you about in the last squirt—he's going to make an alliance with the administration at Jupiter. The general in charge of the occupation force there is an old-school guy who has refused to acknowledge the new government of Greater Brazil. So even if things go well for us here, we'll still have to work out what to do about that.

Macy wrote on, sitting cross-legged on the bed in her pod, lights dialled down to a twilight glow. It was two in the morning, local time. She was dog-tired, sapped by grief and the drag of Iapetus's gravity and the grainy residue of spent adrenalin. After the murder of Loc Ifrahim, there had been a long session with the TPA security council and delegates from the free cities. Macy had been asked to attend, the sole representative of the Free Outers. Sitting near the back, her hair drying from the shower she'd taken to scrub off Loc Ifrahim's blood, she'd listened with increasing impatience to arguments that flowed back and forth with no sign that any kind of agreement would ever be reached. Everyone seemed to be treading old ground and defending positions they'd taken some time ago, showing far too much self-interest and far too little unity or trust. Macy was amazed that no one mentioned the most obvious way of cutting through all the posturing, the single act that would bring the Outers around to the TPA's side. When the meeting was temporarily suspended around midnight, breaking up into little cliques with nothing substantial decided, she went up to Tommy Tabagee, asked him for a few moments of his time, and laid out her idea.

He listened carefully and said, "It is one of the first things we must deal with after this is over—"

"Not later," Macy said. "Now. Maybe I didn't make myself clear. This isn't just about proving to the Outers that you want to reach some kind of reconciliation with them. Although that's important, no question. But what's equally important is that there must be all kinds of talented people locked away in that place. About the only thing people here agree on is that we need more resources. Well, aren't *they* a resource? We're short of pilots. Let them fly some of those ships. Maybe they know where ships and caches of weapons were hidden before the Quiet War kicked off. And maybe, just maybe, they can help you to reach out to the Ghosts and stop this developing into a full-scale war."

They kicked it back and forth. Tommy Tabagee called over the Brazilian ambassador, Paulinho Fontaine, who listened to Macy and then said that while she supported the new government of Greater Brazil and its pledge to free the cities and settlements of Outer system, there had to be an orderly transition and that was not possible in the present crisis.

"The most important thing I learned, living out here," Macy said, "is that when it comes to solving problems the Outers have everyone else beat hollow. They're smart, and they know how to organise and cooperate to get things done. How do you think they survived out here for so long? You don't need detailed plans for handing over power because they can work up solutions to snags and complications on the spot. But you *do* need to get them on your side right now, and show them that Euclides Peixoto's authority has expired. Let him go after the Ghosts if he wants to, and let the Outers help you take care of business here."

Now, two in the morning, she told Newt what had been decided, sent the message, switched off the slate and the pod's lights, and lay down and tried to sleep. She had a long day ahead of her. She had to liberate Paris.

The next day, Macy, Tommy Tabagee, the Brazilian ambassador, and the neuter, Raphael, were on Dione, in a crowded one-room apartment in the so-called New City, the prison tent built by the Brazilians, talking to elected representatives of the Outer prisoners while a drone up in the corner of the ceiling fed the discussion to everyone else.

One of the representatives was Abbie Jones, Newt's mother. Macy had barely enough time to tell her that she'd become a grandmother by adoption before everyone got down to business. They talked a long time. Three hours, four. At first, the Outers' representatives split along expected lines: those who believed that it was a trick, that the Ghosts would be their salvation; those who wanted nothing to do with either the Ghosts or the TPA; and the majority, led by Abbie Jones, who knew that this was their best chance of regaining something like their original independence. Finally, Macy sat back and sipped mint tea and massaged her sore throat, dazed and exhausted, while a referendum was organised. The results came in within an hour: a clear majority in favour of evacuating New City and moving back to Paris.

The Brazilian ambassador made a short and gracious speech thanking them for their decision. "Before you begin to organise your people," she said, "I want to ask you for one favour. We will open links to the other cities in the Saturn System. Talk to their people. Tell them what has been agreed here. Let them know that you have agreed to help us in this desperate hour."

After that, the Outers got to work. Euclides Peixoto's zero-growth policy meant that there were no pregnant women, babies, or small children to worry about. A significant minority who refused to cooperate with the TPA under any circumstances agreed to stay behind as caretakers, along with medical technicians and patients too ill to be moved. Everyone else packed day bags and put on their pressure suits and assembled in streets and squares close to the airlocks. Monitors in charge of groups of twenty people reported to supervisors who reported in turn to the ad hoc committee, until at last everyone was ready, and the evacuation began. Group by group, people cycled through the airlocks, some climbing into waiting rolligons, the rest moving off in a slow and ceaseless procession that overflowed the roadway and spread across the dusty ice on either side, a river of people moving with common purpose, flowing across the floor of Romulus crater toward Paris.

Macy walked near the front of the long column with Abbie Jones and other people from the Jones-Truex-Bakaleinikoff clan, including Newt's uncle, Pete Bakaleinikoff, and Junko and Junpei Asai, members of the little telescope gang she had once belonged to. They told her stories about life under the rule of the Brazilians; she told them about the Free Outers.

"A great thing you did," Pete Bakaleinikoff said, "surviving out there, fighting off the Brazilians and then the Ghosts. Will you all come home, when this is over?"

"I don't know," Macy said, and realised that she hadn't really thought about it. "We've made a kind of home out there, at Nephele. I suppose some people might want to stay there. And I suppose that others might want to go back to Miranda and revive the habitat we built there—or build a new one, if the Brazilians destroyed it. But we have to get through this first."

Everything was at hazard, and yet Macy was happy. It was a fine thing to be walking with her old friends at the head of this great army of people, to have helped to free them, to be leading them home. Rolligons moved at walking pace ahead of the column, carrying supplies and those too old or too infirm to walk, and several trikes skittered up and down, videoing people as they bounded along in a low-gravity lope, talking to each other across the common band, joining in songs that rose and fell down the length of the colourful carnival as it moved steadily through the sombre moonscape under the black sky, with the small bright sun low in the west and Saturn's great globe looming overhead. Macy was unused to walking long distances. Her legs and back soon began to ache, her breath was harsh in the bowl of her helmet, and the stiff pressure suit chafed her at knees and hips, but she was determined to finish the march on her feet.

And so they all walked on, and at last Paris rose above the close horizon, a bright chip set in the dark slopes of the inner edge of the crater's rim. A great cheer went up and the column surged forward, passing through vacuum-organism fields, passing the spaceport, some people running ahead of the rolligons now, leaping like gazelles, eager to be the first through the airlocks.

The big freight-yard airlocks were able to take a hundred people at a time, but more than five thousand had walked to Paris and although the operation worked as smoothly as the evacuation of the New City it took several hours to process them all. Macy, Abbie Jones, and the other representatives waited their turn, and were met by Tommy Tabagee and the Brazilian ambassador on the other side. All around them, Parisians were moving out of the maws of the airlocks and flowing across loading platforms and marshalling yards, still wearing their pressure suits, helmets under their arms and day bags slung over their shoulders. Spreading out into the empty avenues and streets and parks, organising themselves into groups and crews to open up apartment buildings, setting up kitchens in the parks to give everyone their first meal, taking charge of the power and water and air plants, and the rest of the city's infrastructure.

All of this videoed by drones, footage that was edited on the fly and zipped into compressed transmissions aimed at the Ghost fleet and at Neptune.

Late that night, on the top floor of the TPA administration building, high above a city enlivened by the lights and music of a hundred street parties, Macy was stuck in an interminable discussion between Paris's representatives and senior members of the TPA about measures to make sure that Euclides Peixoto's forces couldn't retake Paris—distribution of small arms from the military armoury, organisation of volunteers into cadres, and the disposition of battle drones which had been pulled off patrols around the periphery of the New City. There were fewer Outer ships than expected, mostly scows and tugs left behind by Euclides Peixoto. Former pilots and engineers worked up plans to fit them with rail guns and drones loaded with high explosive, a small but significant addition to the resources that the Europeans and the Pacific Community were assembling as a last-ditch measure against the Ghosts, who as yet had made no acknowledgement of the transmissions showing the liberation of Paris.

It was after midnight by the time everything had been hashed out. Macy ate a meal with Abbie Jones and talked about her gypsy life with Newt and the twins.

"I should send a message," Abbie said. "In fact, we should locate all the families of your people and ask them to send messages too."

It was a good idea, and it kept Macy busy all the next morning. Abbie organised a couple of technicians who aimed one of the dish antennas of the city's uplink station toward Nephele, and a steady trickle of people came in and recorded messages that were transmitted over and again until Nephele dropped behind Saturn.

Macy recorded her own message, scripted with the help of the Brazilian psychologist, appealing to Sada Selene to open up a dialogue. And then, while it was being transmitted to the Ghost fleet and to Neptune on a continuous loop, she used an avatar to appear before the Tactical Group panel on Iapetus, answering questions about the Ghosts and their city.

The next morning, the Ghost fleet was fast approaching the picket line established by the *Flower of the Forest*, the *Getûlio Dornelles Vargas*, and a small fleet of singleships and Outer shuttles and freighters, some hundred million kilometres out from Saturn. There had been no response to Macy's message to Sada Selene, or to any of the other messages aimed at the Ghosts.

Pete Bakaleinikoff and Junko and Junpei Asai had woken the telescope cloud that all this time had been sleeping in orbit around Saturn's trailing Trojan point, and pointed it at the picket line. All over Paris, people huddled around slates or put on spex and watched the live feed. Macy and members of the new city administration watched it on a memo space on the top floor of the TPA administration building. A technician had set up a holo of a clock counting backward to the moment of first encounter. As it approached the last minute everyone in the big round room on top of the administration building fell silent. The whole city was hushed and watchful.

The Brazilian ships were strung in a line a hundred thousand kilometres long that ran parallel to the projected path of the Ghost ships, and clouds of kinetic weapons and laser-cannon platforms and proxies and nuclear and EMP mines had been sown across the volume of space through which they would pass. The four ships were switching their mass drivers on and off at unpredictable intervals, altering their delta vee so that their trajectory couldn't be precisely plotted, travelling one after the other in a sharply curved arc at a velocity of almost three thousand kilometres a second, about 0.1 percent the speed of light. Even though their arc stretched for some ten thousand kilometres end to end, it traversed the Brazilian picket line in a little over thirty-six seconds, smashing through a gauntlet of kinetic weapons and x-ray lasers and conventional and hydrogen bomb explosions whose ragged flowers were still expanding and fading as the Ghost ships ploughed on.

The outer layers of the ice-shields of the first and second ships, which had been closest to the Brazilian picket line, were breaking up in large chunks. But the shields of the others, although cratered by the impacts of numerous kinetic weapons, were largely intact. One instant replay of a magnified section of the general view showed a trio of singleships targeting a Ghost ship as it swept past, firing x-ray lasers into the maw of its exhaust; another showed a swarm of proxies striking the *Getúlio Dornelles Vargas*, flares bursting across the big ship's prow, fountains of debris expanding above rents in its hull; a third showed a kinetic weapon piercing the *Flower of the Forest* from stem to stern, exiting between the vent nozzles of its fusion-motor cluster in a massive plume of flame as glittering sprays of debris expanded from the shattered hull.

Attempts to raise anyone aboard the two Brazilian ships came to nothing. Beyond their shattered hulks, surviving singleships were frantically decelerating, attempting to kill their delta vee so that they could turn around and return to the Saturn System. The Ghost fleet ploughed on, less than nine hours from an encounter with Titan, and then with Saturn.

The first round of the battle for the Saturn System was over. The second would soon begin. Pacific Community ships accelerated outward, preparing to mount a last-ditch attack. Tugs and scows hastily converted to weapons platforms and piloted by remote control hung in synchronous orbits above the cities of the inhabited moons, and in and around the cities crews worked to make ground-based weaponry ready. On the top floor of the TPA administration building in Paris, strategy teams elaborated responses to every kind of scenario. There was still no general consensus about what the Ghosts planned to do. It still seemed most likely that they would slingshot around Titan and Saturn and pass straight through the system, heading inward to Jupiter or Mars or Earth, but as they passed they could aim kinetic weapons at TPA installations and the Outer cities, or release drones and proxies able to decelerate by ploughing deep into Saturn's atmosphere and so achieve a variety of orbits amongst the rings and moons, waging war long after the Ghost fleet had passed on.

People kept coming up to Macy with questions. She couldn't answer most of them; was amazed that she could answer any at all. She'd had already sent video of the Ghost ships running Euclides Peixoto's picket line to Newt, and between interruptions she sent messages describing the ongoing discussions and speculations. He sent back that his surveillance satellites had spotted the H-bomb explosions, said that the Free Outers had held a debate and voted overwhelmingly to recognise the new government of Paris and to begin a dialogue with the TPA administration.

—Too little, too late if you ask me. But we can't do much else. Even if we had the fuel it would take us nine weeks to get there.

—Stay in contact, Macy sent. And you might want to get ready to welcome a bunch of refugees if this goes bad.

She discovered that she was hungry and wolfed down a pouch of CHON yoghurt that tasted faintly of burnt rubber. The holo clock had been reset and was counting backward toward the Ghost fleet's encounter with Titan, less than an hour away. Arguments were breaking out across the crowded room. The Brazilian ambassador and Abbie Jones were standing in front of a memo space, talking to Tommy Tabagee and other members of the security council on Iapetus. Raphael, Sri Hong-Owen's representative, had been discussing something with Pete Bakaleinikoff, and now they picked their way through the knots of people to Macy.

"This one wants me to point the telescope cloud at the rings," Pete said. "Says something's about to happen there that everyone needs to see."

"You must do it now, or you will miss it," Raphael said. Yo's disturbingly beautiful, androgynous face was impossible to read. "And please, Macy, don't ask me about what is going to happen. It is much easier to show it than to explain."

The neuter had volunteered to come to Dione to help supervise the evacuation. Macy had wondered about yo's motivation then, and now she felt a strong pang of unease. A cold snake uncoiling in her guts.

She said to Pete, "Will it take long to swing those telescopes around?"

The old man ran a hand over his pale freckled scalp. "Not long, no. But we'll lose our best view of the Ghost fleet."

"At the moment, what is about to happen in the rings is more important," Raphael said. "There are other telescopes, of course. But yours is the most useful because it is above the plane of the rings."

"I guess it can't do any harm to take a quick look," Macy said to Pete.

"That's what I thought," he said. "But you're the one in charge."

She laughed: a nervous bark. "The hell I am."

"Of course you are," Pete said, and hooked on his spex and began to cut and caress the air with his hands.

The big memo space in the centre of the room turned black and then displayed a view of Saturn's butterscotch globe and the sunlit side of the rings curved around it: a broad bow intricately grooved with threads and bands of varying brightness and colour, tans and creams and spectral greys incised by thin black gaps and the wide sooty stripe of the Cassini Division.

Raphael laughed, stepped toward the memo space with slinky grace, and pointed to a cluster of tiny bright lights near the Keeler Gap, at the outer edge of the A Ring. Five, ten, twenty point sources that were clearly moving outward.

"Ships!" several people said, and someone else said it wasn't possible,

372

there were too many of them and, besides, they were accelerating too quickly to be ships.

"Whatever they are, they're on an interception course," Pete said.

He opened a window that showed a schematic of the inner system, and drew an arc that curved away from Saturn and swept out to connect with the track of the Ghosts' fleet just before it encountered Titan.

Everyone in the room was watching the memo space now. Raphael turned to look at them all, yo's smile broad and happy, yo's hands raised as if to bestow a blessing. "This is a gift from Sri Hong-Owen," the neuter said. "She has chosen to sacrifice these seeds for the immediate good."

"Seeds? They're propeller moonlets," a woman said. "I'm picking up changes in ring-particle streaming right now."

Macy asked Pete what the woman meant; Pete explained that there were thousands of irregular bodies between thirty and a hundred metres in diameter orbiting in a thin belt in the A Ring, remnants of a small moon shattered by collision with an asteroid or comet. Their gravity caused characteristic patterns of turbulence in the ring plane, like the wakes of so many speedboats.

Raphael waited out a clamour of questions, then lifted yo's hands again and said that Sri Hong-Owen's people had not had time to turn all the propeller moonlets in the A Ring into seeds, but they had transformed a significant proportion.

"If the first wave does not overwhelm the Ghosts' defences, then we have more than enough to try again."

People started to ask more questions, and Raphael told them that everything would soon become clear. Meanwhile they should get back to work. "We don't yet know the Ghosts' intentions, so our best hope is to prepare for every conceivable possibility."

"I don't know whether to punch you or kiss you," Macy told the neuter.

"Sri asked me not to reveal this unless it was necessary," Raphael said.

"And you always obey your mistress's whims."

"They may sometimes seem strange or inappropriate, but they are never whims."

Pete Bakaleinikoff put up a blurred video grab of one of the moonlets powering away from the rings. An irregular potato-shaped chunk of pitted ice wrapped with a helical band of fullerene composite, some kind of sheath or cap at one end, a cluster of mass drivers at the other. A scale bar put it at around eighty metres along its main axis, roughly forty metres across. Calculations by various hands started to scroll up beside it. The seed was accelerating at more than 20 g and would consume a significant proportion of its mass as it powered out to Titan, but it would still mass some 60,000 tons when it intercepted the Ghost fleet, and would be travelling at a relative velocity in excess of thirty-five kilometres per second.

"The impact of just one of those things should punch right through their shields," a woman said.

"They could retaliate before they're hit," another woman said. "We can't rule out some kind of suicidal spasm."

"We're expecting that anyway," the first woman said.

Everyone went back to calculating impact parameters and working up defence scenarios. Macy studied the image of the transformed moonlet, wondering what the sheath at the forward end contained. It looked a little like the acrosome that capped the head of a human sperm. Seeds. Packages that contained new life, everything it needed to get started.

She asked Pete what the propeller moonlets were made of.

"Dirty ice, mostly."

"Any carbonaceous material?" Macy said.

"Some, sure." Pete squinted at her. "You think it was spun into fullerene, used to weave the wrappings and make the mass drivers?"

"Among other things," Macy said, thinking of the lovely little habitat circling Nephele.

Twenty minutes passed. Thirty. Someone patched into a feed from a drone more or less directly behind the little cluster of moonlets: chips of shadow in a vast haze of icy exhaust. And now Titan's orange disc rose beyond Saturn, and within two minutes the fusion motors and mass drivers of the Ghosts started up. Clearly, they had spotted the moonlets and realised that they would pass through the volume of space their ships would occupy just before their encounter with Titan. They couldn't change course but they could try to increase their velocity and cross ahead of the trajectories of the moonlets.

Everyone in the room was standing, watching the big memo space, as the arc of Ghost ships powered in toward Titan.

"They aren't going to make it," Abbie Jones said, with grim satisfaction.

Thirty seconds later, the leading Ghost ship was struck by a moonlet. Ice flashed into an expanding ring of white-hot gas brighter than the sun, devouring half the mass of the enshelled ship, flaring even more brightly as the pinch field of its fusion generator let go, this avid star dimming and beginning to collapse on itself as it plunged around Titan and headed on toward Saturn. And now the second ship flared, and the third. Macy and everyone else watched in sombre silence as the fourth and last ship ploughed on untouched. It skimmed a deep chord through Titan's smoggy atmosphere, and its ice shield, heavily degraded by passage through the picket line, broke up. Some of the chunks of debris scored bright parabolas of plasma trails through Titan's smog and impacted along the moon's northern hemisphere, creating a string of raw new craters; others emerged more or less intact, a broken comet tumbling in a line toward Saturn, hurrying after the cooling shells of plasma that were all that was left of the other three ships.

Now at last the tension snapped and everyone in the room fell into each other's arms. Macy hugged Pete Bakaleinikoff; strangers hugged her. And then she was standing in front of Raphael, who pulled her close and said in her ear, "I need your help. Will you help me?"

"Sure."

"Good. I need to go home," Raphael said. "I would very much like you to take me."

"Now?"

"Please. If we don't leave soon, we'll miss the rest of the fun."

Macy took a moment to talk to Abbie Jones. Telling her that she had to leave, asking her if she wanted to come to Nephele to visit her son and grandchildren, to see what they had done and hear all about what they planned to do. Abbie told her that she would come as soon as she could, but there was still much to do right here around Saturn.

"Set up a proper city government. Make links with the other cities," she said, ticking off each point on her fingers. She was perched on a beanbag with a slate in her lap, glazed with exhaustion but determined and coolly focused. "Get ships working again. Make peace with the people of Camelot, and with everyone else who tried to save their own skins by choosing neutrality. . . ."

Macy, cross-legged on the floor in front of her, added a couple of her own. "Deal with the Ghosts. Make sure that the Europeans and the Pacific Community don't renege on their agreement."

"Persuade them to go home," Abbie said. "And find a way of starting negotiations with the Brazilians in the Jupiter System. The people of Callisto and Ganymede and Europa deserve their freedom too. We have planned and talked and discussed what to do when this day came. And now it is here and everything needs to be done at once. Take care, Macy. Get home safely and make sure that my son doesn't go charging off on some wild mission. Make sure he waits for me to come visit."

It was past midnight, but no one in the city was asleep. People sat outside cafés and in parks, wandered the avenues in groups large and small. Laughing and singing as they ankled along arm in arm. In one park a drumming circle had started up and people pranced and leaped like a demented ballet corps.

Fireworks were bursting in the black air above the flat roofs of the old apartment blocks as, dressed in pressure suits, Macy and Raphael rode on a trike to the industrial zone. They hitched a ride to the spaceport on one of the rolligons that had been ferrying stockpiles of arms and ammunition into the city. Macy had flown from Iapetus to Dione in *Elephant*, and the tug had been powered up and refuelled and a dropshell had been loaded into the cargo bay. Macy strapped into the acceleration couch in the control blister, started to run a systems check, and asked Raphael where yo wanted to go.

"Into orbit around Saturn, about a hundred and seventy thousand kilometres out."

"The edge of the F Ring?"

"You might want to make it a little way beyond the edge. And you might also want to incline your orbit above the equatorial plane by ten degrees or so."

"You aren't going to tell me why, are you?"

"I can tell you that something is going to happen. Something wonderful."

Macy spent some time interrogating the navigation AI, then took *Elephant* up, her first real solo flight, powering straight out of Dione's shallow gravity well and accelerating inward toward Tethys; after *Elephant* curved around the icy moon, it would be at the correct velocity and angle to achieve orbit outside the rings at the inclination Raphael had suggested.

She was intensely nervous. The AI had calculated and implemented flight parameters tailored to her requirements, but she knew that she didn't have the experience to figure out her best option if she encountered something unexpected. So when the comms lit up just after *Elephant*'s brief burn at orbital insertion, panic speared her heart. Jesus. It seemed that everyone in the system wanted to talk to her, all at once. Macy bounced the stack of messages to Raphael and asked the neuter if yo wanted to answer any of them.

"They already have their answer," Raphael said. "Look out across the rings, Macy."

The broad arc of the rings fell away beyond and below *Elephant*'s orbit, curving out around Saturn into the planet's vast black shadow. Tiny stars were lighting up inside that shadow, a host or cloud of little lights strung out in an arc. Macy checked the bearings and aimed *Elephant*'s spectrometer at one of them. No doubt about it, they were moonlets lit up by mass drivers, beginning to move away from the plane of the rings. Heading out from Saturn, toward the sun.

"Seeds," she said.

"Precisely so."

"The packages on them, they're components for bubble habitats, aren't they? We built one ourselves. Found the design in the Library of the Commons."

"As did we, although we have considerably modified it," Raphael said. "When the moonlets reach their final orbits, construction robots will use the remaining mass to spin bubble habitats. And inside those habitats, other robots will create gardens from DNA libraries and carbonaceous material. A thousand gardens, all different, all orbiting just inside the snow line, at the outer edge of the asteroid belt."

"Who are they for?"

"Anyone who wants to live there. Sri is a great person, Macy. Isolated by her genius, yes, but the finest gene wizard who ever lived. Finer even than Avernus. This is her last gift to humanity. Now it's time to take me home. To Janus. We still have much work to do there."

Macy consulted the navigation AI again, and at last *Elephant*'s motor lit up and the tug curved inward, toward Janus. She told Raphael that she could match the moon's orbital speed but because of the inclination of *Elephant*'s orbit she'd have to swing around Saturn a couple of times to bring them into the ring plane.

Raphael, fastening up yo's pressure suit, said that it didn't matter. "The dropshell will take me where I need to go. Forgive me, Macy, but at present Sri does not welcome visitors. One day, perhaps. Not yet. But if I may ask a final favour?"

"Ask away. I guess everyone owes you a moon-sized debt of karma. I'd like to reduce mine to a manageable level as soon as possible."

"If you ever meet Avernus, tell her that she is welcome to visit at any time. Sri believes that she and Avernus have a lot to talk about."

"If I ever see her, sure. I don't know what good it will do."

"You saved her life, Macy. She will listen to you."

"And I thought you asked me to give you a ride because you liked me, not because of who I knew."

"You are a power, Macy. Perhaps not as powerful as Sri or Avernus, yet still a power in your own right. I respect you for that. And one day, who knows, perhaps we will know each other well enough to believe that we are friends."

Raphael cycled through the airlock and swung easily around the hull to the hatch of the cargo bay. A couple of minutes later the dropshell drifted away on a whisper of gas, and when it was a few hundred metres from *Elephant* its chemical motor lit and it dwindled behind the tug, shedding velocity. Janus swelled from a fleck of light to a lumpy sphere half in shadow; then *Elephant* fell past it, heading beneath the ring plane at a shallow angle. Macy used the telescope to track the dropshell as it closed on the little moon, skimming toward a huge net slung between a pair of slender pylons hundreds of metres tall. The dropshell ploughed into the net, and the net folded around it as the pylons bowed toward the surface.

Macy consulted the navigation AI again. She was going to have to swing out past Titan, then come back in and slingshot around Saturn so that she could achieve escape velocity. She had a good twenty minutes before the burn that would put her on the trajectory for rendezvous with Titan. She used the time to send a message to Newt and the twins. Telling them that she was coming home.

PART SIX

EVERYTHING THAT RISES MUST CONVERGE

I t was the most important funeral to have been held in Paris, Dione, since the city's foundation. In the sprawling park at the eastern end of the new biome, quickened just a year ago, more than half the population of Paris and many visitors from settlements on Dione and cities and settlements on other moons of Saturn crowded across the Great Lawn. They picnicked and talked, danced in small groups to music played on a common band, sat in meditation circles, got up impromptu games of futzball and tig with their children, and ascended in little one- and two-person dirigibles that floated like schools of tropical fish in the bright air beneath the tent's skin. At the centre of this great gathering, representatives from cities and settlements on every inhabited moon in the Jupiter, Saturn, and Uranus systems and the reefs of the new bubble habitats met and mingled around the canopied platform of the funeral bier with the ambassadors of Greater Brazil, the European Union, the Pacific Community, and several smaller nations on Earth, and scientists, green saints, gene wizards, and former colleagues and friends of the dead woman. Such was the respect for her that everyone had come in person or had sent a human representative instead of defaulting to an avatar. There was even a pair of etiolated Ghosts, talking to no one but each other in a private hand language.

Avernus, born Barbara Reiner in San Diego, California, a city lost to the global floods of the long ago and as storied now as Atlantis or Oz, was dead at the age of two hundred and twenty-two. Everyone said that her heart had been broken by the murder of her daughter. She had refused to renew any of her longevity treatments and had worked on in the research facility gifted to her by the people of Greater Brazil until she had died in her sleep after a brief illness. Although she had been born on Earth and had spent her last years there, she had lived most of her life in the Outer System, and after some discussion her body had been brought to Paris, Dione, where she had famously campaigned for peace before the Quiet War.

Dressed in an ancient white smock coat with hand-crafted pens and scalpels and a slide rule in its breast pocket, her lined face still and calm and empty, Avernus lay on a simple trestle banked with flowers left one by one by those who stepped up to pay their respects. Her funeral was an informal celebration of her life. Anyone could approach one of the attendants and ask for a turn to speak at the lectern in front of the bier to reminisce about the dead woman, to thank her for her work or for some small kindness, or to read out a few lines of poetry or prose. East of Eden's best fado singer sang a long lament. A string quartet from Rainbow Bridge, Callisto, played Barber's *Adagio*. A tin-man robot tottered up, leaking steam at its joints, and in an elaborate mime attempted to plant a flower and sprinkle it with a watering can packed with smoking carbon dioxide—a performance piece by one of Paris's microtheatres. And although Avernus had believed that the Universe had been created by a chance confluence of physical laws and properties, priests and rabbis and imams and monks commemorated her passing in their fashion, chanting prayers or spinning prayer wheels, burning fake banknotes, lighting candles and cones of incense.

Toward the end of the day, Alder Topaz Hong-Owen walked up to the lectern. Drones swooped down to video him and a hush spread across the crowd around and about. He spoke in his usual plain and direct manner, telling the great assembly in the park and everyone watching in the city and the worlds beyond that Avernus had risked her life for peace not once but twice: first in Paris, before the Quiet War, and then after she had returned to Earth and joined the underground movement that had at last overthrown the rule of the great families. She had not only helped the people of Greater Brazil to win their freedom; she had also gifted them with something that allowed them to explore the wildernesses so long forbidden to them. They must still tread lightly on the land, and live for the most part in self-sufficient cities, but their cities were no longer prisons. They were free to embark on wanderjahrs across both rewilded territories and those as yet unre-constructed, travelling from oasis to oasis in a network that stretched across Greater Brazil from the Thirtieth Parallel in the north to Tierra de Fuego in the south. Every oasis was centred on groves of a new variety of people tree that Avernus had created. The trees grew in tundra and grassland, in desert basins and in high mountains, flourishing in places where very little life had been able to survive before, providing food, water, shelter, and clothing. Avernus lives on not only in our memories, Alder said, but in her work. In every plant and animal that she touched and changed, in every biome and garden she created, she still lives.

After his speech, Alder had a private meeting with Raphael, the representative sent by his mother, and talked with half a hundred other people. Some he remembered from the time when he had visited the Jupiter System with his mother, twenty-three years ago. Burton Delancey, who, after he'd seduced her, had taken him on a trek across Callisto's tumbled and shattered moonscapes to one of Avernus's secret gardens, and was now a senior member of the Callistan Senate. The ancient gene wizard Tymon Simonov from Minos, Europa. Macy Minnot, whom Alder had never before met but knew so much about, and her husband, Newton Jones, and her youngest son. They had recently moved to Titan, where she was designing garden habitats and helping with the planoforming project.

The biome's great chandeliers dimmed toward twilight. Fireworks bloomed under the high angles of the tent. Fliers with chromatophore tweaks, their skin rippling in luminous patterns like amorous squid, danced in the middle air. And at last the dead woman was taken up by pallbearers and half a hundred men and women in white breechclouts beat out a slow, deep rhythm on drums hung at their waists as a great procession gathered and wound out of the biome and through the railway tunnel and into the darkened city, along avenues lined with people holding lighted candles, ten thousand points of flickering flame that illuminated every kind of human face. Until at last Avernus's body was carried into the resomation facility, and the crowds dispersed and night and silence settled over the city.

—●—

Alder had been given the task of returning a portion of Avernus's ashes to Greater Brazil, where it would be scattered around a people-tree sapling in the Eixo Monumental in Brasília. But he had some family business to attend to first.

For the past ten years, his younger brother, Berry Malachite, had been holed up in a suite in the hotel in Camelot, Mimas, which had been built to accommodate VIP visitors during the TPA era. His bills were underwritten by his mother's credit and karma; he had no work, and had long ago lost contact with his friends and former business partners; he had never replied to any of the messages that Alder had dutifully sent him every birthday, Gaia Day, and Christmas. Alder wanted to help Berry in any way he could, but according to Cash Baker, who'd travelled to Camelot ahead of him, he would first have to deal with the woman who claimed to be Berry's handfasted partner.

The hotel, located in a cut-and-cover chamber trenched into the cratered plain outside the tents of the city proper, was a biome of rolling grassland that, punctuated by scattered clumps of trees and grazed by small herds of mammoths and zebras and aurochs, appeared to extend to infinity under a virtual sky, the blue sky of Earth. As they rode a cart along a red-dirt track toward Berry's suite, Cash told Alder that during the occupation guests had been allowed to hunt the animals.

"Anything they shot was butchered on the spot and broiled in a barbecue pit. There are fishing holes, too. Pools in the little river that wanders through this place. Of course, the Outers who run this place control the animal populations with contraceptive implants now. When I think back on how it was after the war, the things we did. . . . We must have seemed like barbarians."

The cart, rolling along the track at a leisurely walking pace, made a wide circle around a big stand of bamboos and yellow-flowered mimosa, and there was Berry's suite, a dome turfed over with lush grass, punctuated with little round windows like rabbit holes. Waiting outside the round door at its base, her dark face pinched in a grim expression and her arms folded over the plastic vest laced across her small breasts, was Berry's partner, Xbo Xbaine.

She seemed courteous enough, showing Alder and Cash to sling seats under the shade of an umbrella tree, offering them tea and sushi, telling them that Berry wasn't at his best today.

"Does he know I'm here?" Alder said.

"If I may be candid? I didn't think that it was a good idea to tell him," Xbo Xbaine said. "He's having one of his bad times, and his bad times are very bad now. The shock of seeing you could easily tip him over into one of his fugues. Or worse. If you come back tomorrow, or the day after, he might be a little better. I can't promise anything, of course, but I'll do my best to talk him around. And meanwhile, if there's anything you want to know, anything at all . . . Perhaps this is presumptuous of me, but I like to think that I'm part of the family now. And people in families shouldn't have any secrets from each other, should they?"

Alder saw straight through this clumsy attempt to stall for time, but even if the woman had been looking after Berry only for what she could get out of it, he felt that he owed her something. And he felt a little grudging respect, too, for her attempt to stand up to him. So instead of using Cash's extensive research into her past and present crimes to bludgeon her into submission, instead of telling her that the handfasting she and Berry had entered into was a sham, witnessed by people she had bribed, instead of telling her that he knew about her little scam, selling high-end room-service goods for credit, he talked to her about Berry's good days and bad days, listened sympathetically to her litany of complaints, and asked her if there was anything that she and Berry needed.

384

"Credit," Xbo Xbaine said, with a bold and direct look that surprised Alder. "There's only so much that you can get on room service. With a little credit and kudos I could look after your brother much better."

Alder promised that he'd see what he could do, and said that while Berry might not be at his best he still had to see him.

"Your mother sent you, didn't she?" Xbo said. "You think I don't know what this is all about? Of course I know."

"I want to talk to him because he's my brother," Alder said.

"One of her creatures came here," Xbo told Alder, and smiled when she saw that she'd surprised him. "She didn't tell you about that? How like her. It was a couple of days after they announced that Avernus's funeral would be held in Paris. After, I bet, she found out you were coming out here because of it. Her creature told me that you were visiting her, said that she wanted Berry to go with you. A family reunion. Well, I'll tell you now what I told the creature then. Berry tried to see her once. It was before I met him. Twelve, thirteen years ago. He hired a tug to take him to Janus, and when he got there she refused to see him. That's when he really started drinking and drugging. You know? To numb himself. He was in a bad way when I met him first. Much worse than he is now. But you have to love him because underneath it all he's so sweet and helpless. . . ."

"I know," Alder said.

"She hurt him bad. She doesn't have the right to hurt him again. That's what I told her creature before I sent it away. And now here you are, bothering me all over again."

"It's true that my mother wants to see both of us. But I would have come here anyway," Alder said.

After a moment, Xbo Xbaine sighed and shrugged. "I don't suppose I can stop you. But if you try to talk to him about his mother and he gets upset, don't say I didn't warn you. And your friend better stay here."

She led Alder through the round door in the side of the turf-covered dome, into a big space with halflife grass over the floor and walls and furniture handcrafted from wood and steel scattered about. "I thought this was so choice at first," she said. "The luxury. Everything anyone could need. This way. He's in the pool."

A ramp spiralled down to a basement that was all white tiles and bright light, with a circular pool of water covered in a skin of blue plastic balls that rippled back and forth in slow waves, something big and pink rising and falling in the dead centre. An enormously fat man floating on his back, naked apart from spex and tipset gloves, his fingers twiddling and tapping on the bulging folds of his belly.

"Time to wake up," Xbo said loudly. "Come back to reality, Berry. I've brought a friend to see you."

"I'm in the Ten Thousand Flower Rift," Berry said.

A little drone hovered in the air close by his head, clutching a bulb of thick white liquid. When he lifted his face the drone dipped down and stuck a straw between his swollen lips. He sucked at it noisily, then said, "I'm going to get through to the Beast's chateau this time."

"It's an old friend," Xbo Xbaine said. "A family friend."

"Tell him *in a minute*," Berry said.

Alder recognised his brother then: that familiar squeal of petulant frustration.

"He does love his sagas," Xbo Xbaine said. "Mostly he just lies there, immersed in one or another of them. And he loves his drink, too. Banana margaritas, mostly. He gets through a couple of litres a day. He uses other stuff, too. Tailored psychotropics. I get them by selling off stuff I order on room service."

"I know."

"I have to do it because your brother needs the drugs and the hotel doesn't feature them on its room-service menu. I have to buy medichines, too. To flush out Berry's blood once a month, and clean up his liver. He likes ice cream, and peanut butter sandwiches. That's about all he'll eat, but I slip him supplements in his margaritas. The only other thing he likes, apart from running sagas and maintaining a steady load, is fucking. He can manage it, just about, although it takes some care. That's our life. You think I wouldn't put up with it if I didn't love him?"

Xbo Xbaine fixed Alder with her dark and truculent gaze, daring him to challenge her. Saying, "Can I be candid? Professor Doctor Sri Hong-Owen is very smart. She saved the Saturn System and she gave away those bubble habitats. And rumours are she's turned herself into something radically posthuman out there on Janus. But I don't think she was much of a mother. Not to Berry, at least."

Alder felt that he had to defend Sri, saying, "She loves him in her own way."

"Now you've seen how he is, do you really think he should go see her?"

"You feel that you have to protect him, Xbo. I appreciate that. And I appreciate all you've done for him. I really do. But this is something he has to decide for himself."

"I know I can't stop you taking him away. But please, don't do it unless he really wants it."

"I wouldn't have it any other way."

"All right, then," Xbo Xbaine said. "You go wait outside now, while I coax Berry out of the pool."

Cash Baker was waiting under the umbrella tree, absent-mindedly picking grapes from a vine twisted around its slender trunk. Alder told him what he'd seen, said, "I think we can forget about taking him to see my mother. Or anywhere else."

"What about the woman?"

"She cares for him, in her way."

"She's a vampire." Cash nipped a grape between the contoured plastic ridges that had replaced his teeth when he'd been cut and adapted to fly singleships. "Back in the day, I was taught that Outers had turned themselves and their children into monsters because they believed they were better than ordinary humans. Turns out they aren't so different from us. Maybe they're smarter, and kinder, but that doesn't stop them fucking up their lives and the lives of other people in the same old ways, does it?"

"Living with Xbo didn't make Berry what he is. If anyone is to blame, it's my mother."

"You turned out all right."

"I have advantages that he lacks. I don't mean the tweaks she gave me. When she came out here with Berry, I was left behind on Earth, in charge of the Antarctic research facility. So I was able to escape her shadow. I was able to learn what I could do, who I really was. . . . Berry didn't have a chance to do any of that. The drinking and the drugs, I think it started as a rebellion against her control. And it worked, in a way. But it's ruined him, Cash. He had to destroy himself to get free of her."

A silence fell between the two friends. Alder tried a handful of grapes. They were cool and delicious, each with a slightly different flavour bursting on his tongue. Presently, Berry came tottering out of the door in the side of the grassy dome, pinkly, hugely naked. Pleated folds of fat fell to his knees; his legs were so swollen that he could only take mincing little steps as he followed the machine that carried his bulb of margarita mix.

"Man," Cash said. "You told me he was big, but I didn't think he'd be *that* big."

"Nor did I," Alder said. "Most of him must have been underwater."

Berry managed half a dozen steps, then belly-flopped onto the grass and rolled onto his back, fat rippling under his skin in clashing tides.

The drone drifted down and stuck its straw in Berry's mouth; Xbo

Xbaine knelt beside him and started to rub coconut-scented cream on his legs.

"He can get about if he wants to," she told Alder. "But it hurts him, even in microgravity, so he stays mostly on his back. And because the chandeliers put out some UV for the plants, I have to rub this on him, to stop him burning. If you want to talk to him, you'd better do it now. He'll want his drugs soon, and after that he won't make much sense."

"Let me help," Alder said

He knelt beside Xbo Xbaine, took a palmful of cream and rubbed it into the folds of Berry's neck, over his shoulders. Berry grunted with deep animal contentment.

"Do you know who I am?" Alder said.

"Xbo's friend. Want anything from room service? Just ask her. They let her sign it off for me."

"I'm fine," Alder said, and asked Berry if he remembered the old times back on Earth.

"Not really."

Alder talked about the research station and the fjord and the mountains, and asked Berry if he remembered any of it.

"The Beast's chateau is in the mountains."

"You liked playing in the beech wood, too. And most of all you liked the games you played in the pool with your brother. You remember those?"

"I always beat Alder."

"Yes. Yes, you did. You're a natural swimmer. Like a dolphin."

"Alder was smart and people liked him. But he couldn't swim for shit," Berry said, and giggled.

"Have you ever thought about going back to Earth?" Alder said, ignoring the sharp look that Xbo Xbaine gave him.

"I wouldn't like that."

"You don't have to do anything you don't want to. But did you ever think about it?"

"Xbo and me, we're happy here." With some effort, Berry turned his head and squinted at Alder. "I know you."

"Do you? Who am I?"

"You were here before. My mother sent you. You gave me this place. . . ."

"He gets confused," Xbo said.

Alder said to Berry, "You like it here."

"Xbo and me. Yeah. Why are you here? Xbo? Xbo? Why is he here?"

Berry was trying to get up, pushing to his elbows, breathing heavily, his face congested. Xbo Xbaine calmed him, stroked his forehead and cheeks, and told him that it was all right, no one could take this away from them, and they could stay here as long as they liked. After a while, Berry relaxed and lay down again. The drone fed him its straw, and he began to slurp down margarita mix.

"You should leave," Xbo told Alder. "It isn't good for him to get upset like this."

"I have to ask him a question."

"He won't go."

"I know. But I have to ask it anyway," Alder said, and told Berry that he was going to visit Sri. "Do you want to come with me, Berry? It will take two days at most. If you want, Xbo can come with you. And I will bring you straight back here."

"You shouldn't go near my mother. She's dangerous."

"Do you know what she's been doing, on Janus?" Alder said. "Did she ever tell you about her plans?"

He'd tried to find out about his mother's work, of course, but his spies and agents had failed to get beyond the smokescreen of rumours and fairy tales, and Raphael had smoothly sidestepped his questions, telling him that he would see soon enough.

"It's bad place," Berry said. "Full of monsters."

"Really? What kind of monsters?"

"I don't want to think about it. I like margaritas. They go down smooth," Berry said. "I like dazzle too. It stops the bad thoughts."

Alder tried again, but he couldn't get any sense out of his brother. Berry's brain had been fried by alcohol and psychotropics. Most of the switches jammed open or closed, whole areas dead and blasted. Like a low-grade robot, he was able to follow the tracks of his routines but had trouble with anything outside them. When he grew agitated again, Xbo Xbaine slapped a patch on a fold of skin above his ear and told him it was time to take a little nap. "Sleep deep and don't dream, sweetheart."

"No more questions. . . ."

"No more questions," Xbo said, staring at Alder.

"That woman knows something," Cash said, as he and Alder rode across the grassland toward the hotel's reception area.

"I know," Alder said. "But she isn't going to tell me."

"People like that, they have a price. Pay it, and she'll talk. She'll even tell something like the truth. If you want, I can go back tonight, talk to her alone."

"She won't talk. Because the only power she has over me is withholding information. And because she wants to protect Berry."

"Her sweet setup, you mean."

"They're both locked together," Alder said. "Berry in his head with his bad thoughts; Xbo in that suite with him. Maybe she didn't start out loving him, but I think she does now. She can't let him go. She can't walk away. Not because she wants the stuff, but because she loves him. I feel sorry for her. It's luxurious enough, it has full room service, but it's still a prison."

"So what do you want to do? There's still Plan B."

"Plan B?"

"Sure. There's always a Plan B. Kidnap your brother's ass, haul him back to the Moon, put him in a rehab programme, and clean him up in every way. Say the word—I can put it in motion right now."

"If I thought it would make Berry happy, I'd do it. But I don't think it would."

"So what are you going to do?"

"I'm going to talk to my mother."

◆

The hired tug cut a deep chord across the rings as it headed inward from Mimas to Janus, some sixty degrees around Saturn's gravid curve. Cash Baker paid little attention to the stupendous view, chatting instead with the pilot about trade routes between the various moons. Alder was grateful that his friend had volunteered to come with him. Especially as he still did not know what he would find; before they'd left Camelot, he'd had another frustrating conversation with Raphael.

"She wants you to see her home without any preconceptions," the neuter had told him. "Call it pride or vanity, call it whatever you like, but there it is."

The tug crossed the Cassini Division and swept on above the A Ring. Beyond the ring's outer edge, Janus resolved from a spark to a bead to a pale lumpy sphere. The tug's pilot talked to the traffic control AI and the tug matched the little moon's orbital velocity with casual precision, swinging around it once every forty minutes at an altitude of less than a hundred kilometres: a mountain dimpled with impact craters that held commas of black shadow, the terrain between patched by silvery or black vacuum organisms.

Two immensely tall, whiplike pylons with some kind of net stretched between them stood on the slumped rim of one of the largest craters, close to a dome that shone green with internal light: Avernus's phenotype jungle. Somewhere down on the crater floor was the entrance to Sri's underground lair.

The tug's pilot pointed to the great circle of shafts and boreholes that surrounded the outer ramparts of the crater, where construction robots were burrowing deep into the moon's regolith, then spotted a defence proxy thirty kilometres off their starboard bow and presented Alder and Cash with a grainy image of the deadly little machine, a radar dish and microwave antenna at one end and the swollen bulb of an oversized motor at the other.

"I'd appreciate it if you didn't take too long down there," he said. "Those things make me nervous."

"It will take as long as it takes," Cash told him. "And you'll get paid for every second."

Alder and Cash sealed up their pressure suits, cycled through the tiny airlock one after the other, and clambered onto the impulse scooter that sat on one of the racks bolted to the hull. Cash was quiet as he guided them in, concentrating fiercely on a task he once could have done as easily as breathing, making a wide curve to avoid a plume of debris that feathered up from one of the shafts and painted a narrow, bright ellipse of fresh water ice across the moon's surface.

They touched down on a landing platform two kilometres around the crater rim from the green dome of the phenotype jungle. There was no one waiting for them—Sri's crew lived and worked on Janus's co-orbital partner Epimetheus now—but Raphael had given detailed instructions, and they set off along a broad road that slanted through a dense planting of tall black blades toward the crater's floor.

Alder hadn't worn a pressure suit for many years, and in Janus's vestigial gravity he felt both clumsy and insubstantial; although the road's palely luminous surface was coated with some kind of nanotech adhesive that suckingly gripped the soles of his boots, he shuffled along as cautiously as an old and frail man negotiating a patch of ice. After a couple of minutes, Cash took his arm and steered him through the inky shadows cast by the blades that towered above on either side, out into the weak light of the sun and on across the floor of the crater, past small silvery domes and angled tents packed with jungly greenery, a white cube that Cash said was a fission pile, and something that looked like a chemical refinery, all tanks and pipes, parts of it glowing in infrared, to a circular shaft brimful of black shadow.

Two child-sized figures in fluorescent orange pressure suits waited on a platform slung out beyond the edge of the shaft.

"You have any idea what those might be?" Cash said.

"Not one."

"You don't have to do this alone."

"If I thought this was in any way dangerous I wouldn't have come here."

"Yes you would."

"Well, I don't think it is. And I'm grateful beyond words that you came along."

"I'm just a tourist, is all. Taking in the sights."

"I'll tell you all about it when I get back."

"I hope you will. Remember me to her. Tell her that despite everything, I'll always be grateful to her for fixing me up to fly singleships."

The two small figures in orange pressure suits did not respond when Alder greeted them on the common band. Their faces were masked by the golden mirrors of their faceplates and they did not move as he shuffled onto the platform, which immediately began to descend down a fixed rail, dropping for at least a kilometre and passing through dozens of stiffly yielding curtains, each breaking apart around it in a jigsaw of shards that afterward snapped back into place. The curtains must have formed a pressure lock: soon after it had passed through the last of them, the platform emerged above a horseshoe of cliffs and terraces stepping down to the lumpy green canopy of a forest that stretched away beneath the sharp light of a hundred floating sunlamps.

The platform slowed, gliding smoothly down a track set in the face of a cliff faced with black flowstone that fell to a meadow of tall red grasses on the topmost terrace. Alder's guides jumped off and bounded away like a couple of grasshoppers and disappeared into a belt of lush green forest. His pressure suit informed him that the atmosphere was the standard oxygen-rich mix found in most habitats in the Outer System. When he cracked the seal of his helmet, his ears popped to accommodate a modest difference in pressure. The hot, muggy air smelt of soil and growing plants. He hooked his helmet to his utility belt and ankled through the shoulder-high grass.

He wasn't afraid. Hollow with anticipation, yes. Curious to see what his mother had created here. But he wasn't afraid.

There was no sign of his guides, but he soon discovered a ribbon of black gravel that ran off through ferns and pillowy mosses that sloped down between puffball pines and fan palms and tree ferns. He followed the path through the wood, saw white worms like severed fingers working through patches of rich humus, saw a snake with pale skin and blue, human eyes ripple away into a thicket of ferns, saw a huddle of naked little tarsiers peeking down at him from the crown of a palm tree. The path gave out at a mossy lawn set between palm trees at the edge of a steep drop to another belt of forest.

Alder shaded his eyes with his forearm and stared down the length of the chamber. No sign of any roads or buildings on the ladder of terraces below, or in the thick forest that covered the chamber's floor, stretching away for three or four kilometres under a haze of water vapour. Nothing moving out there except for a flock of birds turning in lazy circles between the bright daystars of the floating lamps, wheeling and swooping toward him, crying out in musical voices. They were more like bats than birds, with leathery wings as wide as his outstretched arms and human hands for feet and shrunken human faces, each turning to look at him as they poured past the edge of the lawn in a dry rustle of wings.

Something twinkled in the air, drifting toward him through the bright air. A naked person—or no, it was an avatar, its white plastic glinting as it glided along, balanced on top of a platform curved like a turtle shell with a fan motor at each corner. As it drew nearer, Alder saw that the face floating in its visor was the face of his mother as she had been on the day he'd last seen her, more than twenty years ago. Before he'd been smuggled out of Brasília at the beginning of the long clandestine journey to the research facility in Antarctica, and she'd stolen a ship and taken Berry off to the Saturn System.

The platform drifted to a stop at the edge of the lawn and the avatar stepped down lightly and easily in front of Alder, who stood bareheaded in the armour of his pressure suit, like an old-fashioned knight at the end of his quest. From thickets of ferns on either side naked children stepped forward, so pale and skinny that they seemed as translucent as cave fish. Their heads were small and wedge-shaped, sloping straight back from skin-covered dimples where their eyes should have been. Their ears flared out like bat wings; their hands had only three fingers, spaced like a crane's grab.

"Welcome to our home," the avatar said. Its voice was Sri's voice, although the face floating in its visor did not move its lips. "What do you think of it? Isn't it beautiful?"

"I think you have acquired an unexpected taste for melodrama."

"You look well. Older, of course, but you are still my beautiful boy. You didn't bring Berry."

"I asked him to come with me. He refused."

"You should have brought him. We could take care of him here."

"I'm sure you could," Alder said. "But he has his own life. His own way of surviving. His own way of escape. And he already has someone to look after him."

"The woman."

"His handfasted partner. The one person who truly cares for him, it seems."

"You think I have been a bad mother."

"I think we've both let him down."

"I did my best, but eventually I realised that nothing I could say or do would help him, so I left him to his own devices. It hurt me to do it. It hurts me still, to know how unhappy he is, how badly he is damaging himself."

"He came here, once upon a time. You turned him away."

"I was . . . changing. That is finished now. I am ready to look after him, but I would never force him to do anything he does not want to do. I would never bring him here against his will."

"I feel guilty about it too. He's my brother. I should have reached out to him long ago, and I didn't. And now it's too late."

"Is he happy, do you think?"

"He is what he is."

"I have followed your career with much interest, Alder. And with no little pride. Perhaps you are angry and upset that I did not answer your messages. To begin with, it was a matter of security. And then . . ."

"You were busy. I understand. I understand you better than you think I do."

"I was busy, yes. There is always much work to do, and too little time. And I was changing, too. We were changing. Changing and growing. We are the clade now. One flesh, one purpose."

"So I see."

"Do you? Do you really understand?"

"I think I have a fair idea of what you've done. But I don't understand why you've done it."

"Walk with me," Sri said.

"I've seen the wood. And the things in it."

"Indulge me anyway," Sri said.

Alder walked with lumbering and infinite care beside the graceful avatar through the green shade under the trees, the two of them followed by the pale blind children and a troop of lemurs that flowed from tree to tree. Things like severed hands shelled in bone lurked amongst tangled prop roots. At the bottom of a deep pool of clear water, nets of pale tubes pulsed and quivered like unstrung arteries across black sand. A flock of hand-sized butterflies whirled around a slanting shaft of chandelier light, their wings covered in pelts of fine black hair.

Sri explained that an early experiment in immortality had gone a little astray. Her body had swollen with tumours teeming with independent life and her crew and a team of expert systems modelled on her own memories and skills had put her in hibernation while they searched for a cure. Although the tumours were under control now, she was confined to a series of vats. It did not matter. She had cloned a family of sister-daughters, and used her genome as a template to fashion dozens of species of animal by engineering and forced evolution: a clade of radically different phenotypes that shared the same genome and filled every niche of the biome's self-regulating ecosystem.

After her sister-daughters had taken charge of the biome, Sri had begun to reshape herself.

She had altered and improved vacuum organisms designed by Avernus to capture sunlight and convert it into electrical energy. As they spread across the surface of Janus, Sri's modified body grew ever larger. Copies of her original body were cached here and there in that great mass, each sharing the same sensory inputs, the same thoughts. They were all as alike as possible, true avatars ready to be sent out to explore the universe.

"We will soon break out of this little moon and leave the Solar System and travel on toward Fomalhaut," Sri said. "It will take a thousand years, but we are capable of surviving voyages ten times as long. There is a ring of dust and protoplanetary debris around Fomalhaut, twice the size of our solar system. Millions of comets and planetoids and asteroids. Planets, too, but we don't care about planets. We will fill the dust ring with copies of our clade, and some of those will move on to other systems where planets failed to form. We are the first true posthuman. A new species. The Outers were a first step, lungfish on the shore of space. We have already gone much further, and we will go further still.

"From the point of view of the individual, evolution is cruel. For in the race to survive, all individuals perish. Most species perish. Only successful genes survive for any significant span of time. But the clade will split into a thousand or a million varieties, all different, yet all one flesh, one genome. We will fill the galaxy, in time. And we will never die."

Alder laughed, and told his mother that he couldn't fault her ambition.

"You are not shocked by what I've told you," Sri said. Her ageless face floated calm and still in the avatar's visor, like a medical specimen in a jar. "I'm glad. So very glad. Your acceptance means much to us."

Alder remembered what Cash had said to him in the world above. "I'm your son. You made me what I am. Cut me with various talents and tweaks so that I could help you to get what you wanted. For a little while, we were a team—or so I believed. I didn't even mind when you left me behind on Earth, because you had given me the responsibility of looking after the research facility. But in the years after the war, when you fell silent, I grew to hate and despise you. Because you had found something new, and had abandoned me for it. Because I realised that all along it was only your work that ever mattered to you. Well, I had my own work, and in time I had my own family too. You no longer had any power over me, and my hate ebbed away. But I never gave up on you. I sent you news about my family. I collected rumours about your work here on Janus, and sifted them for nuggets of truth. And now I know the truth, now I see what you've done, I know that I can let you go. I am amazed by it, yes. But I don't approve of it. You were always remote from other people. Even from me, in the end. And now you've become a true monster. What you've accomplished is amazing, yes. But there's something sad and desperate about it, because it seems to me that you've given up on other people. You have become a nation of one."

"You have your own family now. And I have mine, and it has me."

"When you arrive at Fomalhaut, you know, you might find other people already living there. What will you do then?"

Sri laughed. The pale children around them laughed too, a melodious but chilling carillon.

"You are limited by old ways of thinking," Sri said. "We're beyond that."

"We'll see," Alder said.

He and his mother walked and talked. He told her about his family and his work on Earth. He told her about Avernus's funeral and the people he had met on Dione and Mimas. Sri said that she'd hoped that the old gene wizard would come back to the Saturn System before she died; they'd had so much to talk about.

"But it was not to be," she said. "And I have discovered that it doesn't matter. Because I know now that I am her equal. At least her equal. And we will go on, and do such things. . . ."

"Avernus has her place in history, and you have yours," Alder said.

He could not tell her that she was not now, nor could she ever be, Avernus's equal. It would be too cruel. And besides, there would be no point. She would never acknowledge her faults because she was too proud, too vain. A monster of ego. As she always had been. She might live a thousand years, but she would never change. Never understand people. Like Berry, she had retreated from the world into her own fantasies. But at least Berry had Xbo Xbaine. Sri had only copies of herself.

At last they climbed a winding path to the meadow, and the cliff where the platform waited at the foot of its track.

"We are glad you came," Sri said. "We have changed beyond your understanding, and we will continue to change. But we will never forget you."

"I don't know if I will ever come here again," Alder said. "But I won't say goodbye. We can still talk, you and I, whenever we want."

But he knew that they wouldn't, and he knew that she knew it too.

They made their farewells and the avatar stood still and silent amongst the crew of strange children as Alder stepped onto the platform and it rose up the cliff toward the mouth of the shaft. One flesh, one clade, one family. Dwindling below him, gone. The platform passed through the roof of the chamber and the leaves of the pressure barrier, climbing toward the black sky at the top of the shaft, where his friend was waiting.

2

Twelve years after the death of Avernus, Macy Minnot was still living on Titan, was still involved in the planoforming project. Currently, most of her time was taken up with a scheme to quicken the moon's Hot Lakes. These occupied a string of fresh craters south of the hilly chaos of Xanadu, created by the impact of chunks of ice from the shield of the Ghost ship that had broken up while traversing the outer edge of Titan's atmosphere during the crisis of '31. Ice melted by the impacts had flooded the floors of the craters with ammonia-rich water. Now radiator grids powered by fission piles kept the lakes from freezing solid, and ecoengineers and gene wizards were seeding them with varieties of methanogenic bacteria and cyanobacteria, the first stage of the construction of a simple ecosystem of plankton, kelp, and several species of krill, shellfish, and crab.

When Newt came to pick her up, Macy was working with the nutrient-cycling crew at the research station beside the largest lake, Windermere Lacus. One of her assistants drove her up the steep slope, the lake stretching below, sheeted with brash ice and patched by fog smoking off leads of open water, to the landing pad where Newt's aeroshell shuttle, painted the signature pink of his haulage company, sat like an orchid dropped in a coal cellar. Despite the string of fusion lamps in equatorial orbit and the ongoing injection of a layer of ultraviolet-absorbing chemicals high in the atmosphere to prevent formation of thiolins, the major component of the moon's smoggy shroud, light levels at the surface of Titan were still relatively low. But the sun was clearly visible in the sky now, a tiny ruby in the dust, and so was Saturn, its crescent tipped sideways in the sky above the pale and restless fogs.

Macy and her assistant supervised the robot that unloaded pallets of insulated packages from the rolligon and slotted them inside the shuttle's hold—all kinds of samples for her colleagues at the University of Athena, and for laboratories in a dozen research institutes and facilities on Earth. When the samples had been safely stowed, Macy climbed aboard and Newt took the shuttle straight up, punching through Titan's sky and rendezvousing with the transit station, where Macy and Newt transferred themselves and their cargo to *Elephant*. They were on their way to the Sixtieth Conference on the Great Leap Up and Out, scheduled to be held in eight weeks at Athena, the Moon, but they took a roundabout route, via a comet falling toward Mars.

They had been partnered for more than thirty years. The edges of their relationship had long ago worn comfortably smooth and they had their own private shorthand and habits and accommodations that allowed them to rub along together during the voyage. Macy kept in touch with the research station at the Hot Lakes and the landscaping crew in the new city of Coleridge; Newt dealt with the snags and routine administration work generated by his haulage company, a little fleet of ships that connected Saturn and Jupiter and Mars in a shifting triangle, with a sideline in special deliveries and exotic cargoes. So the time passed equitably enough as *Elephant* fell inward, rising above the plane of the ecliptic at a shallow angle as it crossed the orbit of Jupiter and the asteroid belt, until one day Newt pulled up a view of their destination in the memo space: a faint star off to one side of the tiny red disc of Mars.

Three days later, he took command of *Elephant*'s navigation and drive systems and flew the last ten thousand kilometres by eye and hand. The sun was eclipsed by the spinning sunshade that minimised thermal input—a circle of faint blue light expanding toward them, the comet nucleus at its centre acquiring heft and solidity. A fleck, a seed, a boulder, a small mountain. *Elephant* drifting past its pitted flanks toward the ship that kept station fifty kilometres ahead of it, silhouetted small and sharp against the sunshade's oceanic glow.

The comet was a member of the short-term Jupiter family, a dirty snow-ball massing some thirty-two billion tons, its surface coated in layers of ice flakes and carbonaceous dust as fragile as cigarette ash, its interior a loose agglomeration of pebbly planetesimal material and water ice and pockets of frozen gases. As it fell sunward, its orbit had been perturbed by judiciously creating hotspots that vented jets of gases and dust; in eighty-three days it would intercept Mars and break up above the surface, making a significant contribution to the partial pressure of the red planet's atmosphere, currently thirty-two millibars at datum.

Newt's company had won the delivery contract, and Newt and Macy's youngest son, Darwin, was in charge of the crew that micromanaged the comet's trajectory, countering changes in its delta vee caused by irregular out-gassing as the pulse of thermal energy that had warmed the comet's surface before the sunshade had been unfolded worked its way into the interior, and pockets of carbon dioxide or methane snow explosively sublimed. There was a small blowout under way when *Elephant* sidled up to Darwin's ship, a foun-tain jetting out sideways from the sunward end of the comet, dissipating out-ward for ten thousand kilometres. Darwin was busy organising a correction to the slight spin this had imparted, so his parents didn't meet him and the rest of the crew until supper, some six hours later.

Macy hadn't seen her son for more than a year. It was a small but pleas-urable shock to be reminded of how much he looked like his father. He was a pale and lanky young man with a disordered crest of black hair, bright blue eyes, and a quick, lopsided smile, about the same age, twenty-five, that Newt had been when he'd helped Macy escape from East of Eden. And like Newt all those years ago, Darwin was trying to escape from the shadow of his par-ents' reputation and find his own way in the world. He'd had some spectac-ular rows with them in the past, but he was happy to see them now and they had a fine time exchanging gossip about his siblings and discussing plans to use comets as the raw material for an ocean habitat wrapped around a rocky asteroid. Herding and dismantling the half-dozen comets needed to supply a sufficient volume of water created all kinds of complex and knotty problems, but Darwin reckoned that with the right backing it could be done within the next decade.

"We have enough karma to organise an initial study," Newt said to Macy later that evening, back on board *Elephant*. "We could give it a push, see where he takes it."

"And how would he feel about that, do you think?"

"He should feel grateful, I reckon. It would be his thing—there's no way I want to get involved with the kind of bureaucratic jungle that's bound to grow around a project like that. But we could help him plant the seed."

Sometimes Newt couldn't see anything but the problem at hand. Macy said patiently, "What I mean is, think back to when you were Darwin's age. How would you feel about your parents muscling in on your plans?"

"Hell, I didn't *have* any plans back then."

"Were you grateful every time Abbie bailed you out of trouble?"

Newt laughed. "Good point. But I want to find some way of helping him. Don't you? And it could be a fantastic opportunity for the company. The start-up costs are big, but the potential is way bigger."

"Of course I want to help. But I don't want to run Darwin's life for him."

Newt thought for a little while and said at last, "The kid needs to start up his own company. Then we act as subcontractors. We bring in the karma, but he'll control everything. It'll be up to him to make it happen. Maybe it'll come to something, maybe not. But the kid's smart. He'll pull it off, I reckon, if he doesn't get bored and go off and get into something else instead."

They spent two days with Darwin and his crew. Macy discussed the latest panspermia theories with the exobiologist who had hitched a lift so that he could take cores from the heart of the comet. So far, he'd failed to find any traces of biological activity, but his inventory of organic molecules, deep-frozen since the formation of the Solar System, would add to the vast store of data about conditions in the primordial planetary disc. And Macy and Newt talked with Darwin about his plans for the construction of the ocean habitat, and did their best to support him without appearing to criticise or interfere. Telling themselves that if he failed, it would not be an important failure. He was young, and the Solar System was buzzing with boundless possibility. At last they said their farewells to Darwin and his crew, and *Elephant* powered on, hooking past Mars in a slingshot that sent her back into the plane of the ecliptic, toward the sister worlds of the Earth and the Moon.

Macy hadn't been to one of the conferences on the Great Leap Up and Out for eighteen years—she'd dropped out of research into extrasolar planets because her work on Titan had taken over most of her time. Superficially, little seemed to have changed. The same round of intense discussions about everything from mapping extrasolar planets to the Holy Grail of faster-than-light travel; the same social dynamic, with young delegates looking to make their mark and older delegates defending their reputations. There were even a few Ghosts, keeping themselves to themselves as usual. They were generally regarded as a spent force, pariahs who had at last made peace with the great society of the Solar System but were still struggling with the long and painful process of integration.

Macy knew more than half the delegates, old friends who were a little greyer and slower than she'd last seen them, but were otherwise much the same. A few faces were missing, chief amongst them Pete Bakaleinikoff, who had hitched a ride on Pholus, a centaur planetoid that had been outfitted with mass drivers and was now heading out toward Delta Pavonis, a voyage that would take more than a thousand years. Junko and Junpei Asai were still researching Delta Pavonis's Earthlike planet, Tierra. Using an ultra-long base telescope cloud stretched between the orbits of Saturn and Uranus, they'd refined resolution down to less than a kilometre, and were discussing their findings with Pete and the rest of Pholus's crew—possible landing sites, places where cities could be built, climate models and vegetation maps, and much more.

So that was one very large difference. When Macy had attended her first conference, everything had been theoretical. In addition to Pholus, several other planetoids were being converted into generation starships, and Sri Hong-Owen and her clade were heading out to Fomalhaut inside a chunk cut from the regolith of Janus, still steadily accelerating eight years after departing from orbit around Saturn, deep inside the cometary belt now, some seventy-five trillion kilometres from the sun.

At the end of the conference, loaded with invitations to visit every kind of research project, Macy and Newt rode out from the Moon and fell toward Earth in the ancient free-return trajectory, a slow, lazy trip of three days, the mother planet swelling ahead until at last they were in orbit a mere five hundred kilometres above the equator. Macy pointed out landmarks and mountains and rivers and cities; Newt told her that he knew they'd talked about this before they'd left, but just in case she had changed her mind he'd brought along a couple of exoskeletons: they could hitch a ride down on a shuttle if she wanted. He watched her carefully as she thought about it.

"No," she said. "We have places to go, people to see. And we have to get to Hannah before her time is due. Maybe another time."

"It's so close we could walk it. And I'm curious to see where you came from."

"Where we all came from."

"Not me. I was born on Titania."

"You won't find anything down there you can't find anywhere else. And there's the crushing gravity, impossibly crowded cities, biting insects, diseases. . . ."

"And wind, and rain, and all the rest of the stuff you miss."

"I grew out of missing it. Let's get on."

They docked briefly with one of the stations hung in synchronous orbit around Earth's equator and unloaded their cargo, and then they headed outward to one of the reefs of bubble habitats that, grown from the fugitive moonlets modified and launched by Sri Hong-Owen and her crew, orbited inside the inner edge of the main Asteroid Belt. Thin and interrupted arcs of gardens ringing the sun.

Macy and Newt's adopted daughter, Hannah, lived in one of the largest, Pan-Ku, named for the world-sculpting Chinese demiurge, with her partner, Xander Elliott, and their twins, Abbie and Kit, Macy and Newt's first grandchildren. Abbie and Kit were seven years old now, and Hannah was pregnant again, again with twins. She was carrying them the natural way, as Macy had carried Darwin, and was due to give birth in three weeks' time, which was why Macy and Newt had come to visit.

Pan-Ku was twenty kilometres in diameter and jacketed in a lumpy skin of water-filled bubbles that helped to protect it from solar and cosmic radiation, but otherwise it was little different from the habitat that Macy and Newt and the other Free Outers had built at Nephele. Hannah and Xander's home was a tented garden on the inner surface, with views out across the vast airy gulf where rafts bearing farms and forests, strung along the habitat's radial spars, receded toward the loose shell of sunlamps and the infrastructure that underpinned the habitat's lifesystem.

Xander was a pilot, and he and Newt disappeared off for hours at a time, inspecting ships garaged in the hangars, lost in discussions about microscopic improvements to routes between the inner and outer planets and the latest tweaks to fusion-motor technology. Unlike her brothers—Darwin with his comets; Han with his current enthusiasm for extending and improving the gardens that Avernus had created in the atmosphere of Saturn, which would almost certainly be replaced by an enthusiasm for something else in a year or two—Hannah was sensible and thoroughly grounded. She had made her home here with her partner and children, was part of the crew that maintained the ecosystems, variations on the phytoplankton-krill-fish food chains of Antarctic seas, of the watery bubbles that jacketed Pan-Ku. She loved her life and saw no reason to make any radical changes to it.

One day, while Xander and Newt were mooching around in Pan-Ku's hangars, Macy and Hannah took the twins down to one of the island forests, an expedition that took all morning to organise. It was well past noon when they finally set out, travelling on a cog tram that ran down the centre of one of the hollow spars to the island's tiny station.

The island was a plate of fullerene composite a kilometre across, sculpted in low relief and landscaped with lawns and paths of halflife grass that, overlaid with a web of tethers, wound through heather scrub and thickets of puffball pines and live oaks. Abbie and Kit swarmed ahead of Hannah and Macy, swinging from tether to tether with swift balletic grace, vanishing around a clump of trees and returning a few minutes later, calling to their mother and grandmother, eager to show them the perfect spot they'd chosen. And it *was* lovely, a sheltered saddle of soft turf sprinkled with wild flowers, embraced on three sides by a thick belt of trees, with views across the ocean of air and the linear archipelagos of green islands that arrowed inward all around, like a student's exercise in perspective, toward the glare of the sunlamps.

Hannah settled down with a contented sigh; she was as huge and awkward as a walrus, as she put it, had to spend half of each day in the habitat's centrifuge for the sake of her babies, and suffered from nagging backaches. She and Macy set out the picnic they'd brought and coerced the twins into spending at least some time tethered while they ate, and then there was an argument about how soon they could go flying. Not for an hour, Hannah said firmly, or you'll be sick to your stomachs.

Two of Hannah's ecosystem crew, Jack and Christof, and their son Cho, a solemn two-year-old, joined them. Abbie fussed over Cho, feeding him titbits and giving him sips of chocolate milk, while Kit roved to and fro, collecting beetles for his vivarium, and Macy and Hannah talked with Jack and Christof about the ongoing planoforming projects on Titan and Mars, and the conference on the Moon. Jack and Christof had a sideline in cultivating grapes and making wine; Macy shared a pouch of their latest, a pink Zinfandel.

Kit came back, wanting to show Macy a colony of funnel spiders he'd found, and she got up and hauled herself hand over hand along a tether, into the bank of trees. He watched her critically, said that it would be easier if she didn't try to walk.

"Cheeky pup. I've been doing this longer than you've been alive."

The funnels were gauzy trumpets laid everywhere in the fibrous tangle of tree roots. Kit showed her that the threads from which they were woven were sticky if you rubbed them in one direction and smooth if you rubbed them the other way. So that beetles and other insects could walk in, but they couldn't get out.

"Very clever," Macy said. "Did someone invent these or are they from someplace on Earth?"

Kit shrugged, feigning indifference because he was embarrassed that he didn't know.

"We can look it up when we get home," Macy said.

"I want to get rigged for full net access," Kit said, "but Hannah says I'm too young."

"That's because it's good to learn how to remember things. Stretches the brain."

Macy clung to the tether with both hands, turning to look up at the raking spread of branches and leaves. She was a little dizzy from the wine. If she let go she would fall past the trees into the sky.

She said, "What happens to dead leaves? On Earth, they would drop to the ground. Here they must simply float away. Why isn't the sky full of them?"

"Little drones collect all kinds of junk," Kit said. "They move in flocks, like birds. If you catch one it starts to make this beeping noise, louder and louder. Because it's lonely."

They talked about the different kinds of drones that policed the habitat, and the soil that wasn't really soil but intricate domains of halflife hyperfibre. Macy told Kit that he should come and visit Coleridge, and see how things grew in real soil, and then they hauled themselves back to the others and Hannah helped Kit and Abbie fit on their flying gear: crash helmets, spurs for landing, the ribbed wings of monomolecular plastic that extended out beyond their hands and clipped to their ankles. And then the twins went bouncing away, clambering like grounded bats to the edge of the catchnets that stretched around the edge of the island and kicking off and beating their wings to get up speed, chasing each other toward the next island, Abbie in red, Kit in yellow and in the lead as they dropped beneath the edge of the island and vanished from sight.

Macy's heart gave a little bump when they disappeared. She asked Hannah if she ever worried that the twins might get into trouble.

"Not really," Hannah said. "The wings aren't very efficient, so they can't go much faster than twenty kph. Kit broke his wrist soon after he took it up, because he was trying to show off, but he's better at flying than Xander now. He wants to get the full set of traits, practise in different kinds of gravity, different environments. It will mean a fair bit of travelling if he's serious."

"Just like his grandfather and his uncles," Macy said.

"Just like his grandmother," Hannah said.

Macy laughed, and conceded that she had a point.

They talked about the woman Han was living with, down in the water-zone inside Saturn, about Darwin's plans to expand the comet business. Presently the twins reappeared, small red and yellow shapes far off in the immense sky, Kit chasing Abbie, wings beating steadily as they stooped down and vanished from sight again as they went below the keel of the island. It was more like swimming than flying, Macy thought. Without gravity you had to beat your wings to get up speed, and if you stopped you wouldn't fall—air resistance would slow you down until you came to rest, like a fish hanging over a reef.

Newt called and said that a party was getting up to go visit an asteroid that was due to make a transit just ninety thousand kilometres away.

"It's entirely covered with a garden of vacuum organisms. One of Avernus's. Very weird and beautiful, I'm told. They're heading out in two days and need to know numbers. I said you'd be interested. How about it?"

"You go. I'll see it another time."

"You're sure?"

"I'm sure. Come out here and join us. There's wine, and plenty of food, and the twins are playing tag in the sky."

Macy was content to rest. Tethered on the warm slanting lawn with her daughter on one side, flushed with the hormonal health of late pregnancy, and the two men and their son on the other, the solid two-year-old jiggling happily in his webbing, a glaze of yogurt on his chin.

"You didn't want to go down to Earth," Hannah said.

"Oh, you heard about that?"

"I knew Newt had planned it as a surprise for you."

"One day we'll all go."

"Not me. We have too much to do here. And I'd have to exercise like crazy, and I've already had enough of the centrifuge. As far as I'm concerned, gravity is for losers," Hannah said, shading her eyes as she looked straight up.

Macy shaded her eyes too, saw Kit and Abbie floating high above them, red and yellow wings moving in wide and lazy sweeps as they checked their momentum. And now they both turned and began to pick up speed, wings beating swiftly and steadily, laughing and calling out as they swept low above their mother and grandmother, climbing beyond the treetops so that they could do it all over again.

How they flew!

3

Every day the girls of Crew #1 wake at 0600 and swim from their sleep pods, a school of lithe pale mermaids undulating through the oxygenated liquid fluorocarbon that fills the tubeways and commons and work stations of their ship, a medium far better suited to permanent microgravity than air. At a little less than five hundred days old they are already fully grown. Tool belts are cinched around their waists but they are otherwise naked. The muscular barrels of their chests pump fluorocarbon through booklungs packed with blood-rich fibrils; their arms are long and double-jointed; their fused legs flare into ribbed, fanlike fins. Their faces are round, with small pouting mouths, flattened noses, and large black eyes. Each wears on her right cheek a tattoo of spiky dots and lines that sketch the constellation of Hydrus.

There are twenty-one of them. Two of their original complement of twenty-four died in an accident while working on the surface and a third, injured beyond repair, had to be euthanised.

They collect pouches from the treacher and eat quickly, sucking up a salty gruel rich in vitamins and amino acids and casually discarding the empty pouches, halflife things that, tracking a simple chemical cue, flutter back to the treacher like flattened jellyfish as the girls swim one after the other through a short tube to the equipment bay. Two screens are already lit, showing the faces of the tutelary spirits of the ship: AI constructs animated with personalities derived from the hero-warriors Sada Selene and Phoenix Lyle. They update the girls on the progress of the other crews and give them their tasks for the day, and then the big screen on the other side of the spherical space lights up and with synchronised flicks of their fins the girls turn to face their beloved and benevolent leader, Levi.

Sometimes, while working, the girls fall into intense discussions about whether Levi is an AI construct like the mentors, or whether he is something more. A true AI, or even the image of a real person alive somewhere else in the ship. Not the real Levi, of course, but perhaps a clone. They want to believe that he is with them in body as well as in mind. They dream that when their work is done they will be allowed to meet him as a last reward.

This day as on every other day Levi talks of the great project in which they are engaged. Moving day by day in small but definite steps toward fulfillment of the auguries of the past-directed messages from his future self. The great circle of time ticking inexorably toward closure, and the glories of rapture.

And so on, and so forth.

The girls have heard variations on this theme many times before. Yet on this day as on every other day they give themselves up to it heart and mind. Levi's words vibrate through the fluorocarbon, beat on their skins and the taut drums of their ears, thrill in their blood, in the marrow of their bones.

At last Levi's face fades from the great screen. The girls unclip their tool belts and help each other into their pressure suits and clip on their belts again, and three by three cycle through the airlock and flow away from the ship, out across the surface of the tiny worldlet.

It is a battered planetesimal: a core of water ice and silicates frozen harder than granite and caulked with thick layers of primeval hydrocarbons and pitted with craters. A lonely remnant of the swarming shoals of protoworlds of the early planetary disc; a fossil deep-frozen in the comet-haunted outer dark far beyond the orbit of Neptune. It has been greatly modified since the Ghost ship reached it two hundred and forty-six days ago. Construction robots have excavated pits along its spin axis, and the crews are assembling three huge mass drivers, each with its own fusion generator. Other robots are mining water ice and shaping it into pellets that will fuel the mass drivers, spinning fullerenes and construction diamond wire and other exotic materials from the tarry regolith, digging down into the planetesimal's frozen core.

There is still much to do. The girls of Crew #1 relieve their sisters of Crew #3 and begin their twelve-hour shift with joyful hearts. When the work is finished, the lumpy planetesimal will have been transformed into a tapered teardrop wrapped in a diamond-mesh skin and hung behind a parasol shield of fullerene and aerogel, with fabricators and libraries of genetic information and a community of AIs held snugly in the chambers of its heart.

The girls of the construction crews will live just long enough to complete their work and supervise the start-up of the starship's mass drivers at the beginning of its long, long voyage.

They won't reach the stars. But their brothers and sisters will.

ACKNOWLEDGMENTS

Parts of this novel are based on heavily modified characters and situations that first appeared in the following stories: "The Gardens of Saturn" (*Interzone*, 1998); "The Passenger" (*Asimov's Science Fiction*, 2002); "The Assassination of Faustino Malarte" (*Asimov's Science Fiction*, 2002); and "Dead Men Walking" (*Asimov's Science Fiction*, 2006).

My profound gratitude to the astronauts, scientists, engineers, and flight crews of the Apollo programme, *Pioneer 11*, *Voyagers 1* and *2*, *Galileo*, and *Cassini-Huygens* for the photographs, maps, research, and firsthand accounts that have inspired and informed every part of *The Quiet War* and *Gardens of the Sun*.

ABOUT THE AUTHOR

Paul McAuley's first novel won the Philip K. Dick Award and he has gone on to win almost all of the major awards in the field. For many years a research biologist, he now writes full-time. He lives in London. Visit him online at http://unlikelyworlds.blogspot.com/.

"Desolation Road *is a rara avis....*
Extraordinary and more than that!"
—Philip José Farmer

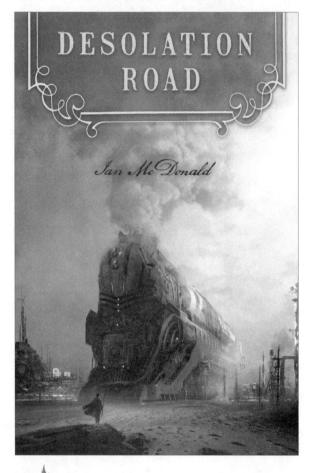

PYB Pyr®, an imprint of Prometheus Books
716-691-0133 / www.pyrsf.com

APRIL 2010

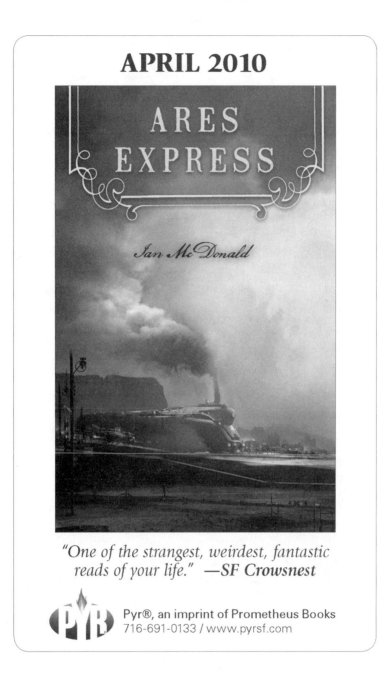

"One of the strangest, weirdest, fantastic reads of your life." —*SF Crowsnest*

Pyr®, an imprint of Prometheus Books
716-691-0133 / www.pyrsf.com

JULY 2010

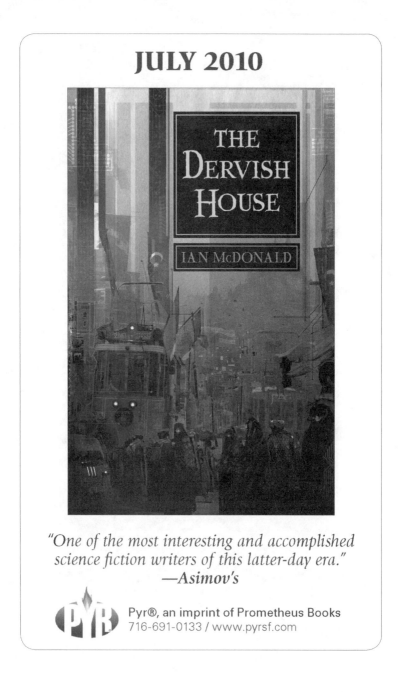

"One of the most interesting and accomplished science fiction writers of this latter-day era."
—Asimov's

Pyr®, an imprint of Prometheus Books
716-691-0133 / www.pyrsf.com